THE ORCHARD

Tony Veale

imprint**arts**

First published in the UK by **snowballpress**, 2004

Paperback edition (2006) published by **imprintarts**
Imprint Academic, PO Box 200, Exeter EX5 5YX

A CIP catalogue record for this book is available from
the British Library

ISBN 1-84540-058-5

Printed in England by Imprint Academic, Exeter

ONE

'Y ou can't say that! Come back! Stop!'
Matt Flight woke up, sweating and terrified.
God! A person could die this way, heart bursting,
overwhelmed by an event conceived in a dreaming brain.
He drew a deep breath and counted one to five. Emptying
his lungs, he felt the fear recede.

His recollection of the dream was vivid. Running from
the gallery exhibiting his work, he'd headed down Cork
Street in the heart of London's West End, pursued by an
angry mob. Trying to escape he'd run faster and faster
until, on the point of collapse, he'd woken up.

Motionless in his studio bed, he clutched his duvet.
The darkness was close: physical, like the ear of a priest.
'What have I done?' he whispered. But there was no
going back. The exhibition had pitched his life into
immediate controversy. And all because of one canvas!

Central to the show, *The Orchard* was a painting of
doves gorging on flesh bursting from the fruit of pomegranate trees. The trees were rooted in bodies – in the
dead of human conflict. To Matt, this symbolized peace
drawing its strength from war, the one giving meaning to
the other.

All I did was paint the truth, he reflected. And what
happens? I cause an outrage!

'How can you paint such a horrible scene?' a woman had cried, tears in her eyes. 'Have you no faith?'

'Yes, it's obscene!' another had said. 'You're a heartless beast!'

He told himself he should have known the image would insult. After all, wasn't it his intention to push the glory train of false hopes off the rails?

Couldn't they see? he thought. The point is to make clear something we've forgotten. Human nature doesn't change! We are what we are – creatures of habit, good and bad.'

He wished he could turn back the clock – remove the picture from the show – anything to reverse the public's indignation.

But Bernie Feltz, the gallery's owner, couldn't have been happier. The private view had been packed and the consternation of his guests gave him reason to feel his latest protégé was a winner.

Lagoon Art had a reputation for notoriety. Regular attacks in the press accused it of using shock to attract attention and of debasing art. By playing on the cognoscenti's flirtation with 'underground' thinking, Feltz had built a good business. His customers were hungry for a place at the high table of metropolitan cool and Matt's work was his latest offering – another plat-du-jour of delectable controversy.

Feltz knew artists backwards – or so he thought. Weaving his way through their layers of conceit and insecurity, he counselled and cajoled them with promises of recognition. It was a matter of mutual trust, he assured them: if they put their careers in his hands, he would lead them to the gilded rostrum of their dreams and the plaudits of an admiring public.

Unable to get back to sleep, Matt turned restlessly. He closed his eyes, re-living the events of the private view which for him had been a baptism of fire.

'Matt, you're on your way,' Feltz was assuring him, as he eased him through the throng on a slow meander round the gallery floor.

'But they hate me!' Matt despaired.

'Hate, love – it doesn't matter a toss!' Feltz insisted. 'With everybody fired up like this, the show'll be talked about all over town.'

'Yeah, and with me dubbed a pariah!' grumbled Matt. His name was already a talking point, leaping from head to head in the gallery in a brushfire of opprobrium. Yet – all he wanted was the love and respect of his fellow men. And the recognition that he had something of value to say, something which might save society from what it had become. For hadn't it gone soft?

Sparring with strangers at the private view, one after another, Matt's discomfort had grown. And Feltz hadn't helped, passing diplomatic asides, careful not to become embroiled. But that was Feltz's party trick of course – get everybody wound up, step back, then referee the action.

'Whatever's going on in your head, to make you want to paint something like this?' someone had shrilly demanded.

'Peel morality away and this is what you're left with,' Matt tried feebly to explain.

'The nitty gritty,' said a voice to his side.

He turned to find a girl engaging him with a wry smile. 'You're a bit of a party pooper!' she said.

'Party pooper?' said Matt, troubled by a feeling that she might not be taking him seriously – or even worse, that she might be mocking him.

'Hey, but don't get me wrong,' she continued. 'It's great work, even if nobody else thinks so.'

People in the vicinity were blinking at each other in dismay.

'Thank you!' said Matt. He wanted to read the girl's eyes, but they were hidden behind dark glasses. He felt awkward, like a suspect stood before a one-way screen.

'How long's your show on for?' she asked.

'Three weeks – if I survive tonight,' he said, sensing she was eyeing him up and down.

The girl laughed, sweeping a hand through her hair. 'OK, I'll come in again. Maybe tomorrow.'

And like a dragonfly she was gone, but her support gave Matt strength to battle on. And the torture lessened as he got into his stride, repeating and refining his patter of justification.

Then, just as he thought it couldn't get any better, he had found himself standing alone. The gallery was beginning to empty. Strains of hostility were giving way to crescendos of merriment, seesawing like a radio fiddled with by a meddlesome child. His ordeal was over: the evening was moving on, the party breaking up into little groups for whom thoughts of dinner were paramount. Mentions of booked tables fell from people's lips in tones of loud subservience to this or that celebrity chef. 'God, we were so lucky! Managed to squeeze in at Mario's! Table for 9.30 – must dash or we'll lose it.'

Back to trivia, he gloomily reflected. Watching the guests file out of the gallery he felt as if they were living in a bubble. The discord of the age, so real to him, was for them no more than a disturbance in the endless round of gossip.

Matt put his hands in his pockets and ambled into Feltz's office. Feltz sidled in after him: 'Hey, hey! Why the long face? You were brilliant!'

On nights like these, the word 'brilliant' would pop from Feltz's mouth again and again, rounding off each remark with overflowing exuberance.

Matt succumbed to his scented hug. 'Thanks. But I could have done without the flak.'

'Comes with the job,' Feltz laughed, slapping Matt on the back. He had good news. None other than Sylvester Rich had attended the private view. That was significant – an endorsement from a great collector, whose own gallery was full of art at the cutting-edge.

'Sylvester admired your work,' beamed Feltz. '*The Orchard* in particular. Says it brings to mind Kiefer and *Nigredo*.' For all Feltz all knew, this might have been some kind of double-act, like a man with a dog that did tricks. He kept his ignorance about the great painter and his *oeuvre* to himself. '

Matt was visibly cheered. 'Great! But has he seen the price?'

'Twenty-grand? That kind of money's nothing to Sylvester. His gallery's open to a paying public. Think of the money he could take with *The Orchard*! Look at the stir it caused tonight. All it needs is a hammering in the press and the punters'll flock to see it. You'll be made!'

Matt frowned. 'A hammering in the press? I need that like a hole in the head.'

'It's what the Rich Gallery gets off on,' said Feltz. 'Their show's the wackiest in town. Really freaky, man! And it makes a great day out for Joe Public. They lap it up.'

'Freaky?' said Matt, the word sticking in his craw.

'Just a figure of speech,' said Feltz. 'Trust me, most artists would kill for a break like this.'

Matt felt insulted. I'm not like most artists, he thought to himself.

'Of course, Sylvester'll need his usual sweetener,' Feltz added, smarting at the discount he would have to offer.

'How much will that be?' Matt asked anxiously. 'I mean, I spent an age on that picture.'

Feltz tapped his nose knowingly. 'Don't get your knickers in a twist,' he said. 'It's built into the price.'

Slippery sod! thought Matt.

Thumbing his lapels, Feltz gave Matt his version of the evening's events. He eulogized the celebrities who had attended. Soap stars, fashion models and a celebrated footballer had all helped give the occasion that show-bizzy buzz he adored. A nice turn out, he said, marred only by a drunk swinging a punch at a man in a lime-green seersucker suit, creation of the fashionable coutu-rier Willie Fitz. And strangely, the bottle count was favourable – on budget, give or take a crate.

'They were all talking their heads off,' Feltz happily observed. And tomorrow would be better still – he'd get a grip on Sylvester, and edge him towards a deal.

Bernie Feltz was addicted to deals, Matt reflected. He was emotionally transparent – a villain from a cartoon strip, loud and theatrical. A transaction in the offing would bring a shine to Bernie's face matching the silky red sheen on his dickie-bow, a clip-on touch harking back to days long before he had a gallery of his own.

Bernie had boasted to Matt about those days. He'd started as simply an agent with flair and a simple philoso-phy: 'Talent alone is not enough. You have to have an angle, a story to grab the public's attention.'

Several years ago, in the course of promoting a young sculptor's work, Bernie had published a poster of two granite spheres, the one in close proximity with the other. Titling it 'Talking Balls' he'd plastered it all over the city, causing a flurry of amusement. Questions were raised in the media; who was the caption aimed at?

'Take your pick!' Bernie had proclaimed. 'People talk balls the world over.' Demand for the poster had soared and the sculptor's name had found its way round the globe.

Not that Bernie was always successful. There were art-ists who blew their chance – 'Fucking me about!' as Bernie saw it. Like the artist who committed himself to a show then disappeared on a grant-aided whim to

Patagonia. Life was 'cool' there, said his e-mail back to the enraged Bernie: mountains and open spaces a perfect antidote to the civilized world. 'The bloody nerve of the guy!' Bernie had shrieked.

In small doses, Matt found Feltz amusing, likeable in his better moods – for example when he received a large cheque. Then he became malleable, like a cuddly toy with bright glinting eyes.

But it was clear that lasting friendships played no part in Bernie's life. Oscillating between euphoria and fits of pique, he would alarm anyone for whom restraint and discretion were the norms of everyday life. Friends and associates alike treated him with wary tolerance, guffawing at his puerile jokes only in fear of offending him.

Approaching middle age and divorced, Bernie lived on his own. The frenzy of business filled his life. Now Matt was a part of that frenzy – a talent on the brink of metamorphosis.

'A word in your shell-like,' Feltz would say, when taking a punter aside. 'A year ago, this guy was nowhere! Now he's five grand a throw and rising. If you're thinking of getting on board, now's the time.'

Matt had heard worrying stories about artists hyped by Bernie. Some had gone off the rails on drug abuse, some had grown absurdly self-important, some had fled the world entirely. He wondered what the future held for him.

TWO

Matt eventually dropped off to sleep. He woke again late that morning to a scuffle of pigeons copulating on the studio skylight. Staring at their feet, he could see clouds drifting way above, carried by the same wind that was humming over his roof in highs and lows as if in sympathy with the throbbing in his head – the aftermath of an evening he would rather forget.

'The Piranha Pool' had taken its toll. It was a favourite haunt of Feltz's, especially for parties after a private view. Its fish tanks and pulsating glitz were well suited to the new money that frequented his exhibitions. Matt had been there, doing his bit for the gallery, but his outwardly genial manner had concealed a strong desire to go home.

Hemmed in between Feltz's guests, high on their cocktails and cocaine, he had prayed for deliverance. It hadn't come until the early hours, when burning Amaretti wrappers ghosted to the ceiling and everybody stood up to leave, tossing him their small change of good wishes amidst a flurry of vacuous farewells.

Come the morning, will they remember anything? Matt asked himself. No: by then, his paintings and everything he'd said would be forgotten, sunk in the stagnant canals of their brains. Bastards!

The phone rang, intensifying his pain. It was Feltz.

'Sorry, mate. Did I wake you?'

'No,' Matt drawled.

'You sound half dead. Are you hung over?'

'Yeah,' he admitted, sliding the earpiece down his cheek to muffle Feltz's cackling laugh.

'Listen,' said Feltz, 'Holly Tree's called me.'

'Holly Tree?'

'You spoke to her last night, remember?'

It's got to be that redhead, Matt thought. 'Yeah, I remember. She was the only one who gave me a break. D'you know her?'

'Sure. She's a bit of a wild child, but she comes to most of the shows. Even helps out a bit.'

'Does she ever buy?'

'Sometimes. If she trusts a guy's work.'

Matt was intrigued. 'So, what did she want?'

'She's coming in for another look.'

'When?'

'Later this afternoon. Can you make it?'

'Yeah. I'm coming over now, anyway.'

Holly Tree. So that's her name, Matt thought, surprised that she was keeping to her word. He remembered how pretty she was. Comforted by the thought that she at least was on his side, he eased himself out of bed.

Picking his way through the chaos of the studio, he reached the kitchenette. The partitioned area offered little in the way of amenities. Switching on the kettle, he turned to the refrigerator with its persistent leak. A tortured sausage and half a carton of milk awaited him, signs of someone who found cooking a waste of time. He sniffed the milk. It was passable – just. The sausage he returned to the cold, like a corpse to the morgue.

A torn foil of aspirin lay on the draining board from the night before. He chewed on a couple more, his face contorting as he tried to drown their bitterness with sweet tea. Somehow this never quite worked.

Holly Tree. What's she like? he wondered. A wild child, whose dark glasses hid the life in her eyes. If red hair was anything to go by, then 'a handful' was the likely answer.

It was midday. Scooping up some change he grabbed his old leather jacket and left for the Underground in a thoroughly gloomy mood.

May was special to Matt – a month when flowering trees brought an air of carnival to the street, scattering blossom in celebration of Spring's union with Summer.

The seasons affected his mood. Bad weather could trigger depression, spilling negative thinking into his work and leading to failures, hard to accept. But today was fine enough and his worries faded when the sun found his face through the panoply of tender green above. He thought, how strange it is; high in these trees is another reality – the life of grubs, burrowing and nibbling through leaf and bark. Their memory span must be so short, nagging anxiety is surely unknown to them.

Lucky buggers, he thought. What a price we humans pay.

On the pavement ahead, a mass of bouquets lay heaped against a wall. It was a common enough sight, but Matt noted the pile had grown since he last walked by. It trailed some distance now in both directions. Ten days ago there'd been a mugging there and someone had been murdered. The papers next day were full of it, regurgitating clichés of concern for the victims of crime.

Matt slowed to read the dedications, now blurs of inky sadness from the previous rain.

'We come up from Sidcup,' someone said to him.

Matt looked up to find a man and a woman standing beside him. 'You knew the guy?' he asked, noticing they'd bought a bunch of flowers.

'No,' the man said. 'But we was at the Natural 'istory Museum, to see that new flappin' pteradactyl they got. Triffic it is too!'

The woman nodded in accord. 'Yeah, real scary!'

'Anyways, as to get 'ere was only a short 'op on the tube, like, we thought we'd come an' 'ave a butchers.'

'Terrible business, weren't it?' said the woman, now shaking her head in disgust.

Matt agreed it was.

To his surprise, the man produced a street map. Opening it out, he said: 'The lady in the tourist kiosk at the station was ever so 'elpful. Look – marked the spot for us, she did.'

'Oh,' said Matt. He glanced at the cross inked in on the map.

'Dunno what the world's comin' to,' said the woman, a questioning look in her eye.

'Neither do I,' said Matt. Leaving the couple to gawp he moved on, wondering which of their visits they'd enjoyed the most. The latter, most likely – an opportunity to share in the national fever of collective condolence. Too good to miss!

In the depths of the station, he stood on the platform, listening to the roar of an approaching train. Excreted from the bowels of the earth it emerged in a rush of foul air. Lacerations of graffiti bore witness to dark hours spent in the purgatory of some distant siding. The doors shuddered open and a muffled call to 'Mind the gap!' reverberated over the public address.

Automated altruism; this is as good as it gets, he thought.

Stepping aboard, he sat down to be greeted by the smell of a spit-roasted chicken. Opposite, a youth sat perched on the edge of his seat. He was tearing at the bird's flesh and stuffing it into his mouth as if he hadn't eaten for days. Oblivious of his fellow travellers, he squinted repeatedly at the route map high on the other side of the carriage. Gaunt-faced and anxious, he appeared to be full of misgivings.

He has to be an immigrant, Matt thought. An illegal, one of the many freed each day from airless concealment only to find themselves on the run once more, in search of Shangri-La. Perhaps for this guy it was Cockfosters, at the end of the Piccadilly Line.

The doors closed on the thin volume of passengers and the train was on the move, a shabby repository of grey faces etched in suspicion and gloom.

At the next stop a man with an accordion walked on. Positioning himself at the back of the carriage he struck up a tune, its rollicking jollity contrasting absurdly with the passengers' pretended indifference. Swaying from side to side he studied the passengers one by one, his eyes narrow from a lifetime of reckoning which 'misery' would cough up and drop a coin in his old paper cup. On approaching Green Park he shuffled round to collect what little was on offer, his gratitude a cursory nod.

Matt walked up Piccadilly to Burlington House. He found himself in a struggle for space on the pavement. The Impressionists were back yet again at the Royal Academy and excited hordes were queueing up. Clambering under the comfort-blanket of retrospection, Matt thought. How can people pass time this way, when all around them is mayhem – their country falling apart at the seams like an unloved teddy bear? Don't they care? Or is it that they just don't see?

In the Burlington Arcade he peered into shop windows. Soft traps of cashmere and silk lay in wait to snare the affluent shoppers who were wandering about desultorily. To Matt they seemed bored and flabby-faced, their wants greater than their needs.

In Burlington Gardens, a beggar thrust a scrap of paper at him with a muttered threat. Barely legible, it was the second claim on his charity within fifteen minutes. Beggars were everywhere. He'd had sympathy once, but not since the menacing started. The police, hamstrung by politics, had little control over these marauders, who sometimes worked in groups, pressurising passers-by until they yielded.

Matt noted the crusted blood hanging from the corner of the man's mouth. Perhaps he'd been in a fight. Doorways in side streets bore daily witness to quarrels over lucrative pitches. Matt eased past the man, tailed by a curse blurted out with such vehemence that it stirred the hairs on the back of his neck. Rather a curse, he thought, than risk a tubercular cough in the face.

Lagoon Art came into view, its fascia prominent in the sobriety of Cork Street. From the street, 'the shop' (as Feltz liked to call it) gave little away. There was no artwork in the window and potential visitors would put their noses to the glass for a cautious peer, nervous about what they might find.

Inside the gallery, focus on the artist was intense. 'Artist's Statements' were writ large on the walls between exhibits. Deliberately controversial, they were part of Feltz's armoury of marketing gimmicks. Supposedly, they provided insight into the artist's persona: their *'raison d'être'* and *'modus operandi'* as Feltz liked to say – foreign phrases which he bandied about to impress.

Only in the rear gallery would a photographic image of the exhibiting artist be revealed, usually much enlarged. This small room was a hallowed sanctum where artists might also be seen on video, their pained facial expressions accompanying sombre expositions of earnest methodology.

Not for Feltz the sterility of silent white walls, but rather a focus on developing the artist as a celebrity. An artist should be as familiar to the public as his work, he would say; sometimes more so.

'Face it – it's about money now. Commission is commission is commission, whether it's on a painting, a sculpture, or an appearance on a chat show. Spread your risk and cash in while you can. Don't talk to me about integrity – that went out with the Ark. Successful artists today are shits with laptops jabbering into mobiles – on the make like everybody else.' Matt would protest at this kind of talk; then Bernie would tell him to come down off his high horse and knuckle down to the reality of earning a living. His bottom line potential could be huge!

On 'The Street', Bernie Feltz was looked at as a Johnny-come-lately from the yellow brick roads. He'd rudely banged on the temple door demanding admittance and now he riled everyone with cocksure opinions on the future of art – globalization being the route to unimaginable riches.

'Why couldn't he have stayed where he was,' the high priests of Cork Street complained, 'trading modish junk along with the rest of the Brit Art crowd in the East End.'

But Feltz wanted 'class,' the cachet of an address known to collectors the world over. And that meant Cork Street. The rents were excruciatingly high, but it was where the real money was. 'You can smell it in the air,' he'd once said to Matt as they stood looking out of the gallery window, watching for likely punters in the street. Some men were passing by; vicuna overcoats draped across their shoulders, they seemed the kind of guys Feltz liked: men about town, flush (he hoped, with fingers crossed) from some lucrative deal.

'Cool, so cool,' Feltz commented admiringly. One of them glanced in the window and Bernie adjusted his cuffs ostentatiously, evidently hoping they would stop and come in. But he was out of luck; they avoided his gaze and walked on.

Sometimes they did stop, and Bernie would be pleasantly surprised – their gambits of enquiry sending him into a spin of unctuous cordiality.

Save for the curse of wealthy foreigners who always demanded a discount, Lagoon Art was for the most part spared the machinations of bargain hunters. Such people insulted his judgement, Bernie believed – just as they used to do, way back when first he started selling artists' work from his house: 'Come on, Bernie, you ain't going to shift this for that sort of money. The guy's an unknown! But, tell you what, I'll take it off your hands for...'

Now that he was the owner of a gallery in Cork Street, Bernie had learned that the higher the price of an exhibit, the greater was its mystique and the easier it was to sell.

Matt put his face to the gallery window and peered in. Feltz was talking to two men in partial silhouette against the illuminated expanse of his masterpiece. He wondered if it was under discussion. It certainly looked that way.

Not wanting to be seen, he walked on a little way up the street. Better not interrupt; besides, Feltz's sales pitch was an embarrassment. His hype and flattery was so blatant; how anybody fell for it was a miracle.

But Feltz had sized up the two men as soon as they entered. They were far from typical customers. A staccato chatter of short wave radios clipped to their jackets was keeping them in a state of harassed readiness, which showed in their gloomy eyes. Presenting their identity cards, they had revealed themselves to be policemen.

'Er, is Mr. Lagoon available?' asked the Detective Sergeant.

'Lagoon?' queried Feltz. 'No. I think you mean Feltz, don't you?'

'Well, it says 'ere, Lagoon,' said the policeman, studying his check sheet.

Feltz shook his head. 'No, that's the name of the gallery,' he informed them.

'And you are, sir?'

'The name's Feltz.'

'Ah! Would you be the proprietor, then?'

'Correct,' said Feltz.

'Well, sir, in that case, you would be the person to whom we wish to speak.'

'Oh?' said Feltz.

'Yes, sir,' the officer confirmed. 'Are you familiar with a revision in the law concernin' the use of nudity?'

'What law's that?' Feltz inquired warily.

'The Depiction of Nudity Act, sir.' With gravitas, he explained. 'You see, there's been an amendment bannin' advertisers from exploitin' a certain category of images. 'Aven't you read about it?'

Feltz remembered. Panicked by the growing use of sexually explicit material throughout Europe in advertising campaigns, the government had rushed a bill through Parliament designed to prevent an outbreak of 'Eurotica' in Britain. Of particular concern was a campaign in France linking the staying powers afforded by a glucose drink to an act of sex between naked aficionados. Their endorsements of the product – *'Encore! Encore!'* – emerged in speech bubbles through sets of unnaturally white teeth.

'There's been extensive publicity,' the officer advised him.

'I remember reading something,' said Feltz.

Libertarian protests – that imagery of this kind had been televised for the best part of thirty years – carried no weight. At least a screen could be switched off, said the critics. Salacious posters weathering on billboards all over the country were quite another matter.

Hysteria was rife. The responsibility for drafting changes to the law had fallen to the Council for Moral Issues, a body appointed by government to act as a watchdog on morality. Now the law was in force; and the police, nervous of being sued for neglect of duty by an increasingly litigious public, pursued incidents of suspected 'Eurotica' with zeal. After scrutinizing Lagoon Art's catalogue for the Flight exhibition, they had no doubt there were adequate grounds for a prosecution.

'Well, whether you're aware of it or not,' the officer continued, 'the ban's a fact of life.'

'I'll take your word for it,' said Feltz. 'But I can't see how all this affects me.'

'On the contrary sir, we have 'ere *prima facie* evidence that suggests your gallery is very much affected.' The Detective Sergeant nodded to his colleague, who produced a copy of the catalogue: 'Matt Flight: Recent Paintings'.

'It's connected with this material, sir.'

'Really?' said Feltz, puzzled.

The policeman coyly circled a finger over the catalogue's cover. 'The law clearly stipulates that advertisin' material cannot carry images portrayin' sexual activity.'

'So?' said Feltz.

'Well, to my eye, the cover of this catalogue does exactly that.'

'You've got to be joking!' scoffed Feltz.

'On the contrary I'm afraid,' said the officer. Then, with a hint of embarrassment: 'To be specific, it appears that tree roots 'ave inserted themselves in all manner of orifices on these bodies, if you get my drift.'

'That's absurd!' protested Feltz.

'To your eyes, maybe.'

'You don't understand,' insisted Feltz. 'What you're looking at is a detail from a picture in this artist's exhibition. Look, we're standing right by it.'

The two policemen glanced briefly at the painting, as if to examine it closely would indicate an unhealthy interest.

'What you 'angs in your gallery is not the problem, sir,' said the Detective Sergeant. 'The possible offence concerns this catalogue, circulatin' freely within the public domain.'

To the policeman's mind, naked bodies violated by tree roots, probing and phallic, was evidence enough of malpractice. 'Sir, it's my duty to tell you that distributin' a catalogue like this is a clear breach of the law.'

Feltz shook his head, exasperated. 'Look,' he said, pointing to the cover, 'how can you say this is sexual? These people are dead! Corpses! Kaput, for Crissake!' Taking pains to explain the allegory, he said: 'Nothing's inserted itself anywhere! Those trees are growing from the victims of a massacre. This painting is about peace growing out of war.'

The officer looked at Feltz blankly. 'Clearly, them roots is penetratin' private parts.'

'They're tree roots, for God's Sake!' snapped Feltz. 'Not pricks!"

'Offensiveness will get us nowhere, sir,' said the Detective Sergeant officiously. 'And if you take my advice, you'll do well to consider your position, as the manner of this paintin' smacks of un'olesome shenanigans.'

Feltz sighed heavily. 'How you work that out beats me.'

But arguing the point was futile. Years of service in the Vice Squad had warped the officer's imagination: he saw phallic symbols everywhere, and Feltz's explanation was mere psychobabble. While his colleague made notes with an obstinate ball pen, he informed Feltz that a report would be sent to the authorities for evaluation. Furthermore, if the matter was referred to the courts and judgement found against the gallery, a fine was mandatory.

Already enraged beyond words, Feltz was further obliged to listen to an address before the policemen took their leave. It bore the usual hallmark of civil service verbiage:

'This law has one prime purpose in this case, namely to uphold the dignity of the human body. By so doin', the baser forms of exploitation practised abroad will be prevented from occurrin' within these shores, where it is the responsibility of the law to safeguard people from the effects of salacious advertisin' which could otherwise undermine the moral fabric of the nation.'

Feltz muttered under his breath: 'And bollocks to the aforesaid.'

But whether he liked it or not, the moral welfare of the nation had become a matter of prime concern for the government. Experts blamed an increasing abnormality in sexual behaviour on the massive growth of internet pornography. Given the nature of the problem, counter-measures were futile. Nevertheless, an information pack was available at health centres nationally; published by the Council for Moral Issues, it was the brainchild of their chairperson Dame Bridget Bradstock. Alias 'Auntie Biddie' to the public at large, she was a one-time agony aunt with a self-proclaimed expertise in the field of human relations. Recently ennobled, she was at the height of her powers; a cabinet position had been specially created for her and she was now Minister for Moral Affairs.

In this climate, the heavy-handed response to Flight's catalogue was hardly surprising.

Matt waited until the two men had left before entering the gallery. He found Feltz flushed with fury.

'Whatever's happened?' asked Matt.

'What a load of crap!' shouted Feltz.

'What is?' cried Matt in surprise.

'Those tossers that have just left,' spluttered Feltz.

'What about them?'

'It was Plod!' he exclaimed.

Matt was incredulous. 'What?' he said. 'I thought they might have been buyers.'

'Fat chance of that!' snapped Feltz. 'Some bastard's put in a complaint about your work and I've been booked for it.'

'On what grounds, for God's Sake?

'Publishing offensive material! Would you credit it?'

'You cannot be serious!' said Matt, dismayed.

'Oh but I am!' Feltz pointed to the cover of the offending catalogue. 'Look, they reckon those roots of yours are shafting the corpses.'

'That's ridiculous!' Matt protested.

'Plod didn't see it that way,' said Feltz.

Matt shook his head in amazement. 'This is crazy!'

'It's all to do with that fucking Nudity Act,' explained Feltz, 'You can't use advertising material that even so much as hints at a sex act.'

'But this painting's not about sex,' said Matt.

'Try telling that to Plod!'

Matt shook his head. 'Incredible, bloody incredible,' he sighed. 'Does that mean someone's put in a complaint?'

'*Someone* must've,' said Feltz. Among his enemies, there was one name which jumped to mind: Godfrey Privett, a columnist whose views on contemporary art had earned him a reputation as a guardian of reason and moderation. Much loved by traditionalists and vicious in his criticism, Privett was a St George thrusting his lance at the dragon of modernity.

'Last night, there were so many people kicking up a fuss, it could have been anybody,' said Matt.

'No,' said Feltz. 'I've got a pretty good idea who's behind it. Godfrey bloody Privett!'

'Oh, him,' said Matt, amused by how the name conjured up the apple-pie order of suburban hedges. 'He's that freelance critic, isn't he?'

'Yeah, but the odd thing is I never spotted him here. He must have sneaked in and out when the gallery was full, the old shit!'

Then – on patchy evidence, the kind of hand-me-down hearsay that can cling like a limpet to a bachelor – Feltz made him out to be a closet queen.

'Oh,' said Matt, not altogether surprised. There had been a number of gays at his private view – single men and couples seemingly more interested in each other than his work.

'Yeah, he's a fudge-packing faggot, no mistake,' sniggered Feltz, pleased at this chest-beating affirmation of his own manliness.

'I should think he's past that, isn't he?' said Matt, reckoning Privett was old enough to be sexually atrophied.

'Maybe,' Feltz conceded. 'But if it is him, you can bet an article'll pop up somewhere, making a meal out of this business.'

'Paranoia,' said Matt, dismissively.

Feltz grinned knowingly. 'You want to put money on it? I can see the headline now: 'Lagoon Art Charged! – Violation of Sex Law!'' Then it occurred to him: a fine was nothing compared to the possible upside. His shoulders hunched in a fervour of enthusiasm; his brain went into overdrive. 'What a fantastic opportunity,' he said. 'Just think of the publicity!'

Matt looked at him nervously. Memories of his nightmare came flooding back. 'God,' he said, running a finger across his forehead, 'if that happens, I'll be in the shit up to here!'

Feltz smirked. 'It comes with the territory, mate. We'll drink to this!'

Bernie sped off to get bottle and glasses and Matt sat down.

So this was life with Bernie Feltz. It was all a far cry from the early stirrings that had set him on the path to becoming an artist. Born to creative parents, he had an aptitude for drawing at an early age and an inquiring mind. He spent hours of owlish communion in books with philosophers of the past. By his early twenties he'd found a truth he could grasp: that the positive and negative are fatally attracted. Good and evil are bedfellows; they can't live apart, the one is the measure of the other. What is beauty without ugliness, or happiness without misery? Lose sight of this and the mind must succumb to vacuous ideals which take no account of humanity's limitations.

With these thoughts in mind, his painting developed through a series of allegorical compositions featuring opposites. To date, *The Orchard* was his finest work.

That fate hadn't consigned him to a life of obscurity among her workaday millions was all due a chance encounter that brought Bernie Feltz, master opportunist, to the door of his attic studio.

Feltz had spotted one of his paintings quite by chance, waiting for a frame in the same shop that Bernie used. Instantly smitten, Bernie gleaned Matt's address from the proprietor. Before the day was out, he had trundled off in a cab in search of his quarry.

At the time, Matt's confidence had been low. Winter drabness was exacerbating a fear that his work would never be recognized. Matt had shown Bernie his canvasses, placing them one after another onto an easel, expecting him to lose interest and go. But Feltz had stood in awe, temporarily silenced, before blurting out in his uninhibited way: 'Jeez, this is mind-boggling stuff!' To him, it stood out a mile: Matt Flight was headed for a spectacular career. Feltz immediately offered him an exhibition. He had never seen work like it. Their dream-like quality reminded him of Hieronymous Bosch and the surrealist Paul Delvaux, but there was something else there too, something he knew he could sell…

Matt's confidence was instantly restored. Here at last was someone who understood. But all too soon, he'd realised Feltz didn't give a damn about their meaning. It was the power of the imagery that counted: the contrasting extremes arresting the eye. Still, the thought of exhibiting – and in Cork Street at that – filled Matt with hope. His shroud of anonymity gone, he would no longer feel like an outsider, like a sad street-wandering psychotic mouthing pleas through plate glass windows to people bemused and deaf to his words. Now at last people would see that he had something of value to say. As for the money, it was a secondary consideration. His intention was noble – to enlighten the world!

Bernie returned with wine and glasses. 'Here,' he said, pouring out two glasses of house white saved from the private view. 'You're gonna have to face it, you know. The game's only just begun.'

Sagging like a rag doll in his chair, Matt stared at Feltz across the vast expanse of the man's desk. 'Game?' he queried.

'Oh, yes! Don't kid yourself it's anything else.'

Matt frowned.

Feltz leant forward as if to confide a secret. 'Look,' he said, 'Lagoon Art's success is down to two things: controversy, and the publicity it generates.' He took a gulp of wine. 'If your work wasn't controversial I'd never have touched it, believe you me! I could never have won the publicity. It's that which puts you on the map. Gives you value.'

Feltz sat back again. 'Now, don't get me wrong when I say this, but in marketing terms your feelings are of fuck-all importance. We're after major recognition here – household name stuff. And to achieve that, we have to build a story around your work that attracts attention and gives you provenance. Without that, you're dead in the water.'

Matt listened intently, more scales falling from his eyes.

'It's all about sensationalism,' Feltz went on. 'That's what sells. Without it, the real money's not interested. Take Sylvester Rich. D'you think he'd be after your painting if it was some frigging little still life? Who's going to pay to see something like that by an unknown? Nobody, I'm telling you.'

'If that's true,' said Matt, 'it makes the whole art scene phoney.'

Feltz shrugged his shoulders. 'So what? Recognize it for what it is and milk it. Believe me, this is the way to go. High-mindedness gets you nowhere. Everything hangs on publicity. The more you get, the higher your profile, and the more valuable your pictures become. Then – hey, presto – before you know it, you're a celebrity!'

'Oh,' said Matt, ruefully.

'So what's wrong with that?' asked Feltz.

'I'd hoped my work would be bought because it had merit.'

'That might enter the equation. But it's not what's important.'

'Investment upside being the main thing,' Matt suggested cynically.

'R-r-r-ight!' said Feltz, drawing the word out, in pleasurable recognition that his message was getting through. 'And here's the rub,' he went on. 'This could go far beyond your painting.'

'How d'you mean?'

Feltz grinned. 'If we play things right, your name will be an earner in itself, maybe pulling in even more dosh than your work.' He paused to allow his words to sink in. 'Do you know how?'

Matt took a guess. 'Spin-offs? Merchandising?'

'You've got it!' said Feltz, stabbing at him with his finger.

Shit! Matt thought to himself. Where is this all leading?

THREE

Holly Tree breezed into the gallery at three o'clock, clutching an early edition of the evening paper. Matt and Feltz were munching sandwiches in the back office and keeping a covert eye on the comings and goings of visitors.

'Holly, luv, you're looking great!' Feltz spluttered through his mouthful. Crumbs on lips, he leapt from his chair to kiss her. Introducing Matt had almost slipped his mind. 'Oh sorry luv, this is…'

'Matt Flight,' Holly interjected. 'Yes, I know. We met last night.'

'Yeah, of course,' said Matt with a smile. He stood up to greet her.

'You were being so serious,' said Holly. Her dark glasses were again disconcerting. He wished she would remove them.

'I was under attack,' he said.

'So I saw!'

Matt turned to Feltz. 'She saved me from the baying hounds.'

Feltz grinned. 'Lucky boy,' he said, thinking (as he often did) how lovely it would be to cuddle up to Holly's breasts. This delight had so far eluded him.

'That was yesterday,' Holly said. 'Today, you've got another problem.'

'Yeah?' said Matt.

'Read this,' she said, passing him her newspaper. It was open on the arts page.

Feltz peered over Matt's shoulder and read the headline aloud. 'FLIGHT'S ORCHARD OF DEATH – AN INSULT TO CIVILIZATION.'

'Godfrey Privett,' said Holly.

'I knew it!' exclaimed Feltz. He looked at Matt. 'There! What did I tell you?'

'What do you mean?' Holly said.

'Sorry luv, I should explain,' said Feltz. 'I've just had a visit from Plod.' Feltz recounted the incident in detail, topping it with a corny remark about having had his collar 'feltz'.

'I simply can't believe what you're saying!'

'Would I lie?' Feltz protested, eyes wide.

Matt meanwhile was immersed in Privett's withering critique, reading and re-reading and feeling increasingly ill. 'Flight's *Orchard* is an abomination, the work of a would-be Antichrist. Its celebration of human conflict is degrading and makes a mockery of those who strive for peace in this world. Its message is nothing but a wild fantasy: base, immoral and subversive. With its palette of vulgar clarity and heinous detail, this work wallows in a mire of barbarism. It should be burned!'

Matt stood motionless, stunned by the fiery *coup de grace*. Holly took the newspaper, sensing even its weight was too much for him to bear.

'What does it say?' Felz demanded impatiently.

Holly passed him the paper. 'Read it for yourself.'

A broad smile emerged on Feltz's face. 'Fantazibobo! Hey! He reckons you're an Antichrist.' He looked up gleefully, as if a pot of gold was stuck to the ceiling. 'Bugger me, if that isn't a libel!'

The tone of the article came as no surprise to Bernie. Privett had a public hatred for Lagoon Art. Bernie could well imagine what he might say about its owner – 'That nasty little man Bernie Feltz! A parvenu of dubious extraction who should have no place in the higher echelons of culture. God!' – with a rolling of the eyes – 'I can hardly bear the mention of his name.'

'Godfrey, you old poof!' Feltz roared. 'You've done us proud, me old son, really proud!' He turned to Matt, waving the paper in the air. 'Wait till Sylvester sees this,' he cried. 'He's gonna love it!'

Matt shook his head and sat down, utterly deflated.

Unmoved by Matt's misery, Bernie was lost in joyous contemplation. With publicity like this, Sylvester was bound to buy. *The Orchard* would bring visitors to his gallery in their thousands, pouring through the turnstiles to see what all the fuss was about.

Holly studied Matt's mournful face. 'It's typical Privett,' she said. 'You mustn't take it to heart.'

'I never imagined people would get so annoyed,' he said. 'I mean, hell, I thought the painting made a valid point.'

'It does,' said Holly. 'But people don't like this kind of truth. It's too uncomfortable.'

'I went too far.'

'No. You've pricked a balloon, that's all,' said Holly, surprised at his sensitivity.

Meanwhile Bernie was pacing the gallery floor, mobile jammed to his ear. 'Sylvester!' he shouted. 'Get a load of this.' Whooping with glee, he read out bits of Privett's article, expanding on it with his usual flair.

'Bernie doesn't give a shit, does he?' Matt said gloomily.

'About you, personally?' said Holly. 'Well, no. His life revolves around money.'

'You mean he doesn't give a toss about art either?'

'He gets a kick out of it, all right,' she conceded. 'But only because it gives him a chance to bullshit with the best of them.'

'You mean guys like me are just cannon-fodder.'

'Listen,' said Holly, finding him suddenly rather tragic. 'Lagoon Art's a business, just like any other.'

Matt nodded despondently.

'It's naïve to think it's any different,' she went on.

'I suppose so,' said Matt. 'It's just that I…'

'Didn't quite see yourself as a commodity?'

'Well, no,'

'Look, controversy is Bernie's stock in trade,' she explained. 'And right now, you're just that. But cheer up! You stand to make a killing!'

But this did little to cheer him up. A killing implied something ignoble, something foreign to his image of himself as a virtuous champion of truth. Yes, he had to earn money: but not 'make a killing'. He wanted recognition: but not to be vilified in the press. He felt exposed, marooned on a rock in a rising tide.

Holly peered at him over her glasses. Then she pushed them up above her forehead. 'Now, show me your work will you?' she said, suddenly firm. 'That's what I'm here for after all – not a counselling session!'

Revealed at last, her eyes astonished him. Arrestingly green, cat-like and invulnerable, they spoke of mischief and a willingness to break rules. Yes, 'wild child' was a fitting description. Drawn in the wake of her seductive scent, he followed her round the gallery, wondering what she would say.

The Orchard was hanging apart from Matt's other work. Holly stood in front of it, finding it just as compelling as when she first saw it. Its haunting imagery filled her with unease.

'You have to admit your thinking's pretty dire,' she said. 'I mean, you're removing all hope of a future without wars.'

Matt shrugged. 'Well as I see it, that's how it is.'

'You're saying we're stuck with it?'

'War?' said Matt. 'Sure! To pretend otherwise is idealistic crap.'

'But idealism must count for something!'

'Not once it's distorted, like now.'

'How do you mean?'

Matt pondered his reply. 'There are wackos out there who'd have us believe that human nature can be changed – that war, if you're civilized, is abnormal.'

'Well, isn't it?' Holly suggested.

'No!' Matt insisted. 'It's normal human behaviour.'

'But, that doesn't make it right, surely?' Holly retorted.

'The rights and the wrongs of it are irrelevant,' said Matt. 'It's what the human animal gets off on.'

'God how depressing,' said Holly, standing back. 'You make it sound like an addiction.'

'It is,' said Matt. 'One we're born with.'

'Horrible!' said Holly, unconvinced.

'And the truth is that with too little war, mankind goes kind of squidgy in the head,' said Matt. 'That's what's happened now.'

'So there must always be fighting?' Holly asked.

'It's part of our psyche, the way we define weakness and strength. Without it we wouldn't be human, just brain-dead androids.'

'At least we'd be happy,' she chirruped.

'Not true,' said Matt adamantly. 'We'd have no concept of happiness.'

'Smartarse!'

Holly grinned at him then she turned to another painting, of a city razed to the ground. Deserted and still, its broken buildings stood humbled before a huge sky all aglow in the evanescent light of evening. Holly studied the work closely. 'Everything's made up of letters,' she said. 'The masonry, the rubble, they're fragments of words. Why's that?'

'It's an allegory. The collapse of a civilization.'

'Ours?'

'Yes. The fragments of letters symbolize all that's left of values we once had.'

'Do you think things are really that bad?' Holly asked.

'Yes,' said Matt.

Holly leant forward to observe the detail of some willowherb Matt had seen fit to include. Standing proud, their pinks and greens contrasted with the buffs and greys of fallen masonry.

'You like them?' he asked, pleased that she'd noticed.

'It's a nice touch, as though you're saying that even where there's devastation, there's hope.'

'If not for us, then for the natural world,' said Matt.

'You think there's no hope for us?'

'Not if we go on as we are. Nothing holds us together anymore. Spiritually, we're bankrupt.'

'Like God's been made redundant,' said Holly, surprised to find herself agreeing.

'Forced into retirement,' Matt added facetiously.

Holly grinned. 'In a bungalow by the sea, maybe.'

Matt smiled with her. 'Yeah, leaving us to live as inmates in a madhouse, our mutual detestation spasmodically erupting into violence.'

'Ghastly!' said Holly, grimacing.

'It's everyone for himself. Unity is dead,' Matt said returning to dolefulness, as if Unity was a matriarchal figure who had held the family together for years but had now regretfully passed away. 'Without some kind of unity, civilizations fall. Show me one that hasn't! Not that anybody seems to give a shit.'

'Why? I wonder,' asked Holly, finding herself seduced more and more into agreement.

Matt gave her a wry smile. 'Too busy frigging around being modern. You know, 'blue-sky thinking' and that sort of crap.'

Holly looked at him with a pensive smile, then back at the picture. It seemed to her there was something sublime about the picture which transcended Matt's dismal message. A fusion of hard logic and poetry put the work in a class of its own, above mere skill and a simple aim to please.

Matt was like no other artist she'd met. Here was someone determined to face truths, yet within him there was clearly a vulnerability. He was easily offended, stunned even, when others didn't see his point of view. A visionary, but naïve; fate had given him a goodly dollop of human failing.

'Do you believe in God?' she asked him.

'As representing what's beyond my understanding, yes,' Matt replied. 'But not like a grand old man with a beard.'

'What then?'

'As a force.'

'With power over good and evil?'

'No, those are human distinctions,' said Matt.

'So it's nonsense to think He might protect us?'

'Yes,' said Matt. 'What have we done do deserve protection?

'I don't know. But I bet if you're in the shit, you're onto Him like there's no tomorrow!'

Matt conceded: 'Well, yeah, we all do that.'

Holly teased him: 'On the off chance He is a guy with big ears who'll hear you cry?'

Feltz, still on the phone, called over to Matt. 'Sylvester says sorry he didn't get the chance to meet you last night. But he'd like us to go over to the 'Rich' tomorrow morning. Can you make it?'

'Sure.'

'Brilliant!' bubbled Feltz, giving his usual thumbs up. 'And Holly, m'luv, my sweetest luv, you couldn't do me the greatest of 'flavours' could you?'

Holly guessed what was coming. 'Stand in for you, here? I suppose so.'

'Good on you, darlin',' he said. 'I'll love you forever.'
Holly's eyes rolled towards the ceiling. She'd heard it all
before.

Feltz returned to Sylvester, their conversation now
turning into the timeless banter of negotiation. An
urgency in Feltz's voice betrayed his desperation to
strike a deal. Opening and closing his fist repeatedly, he
berated Sylvester for suggesting a figure way below the
asking price. He appeared to be making little headway.
Holly could imagine Sylvester on the other end of the
line; he would be smiling to himself, leaning back in his
chair and admiring his manicured nails.

'Sylvester, Sylvester,' pleaded Feltz, in a smarmy
change of tack. 'Listen; I hear what you say, but your
offer is unfair to me and to young Flight. Just look at all
I've done for the guy. No, stop winding me up! His work
is top dollar and you know it.'

Haggling sometimes forges respect between negotiating parties, but this was a one-sided duel. Feltz kept coming back for more only to fall victim again and again, his
every proposal a soft spot for Sylvester's jab. One last
parry from Feltz; then he was forced to retire, bloodied
but remarkably unbowed.

'We'll sort it out in the morning!' he shouted, thrusting
his mobile back into his pocket. 'Jeez, what a tight wad.
Wants everything for nothing, the miserable sod.'

Holly grinned. These tussles with Sylvester were legendary. Feltz's squealing tone was a sure sign to Holly
that he was being screwed to the floor. When Feltz said
he was still confident of getting a good price Holly
thought he was too confident; his judgment was clouded
by gossip that Sylvester – flush from the sale of a Warhol
in New York – was ripe for a 'touch'.

'What d'you think he'll pay?' Matt asked anxiously.

Feltz was evasive. 'Worried about your cut, are you?'

'With good reason,' said Matt. 'I spent months on that
picture.'

'Relax,' said Feltz. 'I'll knock it out for what I can. Trust me, you'll do well enough.'

Matt had emerged from his negative mood. He was amused by Feltz's jargon, with its 'cuts', 'knock-outs' and 'do-well-enough's'. It was as if his painting was bounty fallen from the back of a lorry, to be divvied out between villains. He caught Holly's eye and winked.

'What's so funny?' snapped Feltz.

Matt teased him. 'Nothing,' he said. 'I'm sweet. Well pleased. Sorted!'

Unwilling to share in a joke against himself, Feltz retreated to his office where he sat in a huff prodding at his calculator. Those two would never understand, he thought – Holly with her easy social poise and money she'd never lifted a finger for; and Matt, distanced from the rigours of commerce, perched on a planet of his own, ruminating about God knows what.

What do they know about anything? he asked himself. Fuck all!

For Feltz, life had been very different. Born to a family of immigrant Jews in London's East End, his childhood memories were the harsh realities of survival. His wits were honed at an early age on the wear and tear of the marketplace.

His parents had worked and saved for years before acquiring a shop. It was then that prosperity beckoned and the family went on to build a fortune selling cloth to the world of fashion.

Watching his parents' conspiratorial smiles served to mould his character, giving him a taste for 'naughty' mark-ups and bundles of cash, springy with an energy of their own, so adorable that he would sometimes kiss them before squirrelling them away in secret places.

Using family contacts in fashion and the arts, Feltz had lost no time building a business of his own. The name Lagoon Art, he believed, conjured up an image of tranquil exclusivity, a place of privilege where the wealthy could saunter about and indulge themselves in his discoveries of creative endeavour.

But ask him where the name came from and he wouldn't say – the mundane truth being that he got the idea from an old travel brochure. A picture of a couple dining at the waters' edge on a faraway Pacific island had seemed to him to portray the ultimate point of 'arrival'.

Now, some years on, he'd emerged, as he fancied, a man of the world. To be reminded of his origins made him feel irritable and insecure.

'God, Bernie's a prickly sod,' murmured Matt.

Holly grinned impishly. Wanting to make amends, Matt poked his head round the doorway of Feltz's office. 'Only joking,' he bleated.

Feltz didn't look up. 'I never piss about when it comes to business,' he growled. 'And neither should you, mate.'

Realizing he'd touched a raw nerve, Matt kept a straight face and retreated backwards as if departing from royalty.

'Poor Bernie,' whispered Holly. 'He gets really eggy if you mimic him.'

'I'd no idea,' said Matt.

'It's even worse if he's on edge – like now, with Sylvester roughing him up.'

'You sound as if you're used to him.'

'Helping him out now and then, I've got to know him.'

To Matt, it seemed odd that a man as brash as Feltz should be so sensitive. Holly and Matt exchanged mishievous glances, as children do behind a parent's back.

'He's asked me to work for him, you know,' said Holly. 'Full time, I mean.'

Matt was intrigued. 'As what?'

'Nothing specific, but generally.'

'Would you be selling?'

'Yes, and helping with the P.R. That sort of thing.'

'Would you like that?' Matt asked.

'In principle, yes,' said Holly cautiously. 'But I'd need to find a way to fit my photography in.'

'Oh, so you're into that, are you?'

'Yeah, but it's not a full time thing. Not yet, at any rate.'

'Maybe, he'd let you work a short week,' said Matt.

Holly was hesitant. 'Possibly. But even then, the thought of being stuck in the gallery with him for any length of time is....'

'Is what?'

Holly giggled. 'Well, you know...'

Matt was intrigued. 'You mean he's got wandering hands?'

'Well there are times when he gets a little close,' she confessed, surprised at the intimacy of her admission to a man that she'd only just met.

'Well, so long as he's only looking,' joked Matt.

Holly grinned. 'And I thought I liked you!'

'Well – you can hardly blame him.'

'What's that supposed to mean?'

A touch of indignation in her voice put him on his guard. Did she think he was implying she was a tart? 'Well, you're not exactly one of the Ugly Sisters,' he said.

His veiled flattery floated gently onto her. Half smiling, she relaxed. This moment of flirtation brought them together suddenly, unexpectedly, as if they'd found themselves stuck between floors in a lift. Matt avoided eye contact; he was searching for more words in an imaginary beyond. His face reddened as the silence lengthened into mutual embrassment. It was broken by Holly reaching up and kissing Matt's cheek. 'You're cool,' she said, and she touched his hand.

'Yeah? Well...' said Matt shyly. Not sure how to respond, he cleared his throat and reverted to the subject of Feltz's job offer. 'What d'you think you'll do?'

'About the job?' said Holly, looking up at him as if for ideas. 'I don't really know.'

Matt smiled. Forcing his shyness aside, he said: 'It'd be great to have you on side.'

'You reckon?' she grinned.

'Yeah. For God's Sake, I need allies!'

She laughed. 'It does look that way.'

'D'you think you could talk punters into buying my work?'

'I don't see why not.'

'Well then, you should have a go.'

Acting on impulse came naturally to Holly. She agreed to talk to Feltz in the hope of working something out, something that would allow her some independence. That aside, Matt had ignited her desire. She sensed she would have him – soon.

No girl had been part of Matt's life for months, at least not in any lasting sense. Liaisons tended to flower only briefly before withering in the parched sands of life outside art. Art was a mistress more powerful than any who climbed the stairs to his attic studio and most girls couldn't bear the competition. They would lie alone on his studio bed while he worked through the night hours, his mercilessly bright light disturbing all but the deepest wine-imbued sleep.

But Holly wasn't one to be treated in this way. She liked men to eat from the palm of her hand. And if they bored her, she'd toe them aside and move on, leaving them shocked and bewildered and wondering why they'd been dumped. More often than not it was because they were useless in the sack – 'wham, bam, thank you ma'm jerks'.

Holly and Matt stood close, both fantasizing about what it would be like to bed each other.

36

FOUR

The Rich Gallery stood on a bend in the river. Set alongside a sprawl of modernity whose livid brickwork transformed an area once dominated by docklands, the cake-shaped building of stainless steel rivalled any of the futuristic wonders conceived in the run up to the new millennium. Boatloads of tourists cruising the Thames would shield their eyes from its glinting façade while marvelling at the story of its creation lauded over megaphones into the blustery riverside air.

Those who had lived in the houses demolished to make way for these developments were not impressed. Condemned to live in tower blocks, their sense of community destroyed, they looked out onto a world high on a surfeit of style. 'Bleedin' *café latte*!' they'd complain. 'I mean, wot the fuck's that?'

It was just after ten in the morning when Sylvester Rich emerged from his chauffeur-driven Mercedes. His deep-set eyes darted from side to side, wary of potential assailants. How the world had moved on, he thought. Once, it was only the works of radical artists that were vandalized. Today, even a celebrated impresario of the arts could find himself in the firing line.

The previous autumn he had been the victim of one such attack. He'd staged an exhibition, a celebration of homo-eroticism unsurpassed both in scale and variety. The centrepiece had been a marble sculpture of two men kissing, carved in the classical manner of Canova. The exhibition was well-attended. Gay lobbying groups hailed it as a giant step forward in the incessant struggle to persuade the population that 'back-door' penetration was as normal as buttering bread.

The event led to furious debate in the media. Interviewed on television, Sylvester stated his case, namely that throughout the ages homosexuals had made major contributions to the development of art. Their exploration of what it is to be human was as valid as any other. Like it or not, the practice of sodomy was part of human nature, reaching back to the origins of man. His interviewer took this as a slander against cavemen and their comical television counterparts, loved by successive generations. 'What will we have to put up with next?' he'd asked. 'A gay Fred Flintstone? Yubba, dubba, doo! – No, this is sacrilege, surely?'

Equally offended was broader public taste. Retribution lay round the corner: within days of a televised debate, a group of fanatical supporters of CLASS – the Christian League Against Sodomitic Sex – saw fit to attack Sylvester one evening as he left the Rich Gallery. Masked and gloved, they had forced him to his knees and rubbed excrement over his head before retreating down an alleyway to a waiting van. It had been a humiliating experience, but he had kept it to himself, the public enjoyment of his enemies being better denied them.

Pocketing his hands, Sylvester hurried through a stiff breeze to the circular mouth of glass that was his gallery entrance. Beyond was the complex of temperature-controlled rooms cossetting his collection. Whether figurative, abstract or mixed-media creations, they were all extreme examples of contemporary neo-expressionism.

Sylvester stood in the atrium, bathed in an ethereal glow fit for a god. Pausing for a moment, he pulled back the sleeves of his cotton suit. This calculated dishevelment did little to soften the brutal demeanour of his grey cropped hair – a fashionable touch which he imagined was holding back the years.

Spying him out of the corner of his eye, Feltz stood up from the viewing bench. He'd just been telling Matt in a whisper what a shit Sylvester could be. 'Don't think that just because he's a Jew we get on. We don't! Ours is purely a business relationship.'

Matt stood up too, nervous to meet the great man.

Sylvester Rich approached, his forced smile concealing a sense of loathing – not for young Matt but for Feltz, whose coarseness he abhorred. 'Forgive me, the traffic was diabolical,' he said, glancing at the moon-dial face of his slimmest of gold watches.

Bollocks! thought Feltz. Sylvester's lateness would be deliberate, lending grandeur to his arrival. They shook hands. On Sylvester's part the gesture was regrettable – an invasion of his treasured corporeal space.

'Have you been waiting long?' Sylvester asked.

'No, no,' Feltz lied, determined to give no hint that he and Matt had been inconvenienced. He introduced Matt.

'Ah, l'enfant terrible, n'est ce pas?' said Sylvester, extending his palm. 'You've caused a bit of a furore, it seems.'

'It wasn't intended,' said Matt.

'I don't suppose for a moment it was,' sighed Sylvester. 'But what is done is done and we must make the most of it.'

'Exactly!' Feltz said emphatically.

'I saw Privett's piece,' Sylvester continued. 'Wonderful publicity. What an asset that man is. Though you'll have to be careful – a visit from the Fangos could well be on the cards.'

'The Fangos?' said Matt, reminded of rabid dogs. 'Who are they?'

Sylvester grinned. *'Fans* of Godfrey Privett.'

Feltz explained to Matt: the Fangos were a group of devotees who had taken it upon themselves to organise protest sit-ins in galleries showing art which Privett found objectionable. Artistic purity, standing aloof from the ruinous pressures of commercial exploitation, was their cause and they were becoming increasingly obstreperous in promoting it. Privett was silent on whether or not he approved of their activities.

'They're a pain in the arse!' added Feltz, having had first hand experience of them sitting about, littering his gallery floor with their 'crap'.

'They descended on us only recently,' said Sylvester.

'Really?' said Matt.

'They had this bee in their bonnets about my introducing an Interactivity Hall.'

'Yeah, I heard about that,' said Feltz, smirking at the thought of them squirming with horror. 'Whatever next?' Privett had pontificated. 'Fruit machines?'

'How did you get shot of 'em?' said Feltz.

'It was all most amusing. I had security turn them into an exhibit; put a little rope barrier around them and a hastily concocted sign.

'Performance art,' suggested Matt.

Sylvester chuckled. 'Needless to say, they soon got up and left: rather tail-between-legs, I must say.'

Matt was impressed: then taken aback, when Sylvester asked suddenly: 'Tell me Matt, have you been to my gallery before?'

With some embarrassment, Matt replied that he hadn't.

'Too busy working!' explained Feltz jovially, trying to make light of this unfortunate shortcoming.

'But of course,' said Sylvester, in a pardoning tone. 'It must have taken years to achieve the standard you have. Your study of detail is remarkable.'

'Gob-smacking!' added Feltz.

Sylvester winced at the vulgarism, preferring instead to describe *The Orchard* as a *tour de force*.

'It's kind of you to say so,' said Matt.

With a deal in the air, Feltz was on edge and keen to move the morning on. 'Sylvester, could we have a look at the collection? I know Matt can't wait to see it.'

'Absolutely,' said Sylvester, tilting his head appreciatively. He ushered them in the direction of a huge bronze in the centre of the atrium. 'Of course, Bernard will have to bear with us. There are certain exhibits he will be familiar with. But not this one, I think – eh, Bernard?'

'Oh, yeah,' said Feltz, casting an eye over it. 'We were looking at this before you arrived.'

An enormous sculpture of a parcel, complete with details of knotted cord, towered over them. Its dark polished patina exuded an air of foreboding.

'What do you make of it?' asked Sylvester.

Feltz wrinkled his nose. 'A recent delivery?' he quipped.

'Very droll,' Sylvester conceded. 'I commissioned it specially, as the first thing you see when you enter the gallery. Its title is *Portent* – signifying all you're about to witness.'

'A nice idea,' said Matt tactfully.

They left the atrium and entered the first hall. A party of teenage students was ambling along under the watchful eye of their tutor. An awkward burble of directives and explanation issued from the teacher's head only to be drowned by the students' inattentive babble. The group was heading towards the 'Interactivity Hall'. Now officially open, it housed a collection of mutant forms that visitors could fondle and squeeze. Cast in foam rubber, the artist's intention was to eliminate the feelings of revulsion people normally experience when confronted with the results of genetic malfunction.

To the younger mind, these rubbery mutants presented a chance for nefarious amusement – twisting limbs into knots, forcing others into orifices, creating assemblages of tumultuous depravity.

'Groups of kids like this are a necessary evil,' said Sylvester disdainfully. 'We'll let them get ahead.'

'Grist to the mill, though,' said Feltz, hazarding a guess at the gallery's takings on a good morning.

Utterly typical, thought Sylvester; the man can't stop thinking about money for a moment, not even in the presence of great art.

Like an unwanted cloud the students moved on, appreciative comments from the front being dogged by dismissive comments from the rear.

Sylvester pointed to a cordoned off area of empty floor space. White and pristine, it stretched ahead for some thirty feet. 'Do you know the work of Erik Lindt?' he asked.

Feltz shook his head.

Matt studied the empty rectangle. 'Isn't he that Danish guy with a theory about empty space?'

'That's right. His work is unique,' said Sylvester. 'I'm surprised you haven't heard of him, Bernard. He's probably the most influential artist of his generation.'

'Who says?' said Feltz dismissively.

'I do,' said Sylvester magisterially. It was he who single-handedly established the Dane's reputation. Sylvester enjoyed exposing Bernie's ignorance; it was like pointing out a hole in his sock. It would keep Feltz in his place.

Feltz scowled. 'What's he done that's so brilliant?'

Sylvester hesitated, anticipating a moment of pleasure. 'Nothing,' he said in a hushed voice.

'Nothing!' exclaimed Feltz, his patience eroding.

'No, no, I mustn't,' said Sylvester, rebuking himself. 'I'm not being fair.'

It was at moments like this that Feltz could have slaughtered him. Sylvester's belittling attitude got right up his nose. 'What d'you mean?' he growled.

Sylvester rubbed home his advantage. 'I'm sure Matt understands. The fact that there is nothing happening in this space is as relevant as if there was.'

'Mumbo jumbo!' scoffed Feltz.

'You're so wrong, dear boy. Empty space is as valid as any other subject.'

'Tell us about it,' said Feltz, breathing deeply to stave off his annoyance.

Fearing a heated exchange, Matt intervened. 'I think what Lindt is saying here, is that there are times when we all need space. To be free of worldly demands, if you like. And this emptiness asks nothing of us, except that we enjoy it for what it is.'

'Indeed. The beauty of nothing,' said Sylvester, with reverence. 'Lindt's pointed this out in such a simple way.'

With a possible sale in the offing, Feltz held back his anger and resorted instead to mild cynicism. 'I could get the same result sitting in a bloody deck chair, staring at the sky!'

'You could indeed,' said Sylvester. 'But would you, unless the benefits of doing so were pointed out to you first? In our pressured lives we need reminding of these things. This is what Lindt does. It's a beautiful message, deeply spiritual.'

'Hippy shit,' said Feltz. He turned to Matt for support. 'Do *you* go for this kind of work?'

Matt sat on the fence. 'Lindt's work is much respected,' he said.

'Thank you, Matt,' said Sylvester, graciously. 'I'm only sorry it's so lost on dear Bernard.'

'Lost! I'll say it's lost. There's nothing bloody there!' Feltz persisted. 'I mean, staring at an empty space – that can hardly be a draw in a place like this. You can't tell me Joe Public falls for work like that. It's like saying thin air is art.'

'Not all those who visit the gallery lack sophistication!' was Sylvester's riposte.

Matt hid his amusement. The two men gibed each other as they walked on – Sylvester with a professorial gait, his hands behind his back, and Feltz, the shorter of the two, matching his pace with the studied calm of a man struggling to control his temper.

Despite their mutual antagonism, both men were keenly aware of commercial realities. Whilst feigning disdain for such matters, Sylvester knew he needed people like Feltz; agents and dealers who nosed around the post-graduate shows, searching for talent, moulding it and bringing it to market. They did the donkey work and took the losses when artists let them down – failing to produce work on time on pretexts like the 'vibes' had disappeared. Feltz complained bitterly about such artists, for whom snorting coke, partying and sex, seemed infinitely preferable to getting down to work.

Sylvester bypassed all this hassle. It was much simpler to choose works by artists already in some way accredited: by then, their value was half in the bag. Elevation to the Rich gallery would secure the rest. Sylvester's intellectualized hype would give their work credibility on the international stage. This required gravitas and a convincing show of sincerity – qualities Sylvester was blessed with in abundance. And woe-betide those who mocked him! Mostly, criticism could be dismissed with a patronizing smile that was eloquent in itself: 'I can see this piece of work is quite beyond you.' But his tongue could be even more caustic, if needed.

Once in a while, an attack would actually hit home – though he would be at pains not to show it. An over-heard jibe from a jaded aristocrat had cut him to the quick: 'for all the fellow's airs and graces, he's just another Jew on the make.' Sylvester's inner fury had been as great towards himself for feeling vulnerable, as it was towards the louche, perpetuating old sentiments with the lip-curling enmity of centuries.

Matt approached a low concrete platform on which a small room had been built. In one wall was a security door marked 'Authorized Personnel Only'. A deep window ran the extent of one wall to allow a full view of a brightly lit pink interior.

He peered in at what appeared to be medical equipment arrayed on a trolley. Next to it was a padded bench on wheels. It seemed to represent a room where a medical operation might take place at any minute.

'This will interest you, Matt,' said Sylvester. 'The artist who created this used to produce snuff movies before he turned to sculpture. I'm told they weren't actually real; who knows? But the frisson that people were actually being killed, sold them like hotcakes!'

Feltz smirked. He knew the exhibit of old.

'It reminds me of a surgery,' said Matt.

Sylvester chuckled. 'In the loosest sense, I suppose it is. But, actually, it's an execution chamber equipped for lethal injections.'

'Of course!' said Matt, observing the bench's outstretched arms and buckled restraining straps, neatly at ease across the vinyl upholstery. 'But, hey, what a thing to find in an art gallery,' he remarked.

'Cool bananas, eh?' said Feltz, drawn as usual by the spectacle. 'Now, work like this I can get to grips with.' Pausing a moment to drink in its ghoulishness, he added with a smirk: 'Forgive the pun, but this is knock-out stuff!'

Matt was uneasy. 'Is it the real thing?'

'Oh, yes!' said Sylvester cheerfully. 'All the artist had to do was add the paint.'

'Jesus, what sort of mind can come up with something like this?' asked Matt.

'Pete Kline. He's an American,' said Sylvester. 'An interesting piece of theatre, isn't it?'

'Operating theatre!' Feltz observed, pleased with his intellectual agility.

'But why all the pink?' asked Matt. Every item in the exhibit was painted this colour, as if themed to please the eye.

'It's Kline's sardonic humour,' Sylvester explained. 'A comment on bureaucracy's obsession with appearing as 'Mr. Clean' on the death sentence. As you may know, Kline uses a single colour for each of his works.'

'I like the title,' said Matt. "Death Is Pink Today'.'

Sylvester's eclectic taste was the key to the Rich Gallery's success. Overt statements, challenging enigmas and subtle plays on contemporary thinking took the visitor on a journey that delighted, infuriated and teased. This was the New Art, Sylvester said, and critics of it were just backward-looking. You cannot cloister creativity; to leave the quiet quadrangles of tradition is not to fall off the edge of the world!

'Let them have their past,' Sylvester would say. 'It's not for us.' His doors would never be closed to free thinkers, however uncomfortable their innovations.

Moving on, they came to a sculpture titled 'Black Art'. Cast in black resin, it consisted of a stack of building blocks. Seen closer to, the blocks were made of the compressed limbs of dismembered Africans. An accompanying text said the work signified new nations emerging on the foundations of genocide. 'Hell is on Earth, here and now.'

It reminded Matt of his own work. He leant forward to study it. Here was a fellow artist who, like himself, had fearlessly grasped the inescapable realities of the human condition. He smiled to himself, believing that within the hallowed walls of the Rich Gallery he had found his true artistic home. He crossed his fingers, hoping Sylvester would agree.

'The Devil is in the detail, eh?' joked Feltz, absorbed in differentiating one body part from another.

'It's a tricky piece,' Sylvester said. 'As you know, it's given us some problems.' Feltz smiled; indeed, he had revelled in them!

The forces of political correctness had savaged Sylvester almost daily since he bought the sculpture, forcing him eventually to seek counsel from his lawyer, the sedentary but eminent Royston Rigg.

'Is it wrong to treat genocide as art?' Sylvester had asked.

'In itself no,' Rigg had replied. 'But mention colour and it's immediately a sensitive issue. The problem, I fear, lies in the title: *Black Art*. It implies that blacks have a monopoly on evil.'

'So what do you recommend?' Sylvester had asked. 'Only I may be facing litigation.'

Rigg had given him a wily look. 'Ask Kline to come up with a version in white. After all, whites are fond of massacre too, though we like to think otherwise. Call it *White Lie* – a little play on words, if you will.' Sylvester had phoned Kline the same day to commission a version in white.

'I see you found a way out of trouble,' said Feltz, pointing to the space and a text on the wall that awaited the other half of Kline's balancing act.

'But of course,' Sylvester acknowledged. 'With Kline's work represented in just about every major gallery the world over, we had to. Imagine the ructions there would have been otherwise!'

'I assume Kline makes copies of his work,' said Matt, impressed by the artist's far-reaching influence.

'Absolutely. Once we had installed several of his originals, the clamour for his work was phenomenal,' said Sylvester. 'And to satisfy the demand we created limited editions. They all sold.'

Matt pondered the effects of such exposure. 'Kline must be earning a bundle.'

'A bundle? Ah, well, yes,' said Sylvester, forgiving the young man his vernacular, 'as a matter of fact, he does.'

'And I bet it doesn't stop there,' Feltz added. Yes, it was all very cozy, he felt enviously. Nothing short of a setup. The Rich Gallery's reputation was so entrenched in the minds of curators that many wouldn't purchase new work without deference to Sylvester. His seal of approval was a guarantee that they were spending their budgets wisely.

The prevailing ethos of the day held that classifying art as good or bad was a 'class threat' to the principle of equal opportunity for all. Since anything could pass for art, what was to be applauded? Novelty and shock seemed to be the answer. Genius was redefined as the ability to cause a sensation. The incidence of it rose to new levels, fruiting everywhere like berries in an exceptional autumn.

Lauded by some was an exhibition of sculpture created from human excrement. 'Shame on those,' they cried, 'who mock this valid exploration of the self!'

Among the educated classes, not since the days of Marcel Duchamp's 'La Fontaine' had novelty grabbed so much attention. 'Radical' work had an air of the fairground about it – freakish and voyeuristic like 'The World's Fattest Man'. Mirth or disgust gained an intellectual significance because it was indulged in knowingly. And Sylvester was the high priest of all this.

'The bastard's got it made,' Feltz would say. 'The world's tongue's up his arse.'

Not that he could complain. Without sales to the Rich Gallery, where would he be? Rather worse off, and he knew it. But his share of the cake was rather small when compared to Sylvester's, who would talk up the value of a piece of work to five times what he'd paid Feltz for it.

'OK, Sylvester,' Feltz pushed him. 'What sort of money's involved in an edition of Kline's work?'

Sylvester was evasive, admitting only that twenty-four copies of 'Death is Pink Today' had been built for the international market.

Feltz pressed on for an answer. 'I bet we're talking megabucks?' he said. But Sylvester wasn't to be drawn.

Shyster! thought Feltz. He'll never let on to the likes of me. Meanwhile Matt was reckoning too; the deal must have run into millions of dollars.

Sylvester changed the subject. 'Now, let me show you this: something courtesy of Bernard.' He pointed to an ultra-realistic sculpture of a naked woman. Life-sized and seated, she was encased in glass. Her obesity was falling in folds, like thick custard from a jug, covering all but a wisp of pubic hair reaching from the shadows.

It was the work of Libby Bird. She had made a name for herself while still a student with a huge diptych of two naked women. One was a haunted anorexic and the other a vomiting bulimic.

'I know her work,' said Matt. 'It made headlines a while back.'

'That's right,' said Feltz. 'There was one hell of a shin-dig caused by some arsey feminists she got in with.'

'I remember,' said Matt. 'They crashed her show. Talk about cutting your nose off to spite your face.'

It was this incident that had first brought Matt's attention to Lagoon Art. Two women had forced their way into Libby Bird's private view, where they harangued guests with accusations of gender exploitation and voyeurism. During a spirited attempt to evict them, the antagonists were brought to the floor along with a number of Libby's sculptures, which shattered into pieces on the floor. Their broken limbs and rolling heads gave everyone the impression they were in the middle of a terrorist attack.

At a subsequent trial the defendants argued that Lagoon Art had turned Bird's work into a tasteless freak show of 'unhappily challenged' women. This exacted some sympathy from the judge but even so their action was deemed inexcusable. An order for community service was served and damages awarded to the gallery. But Feltz was cautioned against staging exhibitions likely to incite violence and in this respect the women hailed their action as a victory.

'Libby's show did wonders for the gallery,' Feltz enthused. 'Lit us up like a beacon.'

'Yes. I was lucky to buy this work,' said Sylvester, pointing to the sculpture. 'It was one of the few to escape damage.' He turned to Matt. 'Most of her studies were beyond repair. Her 'anorexics' didn't stand a chance.'

Matt knelt down to read the work's title. '*Bella*,' he said, looking up at the face. 'However did you get like that?' The mournful study of ballooning flesh stared vacantly back.

'Comfort eating, I'm told,' said Sylvester. 'It's a sop for a miserable existence.'

'I notice you've put her behind glass,' Feltz remarked.

'Yes, I'm unhappy about that. I'd hoped that once she was installed here, we'd be able to leave her exposed,' said Sylvester. 'But the truth is, people can't resist the urge to touch.'

'Another 'interactivity' play,' suggested Feltz. 'I bet she got her nipples tweaked!'

Sylvester curled his lip in disgust. 'Regrettably so,' he admitted. 'When a crowd was around it was difficult to stop, even with security present.'

'Well, as long as it doesn't stop her from earning her keep!' added Feltz wickedly.

His tacky inference passed Sylvester by. 'Oh, there's no doubt about that,' he said. 'She's a popular piece. People are fascinated by her.'

'Joy at the misery of others. It makes people feel better,' Matt said.

'Harsh words,' said Sylvester, surprised by his cynicism.

'Is Libby still working?' asked Matt.

'I've no idea,' said Sylvester, dismissively. 'Bernard's more in touch with her than I am.'

Sylvester considered artists an unstable and irrational species. Minimal contact with them was advisable. Having bought a work he would show little further interest, for fear of becoming embroiled in their personal doubts and neuroses. Their novelty was short-lived, like a snowman's.

'Libby flipped as a result of the damage and publicity,' said Feltz. 'Threw a complete wobbly. Didn't speak to anyone for weeks.'

'Where is she now?'

'Hanging out with Holly,' said Feltz.

Matt stemmed his surprise. 'Really?'

'To Holly, it made sense,' Feltz explained. 'She'd been left this big pad in Holland Park by some godfather or other. I met him once – an artist with only one eye. Anyway, after he died she was rattling around the place all on her own.' He paused for a moment. 'Imagine having one of those big houses, in a classy area like that!'

'Lucky girl,' said Matt.

'Anyway,' Bernie went on, 'she felt sorry for Libby after the media had got to her and she'd lost all that work. Holly being Holly, she took her in to give her a break.'

'Amazing,' said Matt.

'Holly's a saint, believe me,' added Feltz. ''Cos that bird Libby's a head case.'

'Really?' said Matt.

'Yeah, Barking!'

Feltz was doubtless exaggerating, Matt thought; artists are often considered mad for their passionate pronouncements.

Sylvester walked ahead to talk to a young attendant. A flickering bulb had caught his eye and the girl was dispatched to 'maintenance' to arrange for an immediate

51

replacement. Such attention to detail was vital, as each exhibit had a specially designed aura of its own.

'Matt, why don't you go on ahead?' Feltz hurriedly suggested. 'I must get to grips with Sylvester about our little deal. You understand.'

'Sure,' said Matt. 'I'll catch up with you later. And hey, good luck!'

Matt walked idly on through the gallery's principal rooms, pausing to study exhibits. As he did so, snatches of conversation caught his ear.

'Yeah, I get the point,' said one awestruck American to another, as they studied a giant hammer stood on its head. Painted yellow and the height of a small tree, it was titled 'Yellowhammer', alluding to the bird of the same name, he guessed.

'Gee, the mind of this guy! He's so darned original.'

Another couple were being deeply critical, coming to the conclusion a work they'd been looking at was 'crap'.

Matt had seen the piece earlier. Half a dozen tenon saws painted fluorescent red were angled onto a green baize board, horizontally lined to suggest they were figures running on an athletics track.

'It's titled 'Running Sores',' said the woman.

'Another play on words,' said the man, twitching his shoulder aggressively.

'According to the blurb it's a comment on the insoluble problems of our times. Racial tension, inner city violence, that kind of thing.'

'Bloody tosh!'

As the couple moved on, another fellow tapped the man on the shoulder. 'People like you should be shot!' he said.

The couple looked at each other in amazement.

'Fascist bastard!' the fellow ranted. The veins in his neck were swelling with fury.

Discretion being the better part of valour, the couple walked away hand in hand, taking care not to make sudden movements. They were on the retreat from a dangerous animal.

Matt followed a little and listened. The couple were muttering to each other about 'crazies' and art having hit the buffers in 'Toytown' and how, in the absence of any fresh ideology to fire things up, there was little chance that a way out would ever be found.

Glorying in Sylvester's reaction to his work and excited by the exhibits he'd seen, Matt didn't share their pessimism. In these works he'd discovered a new world, free from the disciplines of principle he had worked to for so long. Yes, here was a world where anything goes. Intoxicated by the thought that he might soon be a part of it, he felt positively lightheaded.

He sat himself down. He wondered how Feltz was faring – 'ducking and diving', doubtless, in his own inimitable way.

Matt's mind turned to Holly. It was kind of her, to take in that sculptress. He thought of Holly back at Lagoon Art and tried to picture what she would be doing. But in the sultry air, he was overcome by drowsiness.

A voice broke through. 'Are we keeping you up?'

Matt opened his eyes to find Feltz staring into his face.

'Sorry, I was dozing,' he said, blinking his way back to consciousness. 'It's warm in here.'

Feltz and Sylvester sat down either side of him. 'I apologize for the heat,' said Sylvester. 'I feel it too, but if it's lowered, humidity becomes a problem with certain exhibits.'

'Please, I'm not bothered,' said Matt. 'I just sat down to rest my feet and…'

'So what d'you make of it all?' asked Feltz, somewhat distractedly, for the drubbing he'd received in the previous half hour was still fresh in his mind. Sylvester had played with him like a cat with a mouse, batting him about until Feltz gave in, whingeing at the injustice of it all.

'It's mind-blowing!' said Matt, with boyish enthusiasm. 'It's an incredible collection.'

Sylvester smiled like a dignitary about to award a prize. 'Well, I'm happy to hear that, because I've decided to add your picture to it.'

Matt was euphoric. 'I don't know what to say,' he said, feeling like an outcast given a home.

'There's no need to say anything. It's an excellent painting and I'm delighted to have acquired it.'

Matt felt vindicated. The Rich Gallery's purchase would enable him to dismiss Privett's criticism as the ranting of a blinkered fool. But what about the price? he wondered. Was no one going to tell him? He searched Feltz's face for an answer. But Feltz pretended not to notice, looking away and wringing his hands in forced pleasure. The man was concealing something, Matt felt sure.

A probability entered his head – *The Orchard* had been sold for a song. But he dismissed his concern. His spirits were high and a sale of sorts was better than no sale at all. He stood up and outstretched his arms, determined that nothing should sour his moment of glory.

Again, Sylvester Rich smiled. The young artist before him was a model of gratitude and would readily have fallen to his knees in reverence and praise. He read in Matt's face dreams of avarice and glory. And why not? Before him lay the world.

FIVE

olly Tree was watching visitors to Lagoon Art as they moved in silence from picture to picture, their furrowed brows caught briefly in spotlights as if they were characters in a melodrama. After Privett's review and one or two others, the public's curiosity was mounting. Smiling benignly, she eased her way back to Feltz's office where she sat down, thoughts of Matt on her mind.

Barely two days had passed since she'd met him. He was cool, she thought, different from other guys she'd known. A man of ideas, he was vain and over-sensitive perhaps, but that's not unusual in an artist. And as for those brown eyes – a girl could lose herself in those.

More to the point, did he fancy her? She reckoned he did. She'd noticed him colouring up when she was close. Holly laughed to herself, believing her chances of making out with him were good.

She wondered where Matt came from, what his past was. Feltz had only told her he'd dropped out of art school – something to do with his not seeing eye to eye with his tutors. Apparently they'd been 'irredeemable diehards of class warfare.' The catalogue to his exhibition hadn't helped much either. Feltz's laudatory waffle revealed little except for his age, which was thirty-two.

She'd guessed by the look of him that he hadn't a penny to his name. Then again, she told herself, appearances didn't mean much any more. But at least he didn't affect to be plebeian, unlike many of his peers who'd abandoned their articulacy for fear of taunts about 'talkin' posh'.

As for liking his paintings, well, that was more difficult. She did and she didn't. The compositions were faultless, no question; but his subjects were unnerving – doom-laden, impossible to live with.

Opening her handbag, she took out a mirror. The face which looked back was still youthful at twenty-nine, despite a decade of partying and excess. Her eighteenth birthday party had set it all off – and what a night that had been! She had snuck off for sex with several guys in a potting shed in the grounds of her stepfather's country house. It was odd to think now, but who they were had hardly mattered at the time.

As for romance, there were men who fitted the bill, but relationships never seemed to last. Mr. Right remained elusive.

Was it her fault? She wasn't sure. Friends implied that her tendency to throw herself at men in an unbridled way was to blame, and that her bizarre fantasies made men want to make for the nearest exit.

There were times when she wondered if men were worth the hassle. Young guys were the worst: so unimaginative. And though older men could be more understanding – father figures charmed by the babbling brook of her youthful chatter – a future with one of them would be full of problems. Not least, his 'dangly bits' might have seen better days.

Compared to these things, the companionship of women was so trouble-free. Easy talk and laughter over lunches lifted her spirits no end. Outwardly joyful but inwardly sad, Holly felt like someone groping for a door in the dark. If it wasn't for her photography and love of art, life would have little meaning.

And Matt? she asked herself. Is he just another memory in the making?

Only time would tell. For the moment, his combination of looks and talent and his passion to portray the truth had lifted her desire to be with him above the usual wanderlust of a one-night stand.

She had an idea. She would ask him to sit for her in the studio of her Holland Park house. After all, he was making a name for himself and a new set of photographs was needed. Feltz had commissioned the first lot for a knock-down price from some photographer on his uppers. They were naff – more suited to a hairdressing salon than a gallery.

Her work might gain a little prominence from it too. And why not? She had worked hard enough.

A slamming of taxi doors from the street broke her train of thought. Feltz and Matt had returned. She edged hurriedly across the crowded floor to greet them. 'How did it go?' she asked, trying to contain her excitement.

Feltz was noncommittal. 'Tell her,' he said, looking at Matt.

Matt smiled. 'It's sold.'

Holly flung her arms around him with uninhibited glee, unaware of the powerful effect this had on Matt. 'That's amazing!' she cried. 'Well done!' Taking Matt's hand, she turned to Feltz. 'What about the price?' she asked. 'Were you successful?'

'Let me get inside, will you?' said Feltz, unwilling to discuss the matter until he had reached the privacy of his office. There he admitted: things hadn't gone quite to plan.

'So?' said Holly. 'What did he pay?'

'Well,' Feltz shrugged. 'As you know, we started talking around the twenty mark, but…'

Sensing Holly's impatience, Matt intervened. 'It works out at twelve grand,' he said, doing his best to mask his disappointment.

Holly's face dropped.

'Sylvester's a bastard to do business with,' moaned Feltz. 'You know how it is.'

Matt refused to allow a matter of money to mar his success. After all, *The Orchard* was to be given pride of place in the gallery and a specially constructed backdrop of its own.

'My work's in there!' he said bravely. 'That's what we wanted, isn't it?'

'I suppose,' Holly said. 'But it's not much considering the months you spent on it.'

'That's irrelevant,' Feltz said. 'There's no correlation between Matt's time and the price. Sylvester had me by the balls. He knows Matt hasn't sold much work, so a sale was vital to us.' He flopped into his chair like a vanquished boxer. 'It's always the same. I jack the figure up to allow for him knocking me down, but somehow it's never enough – I'm sorry, mate, I'm sorry.'

'What about the Privett article?' asked Holly. 'Surely that made a difference?'

'Don't think I didn't try that argument,' said Feltz, shaking his head bitterly. 'All he did was come back at me about the risk of the painting turning out to be a five-minute wonder.'

'That's so unfair!' exclaimed Holly.

'He's a cunning sod,' said Feltz, relieved to have a little sympathy. Sylvester had had the best of the deal, acquiring Matt's work for little more than half the asking price. For twenty-four square feet of exquisitely painted canvas, what he paid was a steal.

'Come on, there's no point in banging on about it,' said Matt with a shrug. 'The deal's done and we ought to be celebrating.' After Lagoon Art's cut he would receive six thousand pounds. It was money he needed.

'I know. I'll recover,' whimpered Feltz. 'There's some champagne in the fridge.'

Matt picked up Privett's article, still open on the desk. 'So much for this shit!'

Holly returned with the champagne and three glasses. 'Keep that review,' she said. 'It'll make a great start to a book of press cuttings.'

Matt thumbed the cork till it popped, shooting out of Feltz's office into the gallery, where it settled at a woman's feet. Her reproachful stare triggered an apology from him.

'Holly's right,' said Feltz. He selected a cigar from his pearl-inlaid humidor, something he had recently bought to enhance his image. 'Remember what I said about provenance? In Joe Public's mind, that article will be where your story began.'

This didn't seem fair to Matt. If only his work would gather praise instead of disapprobation. Notoriety was inglorious, a reward for cheapskates and tricksters who can't make the scene in any other way. Now, like a branded miscreant, he would carry a warning before him. But grumble as he might, there was not much he could do about it.

Feltz lit his cigar and sat back in his chair. He puffed out a billowing pall of smoke and took a swig on his champagne. 'Things are beginning to roll. We must keep up the momentum – build on it, even.'

'Can't we just let the exhibition run its course?' said Matt.

Feltz guffawed. Never had he heard such naivety. 'With opportunity like this staring us in the face!'

Holly grinned. She could read Feltz – he'd already decided on Matt's next career move. 'Listen, Bernie,' she said cautiously, 'before you go any further, there's something we have to discuss.'

'What's that, m'luv?' asked Feltz, in pliant mood.

'That image of Matt – the one in the rear gallery.' She said apprehensively. 'It isn't right.'

'No?' said Feltz, puffing away.

'Honestly. It makes Matt look more like a game-show host than an artist.'

Matt sniggered. He knew what she meant.

To both their surprise, Feltz offered up his hands in surrender. 'I know, I know,' he admitted. 'I hired the wrong guy, but his quote was just wicked.'

Holly smiled at the feeble excuse, but now was not the moment to chide him. 'Look,' she said sweetly. 'I could do you a retake by the end of the week, if only you'd let me. No fee!'

Holly being an amateur, Feltz had been reluctant to use her before. But now it seemed churlish to deny her, especially when the price was right. 'Alright, m'darlin', you win,' he said, in a rush of magnanimity.

'Great!' said Holly delightedly. 'You won't regret it.'

'I'd better not!' he said firmly. Then, turning to Matt, he asked: 'Are you up for this, mate? Only I've been promising Holly the chance of a shoot for yonks.'

'Sure, I'm cool,' said Matt, sitting down with his glass.

'Brilliant!' said Feltz. 'I'll leave it to the two of you to sort out.'

Holly eyed Matt mischievously. 'This is going to be fun,' she said. 'I've got some great ideas.'

'Like what?' he asked.

Putting down her glass she framed his face in her hands. 'Now that would be telling!'

Matt chuckled. The insinuation in her voice excited him.

Feltz pursed his lips and sent a smoke ring curling up to the ceiling. 'Now what I have in mind is this. We go for some exposure on the telly.'

Matt's heart quickened. 'Television!' he exclaimed. 'Won't that Privett shit put them off?'

'*Au contraire,*' said Feltz, mimicking Sylvester. 'An article like that is manna from Heaven for those guys.'

'I don't know,' said Matt doubtfully. 'Couldn't it just make things a whole lot worse?'

From Feltz's viewpoint, the pursuit of 'worse' was highly desirable. 'Remember the Libby Bird fracas?' he said. 'They did a brilliant job covering that. I called them up and they were round here in a flash.'

'And look what that did to Libby!' Matt pointed out.

'Yeah, yeah, yeah,' said Feltz, unconcerned. 'Sure, what she went through was tough. But there's no comparison. To start with, you're not a neurotic little dyke.'

Holly was furious. 'How can you say that about Libby? It's *so* not true!'

'Chill out!' cried Feltz, throwing up his hands. 'Nobody's criticizing. I'm her greatest fan, but she's a mixed-up chick. Hell, you know that.'

'Maybe, but think what she did for Lagoon Art! Since her show, you've never looked back.'

'I'm the first to admit it,' said Feltz defensively. 'What she gets off on is no odds to me either. AC, DC – I couldn't give a monkey's arse! All I am saying is that in front of the cameras, she comes across flaky; and that's bad news, believe me.'

'You think I'll do better?' Matt asked.

'After watching you at your private view, I know so,' said Feltz. 'And with a little practice, you'll be perfect.'

Matt was sopping up his flattery. 'It's almost as though you knew there'd be trouble.'

'Matt, Matt,' pleaded Feltz. 'You can never predict how these occasions'll go. But I'll admit, it was good to see you can look after yourself. Shrinking violets are a bitch to promote.'

'Well, whatever,' said Matt. Leaning back in his chair, he basked in Feltz's admiration.

Feltz stood up. 'Anyway, we can't take this Privett shit lying down. The man needs a smack, for Crissake! And as for Plod – well, it's a bloody liberty, isn't it? A classic example of the law being an arse.'

'Ass,' Holly corrected him.

'Arse, ass – what's the difference?'

'But, seriously,' said Matt, 'if we hit back, who's going to listen? I mean, let's face it, rubbishing Lagoon Art is a media pastime.'

'You *make* them listen.'

'How? By holding a gun to their heads?'

Feltz ran a finger round the rim of his glass. 'Nothing so radical,' he said smugly.

'Then, how?' Matt asked.

Holly guessed what Feltz was planning. Draining her glass she looked into the gallery, to spare herself the look of horror on Matt's face when he learned what Feltz had in mind.

'By getting them to participate directly,' Feltz explained, obscuring himself in an exhalation of smoke.

'In what?' Matt asked.

'A televised debate,' said Feltz. He swept the fog of smoke aside and Matt could see his eyes were wide with excitement.

'What!' cried Matt. 'Are you crazy? I've never done anything like that in my life!'

Feltz beamed. 'Not until now. But think of it. A slot on 'Torment Tonight' – that's what I have in mind. Cracking publicity!' Feltz rubbed his hands as he imagined the scene; Richard Torment, doyen of television presenters, chairing a debate about *The Orchard* and everybody at loggerheads on issues of morality.

Matt turned to Holly for support. 'This is madness.'

'It'll give you a chance to fight back!' she said brightly.

'Right on!' said Feltz. 'Kick some shit out of the fuckers.'

'Fuckers?' said Matt, puzzled by the plural. 'Which fuckers?'

'Which fuckers? Jeez, man, who d'you think? Godfrey Privett of course, and any other moralizing tossers we can rope in. The country's knee-deep in them.'

In that much he's right, thought Matt. But the idea of sparring with Privett live worried him. It would be hand-to-hand combat with a slippery foe. The man was a media fixture. He knew the ropes; he'd been in the limelight for years.

'Why don't I just write a letter?' he asked.

'A letter!' spluttered Feltz. 'What the poxy Hell use is that?'

'Well, I thought...'

'You didn't think at all!' Feltz cut in. 'No, no, no – we've got to sort these buggers out good and proper.'

Matt looked to Holly: her face was all lit up. It was clear she agreed with Feltz. 'Assuming you get Privett to agree,' Matt said, 'who else would you try and rope in?'

'Well for starters, there's that old dog from the Council for Moral Issues.'

'Dame Bradstock!' said Holly. 'That would be ace. D'you think she'd agree to it?'

'She bloody well ought to,' said Feltz. 'It's thanks to her meddling with the Nudity Act that Plod's got me in the dock for Crissake!'

Holly laughed at the thought of Feltz being led into court. Not that he wouldn't deserve it – if not for this occasion, for all the other times he'd been a rogue and got away with it.

'Go on, laugh. But if I'm fined, they could sting me for thousands!'

'Bradstock,' Matt pondered. 'But she's that government minister, isn't she? And wasn't she an agony aunt at one time – 'Auntie Biddie' or something?'

'That's right,' said Holly. 'She was Dame'd for services to the people.'

'Bloody absurd!' said Feltz bitterly. 'To think – whether I'm fined or not is down to a frigging agony aunt.'

'They say she's a very moral person,' said Holly to wind him up. 'She's an honorary Chancellor at some university, too. There must be something really special about her.'

'Whatever it is, they can keep it,' said Feltz, huffily. 'And what about those dickhead police? I've a bloody good mind to haul them in too.'

'If you make enough fuss, we might get the Commissioner – old Buller of the Yard himself!'

'The Singing Policeman!' howled Feltz, alluding to a moniker the devout Welshman had picked up during an inaugural tour of the nation's sink estates. The Commissioner had had the bright idea of assembling groups of victimized locals and persistent offenders, together with various civic luminaries and local police, and leading them all in singsongs. The idea was to initiate a new era of hope, understanding and togetherness through song.

'I mean, what a plonker!' said Feltz. 'I'd like to put him straight.'

But it wouldn't be Feltz putting anybody straight, thought Matt. No, it would be down to him, and he shuddered at the thought of it. He would be arguing with people of whose ilk he had little experience. Millions glued to their screens would be lusting after his blood like spectators in an amphitheatre. Cameramen would be recording his every twitch and grimace, hoping to catch his death-throes after the fatal cut of some vicious put-down.

Holly saw his doubt. 'Come on,' she insisted. 'You can do it. You've got to!'

It was clear he had no choice. If he refused to co-operate, Holly would think him a wimp. He couldn't risk that – not after that kiss, that embrace. How warm she'd felt! And how she'd cool off, if he crept into a corner, his armour unsullied in battle.

He took a deep breath. 'What's involved?'

'I'll contact Cityvision. It has to be Torment – when it comes to argy-bargy, there's no one to touch him. And he gets audiences of seven million!'

'Only because he's a master of the put-down,' Matt said ruefully. 'That's why people watch him.'

'More likely, it's for the chance of a punch-up,' Feltz chuckled, remembering past occasions when fighting had broken out on air and the studio had descended into chaos.

Matt raised his eyebrows nervously. What would the odd black eye matter to Feltz? It wouldn't be him who'd collect it.

'Think of it, Matt, seven million people!' Holly chipped in. 'The chattering classes in their entirety, glued to your every word.'

'Torment's not for the masses,' added Feltz. 'But then Joe Bloggs isn't the guy we need to win over, is he? No, it's the *cognoscenti* we're after.'

Matt was hesitant. 'If you're convinced it's our best tactic, I'll do it. But I've gotta say it sounds a bit hairy.'

Feltz beamed. 'Game on!' he said, shaking the last drop of champagne into Holly's glass.

Matt felt the fear of God pass over him. What was he letting himself in for?

SIX

Libby Bird, 'Bird' to her friends, stood by the
French windows. She was mesmerized by the
rhythm of water dripping from an overhead gutter
onto the foliage of a potted Hydrangea outside.

A blackbird flew by and she lifted her gaze. Beyond
the flagstone terrace was a small patch of grass overhung
by a mulberry tree. A table and chairs was waiting there
for the onset of alfresco life and summer days.

Except for the recoil of leaves twitching in the down-
pour, the garden of 17 Holland Park Villas was a haven of
tranquillity. It filtered through her senses like a balm
worked gently into the skin. Yes – this was seduction,
lulling and surreptitious, undermining her naturally
rebellious persona.

Kind though Holly had been by taking her in, Libby
considered the house a bastion of privilege. Unaccus-
tomed to the grandeur of fine antiques, she resisted the
temptation to admire them, lest her judgement be cloyed
by the subtle allurements of a class to which she did not
belong – and which she disapproved of.

She had promised herself that before too long she'd
return to her south London commune and the welcoming
embrace of lesbian camaraderie. There, among equals,
she would reconnect with principles, nurtured and grown
tall in the full heat of angry idealism.

But for the moment, those principles could wait. She needed time to herself, 'quality time' to gather up the bits and pieces of her life.

Short and with boyish blond hair, Libby was alone for much of the day. She would wander round the house barefoot, scantily clad and with little reason to dress fully. Pausing to read or sketch in one room or to rest in another, she passed the time in an almost tangible silence broken only by the phone occasionally ringing in the muffling warmth of the kitchen. A crackle of recorded messages would tell her that old friends had rung, pleading for updates: 'Come on, Bird, we know you're there…'

But oblige them she couldn't. Not yet. One day, confidence restored, she would pick up the phone again. Till then, locked in her self-image as a migratory bird damaged in a storm, she would take refuge in Holly Tree's house.

They'd first met during the run up to Libby's exhibition at Lagoon Art. Their friendship had come a surprise to Libby. In theory, she should find a girl of Holly's background an anathema. Holly was the product of a private education and her rounded vowels were a far cry from Libby's nasal intonation and nagging espousal of classlessness.

For Holly, Libby's presence was a positive diversion from the woes which followed from her godfather's death. Holly had been living alone in the house, sorting through his letters and possessions, sitting sometimes for hours in tearful vigils and wondering who to turn to now he was gone.

Things were tricky at first, it had to be admitted. Libby took things rather for granted, believing her presence in the house made little material difference to Holly. Then there was her unkind remark, 'This place kind of mugs you,' implying that a love of beautiful things was wrong, a bourgeois violation of good socialist ideals.

Holly had come straight back at her and told her she was talking nonsense. From then on, each knew where the other stood, and in time Libby's stance softened. Her critical views about 'haves' and 'have-nots', delivered with pummelling intensity, made little headway in the face of Holly's light-hearted refusal to accept them.

It wasn't that Holly didn't listen. She just didn't believe that a level playing field was a panacea for all ills. And by accepting Libby for what she was, Holly could ignore the class hostility and home in on what she believed was the heart of the problem – Libby's troubled soul, and her overriding sense of insecurity.

Over time, this tolerance allowed a bond of trust to grow between the two women. The young sculptress revealed most of her innermost thoughts as they sat on each other's beds on dark winter evenings, comparing the courses of their lives.

Sex was frequently a topic of discussion. Libby professed to believe that from the earliest stirrings of adolescence, sex should be a *carte blanche* affair – an El Dorado of guilt-free abandon, unfettered by dogma as to what is or is not acceptable. Heterosexual or homosexual, consensual behaviour of any kind was a natural fulfillment of desire and should be practised freely without fear of moral reprisal. Holly was surprised by this view, given Libby's prudish condemnation of her godfather's paintings of nude women.

Adorning the stairways of the house, these works marked Uncle Henry's progression from one model to another over the course of his life. Libby asserted that his work was 'on a lower level, completely.'

Libby's view was that her own nude sculptures were art because they carried a serious message. But Uncle Henry's pictures, particularly the fulsome nudes of his middle years, were titillating and bordering on depravity.

Had Henry been alive to defend himself, Holly knew how strongly he would have disagreed. Studies of the female form amounted to so much more, he would say, if there was a sexual frisson between artist and model. A come-hither look, a carefree abandon in the pose would add an earthy quality. 'To paint a woman for her beauty alone is to deny the existence of desire – the very thing that makes the world go round!'

Libby was also scathing of Henry's later work and his use of what she called 'under-age' models. Henry's reaction to this would have been equally vehement. 'How absurd, to suggest painting them is a perversion! They are the most natural sitters in the world! Fresh peachy faces knowing nothing; but who guess and suppose behind sparkling eyes!' And with a flourish of his hand he'd have added: 'In their innocence lies their worth – that virginal purity so quickly lost unless captured by the brush for posterity.' Holly loved it when Uncle Henry was in full flow. A free spirit, he always spoke his mind. Not that Libby would have listened. When the bit was between her teeth, she rarely did.

A drawing hanging in her bedroom was for Libby the most shameful of all Henry's pictures. It was of Holly, aged no more than eleven. Holly loved it. Likening it to a work by Balthus, she praised the way he had captured her sprouting breasts – those little 'bee stings' she'd been so proud of, fondling them in private moments, urging them to grow.

For Libby, the painting was a reminder of how she'd been robbed of her own childhood at an early age, in the interests of gratifying a dirty old man. Come to think of it, he was far worse than that – truly evil! But that was another story – one she never talked about.

These days, she was coming to terms with a different loss – that of her work, the sculpted family of suffering females she'd lovingly created in the squalor of her studio. How rewarding it had been bringing them to life, each of them a different character but all women who'd been through it. Bulimic, obese or anorexic, their glass eyes would gaze back at her in crafted misery that reflected her own.

How ironic, she thought, that at their moment of triumph in Feltz's gallery, established once and for all in the sympathy of the world, they'd had to *die* – victims in the war against gender exploitation. And were it not for a couple of friends who'd got carried away – women in 'the movement' it has to be said – the disaster would not have occurred.

But at least Bella had survived, albeit ending up imprisoned behind glass in the Rich Gallery. Poor Bella: beaten and rejected by the man in her life; as a sculpture she was acclaimed, featured on postcards even, available in the gallery shop. Such irony, such a cruel twist of fate!

Libby felt hard-done-by. Perhaps her destiny lay in martyrdom. She found this pleasurable to contemplate during the long citrus-scented baths which she would take when Holly was out. Staring into the steamy condensation, she would recall the abuse she'd suffered as a child; then the hopeless banner-waving demos of her student years, protesting against nuclear energy, new bypasses and all manner of evils that were still around today. Sad to admit, nothing she'd ever said or done had made the slightest difference to the ways of this rotten world.

Walking back through the drawing room, she paused by a group of framed photographs hanging on the wall. They were Holly's work. One in particular always compelled her attention. It was a monochrome close-up of an old man's eye. The closer she looked, the more it twinkled and, it seemed, lusted after her.

The eye of course was Uncle Henry's. Despite his being dead it seemed to bore into her. Even when her back was turned it was leering at her, she was sure. Once, when she first arrived, she'd wanted to smash the glass and gouge out his retina. Instead she'd lashed at it with her gold studded tongue: 'Men! I hate them!'

Today, her feelings were far less certain. Living with Holly had caused her to reflect on the sterility of her previous life. Her intolerance had softened, to reveal a soul full of misgivings. She accommodated 'that eye' uneasily but with resignation – bristly but silent.

Holly could only guess at the reason for Libby's antagonism. Was it her way of coming to terms with some bitter memory? Or was it all just a front, concealing a desperate search for love?

Whatever the answer, Libby evidently found the tenderness of women preferable to the rougher demands of men. She appeared happy to accept lesbianism as a statement of feminist solidarity, meaningful and focused on issues of independence and equal rights. But Holly gradually formed the opinion that Libby's hostility towards men was more a badge of belonging than a true disposition. She was brainwashed by women preying on her gullibility, modelling for her or chatting her up in gay bars in the hope of an easy lay. No need for men – in their stead were 'little friends' who sprang into life at the flick of a switch.

Libby looked through the window onto the street. 'Cars!' she muttered angrily. She glanced with satisfaction at the vandalized remains of one. Minus doors and windows, it had been there for weeks. What did she care? She loathed cars and the people who owned them – cocooned in their selfish culture of possession and greed.

A glossy magazine lay on the arm of a chesterfield. Flicking through its pages she arrived at the social pages, a pictorial diary covering the 'who, when and where' of jolly events. It was not the first time she'd found herself looking, fighting her curiosity by limiting herself to quick glances. This was part of Holly's world; a merry-go-round of charity bashes and fun; smiling faces that looked through her and made her feel irrelevant. They accused her of feeling envious behind her scowl – an envy she would vehemently deny.

'Bird, you mustn't be so chippy,' Holly would chide her. 'There's no harm in what they're doing. And if money's being raised for good causes, then all's well and good.'

But in Libby's eyes, the girls were la-de-dah, more money than sense. And the men were no better: pop-eyed playboys in louche disarray, or retro-freaks puffed-up like penguins. How she hated them – dancing the night away and pretending to alleviate suffering at the same time. What did any of them really know or care?

But she had grown fond of Holly, who had taken her in, who had talked her through pill-popping tantrums and was now piecing her back together again. 'I must seem really shitty,' she'd say to herself, 'bitching on as much as I do.'

Letting the magazine drop she walked to the fireplace. She read through Holly's invitations and felt like Cinderella, not invited to the ball. Oh for a Buttons, to pop out and comfort her! Turning to the mantel clock, an extravaganza of scrolled bronze and silver-gilt filigree hands, she thought it represented the permanent social barrier which would always be there – if not on Holly's part, then on her own.

It was five-thirty and the clock struck with a genteel ting. Even if she stayed in the house for a lifetime it would never chime for her; only for Holly and her kind, whose ancestors she imagined stretched out on chaises longues for afternoons of leisure in ages gone by.

The key turned in the lock and Holly burst in through the front door. 'Hi Libbs, I'm back!' This abbreviated form of her name had recently found favour with Holly. 'Bird' was reserved for her in spats of moodiness, now thankfully rare.

Holly materialized, wet with rain, in the dim light of the hall. 'God, what a day I've had!' she exclaimed, offering her cheek to Libby's lips. 'You've no idea.'

Libby relieved her of her carrier bags, glancing briefly to see where they were from.

'Diva. Enzo Ghilberti,' she said, carrying them through to the kitchen. 'Sounds cool.' The names had a romantic ring of operas, hot sun and ice cream.

'Aren't I naughty?' said Holly. 'I couldn't resist.'

Libby gave a little shrug. Resisting was quite beyond Holly. Her addiction to spending was legendary. At first it had disgusted Libby: but as Holly's kindness washed over her, those sentiments vanished, engulfed in a swell of relief at being rescued from despair.

'Look, luvvy,' said Holly picking up the bag from Diva, 'I bought you a little something.'

Libby gulped. 'You shouldn't!'

'It's absolutely you, I promise. Here, take it.'

Lost for words, Libby unwrapped the present, reverently peeling the tissue paper back to reveal a yellow micro skirt, bright and provocative in the kitchen light.

Holly bit her lip anxiously, hoping her choice of colour was right.

Libby was overcome. 'Oh, my God! That is so cool.' Picking the skirt up with both hands, she held it against her waist.

'I was worried you wouldn't like the colour,' said Holly.

'No, it's really hip!' said Libby, excitedly.

Holly embraced her. 'I'm so glad you like it,' she said. 'Diva's *right now*, I can tell you.'

'Like it?' said Libby, holding back her emotion. 'I adore it.' *Adore*? she thought, suddenly self-conscious. Why on earth did I say that? – it sounded stupid, not at all her kind of word, but one that Holly used all the time.

They stood in a momentary embrace, enveloped in each other's joy.

But what had possessed Holly to give her a skirt? she wondered. And, a micro one at that – very sexy! Not since she was twenty had she worn anything like that.

Men played no part in her life – she'd already made that plain enough. Yet Holly's gift thrilled her. She was at a loss to understand why.

For Holly, Libby's delight proved that her feelings of womanhood were alive. Holly had suspected as much anyway, from the envy and curiosity in Libby's eyes when she told her about the men she'd made love to.

But there was something else too – a little secret Holly had discovered but said nothing about. Sometimes, when Holly had been out for the day, she would return to the house to find her wardrobe not quite as she'd left it – a dress or a skirt put back in the wrong place. Libby had been trying them on, she was sure.

'How do you know I'll wear a skirt?' Libby asked her. 'I mean, I never do!'

'All that stuff about hating men, the way you used to go on and on – it didn't ring true.'

Libby frowned. 'What d'you mean?'

'It's a gimmick, isn't it?' said Holly. 'Part of this feminist thing.'

Libby said nothing.

'Come on Bird,' she said. 'You're not much more of a lesbian than I am. Not really – admit it!'

'I've been there, lived it!' insisted Libby. 'You know that!'

'So? What's the big deal? We all mess around from time to time. It's like a trip to Disneyland. You go there, live out the fantasy and come back.'

'Disneyland?' Libby looked as if she might burst – into laughter or tears. She did both. Lost for words, they embraced once more.

Libby could do little but accept the denouement Holly's diagnosis had provoked, because Holly had said it not aggressively but in kindness, as a long-overdue disclosure of the obvious.

'Want some coffee?' asked Holly.

'Yeah,' sighed Libby, wrestling inside with her uncertainty: Who am I? – What am I?

Holly smiled sympathetically. Putting on a new face would be hard for Libby. Old friends would be shocked by her abandoning her identity as an amorphous blob in combat fatigues. Her new look would be a betrayal of their cherished ideals.

'Now, look what I bought for myself!' said Holly excitedly, to change the subject. 'Some new shoes. Wait till you see them. They're to die for, handmade in Milan.'

Libby looked in awe as Holly lifted the shoes from the box and slipped them onto her feet one by one. 'There,' said Holly, admiring the soft green suede and low heels, 'aren't they gorgeous?'

'They're great,' said Libby, with a hint of reserve.

'Don't you like them?' asked Holly, concerned.

'Yes, but won't they mark like crazy?'

'God, you're so practical!'

'Well, you know what I mean,' said Libby. She preferred the scuff-resistance of trainers.

'Sure, but you don't have to worry,' said Holly. 'I'll only be wearing them in the gallery.'

'The gallery?'

'That's right,' said Holly, smiling. 'I was about to tell you. Bernie's given me a job!'

'A proper job?'

'Three days a week,' said Holly. 'And hey, this'll make you laugh! From now on, when we're in front of customers, he wants me to call him Bernard. You know, like it makes him sound classy. Yes, Bernard – No, Bernard – Up yours, Bernard!' She grinned.

'The pretentious prat! And rather you than me – remember the way he cuddled me after everything was smashed at my show? It was revolting!'

Libby pretended to hyperventilate at the thought she had ever been close to the man.

'He was doing his best to sympathize,' said Holly, in a half-hearted defence.

'Yuk!' added Libby, indignantly. 'He can keep it.'

Holly laughed. 'Anyway listen, I haven't told you the half of it.'

Libby leant back against the kitchen dresser, folding her arms in readiness for another episode in the life of Holly Tree. She reckoned it must involve a man, for Holly had that cat's-got-the-cream look about her. 'What happened?' she asked, suppressing the teeniest twinge of jealousy.

'I met this guy.'

Libby smiled. 'Not another one!'

'Don't be like that,' said Holly. 'You make me sound like a real slapper. No seriously, you remember the private view I went to the other evening?'

'Which one, darling?' Libby said teasingly – Holly was an habitué of private views all over London.

'At Lagoon Art, for this guy called Matt Flight.'

Holly handed Libby a copy of Matt's catalogue. Libby turned the pages one by one, shaking her head in disbelief. 'This is wacky stuff.'

'I know,' said Holly. 'But I felt the work had something, so I went back for another look.'

Libby laughed. 'You mean *he* had something!'

Holly grinned. 'Shut up, will you!'

'Go on,' said Libby.

'Well, the guy *was* there,' said Holly, sheepishly.

'As if you thought he wouldn't be.'

Holly screwed up her face in an impish admission of guilt. 'I did have the sneakiest suspicion…'

'And don't tell me – he's really cool!'

'Yeah,' Holly said dreamily. 'I quite fancy him.'

'Surprise, surprise!'

'Honestly, you're such a cow!'

'Sorry,' said Libby. 'But it's just that you're so predictable. Anyway go on, tell me what happened.'

Holly leant back against the kitchen sink. 'Well, as it happens, it's all worked out rather well.'

'Oh?'

'Bernie's asked me to photograph him.'

'You mean he's commissioned you?' said Libby. 'At last!'

'Yeah, at last!' echoed Holly.

'So, when's the shoot?'

'Friday.'

'At Lagoon Art?'

'No, here in the studio,' said Holly. 'I mean, here I've got so much more control.'

'Yeah, of course,' Libby said, smiling sarcastically.

'No seriously!' pleaded Holly. 'It'd be a nightmare in the gallery, with Bernie hovering around, sticking his nose in all the time.'

'True.'

Holly toyed with her teaspoon. 'If my hunch is right, Matt'll be quite photogenic,' she said. 'He's got that dark and brooding film-star look, you know?'

'Oh, so it's 'Matt' now, is it?' Then, with an affectionate shake of her head, 'You're crazy.'

Holly giggled.

'I'll keep out of the way while he's here,' said Libby, the warmth of her mug bringing comfort to her cheek.

'No, you can't do that! I'll need your help with the lights.'

'Will you?' groaned Libby.

'Of course! It's much easier if I can stay behind the camera. Anyway, it'll do you good. You haven't seen anyone for yonks.'

'I know,' said Libby pathetically, 'I can't face it.'

'You're such a drama queen,' said Holly. 'Look, the longer you hide away, the worse it'll be. Sooner or later you've got to get a life again. So why not now? Matt's not the kind of guy to bite.'

'How d'you know?' said Libby. 'You've only just met him.'

'He's sweet, I can tell you.'

'What? Have you snogged him already?'

Holly smirked. 'Not snogged, exactly.'

'But you've kissed him.'

'Well, just a peck,' admitted Holly, concealing a sly smile behind her coffee.

'God, you don't waste any time,' said Libby. 'And has he kissed you?'

'No. But he will!'

'You're such a tart!' said Libby, with a toss of her head.

Holly laughed. 'He's coming in the evening, so we can do the shoot and…'

'And what?' interrupted Libby, mockingly.

'Stop it! How should I know?'

'Well, you won't want me around once the shoot's over.'

'Yes, I will!' said Holly, adamantly. 'You can't just disappear back to you room. It'll look too obvious. No, stay and we'll make a night of it.'

Libby paled at her words – Holly's 'making a night of it' was likely to be a full-on frenzy of carnal activity of the kind she'd tried to forget and no longer wanted to be a part of.

'Whatever's the matter?' asked Holly. 'You've gone white as a sheet!'

'Nothing,' said Libby despondently. 'It's just that everything's happening so fast, it's doing my head in.'

'Honestly, you'd think I'd asked a football team over,' laughed Holly. 'Jeepers! It's only one guy. It's not as if anything will happen.'

'Oh no?' said Libby, not believing her for a second.

SEVEN

Matt felt for the cash in his inside pocket. Safe and secure, the slim wad was a modest advance from Feltz against sales.

Typical! Matt thought, thumbing through what he considered was a paltry offering. Anybody'd think he'd been asked for a skin graft!

But grumbling was pointless. Some of the sales had not yet been paid for and until cheques had cleared Feltz would play safe, advancing only small sums. Of course, artists were permanently overdrawn. 'For Crissake,' he'd say to them, 'I'm not a fucking hole in the wall!'

Matt's taxi lurched through the Knightsbridge traffic, making little progress. He squinted at the meter. The fare was mounting, but he was too far from Holland Park Villas to walk. Besides, it was years since he'd afforded a cab. Talking to the driver was fun, a raw insight into the mind of a man who spent his life scouring the metropolis for fares like a dung beetle busy in search of a load.

''Old tight, guv!' said the cabbie, effecting a rapid 'U' turn. 'Sittin' in this lot ain't gonna get us nowhere. I'll try and work me way up Ken' High Street.'

'Days like this drive you mad.'

'Tell us about it, squire. I feel that choked sometimes, I could drive me cab into the river!'

'I don't blame you,' Matt sympathized.

'But then I thinks to myself, wot's the point? I'd never see Chelsea play again. Givin' the Gunners a smack on a Saturday puts everythin' right somehow. So, what's your game, Jon?'

'Not football, I'm afraid,' said Matt, wondering if he'd be instantly ostracized.

'No, mate,' laughed the cabbie. 'I mean your line of work.'

'Oh, I'm a painter.'

'Wot, decoratin'?'

'No, pictures.'

'Oh,' said the cabbie. 'How long 'ave you been doin' that?'

'Years,' bemoaned Matt. 'It's been a real grind.'

'Why's that?'

'Getting recognition was a bastard.'

The cabbie pushed hard down on the accelerator. 'Funny you should say that,' he said. 'I met this bloke once, a mate of me ol' dad's he was, it was the same for 'im.'

'Oh yeah?' said Matt.

'The fella was a pavement artist. 'Chalky' they called 'im. Anyway, doin' the 'Mona Lisa' was 'is thing. Got 'im bleedin' nowhere. Then one day, he did a footballer – the great Georgie Best.'

'He was a bit before my time.'

'I was just a kid m'self,' the cabbie acknowledged. 'Anyway, you know wot? Some fan or other saw 'is work an' went potty for it.'

'What a break,' said Matt.

'Yeah, ol' Chalky,' said the cabbie fondly. ''E was diggin' the slab up to free the picture like, when Ol' Bill cuffed 'im, an' carted 'im off to the nick. Straight up! Talk about laugh – I nearly died when I heard that. Still, that's artists for yer, isn't it? Crazy bastards!' Then, half looking back over his shoulder: 'No offence, matey, ha, ha!'

'None taken,' said Matt, chuckling politely. But to be considered akin to Chalky was insulting. Was the public mad? Were all artists the same to them? That his work should be lumped in with paintings of footballers, running about on turf so sickeningly green it assaults the senses!

'Yeah, poor old Chalky,' said the cabbie, reflectively. 'Brick short of a load, so they say.'

'Sounds like it,' said Matt, wondering how much longer they would stay on the subject of football.

'Still, joke about him as we might,' the cabbie continued, 'he earns a fortune now, doin' pictures of all the top players.'

'Amazing,' said Matt, dispirited. He crossed his fingers in the hope that the cabbie might stop to draw breath. He didn't.

'Yeah. Good luck to the bugger, that's what I says.' Then, leaning back in his seat, he confided: 'What I'd give for an original, eh? I mean, imagine – an original Chalky! You can't do much better than that, can you?'

Matt feigned a smile and said nothing.

'No, Chalky's stuff's out of my league,' the cabbie confessed. 'Still, mustn't grumble.' Then, brightening up: 'But tell you what I 'ave got.'

'What's that?' said Matt, hopeful for a change of subject.

'Postcards!' said the cabbie, with revelatory joy.

'Postcards?'

'Yeah, them comical ones you get at the seaside? I got albums of 'em.'

'What, fat ladies and things?' said Matt, thinking of the work of McGill.

'Yeah – cor, they're a laugh. Been collectin' them for years. Some of them older than you are. Cost an arm and a leg to buy them today, 'specially now there's talk of banning that sort of thing.'

'I can imagine,' said Matt. The Commission for Moral Issues had a team of busybodies specially devoted to extinguishing 'sexist' humour.

''Course, the wife doesn't go for 'em. She's more into soaps and reality TV. Bleedin' women, they're all the same – still, you've got to luv 'em, 'aven't you?'

'Yeah, I suppose,' said Matt. Soaps and the bonds of marital bliss were things he knew little about. But talk of postcards had reminded him of the seaside holidays of his youth, spent more often than not watching rain driven along the promenade. Worthing it was – windswept, worn and weary, the shelters on the seafront full of pensioners sitting huddled together in see-through plastic Macs, mesmerized by the to-ing and fro-ing of an angry sea thrashing the shoreline in cycles of perpetual punishment.

The cabbie let out a long sigh. 'There's summing about the seaside. Candyfloss, donkey rides an all that – I just loves it, you know?'

'Yeah,' said Matt.

'Ever painted it?' asked the cabbie.

'I haven't,' Matt admitted. For him the seaside had spelt boredom, an omnipresent greyness of days. The pier had seemed to promise escape, but it ended abruptly in a thirty foot drop down to the onyx-green sea, lapping against the superstructure as listlessly as his mood.

'So, what *do* you paint?' asked the cabbie

'I've been working with themes for a while now,' said Matt.

'Themes?' echoed the cabbie. 'Blimey, mate! Sounds a bit poncey.'

Matt forced a chuckle.

'No offence, Jon, just kidding,' the cabbie went on. 'To do with what? Nature or summing?'

'More human nature, I suppose,' Matt replied.

'Oh – arty stuff. Above me 'ead, most likely.'

'Not really. I paint things people don't want to face. Truths they'd rather ignore, that sort of thing.'

'Yeah?' said the cabbie blankly. 'Give us an example.'

Matt thought for a moment. 'Well,' he began, 'take war and peace. I believe the one is the key to the other.'

'Like the two go together, sort of thing?'

'Absolutely.'

Having fought his way to adulthood through the mean streets of pre-gentrified Balham, the cabbie readily concurred. 'Cor, I'd vouch for that, mate!' he said cheerily. 'It's bleedin' obvious when you think about it.'

'Sure, it's common sense,' said Matt. 'But you'd be amazed how many people think war's altogether avoidable.'

'Nutters Guv. I mean, it stands to reason, dunnit? Without wars nothing gets sorted. No, grief is a part of life. Least, that's wot I tells me kids – you either gives it out, or you gets it. It's up to you. '

'You could put it like that,' chuckled Matt. It wasn't exactly the point he was making, but he agreed with it. The cabbie had added a new dimension: whatever the wish of idealists, life is harsh – a dog-eat-dog fight for survival.

'Ere!' said the cabbie in a sudden flash of recognition. 'Are you that artist they was goin' on about on the radio? Matt Fright or summing – he did a picture of dead bodies with trees growing out, an' doves stuffin' 'emselves on the fruit.'

Matt's heart missed a beat. 'God! That's me!' he exclaimed.

'Well, I'll be!' cried the cabbie. 'You could knock me darn with a feather. Fancy you being 'im!'

Matt leaned forward on the seat. 'What were they saying?'

'It was the girl what does 'London Diary' – what says 'Bitchy? Moi?' all the friggin' time.'

'Oh, yeah,' said Matt, 'Prilly Prattle.'

'That's the one! Anyhow, she was talkin' about an exhibition; Maroon Art, I think it was; an' sure enough, up pops your name.'

'Lagoon Art! What did she say?'

The cabbie chuckled. 'She'd never seen such 'ghastly' work,' he said. 'Like your pictures should be in the Chamber of 'Orrors.'

'Oh, bugger,' sighed Matt.

'I wouldn't worry about it, squire,' he said. 'People love 'avin' the shit frightened out of 'em.'

Unsure where to place him, the cabbie had addressed Matt as 'guv', 'mate', 'Jon' and 'squire', in the space of ten minutes. Matt thought of what Magritte had said: 'Nothing is so attached to its name, it cannot be called something else.'

Sitting hunched in the back of the cab, Matt felt the desire for recognition and the fear of it coursing through his body simultaneously. A voice broke over the intercom seeking the cabbie's whereabouts.

'Ken High Street mate, an' it's choc-a-bloc.' The cabbie closed the privacy glass.

With the cabbie chatting to his office, Matt looked out of the window. A man roughly his age was thrusting his way along the pavement, shouting above the din of the street into his mobile phone. Scaffolding and building materials were stacked on the pavement, making it hard for him to negotiate his passage. The man appeared unperturbed by the scene of destruction he was passing. After all, it was only the blown-out façade of a restaurant – the result of yet another bombing, so commonplace it was barely worth a glance.

Incredible, thought Matt; incidents like these are just accepted. People should wake up before they themselves become victims, stunned at the sight of their own gaping wounds.

Suddenly, it struck him, deep in the pit of his stomach; that's what he'd been elected to do – wake people up! On air, in a few days time, on 'Torment Tonight'! The prospect was daunting, as it would leave him no alternative but to attack – something he wasn't naturally disposed to do.

Fidgeting nervously, he surveyed what lay ahead. On the following Monday he was due at the studios of Cityvision. 'We'll need you in by nine p.m.,' they'd told him. 'That's an hour before we go live, but Dickie likes an introductory chat with his guests to get to know them. Then of course there's make-up.'

Richard Torment's quick acceptance of Feltz's suggestion had come as a surprise. But morality was a hot topic, and the promise of heated exchanges was too much for the presenter to resist, especially when linked in with a controversy surrounding a painting by a newly discovered artist. Feltz had gleefully assured him that Matt Flight was being dubbed 'the Antichrist' and was anxious to answer his critics – in Feltz's parlance, to 'Kick some butts!'

Matt was worried whether he could live up to people's expectations – especially Holly's, whose impetuous interest in him would surely wane if he failed. Holly had been priming him: 'Don't forget, body language is a giveaway. So be cool. Torment's a foxy shit and once he scents blood there's no stopping him.'

The list of Torment's guests had been confirmed that very morning. Enemy number one was Godfrey Privett. He was certain to be the most aggressive, despite Feltz trying to play him down as an 'out-of-touch old poof'. Feltz claimed to have witnessed, quite by chance one winter's day, Privett mincing along with his pooch at the foot of the Albert Memorial. Wrapped in a scarf and tweed overcoat, Privett had been yanking frantically at the poodle's lead. The animal's anal straining was clearly giving offence to the gilded patrician above, gazing from the lofty heights of a more mannered age.

'Privett's nothing to worry about,' Feltz had boasted. 'He knows Jack Shit about the contemporary scene.'

'Except that he doesn't like it,' Matt added.

Then there was the woman representing the Council for Moral Issues; 'Auntie Biddie', now Dame Bradstock no less. Not being a keen student of form in the quango-cracy stakes, Matt knew little about her as a person, except that she was a moralist with a reputation for big hair.

Lastly there was the Singing Policeman, Commis-sioner Buller of the Yard. He'd agreed to appear after a modest inducement was offered – a mention of his newly released CD. Buller's sing-songs had recently become politically controversial after an ethnic group claimed the roistering accompaniment of a police cadet on the tuba had imperialist overtones.

Matt hunched into the corner of the cab. Torment's guests were assuming nightmare proportions in his mind. Some vindictive, others plainly mad, they were wagging fingers and demanding he denounce himself. It was the Inquisition in full flow: 'Confess your blasphemy and the court will show you leniency!'

To hell with them, he thought. If they refuse to accept what the painting is saying, well stuff it. He comforted himself with the knowledge that his work was going to hang in the Rich Gallery. At least Sylvester Rich had got the message: had he not hailed *The Orchard* as a 'master-piece of perception'?

The privacy glass opened again. 'Seems like there's a demo, which would account for the traffic, like,' said the cabbie.

'What's it about?' asked Matt, worried he'd be late.

'Human rights,' said the cabbie. 'Campaigning on behalf of tossers in the shit with debt.'

'What do they want?' asked Matt, aware of the many thousands in this position.

'They want them that's gone bankrupt to be given holiday vouchers.'

'What?' Matt queried him.

'Yeah. Apparently it ain't *their* fault. They're victims of the system,' said the cabbie. 'An' now they're sufferin' social exclusion. It seems if you can't afford to sugar off to the Costa once in a while, it can damage your self-esteem. So they're campaigning for the right to free holidays!'

Matt shook his head.

'Tell you wot, mate. The way fings is goin', them buggers'll end up better off than what I am. Holidays for tossers – I mean, I ask yer!'

Trapped once more in a gridlock, the cabbie sat cursing his lot, having to live in a country so 'politically correct' that it was throttling itself. 'If I could get me hands on the bastards. I'd soon sort 'em out, believe me! Moanin' minnies. They think it's their right! 'Ow can they respect themselves, bloody spongers?'

The intercom crackled again. The cabbie listened hard then turned to Matt. 'Would you Adam and Eve it?' he said, breathless. 'They've gone an' torched a coach. One of the old Bill's!'

Matt looked at his watch. 'I think I'll have to leg it,' he said. 'I'm running late.'

'Just as you like, mate. Can't say I blame you.'

Matt let himself out. 'Here, keep the change.' He pressed a couple of tenners into the cabbie's waiting palm.

The cabbie beamed. 'Very good of you, Matt,' he said, his passenger's generosity cheering him no end. 'You don't mind if I calls you Matt, do you? Only I feel I've got to know you, chattin' the way we 'ave. Sorry I gave you an earful, only I gets that bottled up.' Reaching for his back pocket, he said hopefully: 'Let me give you me card – I mean, you never know, do you?'

'Wally Root,' said Matt, reading the name. 'Perhaps we'll meet again.'

'Yeah. Nice talkin' to yer, squire. An', be lucky!'

Matt walked on, turning off Kensington High Street and up Addison Road. Wally Root – what a character. Encouraged that the cabbie had sussed out who he was, he smiled to himself: Matt Fright, indeed! Not for much longer would misnomers of that sort occur if the controversy surrounding his work continued to grow. And while the thought was unnerving, he was happy with one thing at least – Sylvester Rich was on his side.

Like other artists whose work Sylvester had collected, Matt felt he was now on a different plane – a novice en route for immortality, chosen from the herd. One of the elect. Amazing, to think that only a few days ago he was just another hopeful peering out from the homogenous mass. How he admired Sylvester's perception in spotting him!

He envisaged himself seated at Sylvester's right hand on high, in a rarified air of intellectual supremacy. 'You're a bringer of light,' Sylvester had assured him.

Matt smiled. Once his appearance on 'Torment Tonight' was out of the way, things would take a turn for the better. The great man's endorsement was an open door to opportunity. No longer would he have to put up with public humiliation. Angry recriminations would pale in the face of his hard-won superiority; he would soon be able to do as he pleased.

He felt full of optimism. Certain exhibits at the Rich Gallery had opened his eyes as to a new way of making art. Take Marcia Mount's abstract *Disillusion*. At first he had thought, is she being serious? A huge frame was filled with tightly packed crumpled-up newsprint. Each little ball, said the blurb, was an expression of disaffection, a comment on media 'spin' turning existence into something without meaning, a rudderless drift through time.

But she must be serious, he concluded, otherwise Sylvester would never have bought it. Yes, she was an artist typical of a new and thrilling era. The confines of legitimacy had been stretched unimaginably far. Given the right meaning, anything could be accorded the status of high art.

Sexual arousal too could be given meaning – and why not? Doesn't sex lie behind everything we think and do? Sylvester Rich had shown them a video artist's film that in any other setting would have been deemed pornographic. The small crowd of onlookers, he said, were themselves an exhibit. Their woeful attempts at coping with their own prurience were hilarious to observe.

'If this is art, I'm a Dutchman!' one had remarked. But did he hurry away in disgust? Strangely, no – he just stood there rocking on his heels, expounding on the offensiveness of the work. 'I mean, what's this guy trying to prove?' he had asked.

'That size matters, I suppose,' another had dryly observed.

Matt turned the corner into Holland Park Villas. The row of stucco Victorian façades spoke of a more genteel age, when such lurid subjects would have been confined to the gas-lit smoking rooms of gentlemen's clubs.

A gaggle of children ran along the pavement towards him. Heads hooded, they passed either side of him, in full retreat from the sound of breaking glass. He walked on expecting to hear some reproachful shout; but the evening air carried only silent acceptance. It seemed people were inured to the wanton destruction of property.

'If you're coming from the Addison Road end, look out for the wrecked car,' Holly had said. 'We're just beyond that. It's the house with the magnolia, you can't miss it.'

Halfway up the street, Matt spotted the magnolia flowering in defiant array against the prevailing sense of doom. Its white bowl-shaped blooms seemed to flag up a promise of good things to come. Walking through the garden gate, Matt looked up at the front door in hopeful anticipation.

For too long now, painting had dominated his existence, enveloping him in the airless confines of self-denial. It was time now for some amends, and to build on his hard-won success.

He hoped that things would work out and that Holly would be a part of his success. But she was a wilful chick, and it would be hard for him to keep the initiative. Bernie had warned him: 'She'll run rings round you if you don't.' Would she, indeed!

EIGHT

It had been a good day for Holly Tree. She'd been phoning friends, keeping up to date with things on the grape vine: the succulence of tittle-tattle and the dead wood of people whose lives had turned sour and who would bang on about it for hours given the chance, boring everyone to tears.

But above all else, shining bright in the nebula of gossip, there was Matt Flight. Everyone had asked her, 'Who is this guy? What's he about?' She'd answered with the suave authority of the informed, in keeping with her reputation. 'Trust Holly to know!'

It was six in the evening by the time she pulled down the blinds in her basement studio. 'I don't want any daylight sneaking in,' she said to Libby.

Libby pointed to the mini spotlights recessed in the ceiling. 'Shall I turn those off for a second, just to check?'

'Sure,' said Holly, standing back with arms akimbo. Libby threw the switch and the room was plunged into darkness.

'Great! That's perfect.'

'How are you thinking of photographing him?' Libby asked.

'Well, what do you think of this for an idea? Matt's sort of arrived from nowhere, right? So I had the idea he should be emerging from darkness.'

'Like a spectre, you mean?' said Libby.

'That's it! We'll start the lighting very low, then increase it in stages. At the same time we'll gradually bring his face into close-up, so when it's revealed it'll be highlighted but still in shadow.'

'I get it,' said Libby. 'A bit like a Rembrandt self-portrait.'

'Yeah. I think it could work, don't you?'

'Sounds cool. Are you shooting in monochrome?'

'Absolutely. I want to capture that moody effect. Like you get in film noir, where there's a humungous story being told but nobody has the foggiest idea what it is. *You* know the kind of thing.'

'Yeah, deep,' said Libby solemnly. 'Like the guy's an enigma.'

The doorbell rang. 'God, that must be Matt!' said Holly. 'I'd no idea it was so late. Look, be a luv and let him in will you; I'll load up some film.'

'Sure.' Libby felt a quickening sense of unease at the thought of coming face to face with an enigma – and a male one at that. Reaching the hall, she stopped for a moment, breathing deeply to calm herself. She looked through the spyglass at Matt's magnified face, bulbous and fish-like. The bell rang again, so loud it made her jump. She opened the door.

'Sorry,' said Matt. 'I didn't think anyone had heard.' In truth he had found the door rather intimidating: a glossy red sentinel with a polished brass nose and letterbox mouth which might not want to let him pass.

Libby smiled, hiding her jangled nerves. 'That's OK. We were down in the studio.'

'You must be Libby,' said Matt.

'Yeah, right! And you're Matt,' she said, giving him the once-over. 'Come in, Holly's just setting things up.'

Matt stepped into the hall. 'I've heard a lot about you.'

'Yeah, I expect you have,' she said coolly. 'If it's from Bernie, don't believe a thing he says. He's a sexist pig.'

'I know,' said Matt, feeling it would be best to sympathize. Libby closed the door with a bang. 'He's a real fan of your work, though.'

'Yeah, yeah,' said Libby wearily. 'My sculpture of *Bella*, I suppose.'

'That's right,' said Matt. 'I saw it at the 'Rich' the other day.'

'Did you like her?'

'It's an incredible piece of work,' said Matt with sincerity. 'Her expression is haunting.'

Libby was flattered. 'Thank you. At least you can see her as she was intended. To Bernie she's just a slag with big tits.'

'That's Bernie for you,' Matt sympathized. 'Who was the model? Someone you know?'

'Yeah. She crashed out with me for a while, when she was kicked out by her old man. Vindictive bastard!'

Matt thought better than to pursue the matter.

'The studio's this way,' said Libby. Matt followed her down a flight of stairs. Was Bernie right about her sexuality? Her hair might be short and boyish, but tripping along barefoot in the chic-est of micro-skirts she seemed as untypical a lesbian as he'd ever set eyes on.

'Holls! Matt Flight's here!'

'Hi! Come on through.'

They went into the studio. Holly was closing the back of her camera. She was barefoot too – as if the two of them were planning on a party game, he thought. Then again, it had been a very hot day.

'So this is where it all goes down,' he remarked.

'Saucy!' chuckled Holly, with a flick of her red hair.

'I didn't mean...' Matt blurted, momentarily flummoxed.

Holly greeted him with a kiss on both cheeks. 'I know what you mean, you wally!'

Libby grinned: the 'enigma' had actually blushed. Perhaps he would turn out to be a safe play after all. On the face of it he seemed harmless enough: almost awkward in their company, as if fearful of what would happen next.

'How about a drink before we start?' said Holly.

'Yeah, great,' said Matt, with an enthusiastic nod.

'What's it to be, then?'

'Tea, coffee – anything.'

'I was thinking of something stronger,' Holly said. She liked her subjects uninhibited.

'Well, if it's no problem.'

'Of course not!' said Holly brightly. 'Perhaps my assistant here would oblige?'

'Sure,' said Libby. 'What's it to be?'

'Wine would be fine,' said Matt.

'Red or white?'

'White, if that's OK.'

'Funny,' grinned Holly. 'You look like a guy who'd be into full-bodied reds.'

More innuendo? Matt wondered.

Libby disappeared to the kitchen.

'Libby's not what I expected,' he said, his voice hushed.

'The less said about that the better,' said Holly under her breath.

'After what Bernie said, I assumed…'

'Bernie talks shit,' Holly interrupted. 'He's as perceptive as a lemon sometimes. Things are either black or white, there's nothing in between.'

'I see,' said Matt, reading her 'in between' to be a hinterland where anything goes.

Libby returned, a glass of Chardonnay in her hand. 'There you go,' she said sweetly.

'Great,' he said, taking the wine. 'But is nobody going to join me?'

'And get pissed on the job?' Holly said. 'No way!'

Was 'on the job' yet another allusion to sex? Sipping his wine, Matt glanced round the studio, cautioning himself against jumping to conclusions. A chair with an upright back faced him, and behind it there was a black backdrop. Lighting projectors gaped down like voyeurs from a track on the ceiling, their 'barn doors' open for work.

'Looks like a set-up for an interrogation,' he said.

Holly laughed. '*Ve have vays*, you know.'

'Is that right?' he said, grinning.

'You'd better believe it!' Holly glanced at him over her shoulder, her eyes glinting mischievously as she placed the tripod well back from the chair. Matt studied her figure. In a loose shirt and denim mini, he found her provocatively sexy.

'What's the game plan?' he asked. 'Do I get to sit in that chair?'

'Ten out of ten,' said Holly facetiously. 'Go on, try it.'

Matt dutifully sat. He relaxed, stretching out his legs and folding his arms. Libby perched on a worktop. She was smiling in anticipation, for it seemed to her that Holly's flirting was really full on – outrageous, in fact. Bending down to lengthen the tripod, Holly revealed a glimpse of her cleavage, then a flash of inner thigh. She might as well be shouting 'Come and get it!' thought Libby. And as for Matt – he was like a boy at a sweetie stall – transfixed and unable to look away.

'What sort of camera d'you use?' Matt asked, trying to arrest a sudden surge of carnal thoughts.

Holly looked straight at him. 'A Canon Reflex. I've had it for yonks.' She feigned indifference to his ogling.

Matt averted his gaze and settled it on his shoes, 'Canon's a great make,' he said, his nonchalance overplayed.

'Well, I like it,' said Holly, locking it onto the tripod. 'It was a present from my godfather.'

Using such an ancient camera in a digital age was unusual, Matt thought; there must be sentimental reasons. Or perhaps retro was 'in'.

'It's got a wicked zoom,' said Holly. Pressing a button, she extended the lens towards Matt's face, like a black inquisitive proboscis. 'If that isn't the business, I don't know what is.'

'Yeah, wicked,' said Matt, bashfully playing along.

Libby tittered as Holly deliberately worked the lens, inning and outing it suggestively. Then Holly peered through the viewfinder. Matt's expression was too serious; she needed to lighten him up a little.

'D'you think you'll need make up?' she asked him, straight-faced.

'What?' said Matt.

'Only with portraits, bad skin can be a menace.'

'I suppose so,' said Matt, assuming Holly's in-your-face manner was routine.

But Holly was trying her best not to laugh. 'By the time a close up is enlarged to poster size, moles can look mountainous. As for zits, yuk! They come out like mini volcanoes.'

Libby was aware that Holly was up to no good. She moved out of Matt's vision lest he spot the laughter in her eyes.

Matt felt his chin anxiously for tell-tale lumps. 'Well?' he said.

Holly studied Matt's face through the viewfinder. 'Mmm. A little make-up might not be a bad idea.'

Matt sat bolt upright. 'You mean there *is* a problem?'

'On your nose!' Holly chortled. 'Whatever is it? Dead skin or a spot? I can't make it out.'

'It can't be,' said Matt, feeling his nostrils for evidence of an unsightly protrusion.

Holly stood back from the camera. Hands on her hips, she convulsed into laughter.

'Shit! I thought you were for real,' Matt said, miffed. Not that Feltz hadn't warned him. 'Watch her,' he'd said. 'You'll think she's being serious, and all the time she's pulling your plonker.'

Holly recovered herself. 'Don't be so stuffy,' she chided. 'It's a wind-up!'

Matt forced a smile. Was this to be the pattern of the evening – one lark after another, played out at his expense?

Hearing a gurgle he looked over his shoulder to find Libby laughing too, quite hysterically. 'Is it really that funny?' he wondered, throwing her a pained look. Then, to his amazement, Libby lost control and burst into tears.

'Sorry!' she wailed. Cupping her face in her hands, she slipped down from the worktop and fled from the studio. They heard her continuing to sob at the foot of the stairs.

Mystified, Matt took a gulp of wine and looked to Holly for a lead. But all she did was put a finger to her lips.

'What's going on?' Matt whispered. 'Is it something I've said?'

'It's nothing,' Holly mouthed, with a shake of her head. 'Give me five minutes and I'll be back.'

He heard Holly consoling Libby, then her voice tailing away as she followed Libby upstairs. Libby's outburst must be a symptom of her breakdown, Matt thought – a 'wobbly', as Feltz would put it.

'Women – a race apart,' he said to himself, baffled as ever by their convoluted emotions.

Leaving his glass at the foot of the chair, he got up and wandered round the studio, pausing to leaf through some journals and books stacked on a worktop.

A celebrated image caught his eye: a man leaping over a puddle, frozen in mid air, the work of Cartier-Bresson. It was evocative; like himself, the man was going places – but avoiding the puddles with the deftness of a gymnast.

Amid the clutter of lenses, film and halogen lamps lay an assortment of body paints. Half-used, they'd been left behind by a dancer for whom Holly had created a portfolio of exotic photographs.

Matt selected a pot of red. Theatrical stuff, he thought. Unscrewing the lid, he examined the contents. Peering into a mirror, he worked some paste onto his cheek and stood back to admire the fiery glow.

Acting must be fun, he postulated. And yet – imagine repeating the same lines night after night! He put the pot back where he'd found it.

Better remove the paint before Holly comes back, he thought. Otherwise she might think him effeminate. There was a lot about that in the newspapers – the galloping feminization of men, a result of oestrogen build-up in the food chain.

Matt rubbed his face with his handkerchief. But the paint was stubborn and the circular patch remained, smudged and now embarrassingly large. Cursing his luck, he opened a door, hoping he'd find a sink and some soap.

A pale red glow lit the room; above the lintel a red bulb projected from the wall. What goes on here? he wondered, noticing a vague smell of chemicals.

'Nosey!' called a voice behind him. 'That's the dark room – strictly out of bounds.'

'I was just looking around,' Matt said, guilt written all over his face.

'I can see that!' said Holly, closing the door. 'You're lucky nothing was being processed. Hey, what's that mark on your cheek?'

'I was killing time and…'

'You're a kinky one,' she said, touching his chin. Her expression was of gentle amusement. 'You've been playing with the face paint, haven't you?'

'I wanted to see the effect,' he confessed sheepishly.

'Do you know what you look like?'

'No.'

'A lop-sided pantomime dame. A sort of 'Widow Wonky'. Honestly, what am I going to do with you?'

Matt shrugged his shoulders.

Having set her heart on seducing him, Holly relished her advantage. Now she could play him along as she wished, drawing him in and throwing him out like a yo-yo.

'Sit down and I'll clean you up,' she said in a matronly manner. 'Libbs'll be back in a minute and God knows what she'll think. Probably that I've picked up a screw-ball!' She endorsed her remark with a triumphant cackle.

Indignant, Matt sat down. Was that what he was – a pick-up? Or a plaything – a doll with a face to be painted in some nursery game? He half-expected a scolding: 'You naughty, naughty boy!' He could have kicked him-self; obviously, he'd thrown away his chance to impress her. All he could do now was to dance to her tune. It was unnatural, unmasculine even. But he only had himself to blame.

But Holly was delighted. In matters of seduction, she believed, men were hopeless at pacing themselves. They needed to be led on circuitous routes, teased and denied, with the promise of reward always just ahead like a carrot before a donkey. Otherwise, what is there – just a farm-yard rut that's over in a flash. And where's the fun in that?

Matt felt his credibility was at stake. He struggled for something to say, but he could think of nothing. 'Shit!' he cursed to himself. 'Shit, shit, shit!' He had no idea how excited Holly had become.

Reaching for his arm, she pulled him back. 'Do you want to know something?' she whispered.

'What?' said Matt, disconsolate.

Holly fluttered her eyelids. 'You give me the hots!'

'Me?' he said, breaking into a sweat.

'Yes, you,' said Holly, drawing closer and prodding him repeatedly in the chest with the point of her finger.

'Jeez!' stammered Matt, his heart pounding.

'Putting on face paint,' Holly went on. 'That's cool.'

'Cool?' said Matt, mystified.

'Yeah,' said Holly breathily. 'Kinky, but cool.' She stood on her toes and placing her hands on his shoulders, she kissed his lips lightly.

Matt was astonished. 'Do you think so?' he stuttered, his pulse racing at the softness of her mouth.

She looked into his face, amused by the sudden squeaky falsetto in his voice – like a little trapped mammal. 'Oh, yeah,' she assured him. And glancing over her shoulder at the door, she added: 'I'd tell you more, but Libbs'll be back in a minute.'

With a squeeze to his shoulders she eased herself away. Matt tried to guess what she wanted to tell him. Was it a confession, perhaps, to some fetish about men who use make-up? Whatever it was, how relieved he was! And how magical her kiss, barely touching; like the caress of a zephyr on a tropical night.

'Quickly!' he said, needing to change the subject. 'Before Libby gets back – what's her problem?'

Holly took a cautionary look at the door. 'She's been hellish mixed up for some time.'

'I can see that! You mean, she had an identity crisis or something?'

'Shush!' Holly listened for feet on the stairs. She didn't really know what the problem was herself, though she didn't want to admit it. 'It's a long story, but the gist of it is this. A while back she went through a crazy time; it was like she became another person.'

'Schizoid, you mean?'

'Maybe,' she said pensively, 'though I hadn't thought of it like that. As if she'd been sucked in by a cult, her head was so full of crazy ideas. She believed women should live without men – like you guys should be sperm donors, shut up in ghettos.'

'I see,' said Matt, laughing. 'Used just for breeding, you mean?'

'Yeah! Imagine, all you guys lining up, waiting to be tapped.'

'Like a row of rubber trees.'

Holly chuckled. 'It was all wacky stuff, but I promise you she was really into it.'

'Yet she's not a lezzie, you say?'

'That's such a crap word!' said Holly indignantly. Then, realizing he'd meant no harm by it, she told him: 'Look, the truth is she swings both ways. But there's no way she's a fully-blown dyke – that's just Bernie stirring it.'

'I see. So how did this all begin?'

'When she was at art college,' said Holly.

'Sort of radical chic?'

'Who knows? Anyway, she got sick of guys and started to hang out with girls. At first it was nothing, just clubbing, then she got into snogging them. For laughs at first – but guess what, she found it cool, a real turn on. Anyway, that's what she told me.'

'Jeez,' said Matt, fascinated.

'Fast-forward a couple of years and she's in this feminist squat, hard-bitten dykes filling her head with lefty politics and the kind of crap I mentioned.'

'Looking at her now, you wouldn't think she was that way at all.'

'That's just a thing with you guys. You think she's cute, so she couldn't be a lesbian.'

Matt changed tack. 'So why the histrionics?'

'Attention seeking, or something like that,' said Holly. 'A couple of days ago I had a go at her. She's bisexual, for God's sake, but she didn't seem to know it. Someone had to tell her. As she's living here for the moment, I thought it was down to me.'

'So what did she say?' Matt asked, fascinated.

'Apart from a few tears in her room that night, not a lot,' said Holly. 'But by the look on her face, she knew I was right.'

Matt was silent, wondering why it was that idiosyncrasies and great talent so often meld together in an alliance of misery. Perhaps it's the price of genius, he thought.

'She'll sort herself out soon enough,' Holly said, looking away. 'I think she turned the taps on for your benefit. She probably fancies you.'

'That's crazy!' Matt was flattered, but he feigned indifference.

Holly saw through him. 'Oh yeah? Libbs is a drama queen. She thinks waterworks will get her anywhere, she's always trying it on.'

'Weird,' said Matt gravely.

'But then she's more likely to get sympathy from a stranger, isn't she? She probably sees me as a nasty old bully and you as a knight in shining armour. I expect she wants to be rescued.'

'Rescued?' said Matt, searching for the logic behind this complicated piece of female intuition.

'I mean it!' insisted Holly, teasing. 'Rescued from herself.' Saying nothing more, she studied his eyes, trying to guess at his thoughts. Did he fancy Libby? – she wanted to know.

Eventually, Matt spoke: 'Look, she's not my type.' His economy with the truth was hidden behind a bland smile. He was attracted to Libby, but not like he was to Holly. Foibles aside, she was pretty enough, and it would be a callous guy who would turn her down. Now, though, it was Holly he wanted – mysterious Holly, with some secret he wanted to know.

Cocking her head to one side, Holly half believed his denial. 'That's lucky, because she's not getting a look in. Not until I'm done with you, anyway!' Moving lithely behind him she blew in his ear, sending a shiver down his spine.

Matt straightened up in the chair. Bloody Hell! he thought. Looking to his right, he found her lips directly in line with his own. With little choice in the matter, he kissed her.

Holly sat on his knees. Placing her arms around his neck, she looked into his eyes like an affectionate cat.

'I thought you said Libby'll be back,' Matt stammered.

'She will be, so don't go getting ideas,' she said. She helped herself up from his lap.

'I wasn't!'

'Liar, liar! Pants on fire!' Tiptoeing to the door to listen for Libby, she whispered back to him: 'Don't you think I can tell?'

Matt went back to their original conversation. 'I was assuming her outburst was down to some kind of withdrawal symptom.'

'To do with drugs, you mean?'

'Well, yeah.'

A flicker of concern crossed Holly's face. 'Libbs likes a puff, but no more than most of us do. No, my guess is, she was just acting up.'

Holly went to the doorway again. She called out Libby's name, only to meet her face to face. 'Hi!' Libby said airily, as if nothing untoward had occurred. She drifted into the studio drawing on the remainder of a joint. 'Sorry,' she slurred, 'I jus' lost it. Dunno why.'

'Forget it,' said Matt. Her expression was glazed, and she was talking in a strong accent.

Libby stared at Matt's face. 'Wow!' she said, bringing her hand to her mouth and sniggering. 'What's goin' on down here?'

'Matt's been playing with face paint,' said Holly mischievously.

Libby subjected Matt's face to close inspection. 'Well, call me crazy, but makin' 'im up could be great,' she said.

'Yeah, really wild!' Giggling to herself, she touched his cheek. 'Not that I go for the red blob.' It reminded her of the drag scene – the crudity of brash raucous blokes.

'OK, so what could we do?' asked Holly. They both watched Libby's little figure drift round the studio in an ostentatious show of concentration, which ended with her coughing and stubbing out the butt of her joint in an old tin lid.

'Well, what's the first thing yer think of when yer look at a picture like *The Orchard*?' she asked, eyes now closed and head tilted back.

Holly thought for a moment. 'Well, death, I suppose.'

Libby cleared her throat. 'Yeah, I know that, but what's the reason for it?'

'War?'

''Course,' said Libby. 'And what goes wiv war?'

Holly looked to Matt for an answer.

'Could be any number of things,' he said.

'War paint!' she cried out loud, despairing at their failure to think of the obvious.

'So, what do you propose?' said Matt, pained. 'Stripes on my cheeks and a stick through my nose?'

Holly quivered with excitement. 'Awesome! Like a tribal warrior.'

'No way! I'd look a total prat.' Matt looked quizzically at Holly: perhaps she had a bizarre fantasy about making love to a savage – a real man, earthy, primitive and lustful, who would ravish her as never before.

Holly laughed. 'OK, we'll leave the stick out and go for just a paint job.'

'I don't know,' objected Matt. 'Is 'primitive' what we're trying to go for here? I don't think so – it's too basic.'

Holly frowned. 'Isn't 'basic' what you're about?'

'OK, but who's going to take a face covered in stripes seriously? Come on, I'd look a joke!'

'I don't agree,' said Holly who, truth be known, was indeed salivating at the prospect of sex with a 'savage'.

Libby blocked her ears: even a hint of negativity would damage the vibes building in her brain. 'Listen, will yer?' she said, trying to bring them to order. 'I'm not saying we paint you up as a savage. Shit, no! We'll do better 'n that.'

'Such as what, then?' asked Matt. 'Apart from tribal warriors, who the hell wears war paint?'

'Football fanatics!' laughed Holly.

Libby held on to her vision; in her mind, she was levitating and free of earthly bonds, and it gave her an advantage over Holly and Matt, so prosaic in their thinking.

'No, seriously! The idea of a warrior is great.' She opened her hands in a slow release of mystical wisdom. 'If you think about it, that's what Matt is. A warrior, on a crusade of some kind – I mean, look at his brochure. His work says it all. It's choc-a-bloc with messages, right?'

Libby hadn't totally grasped the meaning of Matt's work, and his ideas didn't seem terribly sympathetic anyway, but it was obvious he was a visionary. His work was heavy, heavy stuff.

Holly looked at Libby, then at Matt. 'Libbs is right,' she said.

Matt stroked his chin, surprised to find himself warming to the theme. Yes, striking out as he'd done did have a certain soldierly merit. And it *had* been a crusade: his work had taken him years.

'OK. I take your point,' said Matt, with growing excitement.

'So, what do we do with him?' Holly asked.

Libby paced in silence. She half opened her mouth as if to speak, then closed it again with a little shake of her head. Concentrating hard, she walked out of the studio, up the stairs and into the hall, feeling the air as if for something tangible. 'Think, think,' she muttered. 'I gotta think.'

Holly and Matt waited in the studio. 'Oh, shit!' Matt said to Holly. 'Now what are we in for?'

Holly hadn't the foggiest. 'I reckon she's got a mental block.'

'As long as it's not another wobbly!'

'I think the savage look's going to win out,' said Holly.

'No way! If you think I'm going to sit here and let the two of you tart me up like some bongo-beating belligerent, you're mad.'

'Wimp!' said Holly. Silence then prevailed while they waited for Libby to return. After several minutes they heard an exclamation from the passage: 'Gottit!'

Libby returned to the studio, fists clenched in victory. 'You know those helmets the ancient Greeks had, the ones with eye holes and cheek plates. They're like faces, right?'

Matt was struck by the urgency in her tone, so at odds with her earlier air of detachment. 'Yeah, I know the ones.'

'Well, how about painting your face up like that?'

'Clever,' said Matt. The idea of linking him to the cradle of civilization was highly appealing.

'Oh, ace!' said Holly. 'That's brilliant.'

'But, what colour would you use?'

'Blue!' cried Libby 'It has to be blue.'

'A sort of steely blue?'

'No, no, like woad!' said Libby, impatiently.

'Great!' Matt exclaimed. 'Just like the ancient Brits.'

'Brilliant!' said Holly again.

Libby's idea was beginning to snowball. She drew a deep breath. 'And how about this?' she said, holding her head in silent concentration.

'What?' said Matt, avid to know.

'Why don't we give you a third eye?'

Matt looked at Holly.

'Another eye?' said Holly, grimacing. 'Where?'

Libby pointed to her forehead. 'Here!' she said. 'Bang in the middle.'

'Like a Cyclops!' shrieked Holly. 'But why?'

Matt's face was a picture of grave concern. The last thing he wanted was to end up the subject of a sad bloke alert.

'Think 'insight',' Libby said. 'You know, the 'third eye' and all that.'

Holly cottoned on. 'Hey, that's cool. But weren't the Cyclops a race of giants?'

'Even better!' beamed Libby.

It was an incredible suggestion and Matt felt it might just work. His eyes darted between the two girls while they discussed how to produce the right effect. It was risky, he thought, but the possibilities were immense. The image could serve as a startling reminder of patriotism unburdened by contemporary cant. And as for the third eye, God! What a stroke of brilliance – to link him with a race of giants.

'Right,' he said, throwing caution to the wind, 'let's go for it!'

Libby chuckled. 'First, we'd better clean up your face,' she said. 'Can't have this red blob in the way.'

'What a shame,' said Holly mockingly.

Matt was on a high now. He adjusted himself in the chair for maximum comfort. But Bernie was right. Getting the measure of Holly hadn't been easy.

For Holly, the evening ahead was full of real promise. She watched amazed as Libby dabbed Matt's cheek with cotton wool soaked in warm water; only a month ago this same girl would've died at the thought of tending a man like that.

Matt sat back enjoying the attention – Libby's soft touch, that sweet whiff of wacky baccy about her, and Holly re-filling his glass with good wine. Like a pasha among concubines, he was grinning from ear to ear.

'Who's a lucky boy, then?' said Holly, reading his mind.

'I could get hooked on this,' Matt confessed.

Libby approached him with a brush and a pot of face paint. 'It may not be woad, but the colour's pretty close.' She applied the blue in scimitar shaped blocks, one on each cheek.

Holly watched, suppressing a twinge of jealousy as Libby guided the brush over Matt's skin from right to left and then down, filling in the blank areas with soft sensual strokes.

Libby had the habit of sticking her tongue out while she worked. Holly wished she'd put it away lest Matt found it a come on, her gold stud a glistening symbol of wanton promiscuity. Don't be silly, she told herself. You're being paranoid. Matt doesn't fancy her. He said so!

The minutes passed silently, the three of them utterly absorbed.

Libby stood back to eye up the effect. 'What d'you think, Holls?' she asked. 'Is that enough on the cheeks?'

'Great. That's really cool.'

'OK,' said Libby, pleased. 'Now, let's have a go with the eye on his forehead.'

'Will you need some white?' Holly asked her.

Libby walked to the worktop. 'Sure,' she said, rummaging for the colour. 'It'll make the pupil really stand out.'

Matt sat still while Libby painted in the outline. 'God knows what Bernie's going to make of this.'

'He'll go ape,' said Holly, 'and accuse me of losing the plot. But he'll come round when he sees the commercial potential.'

'How d'you mean?' asked Libby, painting away.

'Come on!' said Holly. 'A face like this could become famous. To use it just in the gallery would be sacrilege. If Bernie handles it right, it could be everywhere, like on buses and billboards, you know? Hey, it could even go global!'

'Great,' said Matt dreamily. 'Imagine my face covering the side of a building.'

Holly grinned. 'God, listen to the guy!'

Libby looked up from her work, now almost finished. 'Just think of it. My work, larging it in New York!'

'Why not?' said Holly, excited by thoughts of what such exposure could do for her photography. Silence reigned in the studio, as the hopes of all three ascended to giddying heights.

Eventually, Libby spoke. 'There,' she said, completing the pupil with the tip of her brush, 'that should do it.'

'Awesome!' said Holly. 'Truly awesome.'

'Do I get a look yet?' asked Matt.

'In a minute,' said Holly firmly. 'Just be patient!'

Matt kept his silence. The two girls hovered around him, Libby adding finishing touches and Holly commenting when she saw fit. 'You know what I think would be an ace touch?' she said.

'What's that?' asked Libby.

'We should get rid of his shirt – I mean, what kind of a warrior wears a shirt like that?'

'Yeah, it's minging!'

'What's wrong with it?' Matt demanded.

'Well, it's hardly 'Willie Fitz',' said Holly sniffily.

'Willie Fitz!' cried Matt. 'Who the hell's he?'

Holly was exasperated. 'Honestly, don't you know anything? Willie Fitz is high fashion for you boys – really hip! You'll have to pay him a visit. Won't he, Libbs? I mean your image at the moment is, to put it mildly, crap.'

Before Matt could escape from the chair Holly was unbuttoning his shirtfront, while Libby struggled with his cuffs.

'Oi! Get off me!' he protested.

'Don't be so silly,' said Holly, relishing his embarrassment. 'We've seen it all before, haven't we Libbs?'

'Yeah, 'course,' said Libby, enjoying the fun.

With several quick tugs Holly lifted the shirt clear of his arms. 'Mmm,' she said, as his chest was revealed. 'Nice pecs.'

Crimson-faced, Matt sat in the chair, his torso now on view. Holly walked round behind him. 'Don't be shy.' After a little pinch to his biceps, she whispered in his ear: 'Great body!'

Matt recovered his poise and beamed.

Libby felt a tremor of excitement on seeing Matt's chest – smooth, lily-white and hairless, like the skin of a perfect potato. 'That's made all the difference,' she said.

'Hasn't it just,' said Holly, darting behind the camera to see how Matt shaped up through the viewfinder.

'Well?' said Matt, pushing out his chest.

Holly adjusted the focus. 'You look a jerk!' she laughed. 'Stop hamming it up, will you?'

Matt conjured up a little gravitas. 'That any better?'

'Yeah. But don't go over the top, just be natural.'

'Natural!!?'

Holly looked at Libby. They grinned at each other. Then Libby stepped back, appraising Matt's head, a worried look on her face.

'What's the matter, Bird?'

Libby shook her head. 'There's still something wrong. I know what it is: his hair! I mean look, it flops about all over the place.'

Matt could see from Holly's expression the word 'flop' was calling for another sexual innuendo. 'Don't even think about it!' he said.

'Me?' Holly smiled sweetly. 'As if I would.'

Libby was ignoring their banter. 'His hair needs to be more macho.'

'I agree. It's too long and lanky,' said Holly, running her fingers through it disdainfully, as if it was an old wig she'd found in a dressing-up box. 'It's in need of a serious makeover.'

'Yeah, totally.'

Matt hazarded a guess at their thoughts. 'Well you're not cutting it! Short's not my scene.'

'Wimp!' said Holly.

'Yeah,' drawled Libby.

'I'm not going to walk about looking like a bogbrush!'

'I know what,' said Libby brightly. 'We could sweep it straight back!'

'Yeah, cool!' said Holly, excitedly. 'Like Antonio Banderas in one of those old action movies.'

Libby chuckled. 'If you say so,' she said, uninterested by the antics of film-stars.

'It'll work, I know it will,' said Holly. 'Come on, let's try!'

Matt relaxed. He'd seen the movies and had been impressed by the sultry-eyed man of few words who managed to dispatch villains with magical proficiency. 'Okay. Hair swept straight back would be cool.'

Libby fetched a comb and a bowl of warm water from the dark room.

'Hair's so important, don't you think?' said Holly. 'I mean, unless it's right, nothing's right. Life's a bitch, completely.'

'Yeah, completely,' agreed Libby. Wetting the comb, she drew it back from Matt's forehead over his scalp and down to the nape of his neck. She repeated the action again and again as she progressed from one side of his head to the other, making Matt tingle with pleasure. Matt scrabbled for images to quell his arousal – dead birds, bluebottles, maggots and rats.

'What d'you think?' Libby said to Holly.

'Wicked!'

'When do I get a say in all this?' Matt demanded.

'Okay, go on Libbs, give him the mirror,' Holly said, as if pacifying a fractious child.

Matt hardly recognized himself. He possessed the aura of a classical warrior. There was no mistaking that. And as for the eye: 'Epic!' he said, in near disbelief at its powerful effect.

'It's like you're not the same guy,' Holly told him.

Tilting her head to one side, Libby admired her handiwork. 'Yeah, I'm well pleased,' she said, delighted that she hadn't lost her touch after weeks of minimal activity.

Matt was truly impressed: thanks to the girls' efforts, his sex appeal had doubled in the space of half an hour.

Holly winked at Libby. 'We could fancy the pants off you, couldn't we Libbs?'

'Yeah,' said Libby playfully. 'Not half!'

Matt feigned indifference and concentrated instead on his reflection.

Libby studied his head with a critical eye. 'You know, I think we've created a work of art.'

'I agree,' said Matt, moving the mirror from side to side. To his mind, he was looking at a live exhibit: part painting, part flesh and blood. Much like an actor, in fact. He smiled, amused by the irony of his earlier conclusion that the thespian life was not for him. It was just as Sylvester maintained, he thought: 'Art is a boundless thing.'

Holly interrupted his thinking. 'If the photos work out, you could become an icon,' she said. Looking over his shoulder, she revealed her own face alongside his in the mirror.

'You reckon?' said Matt, looking back at her. He toyed pleasurably with the prospect of multitudes gaping in awe at his alias. 'What d'you think people will say?'

Holly stood back and winked at Libby. 'They'll say, 'Who is this warrior and what is his name?' ' she said. Then, suppressing a giggle: 'Has he come to slay us or to save us?'

'Do you think so?' said Matt, unaware she was taking the mickey.

Tempting though it was to bring him down to earth, Holly refrained. She'd fallen for the soldierly appeal of his made-up face and for that all-seeing eye. What a touch – dominant and uncompromising.

Holly and Libby took the brushes through to the dark-room sink. 'That eye you've painted,' Holly whispered to Libby. 'It's brilliant – really erotic!'

'D'you reckon?'

'I do. Where did you get the idea?'

'From that photo upstairs.'

'Uncle Henry's eye?' Holly grinned. 'I thought it bugged you!'

'It does,' admitted Libby. 'It's the way it looks right through you. It makes you feel naked.'

'I know,' Holly giggled. 'It's one of my favourites. It was the first arty pic I ever took.'

'Yeah?' said Libby.

'I'd been photographing myself starkers in my bedroom, just to experiment.'

Libby could appreciate the sense in that; her earliest nudes too had been studies of herself, done with the aid of a full-length mirror.

'Anyway,' Holly went on, 'one day after Henry had finished working, he popped his head round the bedroom door to see what I was up to.'

'The cheeky git!' said Libby, running a basin of hot water.

'No, no, it wasn't like that!' insisted Holly. 'God, he often saw me in the buff. I mean, as far as that goes, I was just another model.'

'Huh!' said Libby, unconvinced.

'Anyway, he comes into the room, sits down, and asks me who the pictures are for. I say, no one in particular; but if they come out I'll add them to a portfolio – to show people, you know?'

'Yeah, yeah – and what did he say?'

Holly giggled. 'From the pose he'd just seen, he said, all I stood to gain was a 'jolly good rogering', quote.'

'The dirty old bastard!' Libby exclaimed.

'Yeah, he was rather,' agreed Holly. 'But humungous fun.'

'So, how come the picture of his eye?' asked Libby.

'Well, he only had one, you know, and when he made that remark, it really twinkled,' said Holly, chuckling. 'His face was a picture – just wicked! So, I told him to hold it right there. I got the camera as fast as I could. The result was a close-up of his face. From that, making an enlargement of the eye was easy.'

Libby shook her head. For all her supposed class, Holly was quite shameless. But then, having grown up in a household where nudity was flaunted, with Uncle Henry and his models parading about and thinking nothing of it, was that so surprising? Holly had once even admitted her shamelessness. She'd told Libby a story about a geeky cousin of hers. Years ago, she'd found him watching her undress through a hole in the side of a dilapidated beach hut. Holly had fondled her breasts to excite him, then watched the boy stumble in some discomfort across the shingle to douse himself in the sea. The story had had them both in fits.

A question was bothering Libby. For weeks, she'd held herself back from asking it, but now the time seemed right. 'It amazes me, that Henry never... well, you know...'

'Tried anything?' chirruped Holly, unabashed. 'No, he never did. He was impotent, you see.'

'Impotent?' said Libby, astonished.

'Yeah,' said Holly, in her matter of fact way. 'Years later, Mummy told me that was the reason she left him. And much as I loved him, I can't say I blame her – I

114

mean, what good's a man if all that's supposed to go on remains stuck in his head?'

'Yeah, right,' said Libby. She was amazed; who would have thought Uncle Henry might have a problem like that!

Holly went back into the studio and Libby followed. 'Come on!' she said to Matt. 'Let's get you on film – we don't want to stay down *here* all night.'

Dragged out of a stupor of self-regard, Matt tensed his chest for the camera. Libby positioned herself by the light switches and awaited Holly's instructions.

'OK Libbs, let's roll!' Holly looked through the view-finder, her right hand controlling the zoom. 'Take the light right down.' She pulled Matt's face into close-up. 'That's great. Now start bringing the light back up again – slowly, slowly, like we said.'

Matt's face appeared in the darkness like that of a Greek god. There was a feeling of impersonal power about him, thought Holly. She had a sense of history in the making.

NINE

The burden of age had come early to Cyril Pout and looking in the mirror depressed him. Locks of grey hair flopped over his ears like the wings of an exhausted pigeon. A visage of surrender gazed back, the eyes sad like marbles dulled by the years.

Now in his sixties, he was ill and aware of encroaching mortality. Even the advent of summer meant little any more.

The seasons show no compassion, he thought: you hope to die on a sunny day in May, but January takes you instead, winter misery gobbling up your own. It's best just to lie in bed and watch the rain beating on the window panes, like an envoy from God, urging contrition.

Cyril peered more closely into the mirror to examine the pallor of his skin. This was a ritual search for signs of marginal improvement, practised with the fidgety frequency of a man in the grip of anxiety. As usual, there was no change. Standing back disappointed, he turned to a topic of frequent reflection:

'Angina!' he said out loud. 'Such an odd name for a heart condition! More like a girl's name, a Pre-Raphaelite beauty perhaps: sitting in an orchard, she extends a loving hand to the sheep grazing at her feet.'

But for Cyril, angina was the Angel of Death. She brought him terrible spasms of pain, warnings that his arteries were irredeemably furred. A specialist had told him that the risks of yet another operation would be considerable. Cyril sought a second opinion: wearily flicking through Cyril's notes, the second opinion pronounced 'Mr. Pout, I fear surgery is now your only real option. Without it – well, it's impossible to say, but you should prepare for the worst.'

While making up his mind whether to submit to the knife, Cyril depended on beta-blockers for survival. Pills, pills and more pills!

Save for the company of goldfish, Cyril had lived most of his life alone. Divorced early, he had lost contact with his wife and little daughter. But since that unhappy time, he had gone on to lead a blameless if uneventful life in the employ of the Royal Household. The last two years of his career had culminated in his appointment as a senior librarian. The job offered the chance of early retirement and at fifty-five he'd been happy to take it.

His disillusionment with the eroding standards of court life had taken its toll. The Royals were by then exposed to a code of nauseating familiarity. Deference to the monarch and her family was considered undemocratic; the forelock-tugging subservience of yesteryear was quite untenable; the notion of servility was long since outmoded.

So he had vacated his grace-and-favour apartment. Fearful of uprooting himself to the country lest he be too far from a hospital, he had returned to live in his one-bedroom flat in London W.8. It was a sought-after area still, even in these restive times when pavements everywhere were blighted by violence and affray.

His flat was on the second floor. The view, whilst no glorious panorama, was nonetheless good. To left and right were vistas over gardens and beyond them the backs of houses. Bobbing heads and upper torsos, seen over walls and at windows, entertained him with their daily activities; drawing curtains and opening windows and

sometimes doing something altogether more obscure –
'Fun to guess at when you live on your own and have little to do.'

It was the house directly opposite that attracted his
gaze most often, in rapturous anticipation of sighting the
young girl who lived there – one Holly Tree, a paragon
of virtue, blessed with all that is good in this world. Her
smile was as lovely now as it had been when she was little, playing in the garden so many years ago.

For more than a decade there had been no real contact
between them, but sightings of her walking in her beautiful garden helped him bear his loneliness. And should
she wave to him, that would be a high point of the
day – the blessing of a comfort-giving angel.

The other gardens held no such lasting interest for him;
they were either showcases of voguish excess, commissioned from one or other fashionable landscape gardener,
or overgrown jungles, ignored on the grounds that they
were too small to swing a cat in and therefore not worth
the bother. But that was no excuse! The inhabitants were
wealthy enough; but they were a new class of heartless
careerists whose worship of Mammon left no time for the
God-given wonders of nature.

Cyril had an eye for beauty, which he had acquired
during the course of many visits to gardens at home and
abroad. He had developed a particular liking for walled
courtyards adjoining great houses, where parterres and
box hedges, trimmed to perfection, combined to create
oases of ordered charm. He would summon them to mind
as intimate retreats from an unravelling world.

His greatest joy was to sit sheltered from the wind, an
old panama hat on his head, and indulge his love of
poetry, reading or writing it according to mood. Old
Nanny Littlecott had sparked off this interest: her 'Rubba
dub-dub, three men in a tub' lived in his mind to this day.
And rudimentary though his efforts at composition were,
they served to release him from his sorrows.

He had no garden of his own, but he enjoyed the changing seasons, welcoming the lengthening days of summer by filling his window boxes with pelargoniums. Bought from a local nursery, he'd carry them in, talking to them as if they were friends – old friends on an annual visit, for whom there was a comfortable *bed*, in return for their gracing him with their sunny disposition.

A sensitive man, he spent his days quietly; walking in the park, browsing in book shops or visiting the local library where he could read the daily papers from cover to cover if he so wished. But he was rarely inclined to do so, for their contents depressed him profoundly. They spoke of a world in which once-cherished values had changed out of all recognition. Goodness, for instance, was now a metaphor for gratification, instant and taken for granted. He could remember the period of rationing following the Second World War – those 'grateful to be able to get it' days, when his mother would pick up her coupons from the dresser before embarking on shopping trips for basic provisions. He believed the mind-numbing plethora of choices available in the contemporary world had ruined entire generations.

He remembered, too, the courteousness of men in brown coats serving behind marble topped counters, carefully weighing goods and wrapping them with enviable proficiency before offering them into his mother's gloved hands with a polite 'Thank you madam'. And sometimes a genial enquiry: 'How's Master Cyril today? Growing up fast, I see.'

So many niceties have gone, he thought, crushed like so much tissue paper. And the iniquity of prices! Goldfish, once a mere sixpence, now over a pound! – hardly worth it, especially when they turn belly up in weeks!

And the commercialism – the 'bangs for your bucks' – it was endless! Whichever wave-band he switched to on his old Roberts radio, the 'out-now' and 'available-at' of countless advertisements would ring in his ears until he could bear it no longer. This was an age of indulgence, of rolling vulgarity and conspicuous consumption as of right. An age devoid of courtesy and finesse, free of responsibility and obligation to anyone or anything. Respect and manners were outdated, considered effete. 'Yes, common man has won,' he'd despair. 'Permeating every aspect of life with his beastly bravura!'

But short of retreating to a monastery, there was little he could do but endure it. 'Oh, Sam,' he would sigh, peering at the solitary shubunkin circling a bowl in the perpetual gloom of his kitchen. 'How long can I go on?'

People reckoned Cyril an oddity. His gentility, like an outmoded garment, was a left-over from a mannered and fogeyish past. In the twilight of summer evenings he would stand at his open window listening to old recordings; Mahler's Fifth perhaps, or Verdi's Requiem. The notes would transport him into a state of tearful melancholy. Working his way through tumblerfuls of whisky, he'd churn over the past, his memories blurring into a steadily increasing incoherence.

Then when he was able to stand no longer, he'd totter back from the window and collapse into the familiar must of his armchair. There he would wait for darkness to descend before retiring to bed to ride once more the punishing roundabout of fiendish nocturnal anxieties. Would he wake in the morning? Or would he die in the night? And would anybody care if he did?

Now sixty-four, he had but one forlorn hope: that before he died just one of his poems might come to mean something to someone. 'Is that too much to ask?' he would say to a darkening sky. In thirty years, he had nothing to show for his labours save a bundle of rejection slips holed up at the back of his desk, each one a body blow delivered with cutting indifference. 'The Editor regrets...'

'Rejection, rejection, rejection! Have they nothing to say, these editors? No comment to offer at all?'

But to them, Cyril was a nobody – one of thousands of hopefuls whose inadequate work spilled onto their desks in an incessant flow of paper and self-addressed envelopes enclosed 'for the editor's convenience'.

What's so wrong with my work? he would ask himself. Are my thoughts so alien that my only hope of being noticed at all will be at my funeral? Twenty minutes centre-stage in a coffin before being trundled off over rollers and consumed in a finale of fire? God, the futility of it all!

On this particular day, the late May sun was shining with particular intensity. Such single clouds as there were seemed out of place, almost artificial. Even with the windows open, the incoming breeze wasn't enough to cool the rooms in Cyril's flat. So he retreated to Holland Park, to spend the afternoon seated on a collapsible chair in the shade of a catalpa tree.

This was a favourite spot. He'd come to look on it as his own, and all the more pleasant in that it was isolated from a copse of larger trees where, sooner or later, couples would come in order to copulate in the shade.

That park regulations should be broken in this way upset him. But in the eyes of the public at large, indecent exposure was not of much concern. The sight of squirming buttocks invoked more humour than disgust, and at times even a round of applause. 'Quite disgraceful!' he thought.

Notepad at the ready, Cyril put on his glasses and waited for inspiration. He looked up through the tree's heart-shaped leaves at the sky, as if it might arrive by divine delivery. The minutes passed by.

It was the middle of the week and the park was relatively quiet. The most conspicuous sounds were the cries of mating peacocks. Eventually their plaintive calling became a nuisance. Drawing back the sleeve of his alpaca jacket, he looked at his watch, tutting impatiently as if the birds had exceeded their allotted hours. The second hand was jerking its way round the face, chopping off time as he watched. What a waste! Soon it would be five and he hadn't written a line.

He began to panic, shifting uneasily in his seat. He tapped his notebook with his pencil in a slow deliberate rhythm to steady his nerve. The birds went quiet as if by imperial command – or perhaps they were being fed.

'Time,' he mumbled out loud. How odd that sometimes it flew and at other times it dragged, agonizingly even, making one minute seem like ten. He remembered how as a young man, time spent with one's beloved would just whistle by, but times of separation would drag and weigh heavy on the heart. If Time could speak to him, what would it say? He hurriedly penned a line:

I love my little room inside your head.

Yes that's good, he thought. Time is a presence inside me, a friend I can talk to. He chuckled; in that case, my eyes can be windows, which Time can look through too.

He wrote down, *Its rounded windows...*

But what next? Catching sight of a finch as it flew from tree to tree, the answer was obvious.

'Of course!' He put pencil to paper again: *...and ever-changing views.*

He looked up and around, an ecstatic grin on his face. Sharing his life with Time, keeping her abreast of things: he liked it. He thought aloud for a moment: 'Yes, that's fine!' A passer-by, mistaking him for some troubled soul high on drug-induced optimism, muttered wearily: 'Not another nutter.'

His earlier tetchiness shed, Cyril was now in buoyant mood. He thrilled at his own originality. Yes, inspiration had arrived at last, creeping in via a side-entrance to announce itself in the foyer of his brain with softly spoken words: 'You didn't expect me today, did you?'

No, he certainly hadn't. Those peacocks had been really off-putting.

A rush of adrenalin furthered him on. Time's words spilled onto the page in a feverish scrawl:

Heads suit me, I suppose –
Ones like yours that fret and care,
Thinking of me always, each and every day...

'Good, good!' he muttered, excitedly.

Then, sometimes you hate me – Don't deny it!
It's when I'm elusive, isn't it?
– Slipping through your fingers!

That's a great first verse! thought Cyril. On the crest of a wave, he pitched easily into the second:

But, how you love it when there is oodles of me,
And I am on your hands to do with as you
please.

'Oh!' he exclaimed, his heart pumping to sustain his excitement. 'This is too good to be true.'

Reading the words through, he felt sure there was more to come. But not for the moment, he decided. If he pushed too hard, the well of inspiration would run dry.

Standing up, he nodded at the heavens in grateful appreciation. It wasn't every day that words came so readily.

With a view to going home, he took off his glasses and popped them in his top pocket before taking a few paces to stretch his legs. A dog turd flattened under his shoe.

'Oh, God!' he cursed. 'Isn't that absolutely typical!' It was as if fate had conspired to mar his jubilation.

Huffing and puffing, he wiped his sole on the grass, paying fastidious attention to the more stubborn flecks of excrement that held fast even when he angled his foot. Satisfied he'd made the best of a bad job, he took a last look at a blossoming tree, hoping to recapture his euphoria. But it had gone, ousted by the foul odour infiltrating his senses. He folded up his chair and wandered off, scowling over his shoulder at the smear, virulent and glinting in the sun.

'Dogs!' he muttered angrily. Standards of civic responsibility were now beyond the pale. He cast his eye at a Borzoi a short distance away, chomping on the remains of a discarded bread roll. Thin and neglected, the stray was one of hundreds roaming throughout the city, scavenging for scraps. People nowadays! Eating always on the move – hot dogs, bacon butties, chip-stuffed Mac Whoppers, you name it. A whole generation of obese, lip-smacking repulsives.

He felt a tirade coming on. There was no one he could vent it on: timorous by nature, his feelings had to be bottled up. He warned himself not to start, as once he did, he would only upset himself further by noticing other things.

His particular hatred was shaven-headed gum-chewing males – in summertime, invariably dressed in shorts – whose ape-like gait and stares of testosterone-packed insolence he found threatening. Add to that their tattoos and, well, they were the embodiment of primordial baseness. He scurried home.

Refreshed by an early bath, he regained his inspiration. The closing lines of his poem came in a rush. Like a canoeist racing over rapids, all he had to do was steer – a touch of the paddle here, another there, and the words tailed out in an orderly wake behind.

But, just as he'd put his pencil down, disaster! 'God, my pelargoniums!' he cried. It was after eight o'clock and he'd forgotten all about them. They'll be bone dry, poor things, after such a hot day, he thought.

Apologizing out loud, he filled up his watering can from the kitchen tap and hastened to the open window. 'I'm so sorry – it's my fault entirely,' he told them. 'I was writing a poem, you see, and once I got into it, I couldn't stop. You know how it is.'

The plants appeared to acknowledge him, sagging with relief as the water passed over their heads.

'When this is done, I'll read you what I've written!'

His grievous omission forgiven, he put the watering can down and collected his notebook from the arm of his chair. Then, returning to the window, he glanced at the plants and began to recite:

> *'Time*
>
> *I love my little room inside your head –*
> *Its rounded windows and ever-changing views.*
> *Heads suit me, I suppose:*
> *Ones like yours that fret and care,*
> *Thinking of me always, each and every day.*
> *Then, sometimes you hate me – Don't deny it!*
> *It's when I'm elusive, isn't it?*
> *– Slipping through your fingers.'*

Smiling briefly at the plants, he acknowledged their appreciation, then began the second verse:

> *'But, how you love it, when there is oodles of me*
> *And I'm on your hands, to do with as you please.*
> *Why! You forget about me – Go to sleep even,*
> *Only to wake and find that I have flown.*
> *That puts you in a panic, doesn't it?*
> *Tapping the clock like a mad thing!*
> *Don't worry. You know I'll never leave you,*
> *As, truth be told, you couldn't live without me.'*

'I don't think that's bad,' he muttered to himself. Then, familiar with the futility of self-congratulation, he added: 'Not that it really matters.'

At eight-thirty, after feeding on a readymade cottage pie from the local deli, he walked to the window. The blue evanescence of the sky was giving way to a dark and threatening presence of cloud building up in the West.

Swirling the whisky in his tumbler, he let out a measured sigh. He knew his pleasure from the whisky would be short-lived. The coming twilight would bring on its demons, meddling with his consciousness and befuddling his brain just for the hell of it.

Resting his tumbler among the pelargoniums, he leant his hands on the window box. A crescendo of turbines broke the peace; a jet appeared overhead as it circled and waited to land. Probably a charter flight full of trippers, he imagined; lobster-red bodies, back from the Balearics or some such: drunk, abusive, and ''avin a laugh'. Pushing the thought of his disgusting fellow-countrymen to the back of his mind, he noticed the breeze had dropped; the noise of the turbines receded, leaving behind a stillness in which voices could be heard. Every detail of greenery was a freeze-frame of slowly darkening matter.

He looked over the high wall bordering the alley below to the garden of 17 Holland Park Villas – the home of Holly Tree, his symbol of hope in an ugly world. A girl appeared on the terrace, a drink in one hand and the fingers of the other casually tucked below her bare midriff, into the top of a bright yellow skirt. It wasn't Holly, it was her lodger – that strange little girl she called 'Libbs' or 'Bird' – the latter sometimes quite crossly, he recalled.

He'd seen her once during the day, standing at a top floor window and gazing at the sky. Away with the fairies, Cyril thought: she seemed not to notice him tending his flowers across the way.

He'd seen her down in the garden too, dressed in combat fatigues. She had sat at the table, rolling cigarettes. Then she had leaned back, eyes closed and face to the sun while she puffed. Had a rifle been by her side, and her surroundings been shell-holed ruins, she could have been a freedom-fighter taking a breather from the ravages of war.

Sometimes the girl barely moved, as if tranquillized. All in all, Cyril found her a bit of a conundrum.

But tonight she looked different: ladylike, for once. Glancing back up the steps to the open French windows, she called to someone inside: 'Come on. It's still warm out here!'

Confident Holly would be next to appear, Cyril waited, hoping for his usual treat – that little wave of acknowledgement that meant so much. But when it turned out to be a young man minus his shirt, he muttered to himself: 'Most unbecoming! But worse still, whatever has he done to his face? Something very strange. Whatever is the boy playing at?

'Hey, some scene!' the young man said, apparently looking around at the garden in awe. And so he should, thought Cyril, for though a little overgrown, it was a microcosm of formal grandeur, stepped and terraced beds surrounding the small sunken lawn with its gnarled and ancient mulberry tree. On either side paths led to a gazebo in the lee of a retaining wall, whose high greying brickwork played host to a tracery of climbing plants, most in full flower.

At last Holly appeared, putting paid to Cyril's fear that perhaps this evening he wouldn't see her.

'Let's sit down there,' she said, directing everyone to a table and chairs arranged on the lawn.

Cyril waited patiently for Holly to look up. Sweet Holly, he thought, the prickly symbolism of her name in sharp contrast to what he believed was her true nature. From the very first moment he'd seen her, he'd cared deeply about her, as if she was his own. Then, she was no more than a little girl: a doll-like figure enshrined in the innocence of childhood who'd wave to him and smile, or play peek-a-boo from behind the old mulberry tree. She could never be truly his own, but she could be his muse, bringing little ditties to his head as he watched her playing, so often on her own:

'Little Holly in your hat,
I wonder what it is you're at,
And who it is you're talking to
When sitting all alone.
Is someone there I cannot see
With whom you like to play?
Some little person in your head
With oh, so much to say.'

Spotting Cyril at his window, Holly smiled up at him as usual. Now it was a different smile: lovely still, but also seductive and assured – a sad reminder that she was no longer the little girl whom he used to meet in the park with her mother. Nevertheless, the thought that one day she might sell the house was enough to fill him with weepy sentiments akin to the misery of a station farewell.

Cyril watched Holly follow the others down the terrace steps to the lawn. As the trio seated themselves and became absorbed in conversation, he leaned further out of the window, ostensibly to take in the cool evening air, but actually to study the group more closely and hopefully pick up their chatter.

Before long, the rheumatism in his wrists began to trouble him. Wincing in pain, but determined to stay where he was, he pushed himself upright again. His curiosity focussed on Matt's face, he made out what appeared to be a single large eye painted on the forehead.

Abstractedly, Cyril fumbled for his tumbler, only to knock it from where it was precariously balanced among the pelargoniums. 'Damn it!' he swore, as it rolled from the window box to shatter in the alley below.

Pushing up the sash window to its furthest reach, he looked down to the gloom below. As his eyes adjusted, he could make out the faces of two startled figures.

'What the fuck are you playin' at?' shouted one.

'I'm sorry,' Cyril blurted. 'It was an accident!'

He could see they were two men, both white. 'I had this glass, you see,' he tried to explain. 'And it...'

'Fuckin' maniac!' yelled the first, kicking at the fragments of glass. 'You could've killed us!'

Cyril apologized again. 'I'm sorry,' he cried. 'I didn't mean to!'

'Piss off!' the man shouted back. 'Or I'll fuckin' 'ave yer.'

'Yeah, right!' shouted the other. His shaven head moved from side to side in apoplectic jerks of menacing intent.

Shocked by the men's hostility, Cyril came to his senses, withdrawing his head a little so it could not be seen from below.

How he hated the alley! Dark and narrow, it was designated by the local authority as a place where gay men could freely importune. Rough trade was always on offer. On still summer nights, low moans and the crackle of twigs could be heard from deep in the shrubbery of the nearby garden square. Graffiti, discarded syringes and used condoms completed the horror. And oh, those splatters of vomit that lingered for days in dry weather!

'What the Hell was all that about?' he heard the young man in the garden say.

The girl called 'Bird' stood up. 'Dunno, but it looks like it's something to do with the old guy at the window.'

Holly walked briskly to the end of the garden, stood on her toes and shouted: 'Hi! Are you alright?'

Cyril was too terrified to speak. He pointed down to the alley where the two men were pacing about, necks craned, waiting to see if his head would re-appear. Then, like a tortoise retreating into its shell, he withdrew.

Matt and Libby had joined Holly at the end of the garden. Matt was peering up at the window, not able to see if anyone was there or not.

'Who's the old guy you were talking to?' Matt said.

'Window Man,' Holly said.

'Window Man? Why d'you call him that?'

'Because he's always at the window!'

'Really?' said Matt, amused.

They all looked up and saw Cyril's face for a moment, peering down from under a mop of unkempt hair.

'His real name's Cyril. I've called him 'Window Man' since I was so high,' said Holly, levelling her hand a couple of feet above the grass.

'Do you know him?' asked Matt.

'Sort of. He's lived up there for yonks.'

'Oh,' said Matt, curious.

'When I was a child we used to bump into him in the park.'

'We?'

'Me and my mother,' said Holly. 'Actually, she thought him a bit of a nuisance,' she went on softly, 'as he always seemed to find us. He used to give me 5p pieces then tell me to put them in my piggy bank.'

'Weren't you the lucky one?' said Matt.

'Mummy always told him he shouldn't,' said Holly. 'But he said he had no children of his own, so giving me something was a pleasure.'

'If you ask me, he's a weirdo,' said Libby, thinking of the time she'd pretended not to notice him smile at her. 'Yeah, I reckon he's a dirty ol' man,' she added.

'Oh Bird! You're such a bitch about him,' said Holly. 'He wouldn't harm a fly.'

Matt guessed the old man's fondness for Holly was more likely the result of a simple infatuation, her little-girl smile melting his heart.

'Apparently he once worked for the Royals,' Holly said. 'And rumour has it he's a poet, although I've never seen anything he's written. But he's nice. He always waves if he sees me in the garden.'

Holly called again: 'Mr. Pout! Are you alright?'

'Butt out, bitch!' shouted a voice from the alley.

Holly's mouth dropped in shock.

'The cheeky bastard!' cried Libby indignantly.

Matt said nothing. Taking hold of the trunk of an aged wisteria, he climbed up the wall and onto the roof of the gazebo.

On seeing Matt's painted face staring menacingly through the overhanging foliage, the two men in the alley were dumbfounded. Making off at speed, they looked back over their shoulders to see if Matt was giving chase.

With one foot on the roof and the other on the wall, Matt stood erect, pointing after them like an avenging angel – his fearsome third eye bearing down on them until they were completely out of sight.

'Have they gone?' called Holly.

'Yeah they've scarpered!' Matt said, triumphant.

'Must have been your face,' Holly giggled. 'But who were they?'

'A couple of blokes,' Matt chuckled. 'They were scared shitless!'

Full of admiration, the girls watched him climb down.

'What were they doing?' asked Libby.

'I don't know,' he said, shying away from saying they were a couple of poofs lest he offend her.

'Here,' said Holly, reaching for his head. 'You've got blossom in your hair and all down your back.'

Matt stooped for her to remove it. 'What about the old guy up there? D'you think he's OK?'

They looked up at the window again, but they could see no one.

Alarmed by the kerfuffle, Cyril had stepped back into the interior of his sitting room, where he stood listening for some kind of 'all clear' that would tell him it was safe to look out again.

'Seems like he's gone,' Libby commented.

'He's probably petrified. I'd better go and see what all the fuss was all about,' said Holly. She felt the least she could do was to go round and assure him the men in the alley had been sent packing.

'You're mad,' said Libby, gravely. 'He's a weirdo!'

'We've been waving to each other for the last twenty years. He's harmless, honestly! And it'll only take me a couple of minutes to get there.'

'I'll come with you,' said Matt.

Holly pointed to his face. 'No way!' she laughed. 'You're not coming like that. You'd give him a heart attack.'

Matt grinned. 'Yeah,' he agreed. 'Maybe you're right.'

TEN

St. Mungo's Court was the former headquarters of a mission, long since converted into flats. Holly stood on the steps of the building searching for the name 'C. Pout'. She rang his bell but there was no reply on the entryphone. Certain he was there but probably too frightened to answer, she rang again. Still no reply. She turned to leave.

'Who d'yer want, luv?' called a voice from the street.

Holly looked over her shoulder to find a small portly man limping towards her. The man had minimized his baldness by encouraging what little hair he had to grow from a parting above his left ear, up and over his head. Laminated in grease, it stuck to his scalp with all the tenaciousness of left-over bacon rinds clinging to the side of a plate.

Seeing a large bunch of keys dangling from his waist, Holly presumed he was the caretaker, which indeed he was. A compaction of grubbiness and deceit, Gittins would lurk in his caretaker's flat for most of the day. There he had plenty of time to pursue his cultural interests, which were limited to football, internet pornography and trawls for information on penis enlargement. This electronic cornucopia of thrills filtered into his brain morning, noon and night, through eyes bleary from an excess of visual stimulation and ears cauliflowered from ancient paternal beatings.

His was an easy job and his limp had played a part in getting it. The residents' committee were a kindly and sympathetic bunch and they still had no idea that Gittins' limp was a sham, adopted to assure him of continuing sympathy long after he'd recovered from the pain of what had never been more than an in-growing toenail.

As an excuse it worked wonders, freeing him from carrying out favours for residents like walking to the post box or doing light shopping for someone ill with the 'flu. 'Nah, I ain't runnin' around for no toffs!' he'd confide to a sympathetic ear. 'Wot does they fink I am – a serf?'

'Cushy' is the word that sums up his position. His jobs were few and simple: he would check fuses in outdated appliances belonging to residents, more often than not to old ladies whose trip switches regularly cut out; and he would arrange access for tradesmen when residents had to be out for the day.

'I'm looking for Mr. Pout,' said Holly.

Gittins belched. 'Er, sorry 'bout that!' he said, rubbing his tummy to ease the indigestion. 'Pout, did yer say? Yeah, 'e's up on the second floor.'

'I know,' said Holly. 'But he's not answering.'

Gittins reached for his keys. 'Wot are you – Hic! – a relative or summin'?' Here's a tasty bit of totty, he thought to himself.

'No, a friend.'

'Strewth! Lucky ol' Poutie,' grinned Gittins, casting a lustful eye over Holly as he eased past her to open the door. 'Who'd 'ave believed it, eh?'

Holly was used to older men dropping asides on the off-chance of eliciting that come-and-take-me look and she smiled tolerantly. Men are such dreamers, she said to herself; especially specimens like this – sweaty, balding and reeking from the aftermath of some filthy meal.

'Known 'im long 'ave yer?' asked Gittins, inserting his key in the lock. Turning to face her, his double chin bulging against his shoulder, he eyeballed her cleavage and said: 'Only, I don't fink I've seen yer 'ere before.'

'I haven't been here before.'

The door unlocked, Gittins stood in the entrance jiggling his keys. An ignoble notion entered his head. 'I ain't supposed to let you girls in, yer know,' he said confidentially. 'Not orf the street, like! But if yer was to...'

Holly's nostrils flared. 'What do you mean, 'Off the street'?' she angrily demanded. 'And, if I was to do what?'

'Come on, luv,' said Gittins. 'I weren't born yesterday.'

'You cheeky bastard!' screamed Holly. 'Is that what you think I am? A tart!'

Gittins leant towards her, his voiced raised. 'Now don't go gettin' all hoity-toity!' he said. 'I ain't got nuffin' against tarts – Hic! – It's just that I ain't supposed to let 'em in.'

'You bloody pervert!' shouted Holly into his face. 'Get out of my way!'

Attracted by cries of 'Bastard!' and 'Pervert!' ringing through the air, a group of people formed on the pavement in hopeful anticipation of a fracas. 'You tell 'im, darlin'!' shouted one. 'Yeah, give 'im wot for!' yelled another.

Emboldened by their vociferous support, Holly pushed Gittins aside with both hands and entered the building. The small gathering cheered, hailing her action as a 'result'.

Baffled by the sound of applause, Gittins hurried to close the front door behind him, cheating two would-be assailants by a whisker. 'I'm jus doin' me job!' he protested as he disappeared from view.

'You want locking up!' shouted a woman, banging on the door after him. 'Harassing young women like that.'

Unbowed, Gittins retreated in haste to his basement office. This was an airless den. Rank with the odour of flatulence, it was a pocket of contagion to which Gittins had the only key. And jealously guarded it was, from residents in particular, who were always kept at bay when they popped down to see him on some domestic matter. No chance one of them getting a peep round the door!

'Silly ol' bugger,' muttered Gittins, reaching for the house phone. 'Fancy calling up a tart at 'is age. Friggin' disgustin!'

'Mr. Pout? Er, 'ello, Gittins 'ere!' he said shrilly, wicked thoughts running amok. 'Sorry to bovver yer, but there's a woman on her way up.'

'Oh,' said Cyril, alarmed. 'Did she give a name?'

Gittins placed his hand over the mouthpiece to block off an ill-suppressed snigger. 'Nah, she juss pushed her way in,' he answered, enhancing his words with phoney concern. 'Says she knows yer.'

Cyril shook his head. 'Oh dear,' he said woefully. 'Couldn't you stop her?'

Stop 'er! Gittins said to himself. Jus' listen to 'im.

'Like I said, Mr. Pout,' he continued in mock respect, 'she just pushed past me. I've a feelin' she's one of them wimmin.'

'What women?'

Gittins convulsed silently. 'Y'know! Them sort of wimmin!'

'What, a prostitute?'

'Well, yeah! Wearin' ever such a short skirt, she was.'

'Oh, very well,' Cyril tutted. 'I'll have to pretend I'm not in.'

Gittins put the phone down. 'Pretend I'm not in, my arse!' he scoffed out loud. 'Tell us annuver one, Pouty!'

Hot and harassed, Holly ran up the stairs. She looked over the stairwell to make sure Gittins hadn't followed, then she ran her fingers through her hair to make herself presentable.

'Now which flat is it?' she wondered, walking from door to door along the landing. Guessing it must be the last one on the left, she rang the bell.

Inside his flat, Cyril stood motionless, his mouth ajar and one ear inclined to the door. He was determined not to answer.

Holly tried once more, only this time she knocked – a gentle tap, less alarming than the ring of a bell. 'It's me, Holly Tree,' she said, her voice close to the door. 'You know – I live opposite, in the Villas. I came to see if you were alright.'

'Holly?' said Cyril, astonished. 'Well, I never!' Cautiously, he opened the door to the extent the slip-chain allowed.

'Mr. Pout, isn't it?' said Holly, peering in through the gap to be met by his face, which seen close to was rather shocking – more deeply lined than she'd imagined.

'It is,' said Cyril. 'But Heavens! What are you doing here?'

'Well, I was out in the garden with friends and there was all that shouting. We wondered if you were all right.'

'My, but that's so kind!' said Cyril excitedly. 'Well, you'd better come in and I'll tell you all about it.' Releasing the slip-chain, he opened the door fully.

For Cyril, seeing Holly close to after so many years was rather daunting. Standing in the doorway, her green eyes gazing at him, she took on a new reality. Her figure, so long seen only in the distance of her garden, was taller than he'd thought.

Holly stepped into the hall onto a threadbare runner.

'Mind you don't catch a heel in that,' Cyril warned. 'I'm afraid it's seen better days.'

'Thank you,' said Holly.

'How good of you to come,' said Cyril. He hovered for a moment, unsure what to do with his hands.

'It was the least I could do,' Holly assured him.

Cyril smiled. 'Well, come on through to the sitting room. It's so dark out here.'

'Fine,' said Holly, conscious of a must of antiquity which grew stronger as she followed him. They went into a room where time, it seemed, had stood still.

'It was all my fault, I'm afraid,' Cyril began. 'Those men had every right to shout.'

'Not like that!' insisted Holly. 'It was totally unnecessary.'

Cyril shrugged his shoulders with calm resignation. 'Ah well, that's life for you today, it would seem. Anyway, do sit down, please – wherever you like.'

She sat upright on the edge of a sagging sofa, her knees demurely together. She felt like a little girl again, conscious that this was perhaps how Cyril still saw her.

Cyril walked to the window and recounted the incident in detail. He pointed and gesticulated while telling her how clumsy he'd been, his brow furrowed by feelings of guilt.

Holly tried to console him. 'It was an accident – it could have happened to anybody.'

'Of course, but it was stupid. I might have hit one of them on the head.'

'Perhaps,' said Holly, unconcerned. 'Anyway, they've gone now. They ran away.'

'Oh, good! Do tell me, was it that young chap in make-up they saw?'

'Yes! That's Matt!' She laughed. 'When they saw his face glaring down at them, they just bolted. Wasn't he brave?'

'Very!' emphasized Cyril. 'Why, only the other night a man was beaten to death just round the corner from here, outside Wasim's Washetaria. I presume it was a racial attack, but I don't really know.'

'I think you're right,' said Holly. She'd learnt of the matter from gossip in the deli. Apparently a Scotsman, who'd been swigging whisky whilst watching his washing tumble round, had jocularly suggested to an Afro-Caribbean, similarly engaged, that he hop into the machine himself. 'Aye, mon,' he reportedly said, 'coloureds come up a treat!'

The black man had taken the remark in good heart. But another white male had accosted the Scotsman. 'Yer filfy racist fuck!' he had screamed. After knocking the Scotsman down with demented ferocity, he proceeded to jump up and down on his chest until all signs of life in him were extinguished.

Holly reflected on the incident. 'It's a madhouse out there. But what can you do?'

Cyril looked at her sadly. 'My dear,' he said. 'If I knew the answer to that!'

Holly changed the subject. 'Matt's an artist,' she said smiling.

'I wondered what he was,' said Cyril politely. Then, allowing himself a little grin: 'I thought perhaps he might have been an actor.'

Holly giggled. 'He's vain enough,' she confided. 'But actually, he paints. His work's very much in the news at the moment.'

'Lucky fellow,' said Cyril, a little envious. 'I hope he realizes how lucky he is.'

'Oh, I think he does,' said Holly. 'He's been out in the cold too long not to.'

Out in the cold too long! Cyril thought, the words clattering round in his head. That's rich – what possible understanding could one so young have of such a thing? Take himself... decades of waiting for a letter of acceptance that would never arrive. But best not to dwell on the matter; the hurt ran too deep.

'Where did you meet him?' asked Cyril.

'At his private view. He's got an exhibition at Lagoon Art.'

'Lagoon Art? Oh, yes, I've heard of it,' said Cyril. 'It's that place that's always in the papers, isn't it?' He refrained from revealing his distaste for the kind of gimmicky work it promoted.

'It's a really cool gallery!' Holly emphasized.

'Well, I wouldn't know,' said Cyril evasively. 'I'm afraid I'm rather out of touch these days.'

'You ought to go there. Matt's work's a real eye-opener!'

'I'm sure it is,' said Cyril, fumbling with his cuffs. 'It's just that I don't get out to that sort of thing any more.'

'I see,' said Holly, saddened by his shuffling decrepitude.

Cyril changed the subject. 'The alley is truly disgusting,' he sighed.

'I know, it stinks,' said Holly.

'Doesn't it just,' agreed Cyril. 'But I was thinking more of the awful men who use it.'

'Oh, I see,' said Holly. Then, realizing someone of his generation was probably homophobic, she smiled sympathetically and said: 'But there's nothing you can do about it, now it's a designated area. They've even put a sign up. Have you seen it?'

'Yes, a pink daisy on a black background,' said Cyril. 'I hate it!' To think that the sign, bolted to a street light at the entrance to the ally, was official! That was the worst thing. 'It seems we must all learn to accept such things,' he sighed. 'Gay Pride – it's quite bewildering.' He found the open promiscuity and the endless celebrations oppressive. It was as if a rampaging army was on the loose, spreading death by Aids around the world.

He made an effort to switch the conversation to something more cheerful. 'It's such a thrill having you here, I hardly know what to say. You know, I can still picture you as a little girl. In Holland Park with your mother, remember?'

'Yes,' said Holly, transported back over the years, 'I must have been five or six…'

'I know,' said Cyril wistfully. 'It was all so long ago.'

'You always waved when you saw me in the garden.'

'I did,' said Cyril. 'And you would wave back. You've no idea how happy that made me.'

'Really?' said Holly.

'Oh, yes! You see, when I moved here, my wife had just left me and taken our young daughter with her. It was your little face that cheered me up.'

Holly smiled.

'Do you remember playing peek-a-boo with me?' he asked.

'Yes, behind the mulberry tree,' said Holly, bashfully. 'I used to call you 'Window Man' then.' She stopped short of confessing that she still did.

Cyril chuckled. 'Of course, I remember. Wasn't that funny?'

'That was in the days when my mother and Uncle Henry were together.'

'Ah, Uncle Henry,' sighed Cyril, reflecting on a sad afternoon not so long ago when Holly's garden had been full of relatives and friends mourning Uncle Henry's passing. 'You know, at first I thought he was your grandfather, and your mother his daughter,' he went on.

'He was actually my godfather,' said Holly. She was still prone to sadness at the mention of his name.

'I know that now,' said Cyril. Over time he had come to believe that Holly's mother and he were probably lovers. Uncle Henry was a splendid fellow, he remembered, an artist who wore a patch over his left eye – the result of a war wound, he fancied. Raffish to look at, Henry would appear on the terrace in paint-stained trousers. With a glass of wine in his hand he would enthuse airily about the good things in life to Holly and her mother. They would listen patiently, their gentle smiles of forbearance passing him by.

Watching the trio from his window, Cyril would envy them their contentment, especially in summertime when his loneliness was acute and the happiness of others most visible. Uncle Henry would take Holly's mother's hand and kiss it as they sat together, while Holly played at their feet with Romeo the cat. It was an idyllic scene: one that brought tears of self-pity to Cyril's eyes, alienated as he was from such familial delights.

Not that it lasted, as Holly's mother soon left for reasons Cyril never learnt. And once she'd gone, Holly would be away for long periods, returning only during school holidays, sometimes for as little as a week. Even so, those were magical days that arrived randomly, lifting his spirits and giving him the feeling that the air at his window wasn't so bad after all.

Noticing sorrow in Holly's expression, Cyril apologized. 'I never meant to upset you,' he said.

'I know. It's just that Uncle Henry and I were so close. He was like a father to me.'

Cyril offered her a drink. 'Whisky? It's about all I have, I'm afraid.'

'No, I'm fine, thank you.' Brightening up, she looked about the room. How could he tolerate such dowdiness? she wondered. Letting things go… it must be like watching a ball roll downhill and not bothering to stop it before it falls in a lake. Would she one day feel the same? That nothing matters any more, and all that's left is to see out one's days in shabby obscurity?

'A penny for your thoughts,' said Cyril, watching her eyes settle on a crack in the ceiling.

'Nothing, really,' she said, returning his gaze.

Cyril nodded. 'When you get to my age, you tend to put things off. Not to bother, you know?'

Holly smiled. 'Well, as long as the plaster doesn't fall on your head!'

'The crack is superficial, I'm sure,' said Cyril, looking up at the ceiling, unwilling to admit that he simply didn't care.

Holly pointed to a photo in a tarnished silver frame. Standing among others of the Royal Family, she guessed it had been taken in the nineteen sixties. 'Was that your wife?' she asked.

'That's right,' said Cyril, sitting himself down. 'And that's little Chloe by her side. She was six at the time.' Half smiling, he paused to reflect. 'She was a lovely little child – like you, a redhead and pretty as a picture.'

At a loss for what to say, Holly blushed.

'I'm sorry, I've embarrassed you,' said Cyril, ashamed of his forwardness.

'No, no,' said Holly, looking up from her lap. 'That's the nicest thing anybody's said to me all day.'

Cyril smiled. 'I'm an old fool sometimes!'

Holly changed the subject. 'Do you miss working for the Royals?'

'I miss them as people,' he said. 'But not what they've been forced to become. As you know, the institution is now a shadow of all it once it stood for.'

Holly sighed. Even in her short life, the pace of change had been remarkable. The Royal mystique had gone, eroded by the smiles of 'conniving poseurs', as Uncle Henry used to call the politicians plotting for the birth of a presidential regime.

Seeing little could be gained by dwelling on the matter, Holly asked Cyril if it was true he was a poet. 'It's what I've heard,' she said breezily.

'I've tried to write poetry ever since I was a boy,' Cyril confessed. 'But I'm not much good, I'm afraid.'

Cyril seemed so pitiful in his sadness and his modesty, and so like family from their long acquaintance, that Holly got up and walked over to him. She placed a hand on his shoulder. 'Will you show me some? I'm mad about poetry.'

Cyril was surprised by her familiarity – and even more by his own, when he found himself placing his hand on top of hers. 'Oh, I don't know. It's pretty awful stuff, I think. Nothing's ever been published.'

'I bet it's not awful. Please show me.' Leaning forward, she kissed him on the forehead in a spontaneous gesture of affection. It was as though he'd been close to her forever – a loving and selfless presence far more than a face at the window.

Cyril looked up at her; scarcely able to believe he'd been kissed. With watery eyes he appraised her sincerity, hoping she meant what she said and wasn't just being polite. Her open face, round and cherubic, convinced him. He pushed himself up from his chair. 'Well, there are a few; written over the years, you know.'

'D'you have them to hand?' she asked.

'Oh, yes,' said Cyril, with resignation. 'They're always to hand.' He walked to a bureau and pulled open the top drawer. Peering into it, he retrieved a small leather-bound book embossed with his initials. 'For what it's worth, most of what I've written is here.' He handed her the volume. 'Dare I say it, there are several little ditties about you!'

'Really?' squealed Holly, taking the little book back to her seat.

'They're in there somewhere,' said Cyril. 'Near the front, I think.'

'Ah!' said Holly, flicking through the early pages, 'This must be one. 'Little Holly, in your hat…' '

'Yes,' said Cyril, coyly.

'But it's sweet!' said Holly, reading on. Then realizing the poem was about the imaginary friend she used to talk to as a child, she was suddenly self-conscious.

'It's about my pretend friend…'

'I hope you don't mind my noticing…' said Cyril.

'No. But how clever of you to know!'

'Not really,' said Cyril. 'You see, when I was that age, I also had an imaginary friend.'

They looked at each other and laughed. Cyril succumbed to a cough before regaining his composure.

'Have a look at the poem on the opposite page. It's called *Chair* – it might make you smile.'

Holly read it:

Chair

Stop staring at me, chair!
With your ornate back
And fiendish grin,
Or I'll face you to the wall!
Better still, I'll sit on you,
And squash the air from your lungs.
Oh yes I will, just wait and see:
I'll catch you unawares!

Cyril was happy to see she was amused. 'Do you know, I still have the very chair. Look, it's over there. If you concentrate on the carving you'll see a face – it's quite hideous!'

Holly focused her eyes on the intricacies of the chair-back. Cyril was right; two eyes, a nose and a mouth seemed to emerge, making an ugly expression like a medieval gargoyle's.

'Does it really seem like a person to you?' Holly asked.

'When you live on your own, inanimate objects can take on the significance of people,' said Cyril, hoping she wouldn't think he was mad.

Together, they sat observing the chair. It seemed to Holly that its bow-legged form was ready to pounce and assail them.

'Perhaps you ought to sell it,' she suggested.

'No, no, I couldn't do that,' said Cyril. 'It was in the family, you see.'

To live with something hated was beyond Holly's comprehension. She read on. There was a poem about cumulus clouds with an allusion to them copulating: 'Heavenly bodies heaped on one another'. It was humorous and she was surprised someone so seemingly pi was its author. Perhaps he wrote it a long time ago. Or was it the fantasizing of a man in denial?

'This one about cumulus clouds is fun.'

'Oh yes, I'd forgotten about that. It's a bit rude, I'm afraid!'

Holly grinned. Turning the page, she came to a poem about autumn leaves, described as 'the auburn pages of a summer's past'. She liked the idea, and the next line too, where the wind lifted the 'pages' from the worn grass of the park to spiral in the reverie of a last dance before being swept up into mass graves.

'This one about autumn leaves is good too.'

But the more she read, the more the book seemed like a box of old jumble: all the sentiments were bedded in the past. Not that she'd make any comment; she must do her best to cheer him up.

'It must have taken years to write all these.'

'Yes, I suppose it has,' said Cyril. He was tempted to recite his latest offering, *Time*, but reserve got the better of him. He crumpled the poem surreptitiously and slipped it back into his pocket.

A thought came into Holly's head. She would ask Cyril to come back with her. It would do him good, and he could bring his book of poetry along. How awful, that his life's work should be shut away in a drawer!

'I love your work,' she said, in a tentative preamble. 'Really I do!' Then, after a pause: 'I was thinking – I wish you'd come back to the house. Matt and Libby would love to meet you.' This was conjecture, but he wasn't to know. 'They'd love your poetry, I'm sure.'

Cyril appeared flustered. The thought was terrifying: sitting in *her* garden with other young people; their energetic talk, their unfamiliar language; no, he decided, the generation gap was far too wide – he'd feel a fool.

'You're very kind,' he said. 'And I'm flattered you should ask me, but…'

Holly cut in, looking earnestly into his eyes. 'No, no! It would mean so much to me, really.'

'The thing is,' Cyril struggled to find a way out. 'You're all so young and I'm so, well....'

'What's age got to do with it?' Holly interrupted. 'Poetry transcends that.' Then, noticing him blink in astonishment: 'You must come!' she begged him. 'Pleeeze!'

My work – *transcend*? Cyril thought to himself. He felt lifted as if on a hot thermal from his ground-hugging diffidence. He looked up at Holly and smiled elatedly. 'You're a very persuasive young woman!'

'So you'll come. Wonderful!' Jumping to her feet, Holly ran to clasp his hands.

Cyril found himself short of breath, almost gasping. Transcend, eh? Well, would you ever? He sat tapping the arm of his chair to calm himself. Could this be the moment he'd yearned for? – the leap into the limelight, so long denied him?

Half an hour had gone by when Gittins saw Holly again – this time, leaving the building with Cyril Pout. 'Friggin' 'eck!' Gittins muttered, stuffing a finger up his nose. He was sure the 'ol' git' had been 'porkin' the girl'. With his armchair strategically positioned in the bay of the basement window, he missed nothing; 'Toffee-nosed cow,' he said, eyeballing Holly's legs as she descended the steps. 'I could show 'er a thing or two!'

Cyril Pout followed, taking care not to slip. 'Surprised the ol' bugger's still walkin!' Gittins' salacious mutterings tailed off into a gurgle, erupting from his mouth like the sudden release of a blocked drain.

Passing by the railings, Holly glowered down at the basement window. That pernicious hobgoblin of a care-taker was surely there, she thought, lurking in his lair; but through the yellowing net curtains she could see nothing but the flickering blueish light of a screen.

Gittins rose from his armchair and craned his neck after them, trying to guess where they were off to. Perhaps the old fool had managed to talk her into joining him for a meal. 'They're orf darn that Eyetie joint, I'll bet.' He had often seen 'Poutie' seated in a corner there, scribbling away in his little book between mouthfuls of 'spag boll'. Gittins was familiar with the book; he'd picked it up and leafed through it one day while 'the ol' git' was out.

'Gawd 'elp 'er, if ol' Pouty bends 'er ear wiv that lot!' he sniggered. Then, lighting a cigarette, he seated himself at his computer. 'Still, serves the lit'le minx roit,' he sneered. Settling back, he steered himself via a grubby 'mouse' to something altogether more accessible – the jerky joys of cyber-sex at 'www.orgies'r'us.com.'

ELEVEN

Cyril Pout stood on Holly's terrace, clutching his book of poetry. What madness had convinced him to come? Libby and Matt were both obviously surprised by his arrival. He wanted to complain of feeling a little faint and go home. But with Holly by his side, he found strength to afford them a smile in return for their looks of dismay.

'Come and meet Mr. Pout!' said Holly gaily. 'He was up at the window there, remember?'

'I do hope I'm not disturbing anything,' said Cyril meekly.

'Ah, Window Man!' said Matt, proudly conveying his knowledge of this intimate aspect of Holly's childhood years. He bounded up the garden steps to greet him, and Holly regretted she hadn't kept her mouth shut.

'Is everything all right now?' Matt asked him.

Cyril shook Matt by the hand. 'Thank you, yes,' he said quietly. 'Everything's fine – and all thanks to you, it would seem!'

Matt smiled happily.

'It was his great ugly mug that did it!' joked Libby from her chair.

Cyril was assimilating the effects of Matt's make-up. Close to, it was as bizarre a sight as he'd ever seen.

'I told Cyril you were here for a photo shoot,' Holly explained.

'I've been given the 'warrior' treatment!' said Matt proudly.

'So I understand,' said Cyril. 'A Greek one, it would seem, only I never gathered why.'

'It was an idea of Libby's,' explained Matt. 'For a portrait.'

'A portrait?' said Cyril, his confusion deepening.

'We wanted something different,' Holly went on. 'An image linking Matt to his paintings.'

'Ah, image,' said Cyril, barely concealing his loathing for the word. It seemed artifice was at the heart of everything. 'I suppose it's all about image now. Good for one's image or bad for one's image – that sort of thing.'

'Well – that's how it is, these days.'

'I know, I know,' said Cyril with a sympathetic sigh.

'Matt, fix Cyril a drink will you?' said Holly. 'I'm sure he'd like one.'

Cyril eyed the bottle of wine. 'That would be nice!' Still a little breathless from his walk to 'The Villas', he took Holly's arm and allowed her to guide him down the steps to comfort of a Lloyd Loom chair, close to the girl called Bird.

'There,' said Holly, helping him into it. 'This was Uncle Henry's favourite chair.'

'How lovely,' said Cyril. 'There aren't many of *these* about nowadays.'

Libby eyed Cyril's cracked black brogues and the frayed cuffs on his alpaca jacket and decided he was something out of the Ark. His obvious lack of enthusiasm for her makeover on Matt didn't help. Feeling obliged by his proximity to say something, she asked him how long he'd been living in his flat. It was the kind of small talk she abhorred, and any answer he'd come up with would be of no interest to her whatsoever.

'More years than I care to remember,' was the reply. 'Nearly twenty, I suppose.'

Matt passed Cyril a glass of wine, for which he was thanked with a courteous nod and the words, 'How kind.'

Libby felt she was being included against her will in an old black-and-white movie, the kind in which everyone was 'awfully nice'. She would love to have mimicked Cyril's accent, but in deference to Holly she held back.

'Cyril's a poet!' Holly said brightly, sensing the onset of an awkward silence.

'Oh, I don't know about that,' said Cyril, a little flustered.

Matt lightened the moment with a smile. 'Holly was telling us about you.'

'He's written some great stuff,' said Holly. And picking up her wine, she sat down next to Cyril, close like an adoring acolyte.

All eyes were centred on the leather-bound book Cyril was clasping to his chest. Oh, God, what have I let myself in for? he asked himself. Looking up at the sky, he wished a great bird would descend and clutch him away.

'You must read some to us,' said Matt. Poetry was not his thing – but then, it could be interesting; images and ideas were the subject of poetry and of his work too.

'I'm afraid most of them are rather old and not very good,' said Cyril.

Libby was predisposed to agree with him. How could a man who looked like a fusty old vicar have anything to say other than sugar-sweet ramblings on a totally 'anal' existence?

Terrified, Cyril put on his glasses and opened his book, which was suddenly the most terrible liability. If only it could be made to vanish under the tap of a magician's wand – up in a puff of smoke, never to be seen again.

'Can you find that one about the cumulus clouds?' Holly said, seeing him shake all over. 'It's really wacky!'

'If you like,' said Cyril. Then, fumbling for the page with all the calm he could muster: 'Ah, here it is.'

Supporting the spine of the book on the edge of the table, he began to recite. His words emerged in an unnatural flow, squeezing through a restriction that had suddenly developed in his throat.

> *'Comely is the Cumulus*
>
> *Heavenly bodies heaped on one another,*
> *Eating, drinking, and puffed up with mirth.*
> *Such lucky fluffy things you are*
> *To float above our crippled earth.*
>
> *Now, look! You've reached the limit!*
> *If what I think you're doing is right,*
> *You should confine it to your bedroom*
> *In the darkness of the night!'*

Holly led the applause with a giggle. 'That's brilliant!' she cried, addressing the others. 'Don't you think?'

'That's cool,' said Matt, grinning. Images found in clouds had always intrigued him. And yes, he'd often seen those buttocks and breasts piled high in the sky, as fleshy as any on a Rubens nude. He chuckled quietly, amused and looking at Cyril in an unexpected light.

The poem took Libby by surprise too. 'It's great, Bird, isn't it?' Holly said, to encourage her look of puzzled approval.

'Yeah.' Libby's condescending tone failed to conceal a certain admiration. Cyril had struck a deep chord, not so much with his idea about what the clouds were up to, more his feelings for 'our crippled earth'. She almost begrudged him, as if he'd stolen the sentiment from a *cause célèbre* of *her* generation; but that was unfair and she knew it.

"Crippled earth' is cool. Yeah, really cool.'

'It's kind of you to say so,' said Cyril, relieved. As well as amusing the others, he seemed to have touched the soul of this strange little creature. He reached for his wine and imbibed heartily.

'What else have you got in there?' asked Matt. The book suddenly seemed like a treasure chest, yielding up its goodies after years under ground.

'There's another one Holly liked, about autumn leaves…'

'Oh yes, that one's great!' said Holly.

Cyril issued a further apology while he searched for it. 'This too is one of my earlier efforts. Anyway, here goes:

'At Season's End

Auburn pages from summer's past
Lift from the balding park, so fast!
In fleeting spirals, round they whirl,
One final dance, one final twirl,
Before their fate is come to pass
Heaped high on thin November grass.

Now stripped of purpose, naked trees
Look on forlorn and ill at ease,
As once in leaf but now made bare
They stand alone with naught to wear –
In dread of winter's mocking looks,
Her testing gales and rocking rooks.'

Holly led everybody into applause. This time it was a touch forced, but Cyril didn't notice. 'You're very kind.' He looked at each of them, his spirits soaring.

Matt's imagination was again caught. He could see the fallen leaves whirling like dervishes in the wind, as if a last-minute potency could save them from the sweeper's broom. And yes, it *was* like they were telling a story, the lime-green ebullience of spring drying to the russet shades of winter – old manuscripts, brittle and holed by bugs.

And, what of 'rocking rooks'? Yes, that was fun too – the birds swaying to and fro, struggling to hold on in a force-eight gale.

But Libby was less enamoured, disturbed even. Cyril's 'balding park' reminded her of an incident in her childhood she'd tried to forget. The memory kept popping up like a jack-in-a-box, triggered by words or even the hint of an odour – an aftershave perhaps, or the rank exhalation of tobacco smoke.

It had taken place on a hot August afternoon in the People's Park near where she used to live. Thistledown was rising; the poplar trees in the distance were a mirage of movement against the hazy sky. In the foreground was the play area, echoing to the sound of children's voices and scuffed smooth by the relentless passage of young feet.

The roundabout she was on with her friends was slowing down. The man who had powered them joyfully round withdrew, 'knackered' as he'd put it and in need of a 'ciggy'. None of the children had seen him before, but he seemed friendly enough.

Walking back to his car, parked at the kerb, he reached in through the driver's open window for a packet of cigarettes. Resting his backside against the door, he lit one up, motioning for Libby to come and join him.

She shook her head and he shrugged his shoulders, as if to say: 'See if I care.'

'Chicken!' one of her friends taunted her. 'Yeah!' said another, taunting her into a danger they were all familiar with from endless warnings on the TV. 'See wot 'e wants.'

Faced with the challenge, Libby wandered gingerly towards him, halting occasionally to look back at the others, only to be egged on again, until she stood before him, coyly swinging her arms.

'Pretty, ain't yer?' said the man, looking from side to side, while drawing heavily on his cigarette. 'So where's yer mum then?'

'Down Tesco's,' Libby replied, looking up at him and shielding her eyes from the glare of the sun.

'Shoppin?' asked the man.

'Nah, she works there.'

'All day?' probed the man, checking.

'No, juss in the afternoon,' Libby replied, glancing back briefly at her friends who stared back waiting to see what she'd do next.

The man flicked the ash off his cigarette. 'So, what's yer name then?' he asked.

'Libby,'

'Libby, eh? Well, tell yer what, Libby. What say you and me nip up the shops in me motor? Get some ices, like.' Seeing her hesitate, he added: 'For you, me and your mates, yeah?'

The events that followed were to change her forever, her innocence evaporating in the smoky confines of the paedophile's Ford Mondeo.

More poems followed, Cyril reciting them loudly between gulps of wine which he swigged down with a flourish. He was feeling a growing satisfaction with the sound of his voice, a relaxed and mellifluous bass that he felt was enhancing his performance no end.

On and on he read, taxing the three of them for the most part of an hour. He slipped further and further into the embracing arms of his chair. Soon, nobody else was listening. Even Holly could see that for the most part his work was a litany of pitiable gibberish, each poem an introspective step on a journey leading nowhere. Poor man! Holly thought. All those years spent on his own!

Failing light and the cool of the evening was bringing on the shivers – for everyone except Cyril.

'I think we ought to go in,' said Holly, clutching her arms. 'It's getting chilly out here.'

Cyril blinked. 'Yes, of course.' A trifle disappointed, he hoped that after an interval – time for people to stretch their legs – they would settle in the drawing room to hear some more. Warm in his mantle of sozzled confidence, he felt on top of the world. What lovely youngsters!

Matt helped Libby collect the empty glasses while Holly pulled Cyril up from his chair – more a process of extraction than a provision of assistance. Cyril swayed from side to side, arms searching wildly for support. Luckily a chair back was to hand; grinning inanely, he paused for a moment, holding on tight. Holly took his arm and led him back up the steps, through the French windows to another chair, in which he landed rather than sat.

'You've read us some lovely poetry,' Holly said.

'You're kindness isself,' Cyril slurred, patting her hand.

'Now, just sit there and relax.'

'He's rat-arsed!' whispered Libby.

Cyril opened his book of verse in the hope that silence would fall and he could begin again.

'You've got to stop him,' Matt whispered. 'He'll go on all night!'

'And I'll go nuts!' added Libby.

'Don't worry,' said Holly, observing his faltering eye-lids. 'I think you'll find he'll soon stop by himself.'

Her prediction was correct. Nearing the end of a short verse about a dripping tap whose spout he'd portrayed as a nose, Cyril's voice faded and he fell asleep. The cherished book slid from his lap to the floor.

'Phew!' said Libby.

'Poor old boy,' added Holly. Noticing his glasses had slipped under his nose, she deftly removed them and placed them in the top pocket of his jacket.

Matt knelt down to pick up Cyril's book. 'Well, what a lot of twaddle.'

'Yes, but be fair,' said Holly. 'He did have some good ideas.'

'Oh yeah. I don't deny that.'

'He got to me here and there, too,' admitted Libby, sitting down and hooking her legs over the arm of the chair. 'But blimey, he did go on a bit!'

The three of them laughed. Cyril had been relentless: like a creature with only hours to pass on its genes before dying, he'd made use of every moment to imprint himself on the memory of his audience, reeling off poems with the withering persistence of a singing cicada.

'It's living on his own that does it,' said Holly.

'I'll say!' said Matt. He knew the feeling. Working alone in his studio was akin to solitary confinement – the passing weeks seamless and silent. When at last he would let himself out he was inclined to be garrulous, spilling his thoughts into any obliging ear.

Matt collapsed onto a sofa with Holly by his side. Curiosity getting the better of him, he read the final lines about the dripping tap:

'Tap!

Your nose is dripping again,
Driving me mad.
Last week, I twisted your neck
Till I hurt my hand.
You must have felt it,
As you stopped for a while.
Now, you're at it again –
How much more can I stand?'

Chuckling to himself, he closed the book. Then, suddenly pensive, he said: 'It's odd when you live on your own, how objects can become ultra-significant. Even a room can have a sort of active presence, like its walls are waiting for your words.' Then, looking to the girls for a reaction, 'A bit like the padding in a lunatic's cell.'

'Exactly!' said Libby, relieved to hear sanity prevail.

'Cyril has that kind of thing going with an old chair,' said Holly. 'He ticks it off for staring at him.'

'The guy's gotta be wacko!' said Libby, who was rolling a joint. She laughed, happy that reprimanding furniture wasn't among her failings. 'What you staring at,

157

chair?' she mocked. 'You lookin' for trouble, or summin'?'

'No, seriously!' Holly insisted. 'He's written about it in one of his poems. Look, I can show you…'

'Please God, no!' pleaded Libby. 'I've had enough for one night.'

'Talking to a chair beats talking to yourself!' said Matt flippantly.

'You're a nutter,' Libby grinned. 'That's exactly the same thing!'

They all laughed.

'I don't think he's very well,' said Holly, looking at Cyril who was twitching in his sleep.

'He certainly doesn't look it,' said Matt. 'In fact, I'd say he's on the way out. The colour of his skin is, well – look, you can see for yourselves.'

'You morbid sod!' Libby said. But looking at Cyril's head tucked into the wing of his chair, spittle running down his chin, she felt obliged to agree. 'He does look a bit rough, doesn't he?'

Matt had seen that pallor before – on the face of an old down-and-out who used to sit by the cash dispenser near his studio. He was a reasonable guy who begged with a genuine smile and he was always at his pitch whatever the weather. Then one day he disappeared, never to return.

'He popped his clogs,' the bank clerk had told Matt. 'Natural causes, so we heard.'

Holly leafed through Cyril's book while Libby and Matt rambled on about age and the inevitability of death. Perhaps a time would come, Matt suggested, when people like Cyril could be put on ice until science could return them to rude health.

Meanwhile a couplet caught Holly's eye:

In the garden, in the rain,
I saw you fall – I too felt pain.

Her heart jumped. The 'you' had to be herself. She could even recall the day that must have had inspired it. It was the morning of her sixth birthday and there had been a light drizzle, enough to make the flagstones in the garden slippery. Her mother was busy organizing a party for her and had sent her to play outside. Wearing little red boots, a raincoat and sou'wester to match, Holly had run to find Romeo the cat, who was asleep in his usual place on a bench at the back of the gazebo.

Vigorously stroking the cat's head she'd woken it up. 'Come on, Romeo! Wish me Happy Birthday!' She'd given his tail a little tug and the cat had obligingly meowed before skedaddling to the mulberry tree to escape what would have otherwise been a forceful hugging.

Holly had run joyfully to tell her mother of the cat's felicitations only to slip on the terrace steps. Bleeding heavily from a cut lip, she'd screamed commensurately and a visit to the doctor's surgery had been necessary, complicating her mother's day no end.

Holly remembered how she used to puzzle over Cyril. Who was he and why did he wave? 'He's just a nice man who lives there,' her mother had said. That explanation was enough when she was small and the name 'Window Man' had completed his place in her world.

By the time she reached adolescence, his waving had come to annoy her. It was overdone and it took no account of the fact she had grown up. It was as though he was stuck in a time warp, still thinking of her as a little girl.

For several years 'Window Man' had been *persona non grata* to use Uncle Henry's words – she'd wished he'd 'get lost'. But looking at him now, slumped and out for the count, he was tragic – and comical too, his mouth ajar as if to let in flies.

He must have seen everything that day, she thought. A lump came to her throat. All those years ago Cyril had perhaps cared about her more than anyone else. The rowing between her mother and Uncle Henry had got worse and taken its toll, leaving her insecure and playing alone for long periods.

Did Cyril still care? she wondered. She looked at him fondly, certain that he did. She thought how incredibly sad it was that a morsel of contact – just the wave of her hand – could have been eked out by this old man to give substance and meaning to his life. And for so long too! Poor Cyril – another of life's lonely people, forever denied love and understanding.

Leaving him to sleep, she got up and went to the kitchen to put together a meal. Libby and Matt followed, both in a contemplative mood.

'It looks like eggs or eggs,' said Holly, coming out of the larder. 'How about an omelette? We've tons of mushrooms!'

Agreement was quickly reached and the kitchen became a hive of activity. Matt diced huge Portobello mushrooms and Libby beat the eggs while Holly melted butter in a pan, all to the retro-sound of Nina Simone's 'My baby just cares for me'. They bobbed up and down, singing along while they worked.

Meanwhile the delicious aroma of herbs, mushrooms, sizzling eggs and butter drifted up the basement stairs to reach Cyril's nose. Drunkenly half-asleep, half-awake, he was transported back to the dining room of the Hotel Lago, a small and intimate retreat on the Piedmont shore of Lake Maggiore. His nose twitched in glorious anticipation of the first mouthful of his favourite dish, *'Fegato alla Salvia'* – calves' liver, pan fried in butter and sprinkled with sage, tasting so infinitely better when abroad.

The hotel had been a home from home for him, before illness made him unable to travel. *'Signor Pout'* was much beloved by the proprietress. He was an Englishman of the old school – courteous and respectfully dressed, unlike the other English tourists, who would throw him mocking glances and nudge one another when they sighted him.

Not that Cyril noticed. Eating heartily at his table by the window, he would be absorbed in watching the crested grebes as they dived for small fry in the lake. Hungry little devils, they never seemed to stop! Or perhaps a ferry would arrive at the terminal; there would be a clatter of gangplanks, and shouts and hustle and bustle, then next time he looked the scene would have evaporated as though it had never been there. The ferry would be a dot on the horizon once more, chugging its way to the likes of Ascona, Pallanza and Baveno, any of whose charms might serve as a glorious treat for the morrow.

Cyril was blissfully happy and each heavenly mouthful of imaginary *fegato* brought a little twitch to his lips. Soon he sunk into a satisfied slumber. From this he woke all of a sudden some hours later, when a French window crashed open in a flurry of night air. Still half-dreaming, he was surprised to find himself alone in Holly's drawing room. A remark from the proprietress *'Il vento é cambiato, Signor Pout – Si?'* (*'The wind's changed, Mr. Pout – Yes?)* was still hanging in his mind. Ah, the variable lakeside weather!

He rubbed his eyes and returned to reality. How sad 'La Signora' had vanished. A lovely dream; an out-of-body excursion he wished could have gone on forever. If only all dreams were like that!

Save for a picture light above the mantlepiece, Cyril was in darkness. Feeling some discomfort round his neck, it occurred to him he must have been asleep for several hours. His watch said it was past midnight. 'Heavens,' he murmured. 'I had no idea it was so late. They must all be going to bed.' Heaving himself to his feet, he made his way towards some sounds emanating from upstairs.

Embarrassed at having fallen asleep, and having outstayed his welcome by a mile, he stood and listened at the foot of the stairs. Gripping the handrail firmly, he walked slowly up to the first floor. Finding no one around, he went on up to the second, where he was greeted by soft Latino music and a sweet smelling haze – possibly of joss sticks, but he wasn't sure.

Puffed from the climb, he took a deep breath. Shifting from foot to foot he hesitated, wondering where Holly might be. He couldn't leave without saying good-bye – not after she'd been so kind, inviting him to meet her friends and recite his poetry in her garden. Such a treat it had been!

To his left, down the corridor, a door stood slightly ajar – enough to reveal at least part of the room's interior. He walked along to investigate and the music became louder as he approached.

On the verge of announcing his presence with a polite tap, Cyril found himself stepping backwards in horror.

He wondered if his eyes had deceived him. Taking a deep breath, he stepped forward to look again.

The bamboozling configuration of bodies, three of them all naked and writhing, was, save for a ball of toads he'd once observed in a lily pond, like nothing he'd ever seen. Matt's painted face at its centre was the incarnation of devilry.

'Holly, how could you?' he muttered to himself: shaking his head in disbelief at the sound of her rapturous exhalations.

His cherished illusions shattered, there was nothing he could do but turn his back. He began to weep – his shock mixed with a disappointment so deep that he wished he could die. Stifling himself so as not to be heard, he looked up through the stairwell to the skylight, black against the night, hoping for a redeeming light from God – an admission that the spectacle he'd just wit-nessed was a terrible mistake.

But there was nothing. His little girl had been taken away and become someone else – a stranger, consumed

162

by lust, her body yielding to both male and female attentions. How could she? he asked himself, again and again. How could she?

He turned to take a last look at the scene, but through tears he saw little. He descended each flight of stairs with care, his head bowed and dejected. This was the end, the parting of the ways – that final goodbye whose arrival he had always feared.

Why now, of all times? he cried out inside. Like a bolt from the blue! And within hours of my meeting her, after such a long time. How cruel can fate be?

The front door stood before him – an exit from hell. He opened and closed it with care so as not to be heard. Pausing to wipe away tears, he shuffled down the steps, through the front garden and into the street. The light was stark, like the truth he had to face: that innocence, like beauty is transient. It exists in the eye of the beholder as much as anywhere and life, like a robber baron, takes all in the end.

Life? He wanted nothing more to do with it: no more wishing, no more yearning, and above all no more heartache. Standing on the pavement, he wished he had never been born. Looking up at the starless night, he challenged the heavens: was God really there, a munificent being with everyone's interests at heart? Or was He a myth, a cruel and damnable lie for the gullible, desperate for succour in a world of uncertainties?

'There's nobody there! There can't be!' he shouted out loud. Then racked with guilt at having blasphemed, he recanted, burying his face in his hands: 'I'm sorry! I'm so sorry!'

But it was too late. An apology was useless, he knew; a last-minute calculation, insolent in its assumption that his sin could be so easily forgiven. Gripped by a sudden pain in his chest, he staggered forward, reaching desperately to a bollard for support.

Across the street, a youth lurking in the shadows heard Cyril's cry. He saw the old man fall to the ground. Assuming he was a drunk, and salivating at the prospect of easy pickings, the youth ran to investigate.

Meanwhile two other youths running from a street fight stopped to boast of their exploits – they'd been 'sortin' some Pakis out', 'kickin' the bastards' 'eads in' and 'cuttin' some uvvers'. Seeing the first youth astride Cyril Pout's body and rifling through his wallet, they went to see what was going on. Cyril's lifeless form impressed them; face down on the pavement, his head askew, his eyes looked like a flounder's on a fish-monger's slab.

'Fuckin' 'eck! Topped 'im, 'ave yer?' blurted one of them.

'Nah, I farnd 'im like that.'

'Wot, dead?'

'Yeah. I was standin' over there finkin' I might turn 'im over, an' fuck me if 'e don't 'it the deck before I gets the chance! Saves me the bovver, like.'

The trio sniggered nervously, their amusement tempered by shapes imagined in the night – a figure at a window or shadows seeming to move.

A siren wailed. It was uncomfortably near. Its *'wow, wow, wow!'* sent shivers down their spines.

'We'd better fuck off,' said one, nervously hitching up his crotch. 'If the 'Filth' find us 'ere, they'll 'ave us for doin' the geezer in.'

The first youth pocketed Cyril's cash. About thirty quid, he reckoned. Dropping the empty wallet down a drain, he followed the others in a frantic dash for the cover of a side street, there to melt into the night.

At three a.m. two policemen in a patrol car approached the junction at the end of Holland Park Villas. Spotting a dog in the distance, sniffing at the shadowy mass of Cyril's body, they pulled up alongside.

A constable stepped from the car. 'Another flamin' wino, I reckon.'

His colleague wound down the window and sticking his head out, said: 'Looks like it.' Pushing back his cap, he remarked: 'It right pisses me off, havin' to pick up these jerks!'

'Yer can say that again,' said the other. The routine collection of drunks attracted no kudos at all. After a cursory walk-round, the officer stooped to detect for signs of life. There were none. 'Hell! I reckon we've got a stiff on our hands.'

'Blimey,' said his colleague. 'I'll call for back up.'

'Yeah, do that. An' while you're at it, get an ambulance.'

With nothing more to be done but await the arrival of 'Uncle Tom Cobley and all' – the constable's collective appellation for the duty D.I., some quack and the boys from forensics – the driver settled back in his seat, peering out for another look at the body.

'Is that blood on the pavement?' he asked, thinking they might have a murder on their hands.

'Where?'

'There! Near the bloke's collar.'

The constable knelt down by Cyril's head.

'Dunno wot it is,' he said, looking closely. 'But it ain't blood.'

Sodding dog, I shouldn't wonder, thought his colleague.

TWELVE

Hell, thought Matt. Willie Fitz this, Willie Fitz that! Holly had been lauding his name since tumbling out of bed in a panic, the morning half gone.

'Willie's the come-back-kid of glam,' she asserted. 'He's right back in style!'

Matt retreated to the shower, still fazed by the night's events. He was wondering where he stood: the imbroglio of the night before had left him physically satiated but emotionally in limbo.

Holly was her usual self: bright, breezy and unconcerned. Matt supposed that for her, the night was just the result of a natural breakout of pheromones.

'Willie's brilliant!' Holly insisted from the bedroom. 'You *have* to go and see him.'

With Holly in an organizing mood and her mind focused on Matt's future, Libby had thought it best to slip back to her room. Besides, she hadn't had much sleep and she felt the need to lie alone, numb in the bliss of somnolent reflection.

But for Matt, even in the shower there was no escape.

'You're not going on that programme looking like crap!' Holly shouted, the edge in her voice cutting through the hissing shower-jets. 'The Torment show is your chance to make a huge impact. For Heaven's sake, use it!'

Feltz had said as much too, thought Matt: Willie Fitz was just the man to smarten up his image. Not that Bernie would ever go to Fitz's place himself – 'It's heaving with poofs, for Crissake!'

Matt's resistance collapsed. 'OK, OK, whatever you say!' he called back.

'Willie'll lend you an original, I'm sure. Especially if I tell him you're going on telly!'

Matt stepped from the shower. 'An original what?'

'Jacket, of course,' said Holly.

'Oh,' said Matt, with a sigh of relief. At least he could keep his familiar comfy jeans.

So it was agreed. Willie Fitz was to be allowed to create an illusion of 'cool' around that part of his body most visible to the cameras. Come the afternoon, after Holly had processed her film, they'd go and see him together at his premises in Soho. 'You'll love him,' Holly said.

Matt took her word for it. Drying himself, he walked to the bathroom window. 'I wonder how Cyril is this morning,' he said, looking across to the windows of St. Mungo's Court.

Holly chuckled. 'I bet he's got a dog of a hangover,' she said, pulling on her jeans. 'He was really hammered, wasn't he!'

'I know,' said Matt, noticing the sash window still open.

'I feel terrible, not taking him home.'

'It was best to let him sleep it off,' said Matt.

'I suppose so,' said Holly. Then, brushing her hair: 'Did you hear him leave? I didn't.'

'No.'

'I wonder why not,' said Holly facetiously. Dressed, she entered the bathroom. 'You're a randy sod, aren't you?' she said, snatching his towel away.

'Hey, give it here!'

Holly giggled. 'Oh, but look now. The little bald monkey's all shrivelled up!'

Matt tried to be serious. 'Come on, give me my towel.'

'What's the matter?' asked Holly in a baby voice. 'Is he a sleepy boy, then?' She threw him his towel and left the room. 'All this excitement – it's obviously too much!'

Eager to develop the pictures, she hurried down to the kitchen, grabbed a cup of coffee and disappeared into her studio.

When Matt came downstairs, he found himself alone in the kitchen. He had a vague sense of guilt, mixed with concern – where was his relationship with Holly going? Most likely nowhere, he thought. Her feelings seemed dogged by ambiguity and his own were rocked by surprise, at his unexpected willingness to go along with her. But how odd too, that she hadn't objected to his getting it on with Libby. It was all strange, so strange.

He put his feelings to one side. He had to. What had happened had happened. And the girls expressed no concern, so why should he?

Breakfasting alone, his mind turned to something more worrying still – his coming appearance on 'Torment Tonight'. Day by day it got nearer; the following Monday would surely be a 'Bloody Monday'.

He found it impossible to relax. He stood by the kitchen window, toying with a bowl of cereal, then he took himself into the drawing room. In a grave frame of mind he ambled up and down, formulating responses to angles of attack which he imagined having to face.

At eleven, Holly rushed into the room. 'These are amazing!' she cried. She passed him some contact sheets. 'Completely amazing!'

Matt feasted his eyes on multiple images of himself. 'Wow!'

'Great, aren't they?' said Holly, delighted. 'They really sex up your image.'

'Fantastic!' said Matt. 'But will anybody know it's me?'

'Does it matter?' said Holly, looking through for the best shot. 'I think the image is strong enough to stand on its own.'

'Slightly defeats the object of the exercise, though.'

Holly disagreed. 'Not if you forget it's a portrait.'

'How do you mean?'

'Think of it as symbolizing what you stand for.'

'Like the image is a front for something?' said Matt.

'Yeah. A front for a campaign.'

Taken by the idea, Matt nodded in agreement. A military campaign, with him as its iconic leader.

'It makes sense, doesn't it?' said Holly.

'Yeah!'

'Of course, a campaign should have a name,' she went on. 'But that's not too difficult, it just has to summarize what you're about.'

'It would have to be succinct,' said Matt.

'Of course. An abbreviation of something, maybe.'

Matt thought hard, leafing through the sheets of images, all of himself. He reckoned his mission boiled down to one thing – bringing people back to reality. Reality, violence... 'Hey,' he said, gripped by a sudden inspiration, 'How about 'R – I – O – T: riot?'

'Riot?' Holly echoed him. 'Why Riot?'

'Think about it,' said Matt. "R – I – O – T'. What could that stand for?'

'Dunno.'

Seeing Holly perplexed for once, he grinned. 'Reality In Our Time! Isn't it that exactly what I'm trying to bring about?'

Holly was impressed. She too was attracted by the implied militancy. 'That's ace! But you're going to need a slogan as well – something that people can instantly identify with.'

To Matt, the solution was obvious. 'Why not 'Get Real!'? There's no mistaking the message in that, is there?'

Holly looked doubtful. 'Isn't that a bit too *everyday*?'

'Not if it's shouted through megaphones,' said Matt.'

'Oh,' she said. 'You mean, like really loud.'

'Right! Imagine it echoing through the streets at full volume. It would make people stop and think!'

'It would.' Holly pictured crowds of people, all craning their necks to see where the message was coming from.

'But on second thoughts, I don't know,' Matt said nervously. 'Think of the flak we'd pick up.' Defending a painting was one thing, but actively campaigning in the streets was something else: risking arrest, just for starters.

'Come on!' said Holly. 'It can't be any worse than the flak you're picking up already. And it's such a brilliant idea!'

True to the soldierly images in his hands, Matt hid his reservations behind a smile.

'I think this one's the best,' said Holly, pointing to one image in particular. 'It's awesome, don't you think?'

'Yeah,' said Matt, studying it closely. The composition was excellent. The balance between light and dark captured in his expression a reproachful air, bordering on rage. Quite flattering, Matt thought. 'How do you reckon it'll enlarge?'

'Should look good,' she said. 'I'll have a shot at it now.' Then, collecting up the contact sheets, she was gone.

The doorbell rang. Matt waited to see if anybody would answer, but both girls were busy – Holly in her studio, and Libby lying comatose in a bath at the top of the house.

Matt opened the front door to find Bernie Feltz on the doorstep.

'Shit, man!' Feltz panted. 'Where have you been? I thought I'd find you at your studio.'

'Yeah?' said Matt, nonchalantly. 'Well, I was here.'

Feltz thrust past him into the hall. 'I can see that, you twat! Listen, I need to know how the shoot went. The press is pushing me for more info on you. First Privett's article, now that Prattle bird lambasting your work on the radio – things are humming mate, I can tell you!'

'It's been so quick,' said Matt.

'Quick?' barked Feltz. 'Of course it has! In this game, one thing leads to another: all at the speed of greased lightning. I tell you now, if we're to keep on top of this you're gonna have to sharpen up your act. The ball's rolling and nothing's going to stop it!'

Matt decided it would be unbecoming to join Feltz in panic. His new image of himself demanded outward self-control.

'So, where are they?' Feltz demanded.

Matt suppressed a yawn. 'The photos, you mean?'

'What else, you dozy pillock! Jeez, man, what's up with you? You look half-dead.'

'Don't panic,' said Matt. 'Everything's cool.'

'Well, come on then, give us a butchers. 'Cos if they're any good, I'll release them to the press right away.'

'I can't. Holly's still working on them,' Matt explained. 'But give her half an hour and she should have something.'

'Shit, she'd better have!' Feltz said, forging through to the kitchen. 'Only those media guys work to deadlines, and when they need copy you jump.'

'Sure, I understand,' Matt said soothingly.

'*He* understands, he says,' said Bernie mockingly. He helped himself to a large mug of coffee and heaped in spoonfuls of sugar to thicken it to the syrupy consistency he loved. 'Anyway, what's the story? How did she take you?'

Matt hid his amusement – 'take', as the evening had turned out, being the operative word. 'Well, they came up with a wacky idea,' he said.

'They?' said Feltz, worried. 'Who's 'they'?'

'Holly and Libby.'

'Libby? Why Libby?'

'She was working the lights.'

'Oh,' said Feltz, disappointed to hear she had got in on the act. Her instability would be more likely be a hindrance than an asset. 'So what was this wacky idea?'

'It's no good me trying to explain,' Matt said. 'You must see for yourself.'

Feltz looked at his watch. 'But you liked it?'

'Er – yeah.'

'You don't sound over the moon about it.'

'Well, it's different from any kind of PR you'd normally associate with a painter.'

Feltz swallowed his coffee in quick gulps. 'OK, so let's hope it worked. Anyway, whatever time did you get here this morning, for Crissake? It must've been bloody early!'

'I didn't.'

'You mean you've been here all night?'

Matt confessed he had.

'Shit, man!' said Feltz, immediately concluding that Matt had slept with Holly. 'No wonder you're half asleep.'

'It's just the way things panned out.'

'You jammy bastard!' Feltz said enviously.

'We got a little high,' Matt confessed. 'And one thing led to the other. I didn't get to sleep till after four.'

'Was there a party?' asked Feltz, fearing he'd missed out.

'No, nothing like that,' said Matt. 'It was just the three of us.'

'You mean Libby was around?'

'Sure,' said Matt. 'She supplied the weed.'

'So how did you get rid of her?'

'We didn't,' said Matt.

Feltz had a puzzled look on his face. 'So, what happened?'

Matt shrugged his shoulders, reluctant to explain. He was proud of what had happened, but a bit ashamed of being happy to let Feltz know.

'Are you telling me Libby hung around?'

'Well, yeah.'

'Eh?' said Feltz, mouth open.

Matt leant back against the dresser but said nothing.

'Am I reading things right here?' asked Feltz.

'I don't know,' said Matt, wishing he'd drop the subject.

'Are you telling me she was in on things?' Feltz's eyes narrowed.

'Well, yeah, since you ask.'

'What, getting it on?' Feltz asked bluntly, his mind racing.

The look on Matt's face said it all.

'You're joking, man,' said Feltz, incredulous.

'No,' said Matt innocently.

'But she's a dyke, for Crissake!'

'Up to a point,' said Matt, strangely relieved by this chance to divulge what had happened.

'So, what went down?' asked Feltz.

'Come on, do I have to spell it out for you?' said Matt.

Feltz struggled to build a picture in his head of who had done what and to whom. 'You mean, all three of you were at it together?'

'Yeah!' exclaimed Matt, astonished himself at what had happened.

'But what about Holly?' Feltz asked him. 'I can't see her making out with Libby.'

Matt walked to a chair at the kitchen table. 'Oh no?' he said.

Feltz joined him. 'Well, fuck my old boots,' he sighed, loosening his collar. 'Holly, of all birds, into that kinda scene.' Then, sitting back: 'No wonder I get an earful whenever I say anything about Libby.'

Feltz looked at Matt to see what a man might look like after such a night. To his surprise, Matt seemed not entirely happy. 'Jeez, man, what's your problem?' Feltz said.

'Nothing,' said Matt, declining to admit that the girls' activities had thrown him into a quandary.

'You should be so lucky!' said Feltz in anguish. All *he'd* ever had from those two were insults from the one and brush-offs from the other.

Holly entered the kitchen. The completed enlargement was concealed behind her back. 'I thought I heard voices!' she chirruped.

'Hullo, m'luv,' said Feltz from his chair. His usual exuberance was muted by a feeling of loss deep inside. 'Sorry to crash in on you, but I had to know how the shoot went.'

'The shoot?' said Holly, looking at Matt and playing on the word with a lascivious smile. 'Groovy, I'd say, wouldn't you?'

Matt chuckled. 'Yeah, groovy's about right. Why don't you show him the result?'

'Sure,' said Holly. And, with a waving of arms and a loud 'Durrah!', she produced her finished work.

Feltz struggled to focus on the matter in hand. He leaned forward to examine the portrait. 'Shit! Who the fuck's that?'

'Matt, of course!' said Holly, brightly.

Feltz thumped the table. 'For Crissake, you cannot be serious!' he shouted angrily.

Holly was unperturbed; she knew he'd react in this way. 'What's wrong?' she asked, a picture of innocence.

Feltz smacked his forehead, struggling for words. 'For a start, it looks nothing like Matt. Any fool can see that. And secondly, he looks a right dickhead.'

Holly turned to Matt. 'I said he'd go ape, didn't I?' she said.

'Give her a break,' Matt said. 'A hell of a lot of work's gone into this.'

'I commissioned a portrait, remember?' said Bernie, not to be coaxed off his high horse. 'Can you blame me for losing my rag?'

Holly stamped her foot on the floor. 'Bernie, you're missing the point!' she cried. 'Just listen for a moment.'

Feltz looked to Matt. 'Matt, Matt! How could you let her do this? I mean, you look a right prat!'

Sensing a full-scale barney developing, Matt raised his hands to calm them both down. 'Let her explain,' he said. 'It's only fair.'

Feltz reluctantly acquiesced. 'So go on, hit me.' He hunched his shoulders as if to say nothing could convince him. 'I'm all ears.'

Holly paced round the kitchen. 'OK, OK, here it is. If you hadn't a clue who the person in this portrait was, would you think it was a good image?'

'But I *do* know who it's of, don't I?' said Feltz acidly.

'But supposing you didn't!'

Other people's 'supposing' always gave Feltz the feeling he was about to be conned. 'I might,' he conceded, eyeing them both with suspicion.

'Good,' said Holly. 'Well that's a start!'

'The composition's superb,' Matt said grandly. 'It really is. I mean look at the way she's captured the light falling on the face. It's amazing, isn't it?'

Feltz reached for the photo. 'Here, let me look at it again.' His aggression was beginning to melt.

'We had this idea of a blow-up...' said Matt.

'You know, big time,' Holly continued. 'Maybe on the side of a building. It would look ace, a real eye catcher we reckoned. Like, making a statement for the world to see.'

It slowly dawned on Feltz that there might be some merit in what they were suggesting, the kind of merit he would normally pride himself in spotting. Yes, forget it was Matt's face and the portrait became something else – a piece of pure theatre. The image was a paradox; trivial at first glance, yet strangely threatening. It was an image that could get people talking – 'Who's face is this? And what's it all about?' The kind of thing the media would die for, if some way could be found to make it seem significant.

'OK, suppose there's something in this,' said Feltz cautiously. 'Where's the story? What do I tell the press?' He smiled complacently, confident his question would back-foot the pair of them.

'Over to you,' Holly said to Matt.

Matt knew his answer must be succinct. Anything less and Feltz would dismiss it as mumbo-jumbo, useless to the press who liked their stories simple. He gathered his thoughts.

'Right. What kind of vibes d'you get, looking at that photo?'

Feltz cast his eye over the image again. 'Pretty weird.'

'Like what sort of weird?'

'Weird as in scary. The face kind of looks into you.'

'You mean, critically?' said Matt, pushing him to explain.

Feltz studied it hard. 'Yeah,' he said slowly. 'I reckon so.'

'I think it's an angry face,' commented Holly. 'Kind of reproachful.'

'Yeah, that's just it!' said Feltz, concentrating hard.

'Good,' said Matt. 'But, what's the face angry about?'

Feltz gave him a blank look. 'You tell me,' he said. 'It's your story.'

'It's angry about what we've become,' said Holly, adhering to the story line they'd previously agreed.

'We?' queried Feltz. 'As in – us?'

'Not directly,' said Matt. 'But you know what I'm saying. This is for everyone, even people who don't know what they're feeling.'

'OK, OK,' said Feltz. 'So what have 'we' become?'

'Simpletons,' said Matt. 'Just look at the kind of shit we put up with everyday. Who else but halfwits would take it?'

'Like Plod's visit, you mean?' said Feltz, his eyes darting between the two of them, wanting to see the point.

'Exactly,' said Matt. 'A typical example of bureaucracy gone mad. But that's only the half of it, isn't it? Just look at everything else that's going on.'

'Like the bombing and the shootings,' Holly interjected. 'Things are out of control.'

'Right!' said Matt, wholeheartedly. 'People are so daft they've come to accept this as the norm.'

Uh-oh, thought Feltz, Matt is climbing on his hobbyhorse again. The emasculated state of the nation was not something he wanted to hear about, now or ever. His mind was focussed on where there was money to be made, not sorting out the state of the bloody world. 'Hmm,' he said, looking at Holly for support. 'I think we get your drift.'

'Let him finish,' Holly implored him. 'This bit's important.'

'It's like pragmatism's been abandoned,' Matt continued, 'just for the sake of appeasing anyone who has a mind to object about anything.'

'That's right!' said Holly.

'I mean, look around you,' said Matt. 'Every day of our lives we're at the mercy of hotheads from one group or another – or control freaks in government, whose grip on reality is zilch.'

For a moment, nobody said a word. Matt added, a touch theatrically: 'I tell you, if we let things go on the way they are, we're finished. Isn't this what this face trying to tell us? 'Get real, before it's too late!'

Feltz had an uncomfortable feeling. This was getting too much like politics. Where was the money in that? But what was it his father had said? 'Son, if people aren't getting what they want, there's a good margin in finding it for them.' Perhaps, after all, there was a business opportunity here.

"Get real',' he said pensively. 'I like it, I like it.'

'We reckoned it would make a great slogan.'

Feltz nodded, his mind on the percentages.

'We thought we could link it to what Matt's all about,' said Holly, following on quickly. 'Like he's the leader of a movement, one that'll really shake things up!'

'We could call it 'Riot!' said Matt, cueing Holly to add the next bit as pre-arranged.

'Riot?' Feltz queried him. 'What's 'riot' got to do with it?'

Holly spelt it out: 'Reality – In – Our – Time. It's what the letters stand for. Geddit?' Then, pointing at Matt, she added: 'Isn't this exactly what Matt's work's all about? Waking people up to reality?'

Feltz's face began to glow. The politics did not interest him one bit but the commercial possibilities stood out a mile. A percentage on every poster, every T-shirt; national campaigns, maybe even global. This image coupled to a slogan like 'Get Real!' could be a marketing man's dream.

'We thought we could cruise the streets in an open top car,' Holly went on. 'You know, using a loud hailer: 'Get Real!' – 'Get Real!' – that sort of thing.'

These kids – full of ideas, but with a bit of management they could be onto something. Maybe in his hands rested an icon in the making. Studying the image again, its implacable gaze seemed to admonish him for his hasty denunciation.

'I may have over-reacted,' he said with uncharacteristic humility. Then, back-pedalling furiously as his enthusiasm grew: 'This is a brilliant wheeze!'

Adding weight to his excitement was something else too – something disturbing, even sinister. He found the eye on the forehead strangely hypnotic. Exerting a subliminal authority, it reminded him of the famous poster of Kitchener, his fearsome face exhorting young men to join up for service during the First World War. Coupled with the words 'Your Country Needs You' it had an eerie power. He wondered if the eye affected Holly and Matt in the same way.

'This eye,' he said. 'It's hard to stop looking at it.'

'Yeah,' said Matt, 'I noticed that too. Its effect is mesmerizing.'

'Bloody clever,' said Feltz. 'Yeah, we're definitely on to something here!'

'It was Libby who started things off,' said Matt, giving credit where credit was due.

'Libby?' shrieked Feltz. 'Bloody 'ell! I thought her only input had been flicking the lights on and off.'

'Oh no!' said Holly gleefully, riding high on his amazement. 'She painted Matt's face.'

'Eh?' said Feltz, his jaw dropping with incredulity.

'Only you would find that surprising,' said Holly, sarcastically.

'Leave it out,' said Feltz, resisting the urge to snipe back. 'I just didn't realize she was back on the scene. You know, working and that. That's all I meant.'

Holly was happy. She had won the day. She walked to Matt's side and put an arm round his waist. 'Didn't I say, Bernie would come round to the idea once he'd thought about it?'

Feltz did his best to smile. 'OK, OK, you've made your point.' Noticing the closeness of Holly and Matt, the two of them now obviously an item, a sinking feeling overwhelmed him. His hopes that one day she might fall for him were dashed.

'Hey,' he said, somewhat subdued, 'if you can just make me some copies of this I'm outa here. Shit! Will you look at the time!'

Holly suggested that they have a run of posters printed. 'We could plaster them all over town,' she enthused.

'That's my department,' Feltz cautioned her curtly. 'Not yours.'

Holly smirked. 'Of course, Bern*ard*,' she teased. 'I wouldn't have it any other way.'

THIRTEEN

As the taxi rumbled towards Soho, Matt stifled another yawn. Once again, the conversation was revolving round Willie Fitz.

'His real name's Fitzmaurice,' Holly airily revealed. 'But he dropped the 'maurice' bit donkey's years ago.'

'Why's that?' Matt asked, idly turning his attention to the cab's internal video, where a character called Tubby Scoff was endorsing new eateries.

'Well, being gay, he got peed off with endless jokes about Willie fitting Maurice – that sort of crap.'

Matt laughed unsympathetically. Holly admonished him for it with a little smack to his hand. 'Don't be so unkind! After all, he is lending you one of his jackets.'

Not that he wanted a jacket, Matt thought – some poncey creation to better his image. But Holly had insisted and for the sake of peace he was going along with her. Fashion – in all its triviality.

But then, in the space of a week everything had changed for him. His old prejudices were being stretched to the limit. Gays, for instance; in the world he came from, they were spoken of in murmurs or in jokey asides. Suddenly he was among people for whom minority sexual preferences were not taboo. In fact, homosexuality appeared to be a virtue – hot on the agenda, like a piquant sauce to be savoured with shrieks of delight.

With his experience from the previous night fresh in his mind, Matt felt he was in a new world. What had been buried was suddenly on the surface and he was expected to join in a burgeoning bonanza of novelty.

'So you know this Fitz guy well?' he asked her.

'Sure. He's a real gas! You're going to love him.'

Matt wondered if she'd been to Willie's 'little eyrie' often, treating other guys to his creations perhaps, guys she had bedded before him. The thought niggled and stirred up another prejudice; that spreading oats was strictly a male preserve and that girls who put it about were for that purpose only – ports of call in the quest for sex, untrammelled by obligations of love.

The notion was archaic and he knew it. Holly was a free spirit, outspoken and unhindered by convention. In many ways she was more of an island than himself and that's what he loved about her. She had tempted him into a garden he'd never have discovered on his own. It was going to take him a while to understand her.

Meanwhile, he was uneasy. What chance did he have of holding on to her? Her appetite for variety seemed so compelling. Take her fooling around with Libby. Was it just a game, a one-off performance brought on by the effects of marijuana and wine? He determined to find out.

'I'd no idea you and Libby were into each other,' he said.

Holly laughed. 'It's nothing heavy. Why, do you mind?'

'It isn't that,' said Matt, not wishing to appear starchy.

'Then what?'

'Well, it's just not what I expected.'

'You didn't seem to mind!' said Holly, her eyes lighting up. 'From what we saw, you found it a turn-on.'

Matt grinned sheepishly. 'I did.'

'No problem, then!' said Holly brightly. So the matter was closed, with Matt none the wiser as to whether he was her plaything or her lover.

'Will Libby be sticking around long?'

Holly gave him a mischievous look. 'Why, do you want a replay?'

'That's not why I asked,' he said, surprised by her insouciance. 'I just wondered how she gets by if she's not working.'

'You're so serious sometimes,' she chuckled. Then straight-faced, she said: 'Well, for starters, living with me doesn't cost her a thing. Don't forget, she netted ten grand for *Bella*.'

'That's not so much,' said Matt, thinking it a paltry sum for such a magnificent piece of work.

'But add to that the payout from the insurance and I reckon she collected near on forty grand.'

'Wow! That's a shed-load of cash.'

'If it wasn't for those silly bitches crashing her show I reckon she'd have earned near twice that,' Holly said. 'Other serious collectors were after her work besides Sylvester, and because of what happened they were unable to buy.'

'That must have been tough.'

'But the irony is, all that publicity pushed her into the big time. Once she starts work again, she can ask what she likes.'

'Amazing!' said Matt. He could soon be in that position too – in the money, and free to work in whatever way he pleased. He drew a deep breath to curb a swell of nervous anticipation.

'Willie's so totally camp,' laughed Holly, turning the conversation back to him yet again. 'He asked me, were you another homophobe I'd got in tow and would you turn rigid with fear when he measured your inside leg?'

'And you said?'

'I told him, we're not after trousers. He said, 'Shame on you girl, denying me my little thrills!''

'Woofters,' muttered Matt derisively. And what was the 'in tow' bit? Was he to be Holly's little lapdog, tugging along in her wake? If so, that was a bloody liberty!

He drummed his fingers on the cab door and glowered at the traffic. They were in the congestion of Soho, passing through the security checkpoints round theatre-land.

'He can make anything, really,' Holly went on. 'Waistcoats, suits, even hand embroidered shirts. Oh, and for Christmas he does the wackiest little prezzies.'

'Yeah?' said Matt, bored.

'Glitter-spangled party socks! In all sorts of lovely patterns – they've been a Fitz speciality forever.'

'Jeez!' exclaimed Matt. 'Who the hell goes in for those?'

'Not just gays, if that's what you're thinking.' Holly peered through the window. 'This security's a pain. Before that last gas attack in the Haymarket I could get up to Willie's place in twenty minutes. Now, look – we've been in this cab for nearly three quarters of an hour!'

'A sign of the times,' mumbled Matt gloomily. Soldiers in flak jackets were checking vehicle after vehicle for explosives. Yet another initiative the government was buying itself into; the management of fear.

Holly shouted to the driver, 'Can you drop us over there on the left?'

Pulling up short of where she'd said, his exasperation was plain. 'Can I drop you 'ere?' he asked. 'Only, then I can 'ang a right an' get out of this friggin' jam.'

'So where's Willie's place?' asked Matt as they got out of the cab.

'Just along here.' Weaving their way along the crowded pavement, they came to an opening through an archway into a cobbled alley, where they arrived at a scratched steel door.

'A bit seedy, isn't it?' said Matt. A strong smell of urine was emanating from a garbage-strewn corner to their left.

'It's a crap location. But wait till you get inside!'

The door bore only a number – no other hint that here was to be found the renowned Willie Fitz.

'Willie works up on the top floor,' Holly said reverently.

Matt followed her up three flights over cracked linoleum treads and past chipped and finger-marked walls. 'What a dump!'

'Willie's got nothing to prove. People would flock to him anywhere.'

She rang the bell. The squawk box crackled: 'Yeah?'

'It's Holly Tree, with Matt Flight.' Holly kept her fingers crossed, hoping Willie hadn't forgotten. Appointments tended to slip the master's mind in the intensity of his creative endeavour.

The door-lock was released and they entered, to be hit by a wall of warm air and the irregular whirr of a fan struggling overhead, its oily motor caked with fluff. From the muffled depths of a storeroom an assistant stammered: 'Mr. Willie'll be out in a minute.' Matt resisted the temptation to laugh.

'Fine,' said Holly, catching a glimpse of the boy's face. 'That's little Warren,' she whispered to Matt. 'He's one of Willie's trainees. Actually I'm amazed he's still here. None of them last for long.'

'You know what Bernie says about that,' said Matt.

'High bend-over rate… typical Bernie! He thinks he's being funny. Really it's because Willie's a perfectionist – nothing more.'

'OK, OK, cool it!' Matt whispered.

Holly pointed to a wall lined with yellowing newspaper cuttings and photographs curling with age. 'Look over there. It'll give you an idea of Willie's client base. It's unbelievable! Celebs, every one.'

Unimpressed, Matt chose instead to study a collection of bounced cheques mounted on red baize board.

'Bad debts must really knock him back,' Matt said. 'I mean, here's a cheque for over five grand!'

'I know,' said Holly. 'Some people are real shits.'

Materials lay everywhere. Rolls, off-cuts and pattern-books were piled so high and in such haphazard heaps that a nudge would send them cascading to the floor.

'This is really wild,' said Matt, fascinated.

'Cool, isn't it?' said Holly.

This must be the secret of his creativity, Matt thought. Out of chaos, order: the shrieking contrasts of fabric demanding new life in funky marriages of texture and colour.

The door to the cutting room opened and out came Willie Fitz, an elfin figure whose tiny feet and boyish face belied his age. Matt thought how effective he'd look flying round a stage on the end of a wire – a creditable Peter Pan.

'Holly dahling! How absolutely lovely to see you!' squeaked Willie, his shaven head a roundel of light. He was fussing to remove snippets of cotton from his waist-coat, a creation in cross-banded silk of many colours. Unbuttoned for work, it revealed a collarless shirt.

'Forgive me for keeping you waiting. Was working on an evening coat – bit of a rush job, don't you know?'

'Oh, who for?' asked Holly, lowering her face to accept his kisses.

'Mustn't say, dahling,' said Willie, pecking both her cheeks. 'Mwah! Mwah! You know how it is.'

Over client confidentiality, Willie was a stickler. And for good reason: leaks could all too easily find their way into the gossip columns, ruining the element of surprise his A-list celebrities needed when, for instance, seeking to trump a rival at a film premiere.

'I know, darling,' Holly said. 'It was naughty of me to ask. Willie, this is Matt. Remember?'

'Of course, absolutely!' Willie extended a limp hand-shake. 'Welcome to my little emporium.' Mischievously fluttering his eyelids, he stood on tiptoe and planted a kiss on Matt's cheek. 'Any friend of Holly's is a friend of mine.'

Holly relished Matt's embarrassment. 'Now Willie!' she warned. 'Don't go getting ideas. Matt's mine.'

'Ooh, are we possessive?' Willie said. Then turning to Matt: 'You must be very special.'

'Honestly, Willie,' Holly laughed, 'You're such a flirt!'

'If the cap fits, wear it!' said Willie.

Uncertain how to join in the fun, Matt's expression was one of stilted amusement. Pocketing his hands, he hoped it wouldn't be long before the two of them got down to business.

'Anyway, my luvs,' said Willie, 'enough idle banter! I've been having a little think. From what you told me, Matt needs to stick out a million miles from the others on the show. I understand, not to put too fine a point on it, they are rather more mature. Am I right?'

'Completely,' said Holly, looking at Matt. Matt gave an obligatory nod.

'He's ever so quiet, your Matt! Has the cat got his tongue, or is he just shy?' Then, with a little touch to Matt's forearm: 'Don't mind me, I'm a terrible tease.'

Matt managed a weak grin.

'Anyway, where was I?' said Willie. 'Oh, yes, I know – Matt could be in for a hard time. So perhaps he should come across as rather intimidating. Something bright, even garish, dare one say. What we need is a gob-smacking creation to take the wind out of their sails.'

'Great!' said Holly. 'Make them think twice before attacking him.'

Willie turned to Matt. 'Dahling, cease your worries. You'll look like a tropical butterfly once I'm done. One of those big bright jobbies that frighten the birds away.'

'Brilliant!' exclaimed Holly. 'As well as Richard Torment he's got that art critic Godfrey Privett to contend with.'

'What?' shrieked Willie. 'Old Lollipop? You're having me on!'

'No, it's true!' insisted Holly. And in a flash: 'But why do you call him 'Lollipop'?'

'Yeah!' said Matt.

'That's brought him to life, hasn't it?' said Willie, glancing at Matt. 'It's what the rent boys used to call him, silly!'

'Oh,' said Holly and Matt as they cottoned on, their voices drawn out in unison.

'Didn't you know?' said Willie. 'Oh, yes, our Godfrey was a shocker in his day.' Putting his hands on his knees, he burst into laughter.

'The old perv!' Holly said, grinning as the connotations of 'lollipop' sank in.

'But how do you know?' asked Matt.

'Remember, more like,' said Willie, pensively. 'It's a long time ago, and largely forgotten now. But at the time it was a bit of a scandal.'

'Really?' said Holly.

'Oh, yes!' said Willie. 'Not that it *ever* reached the papers.'

'Why not?' Holly asked.

'Well, Godfrey wasn't a name in those days, but he did have influential friends. He was the talk of the gay community.'

Holly chuckled.

'Yes indeed! Our Godfrey was put inside,' said Willie, recalling the drama.

'Really?' said Matt, incredulous.

'For several years, poor dear. But the reason the name 'Lollipop' stuck was a bit of a giggle. There was this song around at the time of his trial … you'll be too young to remember, but it was Number One in its day.'

'Go on, try us,' said Holly, hoping for an impromptu performance.

'Well, if you insist!' Willie grinned. He was famous among friends for his mimicking of singers. Bringing his feet together in preparation, he looked up at the ceiling. Snapping his fingers brought the lyrics to mind:

'My boy Lollipop – duh, duh, dah, dah!' he began. 'Remember?'

'Of course!' said Holly, stifling a laugh. 'It's an old sixties classic.'

'By Millie, wasn't it?' added Matt.

'Right!' said Willie, pirouetting in little circles as he sang: 'He makes my heart go giddy up – Duh, duh, dah, dah!'

The high falsetto of his take off had them in fits.

Holly caught her breath. 'Honestly,' she cried, wiping tears of laughter from her eyes, 'is that true?'

'God's Honour! Would I tell you a lie?'

'Lollipop, eh?' Matt was much cheered by the revelation.

'Well, dears,' said Willie, 'there you have it, for what it's worth. So if Godfrey comes on all holier-than-thou, you can put him in his place, the old queen.' Then, regaining his composure: 'Honestly, all these distractions! It's a wonder I get anything done. Come on now, back to business.'

Holly pulled herself together. 'Do you think you've got something?'

'Well as it happens, I just might have!'

'Great!' said Holly, digging Matt in the ribs to stir some enthusiasm.

'Warren, dear,' said Willie, 'fetch me that jacket, will you? The one the lead singer of 'Gameboy' commissioned – Jimmy somebody or other.'

'Garridge,' said Matt, 'Jimmy Garridge.'

'That's the one!' said Willie, impressed. 'Silly boy went and killed himself before he could collect it. My! Matt dear, you are up on your pop stars.'

Matt shrugged. He'd remembered Jimmy Garridge because the name 'Gameboy' had seemed so fitting. High on crack cocaine, Jimmy had managed to crash his 'Yama' and kill himself while attempting a river jump at an outdoor concert. 'Mad bastard, great guy,' his fans had lamented.

'Well, his loss could be your gain,' said Willie. Raising his eyebrows, he pointed to the jacket, now clearly visible in the doorway of the storeroom.

Shit! thought Matt. The scarlet brocade hit him between the eyes. The jacket drew alarmingly near, suspended on a hanger at the end of Warren's arm.

Holly put her hand to her mouth.

'Shocked?' said Willie. 'Don't be! It'll look a dream once it's on.'

Holly believed him, but Matt's expression said he believed otherwise. She struggled to raise his enthusiasm. 'Look, it's a Nero,' she went on. 'They're really hip!'

Matt felt the textured sheen of the material. Not that he was any judge of cloth, but with Holly giving him dirty looks he felt obliged to do something.

'It's wild silk!' Willie enthused. 'Hand-stitched all the way.'

'Come on, Matt, put it on,' said Holly, losing patience.

Warren moved to help him out his beloved leather jacket. 'I can manage,' said Matt edgily. He handed it to Holly, who flopped it disdainfully over her arm. It was so shamefully scruffy she would prefer to have binned it.

'My guess is it'll fit a treat,' said Willie. 'Your build is so similar to Jimmy's.' Then standing back, he reflected sadly: 'Silly boy, fancy going and doing something like that. Such a *terrible* waste!'

Assisted by Warren, Matt eased his arms into the shimmering creation while Willie stood by, waiting to see if the length was correct.

'Ooh!' he said, delighted. 'If that isn't cool, I don't know what is. And that red! It positively frightens me to look at him.'

'It's fab, Matt,' cried Holly. 'Really, I mean it!'

Matt stood there, examining the deep cuffs with disdain.

'Come on,' said Willie, 'see for yourself.' Taking his arm, he led him to a full-length mirror.

Matt hardly dared look at first. When he did, he was pleasantly surprised. The angle of the mirror lent him the air, he fancied, of an emperor looking down on his subjects. 'Should I do the jacket up?' he asked, fingering the row of many buttons.

Holly was relieved to see the beginnings of a smile creep onto his face. 'No, leave it open,' she said. 'It's more hip that way.'

'You know luvvy, for a minute I thought we had a 'no',' said Willie in a whispered aside. 'But now look at him. He can't get enough of himself.'

So engrossed was Matt, presenting his profile first one way and then another, that he failed to catch the remark. Turning to Holly, he asked for her opinion of the fit.

'It's perfect! And the red suits you. Don't you think so, Willie?'

'Absolutely,' said Willie. 'It's *so* macho!'

'But, ugh! That shirt,' said Holly, annoyed by Matt's fondness for old clothes.

'OK, OK,' said Matt, 'we've been down that road already.'

'Now, luvs, no quarrelling!' said Willie. 'There's a simple solution here.'

They looked at him expectantly, awaiting his arbitration.

'With a jacket as striking as this, a simple contrast is needed. And what better than the trusty old T-shirt?'

'Brilliant!' exclaimed Holly.

'It should be a white one, mind,' advised Willie. 'It'll offset the scarlet a treat.'

Matt had to agree. With a jacket as punchy as this, a white T-shirt was all that was needed.

'You could even print a logo on it,' Willie suggested.

Holly's face lit up. 'That's a thought,' she said to Matt. 'We could use it to promote the new image!'

'Right!' said Matt, elated by the way things were falling into place.

'Willie, you're a genius!' said Holly. Gripping him by the arms, she pulled him towards her and kissed him smack in the middle of his forehead.

'Ooh!' said Willie, glancing at Matt. 'This babe will turn me yet!'

Matt looked at Willie and hoped Holly wasn't planning another ménage à trois – there were some lines he had no intention of crossing!

FOURTEEN

Matt kept himself out of sight until the very last minute. Peering furtively round the door to the television studio, he could see his adversaries seated at a crescent-shaped table, sipping water and chatting while they waited for Richard Torment to appear.

Godfrey Privett's face was familiar, wizened and reptilian like and old salamander's. His mouth looked pulled tight as if by a drawstring that, when loosened by his smile, opened to reveal a palisade of yellowing teeth. Matt imagined them gummed up and rank with the residue of old victims.

Next he spotted 'Auntie Biddie', the amply-proportioned Dame Bradstock. She was directing her large double-chin away from Privett and starting an earnest discussion with Buller of the Yard. Her eyelids were a-flutter and her pudgy fingers moved like putti over her hair, pushing and patting it to shape. Leaning towards her, head bowed and attentive, the Commissioner seemed deeply impressed – as, indeed, did Dame Bradstock too.

Matt noted the Commissioner's uniform. It gave his figure a bollard-like shape of Babylonian massiveness. Topped off with a square-set head of bovine solidity, surely this was a policeman on whom the nation could rely. Yet what an illusion! In the towns and cities, law and order had broken down. People were running amok, doing just as they please. Buller was imbued with the sophistry of his political masters and he followed in their footsteps like a large obedient dog. His policy of tolerance was a failure and his singsongs were a national joke.

While Matt waited nervously in the wings, the great man himself – Richard Torment, doyen of the chattering classes – was in his dressing room. 'Torment Tonight' was Cityvision's pride and joy, its flagship show, streets ahead of all similar productions in the liveliness of its debate and in the flair of its presenter.

Torment had graduated from Oxford many years ago. Armed with youthful idealism and a degree in sociology, he was swiftly garnered into broadcasting. There he evolved smoothly and shamelessly from a young man hot-under-the-collar about flagrant social injustice into a heavily remunerted media darling. On a whim, he could demolish a guest with such aplomb that it seemed he was not of this world, but rather a god. His patronizing manner humbled all; confrontational and vindictive, viewers flocked to him in droves.

'Five minutes, Dickie!' How often he'd heard that call. 'Make-up' was still titivating his hair, a well-groomed thatch with a dark widow's peak resembling a spearhead at the ready, to be guided in assault by the swivelling turrets of his cold, steely eyes.

As Torment walked onto the set he focused his attention briefly on the audience. Among the rippling sea of lesser minds he spotted that of Bernie Feltz – that frenetic little hustler who'd bounced into his office wildly enthusing about an idea for a show. To give him his due, it was a good one. Aggro was in the air, he could feel it; a sure fire ratings coup, with any luck!

Next to Feltz was a pretty redhead. Flight's girlfriend, Torment surmised. But where was Flight? He was not at the panel table. Two minutes to go! Then to Torment's relief, Matt walked on, greeted by a gasp of surprise from the audience.

Some jacket! Torment thought to himself. Just the sort of thing the camera loves.

But the other guests glowered, thinking as one: how dare he upstage us like this! Arriving late, in a ridiculous red jacket to boot. They turned and gazed at Matt, rigidly like centaurs in a frieze, their bowstrings drawn. Matt imagined their thoughts: We're not putting up with this. That young man Flight must be put in his place!

The floor manager flitted to and fro like a little bat, appealing for quiet in the auditorium. Within seconds not a murmur was heard, the studio hushed and expectant.

Matt stared at his notepad, its whiteness blank as his mind. What happened now was in the lap of the gods.

Seated between his guests, Torment awaited his cue. His jaw was firm and his notes on the evening's agenda were laid out before him. Words from the director crackled in his earpiece: 'Cue Dickie! Five – Four – Three – Two – One – and – '

Such an institution had Torment become, he'd long since dispensed with a saccharine 'Hello' in favour of a perfunctory 'Good evening' delivered without the shadow of a smile. With condescension he waited for the applause to die down. Then he began.

'On Torment Tonight we ask these questions: Is our society morally bankrupt? Are the values we now cherish based on false precepts? Is our liberal age wrong, to be scornful of principles that our forebears held dear?'

There was a rumble of murmured indecision from the audience.

'To help answer this question,' he went on, 'we have on the show tonight four distinguished guests. Godfrey Privett is known to many for his tireless crusade against what he believes is the vacuous quality of much contemporary art.'

A round of applause; Privett smiled: he was revered – unlike the flashy young upstart at the opposite end of the panel!

'Next we have the redoubtable figure of Dame Bridget Bradstock. A government minister and Chairperson of the Council for Moral Issues, she is, of course, remembered by most of us as Auntie Biddie – a lady famed for her commonsense views.'

Dame Bridget beamed, greeting the applause of her fans with dinky little waves. She was anxious to show that her recent ennoblement hadn't gone to her head. Underneath, she was still the same Auntie Biddie they knew and loved, whose deep and gushing concern for humanity ought to bring tears to their eyes.

'And to my left,' said Torment, 'we are fortunate to have with us the Commissioner of Police, Commander Buller.' Then with a knowing smile and a hint of sarcasm: 'The face of modern policing, he is, of course, known to many of us also for his faith in the power of song.'

The audience tittered along with Torment, who continued in barely concealed contempt for the Singing Policeman. 'The Commissioner's voice can now be heard on a recently released CD, entitled 'A Policeman's Lot'. It was recorded live at some of the many singsongs he and his force have staged up and down the country.'

The suggestion sank in – Buller of the Yard was a victim of gross personal vanity. The audience nudged one another, sniggering and muttering: 'What a plonker!' 'He thinks he can make it to the charts.'

Torment smirked. 'The CD is out now, and of course full details can be had on our Cityvision website.'

Failing to see anything amusing, the Commissioner upheld the dignity of his office by responding with a courteous smile, his hands clasped in grateful appreciation of the plug.

Scarcely had the audience quietened than Matt felt his heart begin to thump. The camera glided towards him, its black eye navigating his face in small and soundless manoeuvres. There was no going back: for better or for worse, he was on air.

'Last, but by no means least,' Torment proclaimed, 'on my right in the very fine jacket we have the young British artist Matt Flight. He is also the founder of RIOT, a movement to bring a sense of reality to – and I quote – 'a society whose morality has succumbed to lunatic senti-ment, which judges what is bad to be good and vice versa.' He is here tonight to defend one of his recent paintings which, as you can see, is represented on the screen behind me.'

Apart from whoops from some followers of fashion, Matt enjoyed little applause.

Torment continued: 'Titled *The Orchard*, this painting has been called corrupting, perverted and degener-ate – words used, indeed, by a member of this very panel.' Glancing at Privett and then Dame Bridget, he continued, 'The Council for Moral Issues is now adjudi-cating on whether *The Orchard* is in breach of the Nudity Act as a detail of the painting, allegedly overtly sexual, has been used to advertise the current exhibition of his work.' Looking appropriately grave, he added: 'Those of you familiar with recent amendments to the Act will know that such practice is now illegal.'

Holly nudged Feltz and pointed: Matt was on the over-head monitor. 'Look! And what an ace shot of the T-shirt!'

'Yeah, get that 'eye'!' said Feltz. It looked mesmeriz-ing on screen – just like when he'd first seen it. Maybe by the end of the show millions would be hooked, and the campaign on everybody's lips.

Torment swung round so he could see the screen. 'For those of you unfamiliar with the painting,' he said, 'may I ask you, distasteful though you may find it, to pay atten-tion to it, as what is portrayed is central to tonight's debate.'

All eyes turned to the screen and the audience reaction was in line with Matt's expectations – the corners of their mouths drooped in universal condemnation.

'Dame Bridget,' said Torment. 'May I begin by asking you: Do you find this painting offensive?'

The Dame responded with a mild rebuke, fragments of her north-country accent surfacing occasionally like stones in a manicured lawn. 'Tut-tut, Richard, you of all people ought to know better. I can't possibly pass a personal opinion, because, as all of us know, the case surrounding this picture is sub judice!'

Torment smiled a crocodile smile which lingered as the Dame wagged her finger censoriously.

'But let me say this much,' she said, with a look of serious concern. 'Looking at the picture, I do find it deeply distressing that such a *yoong* man should 'ave it in him to paint *sooch* a terrible scene!'

Thrilling at the onset of battle, the audience applauded loudly.

The Dame allowed herself a grin of satisfaction. 'I mean, of all the things he could have painted, he chooses a pile of dead bodies and Heaven knows what else, when there are *soo* many other things in life – happy things, you know?' She looked into the audience and widened her eyes for maximum effect. 'Coom on, I'm right, aren't I?'

Matt suppressed his irritation and smiled tolerantly. Happy things, indeed! – Like saying all's well, when it damn well isn't!

'Smile if you like, yoong man,' the Dame persisted, an air of patronising menace in her voice. 'But if you take my advice, you'll do yourself a favour by getting out more into the real world!'

Torment turned his facial turret on Matt. 'What is the purpose of a painting like this?' he asked coldly and superciliously.

Matt was astonished by Torment's aggressive tone. The question was like an incision. During their chat before the show, Torment had been gentleness and courtesy personified. He had listened quietly while *The*

198

Orchard was explained to him. And to round things off he'd even offered encouragement: a touch patronizing, perhaps, but amicable enough in its way. Now he was the master inquisitor; playing to the crowd, asking questions for effect, hoping to reduce his victim to a state of confusion.

Trying hard to keep ahead of the game, Matt replied: 'My aim was to portray a bitter truth.'

'The bitter truth being what?'

Then Matt unexpectedly found an equilibrium within himself. The cameras, it seemed, were a conduit between himself and the outside world. He felt joined to the millions he knew were watching. 'War and peace are interlinked,' he calmly explained. 'Inseparable halves of the human experience.'

'Highfalutin' stuff!' said Torment. 'Can you be more explicit?'

Matt shrugged his shoulders. 'It's simple. If it weren't for war, we'd have no understanding of peace.'

'Are you saying one feeds off the other?'

'Exactly!'

Torment turned to Godfrey Privett for a comment. But the old critic looked away, preferring to sit and make notes, his face a picture of stilted absorption. He was biding his time, thought Torment – a butcher sizing his beast for the slaughter.

Then Dame Bridget interrupted. She was worried things were about to go over her head, engulfing her in a wave of intellectual obfuscation.

'Look,' she pleaded in a mumsy way, 'I don't know about any two halves and sooch like. For my part, I'm woon whole. But there's not an ounce of me that would have truck with soomthin' as barmy as war. It's morally indefensible!'

Applause and whistles erupted from the auditorium.

'Would that be your feeling too, Commissioner?' asked Torment. The immaculately turned-out policeman was sitting bolt upright, his opinion ready to pop.

'I wholeheartedly concur!' the Commissioner boomed. 'Looking at it from here, this *The Orchard*, so called, is as ungodly a vision of humanity as you could ever set eyes on!'

More applause. 'Thank you, Commissioner,' said Dame Bradstock, giving him a coy smile. 'My feelings entirely!' She leaned forward, taking the audience into her confidence, 'You know, I always say there's nothing in the world that can't be resolved by getting round a table and talking – over a cuppa of whatever you fancy. For Heaven's Sake, nobody needs war! It ain't natural now, is it?'

Matt shook his head, resisting the urge to intervene. Not natural? he said to himself. For God's Sake, our appetite for conflict is in the very marrow of our being. Without it we wouldn't be human!

'Matt's keeping his cool,' Holly whispered to Feltz.

'Just as well,' Feltz whispered back. 'If Biddie Bradstock gets to flip him, imagine what Privett will do!'

Leaning back in his chair, Torment gazed at a point somewhere above his head while phrasing his next question. 'Godfrey Privett,' he said. 'Turning to you now, is there absolutely nothing this painting can teach us?'

Privett looked up casually from his notepad before speaking: 'Dickie,' he said, assuming instant familiarity. 'Let me say first of all, that I have already penned a critique on this, so you'll appreciate that a great many people already know my views.' His devotees in the audience clapped.

Matt scowled at him; Privett's cruel words were still fresh in his mind. Privett threw an angry glance back, a ranging shot over the top of his horn-rimmed bifocals, balanced pretentiously on the end of his nose. He was warming up the audience for a treat – the very public devouring of a young upstart who had the temerity to challenge him in open debate.

Lowering his eyes, Privett referred to his notes. 'For those of you who missed my article, the answer to Richard's question is emphatically 'No!' A painting like this can teach us nothing. And for this reason: Mr. Flight's analogy implies the pursuit of moral values is pointless and what we experience is beyond our control. To say such a thing is arrant and offensive nonsense, a denigration of human intelligence – just the sort of thing we have come to expect from attention-seeking young flash-in-the-pan's!'

Privett's supporters clapped heartily.

'Arrant nonsense?' said Torment, tossing the ball back to Matt.

Matt decided to ignore Privett and direct his answers to the audience. He felt his left foot begin to twitch, a sign of mounting irritation. 'I have never questioned the need for moral values,' he said, outwardly impassive. 'But I do question what we've allowed them to become.'

'Would you care to elucidate?'

'Morality has become a matter of indulgence.'

Privett stiffened. Did this 'boy' intend to ignore him – responding to his criticism not to his face, but by way of a general address? His grip tightened on the pencil he was playing with and it snapped loudly in two.

Torment raised his eyebrows and addressed Matt facetiously: 'Morality, an indulgence – well, well! Like a box of chocolates, perhaps?'

Cackles rose from the auditorium. Matt drew a deep breath. Torment's analogy was fortuitously appropriate, he felt. 'Exactly! One we've eaten so much of that we've made ourselves sick!'

Torment raised his eyebrows. 'Sick?'

'That's right,' said Matt, feeling rather clever. 'Too many soft centres!'

Feltz looked at Holly. 'Chocolates? Soft centres? What's he on about?'

'Shhh!' said Holly.

'Soft centres!' Privett sneered. 'For pity's sake, this is supposed to be a serious debate.' Dame Bridget and the Commissioner were both lost by the analogy. They stared blankly into the audience, who appeared equally bemused.

'All right, let's put it another way,' Matt said. 'Morality has become a pick-and choose affair, a matter of what suits us rather than something which is good for us.'

'Ah, now we're getting somewhere,' said Torment. 'What you're saying is, we've lowered our standards.'

'Worse than that. We've discarded them!' said Matt.

'Poppycock!' growled Privett. 'To anyone with a brain, the do's and don't's of moral conduct are perfectly clear.'

'Privett's got the hump,' Holly whispered.

'Yeah, great!' said Feltz, rubbing his hands.

Matt struggled to keep his cool. 'That's not so! Morality's become a soft option – we shape it how we like.'

'And how do you suppose this has come about?' Torment asked Matt, casting a weather eye at Privett in the hope he might be preparing a broadside. The old critic threw his eyes to heaven with a look of exasperated disdain.

'We've gone gaga!' Matt said.

'You think so?' said Torment.

'Our brains are addled,' said Matt. 'And you know why? Because we've had it easy for too long.'

'In what way?'

Matt thought for a moment. 'How long is it since we've been hit by a major catastrophe? One that's affected every man woman and child in the country.'

'On the scale of a world war?'

'Yes,' said Matt.

202

'Well, there's been nothing I can think of,' said Torment, looking around for confirmation. A murmur of accord reverberated around the auditorium.

'There you have it,' said Matt, opening out his hands.

Torment raised his eyebrows. 'Have what?'

'We've lost our sense of reality, of proportion. Of things that are really important, like our very survival. We take such things for granted and we don't want to hear about reality.'

Torment thought for a moment. 'Tell me, what is reality to you?'

'What's true,' said Matt. 'Just that – the truth.'

'Ah! The truth,' said Torment, affecting a worldly-wise air. 'And you're claiming we can no longer recognize it?'

'Exactly,' said Matt. 'Because we've lost the necessity to do so. We have no real experience of deprivation and suffering.'

'Good riddance, I say!' Dame Bradstock interjected.

'But you're wrong!' insisted Matt. 'Like it or not, adversity is the making of us all. It gives us strength, focuses our minds on essentials – things that really count.'

Torment reflected. 'And you maintain that as a society, we no longer do that?'

'That's right. Ask any survivor from a war and they'll tell you we're living in cloud-cuckoo-land. Our priorities are crazy.'

Torment nodded. He more than anyone knew that Matt had a point. Night after night on his show, loony and emotive concepts of right and wrong were on parade, like fungal infections of the liberal brain.

Dame Bridget had something to say. 'What Mr. Flight is forgetting, is this: those very same people who know what it's like to be bombed would never wish to go through it again. Heavens, no!'

'True, but they're not the one's who've lost the plot,' Matt countered.

'Nonsense!' said the Dame. 'All of us know the horrors of war.'

'Oh yes? How?'

'We see it on the telly all the time!' She looked at the audience again. 'I mean, really! This is *sooch* a silly argument we're having.'

Matt summoned up his most sarcastic tone. 'Oh, yes, the telly. Of course, I was forgetting!'

'There's no need for that tone of voice!' snapped the Dame, her double chin wobbling like pink blancmange.

'Is watching war on a screen the same as seeing it for real?'

'No, but you can sense what it's like!'

'But for it to change your life, you have to have lived through it,' said Matt. 'Be bloodied, if you will.'

'Be bloodied indeed! You mean, we have to survive a bloodbath before we can know about morality? You're potty! Quite mad!'

With the audience now giggling, Torment intervened. 'Let's keep things in perspective, please. As I see it, Matt Flight's point is this: anything apart from first hand experience is too remote to affect us in a meaningful way.'

'That's right,' said Matt. 'It's like with a road sign. It can warn people that a bend is dangerous, but it won't tell them what it's like to be in an accident.'

The Dame missed the point. 'But surely, if there's a sign, that should be enough.'

'My sentiments entirely,' said the Commissioner, insulted by this challenge to the efficacy of cautionary signs. Thanks to his input on numerous safety committees, they were increasingly popping up everywhere.

Matt's patience was wearing thin. 'Listen, isn't it time to get real?' he said, tentatively introducing his slogan. 'We have to put to one side what we imagine we are and come to terms with what we really are!'

'Which is?' Torment asked him.

'Creatures tied to patterns of behaviour that we cannot escape from. Until we accept that, all we have going for us is a one-way ticket down the tubes.'

Dame Bradstock was not used to such uncouth vernacular. 'Down the tubes?' she said.

'Yeah, flushed away, never to be seen again,' said Matt. Then, pushing back his chair, he cried out: 'Jesus! You people at the top have gone gooey in the head!'

At this Privett came to life, shaking his head and one hand fiercely like a bear plagued by a persistent mosquito. 'That's an absurd observation!' he shouted.

Commissioner Buller bridled also. Cerebral gooeyness was not a quality to be associated with himself. Fair-mindedness yes – but not goo! 'I can see you don't live in the real world, coming out with that sort of talk.'

The Dame chipped in too. 'My feelings entirely, Commissioner! What Mr. Flight doesn't understand, is that life is about compromise.'

'You mean giving in!' Matt said. 'To anybody who has a gripe about anything.'

Torment coolly seized the opportunity to exacerbate things. 'If that were true, it would be recipe for disaster, would it not?'

'But it's *joost* not the case,' the Dame argued.

'It is!' insisted Matt, his irritation beginning to show. 'Everything is appeased, nothing gets stood up to. You're like bathers, asleep on your lilos – bobbing about, oblivious of danger.'

'That's outrageous!' puffed the Dame. Was she not common sense personified? Secure in the ample bosom of Dame Bradstock's wisdom, the Commissioner wholeheartedly concurred yet again. 'Listen to Matt Flight here, and anybody'd think we'd all lost our marbles, ha, ha! Of course, that is plainly absurd.'

'Then how do you explain what's happening on our streets?' Matt asked. 'Radicals are everywhere, doing exactly as they please – bombing, disrupting, defiling things.'

'That's democracy in action!' the Commissioner said proudly. 'Things do have their price, you know.'

'Precisely!' said the Dame. 'Democracy, Mr. Flight – Have you ever heard of it?'

'What we have now isn't democracy,' Matt replied. 'It's a sham! Do you think this is how people want to live? With mayhem so commonplace and the authorities just accepting it?'

'I'm not listening to this!' said Dame Bridget, looking the other way.

'Nor me either,' said the Commissioner.

'You know what this all boils down to?' Matt said.

'No, but I'm sure you're going to tell us,' said Torment, smiling approvingly.

'Tolerance,' said Matt. 'Let everybody do as they like, and they will do just that. What we have now isn't democracy, it's a shambles! Democracy has faded from view, like the dying of a glorious supernova!'

At this last observation, a woman in the front row of the audience was moved to get out her handkerchief.

'And what has taken its place?' Matt continued. 'A paranoid obsession about personal rights, which can lead to only one thing – the entire population at loggerheads!'

'Anarchy?' Torment suggested.

'Yes,' said Matt, 'of a kind we haven't seen for centuries.'

Holly whispered: 'Matt's really laying it on the line!'

'Yeah, the boy's doing good!' said Feltz.

Some of the audience seemed to be latching on to Matt's message. There was spasmodic clapping, heads nodding in mutual accord.

But the Dame wasn't going to take this lying down. 'Anarchy? No, no, no we've moved on from that. What we 'ave today is a caring and sharing soociety. And it's the personal rights we've all struggled for that make it so.

If that isn't democracy, I don't know what is.' Turning to Torment, she said: 'Honestly, forgive me for saying this, Richard, but this yoong man has soom very strange ideas.'

Torment spun to face the Commissioner. 'Strange ideas, Commissioner?'

'I wholeheartedly concur with Dame Bridget,' he said. For him, personal rights were sacrosanct – to be upheld even at the risk of – dare he say it – the occasional bomb going off!

'I believe, I believe,' the Dame continued, straining to take complete possession of the moral high ground, 'personal rights are the very *basis* of civilized soociety!'

'Just there for the taking?' asked Matt. 'Like loot through a broken shop window? So no one has to earn them, just smash and grab? None of you seem to give a damn!'

The Commissioner squared his jaw, and let rip: 'Balderdash, boyo!' he boomed. 'I've dealt with young men like you in my time, trying to spoil things for the majority. And I can say to you, that's not the case. No, not the case at all!'

'Oh no?' Matt turned to the audience for their opinion. 'What do you think? Isn't what I'm saying obvious and unavoidable?' Encouraged by some cheers, he went on: 'In fact, anyone blind enough not to see it must be a blockhead!'

This seemed an apt description of Buller and amid a gale of laughter Torment felt obliged to apologize for Matt's rudeness, despite his having enjoyed it as much as the audience.

'Don't worry on my account,' said the Commissioner, restive in his seat. 'Sticks and stones – they're water off a duck's back to me.'

Torment was enjoying Matt's forthrightness; it was a welcome change to the insincerity of celebrities. 'So who has an answer to all this?' he asked, looking at each of the panel in turn.

Matt was the first to speak and he did so with passion. 'It's simple,' he said. 'People have to face the truth and embrace values we've forgotten for years.'

'Any comment from you, Godfrey?' Torment asked.

'Hardly!' said Privett, in supercilious disdain for the universal stupidity on display.

'That's unlike you!' said Torment. Things were crackling along nicely, but he knew there was mileage yet to be had from Privett. His director thought so too, for he sent him a message via the discreet prompt in Torment's ear: 'It's time to dish the dirt, Dickie.'

Torment knew just what he had to do. Feltz had informed him of Privett's sordid practices with young boys and though they happened a long time ago he considered them fair game. This was a show about morality after all, and they were relevant. But to avoid accusations of unfair advantage, it would be best not to confront Privett directly. No, an oblique cut would suffice.

'So, Godfrey,' he said, relaxing his prey, 'I take it you've not succumbed to the so-called moral indulgence Matt Flight has spoken of?'

Privett smiled. Was he not the shepherd of good taste, in whose pastures of rectitude fans had been grazing for years? 'I think not,' he said complacently. 'This kind of juvenile prognosis is rather wide of the mark, don't you think? When Mr Flight has grown up a little, we might find him worthy of rational disagreement.'

Torment nodded, then continued with a sly grin: 'Possibly. But, at the end of the day, I suppose it all depends on where you're *coming* from.'

A ripple of sniggers swept the audience. The slight emphasis Torment put on the word 'coming' told them a sexual innuendo was afoot. Moreover, the deadpan authority of his delivery indicated that he was confident of his ground and that perhaps a nasty revelation was about to devastate the life of old Privett – who suddenly looked the part of someone with a guilty past.

In the hands of such a master as Torment, thinly-veiled lewdness could work wonders. He put his hand to his mouth to conceal a sly smile.

Privett was mystified. He failed to pick up on the source of the audience's amusement, so he charged ahead regardless. 'To infer we're no longer capable of making truthful assessments of what is right or wrong is plainly absurd!'

Torment raised his eyebrows at the audience and they sniggered again. Now they knew he had something up his sleeve! Matt of course knew what that 'something' was and he looked at Privett in triumph, the words 'old Lolli-pop' running round in his brain like a Circle Line train.

Privett scanned faces desperately for clues to what was going on and was transfixed by Matt's triumphant smile. It was a moment of horror, of sick realization! A question flashed into his head: had his past become common knowledge? Dear God! But if so – how?

The answer wasn't far away. A glance at the audience revealed his *bête noire* Bernie Feltz looking at him directly and tapping his nose. Grinning from ear to ear, Feltz mouthed grotesquely 'Lollipop' – a word that Privett had hoped never to encounter again. His heart sank. Feltz! he seethed: God, I might have known! He fell silent, his contribution to the debate at an end.

'Look at Privett!' whispered Holly.

'Shafted good and proper!' Feltz gloated. 'All thanks to Willie Fitz, eh?'

'He's so naughty, that one!' said Holly with a giggle.

Matt sighed with relief. For days he had dreaded the confrontation with Privett. And what had happened? He'd been spit-roasted on his own guilty conscience, that's what, the old fraud! Matt saw Holly and Feltz egg-ing him on with little thumbs-up of support.

The message in Torment's earpiece was unequivocal. 'Nice one, Dickie! That worked a treat!'

Grinning fiendishly, Torment turned his attention back to Matt, now clearly the star turn. 'This painting of yours is all very well, but it doesn't offer much hope, does it?' He swivelled his chair again to contemplate the huge screen showing *The Orchard*. 'The fact of the matter is, this is *bitter* fruit, is it not?'

The audience was quiet for a couple of seconds, concentrating on the image: white doves of peace, frozen in time, gorging themselves on the harvest of seeds bursting free from the fleshy redness of pomegranate fruit. Below them tree-roots drew succour from dark decomposing flesh, their sinuous tentacles invading every orifice of the contorted dead.

'It was never my intention to offer hope,' said Matt.

Torment addressed the audience showily: 'I think that's abundantly clear to us all!'

'But how did we get into this mess?' Matt said. 'Isn't it time we all stopped kidding ourselves? Isn't it all the fault of Dame Bradstock and her ilk, who've turned us gaga with their half-baked ideas on how we should live?'

'Gaga?! How dare you!' snapped the Dame.

'Please! For heaven's sake!' Torment said, half-concealing a wry smirk. 'Let's have some respect.'

'Do you really believe that's what I've done to you all?' Dame Bradstock cried to the audience. Nobody said a word; it seemed they were happy to believe she had. 'Coom on, it's me, Auntie Biddie,' she said, her puffy arms splayed out in a pitiful appeal. 'Remember?'

Commissioner Buller applauded her loudly but the audience was unmoved. Dame Bradstock looked at Matt. How could that young man be persecuting her so? He was so unlike the nice artist who, upon her ennoblement, had painted her portrait. He'd been a real pet! He would offer her tea at the end of each sitting and compliment her on the beauty of her skin.

'Yoong man,' she said, summoning up all her power and dignity to humiliate him. 'I cannot believe you mean what you say! Can't you see how you've insoolted all those of us who have spent a lifetime's devotion bettering the lives of their fellow-citizens?'

'You mean puffing yourselves up on the misery of others,' said Matt. Then he shouted. 'Get real!'

At this the audience stirred. Their affirmative murmur sounded like a herd on the move. The Dame began to panic: was that rare privilege – to be one of the people, yet aloof – going to be snatched from her? Oh, tragedy, tragedy! she whimpered inside.

Torment could scarcely conceal his delight. 'Come on, all you out there! Let's have your verdict on this. Are we gaga, as Matt Flight would have us believe?'

Until that moment the audience had only to enjoy themselves at the expense of Torment's guests. Now they wavered, called to account under the craning arms of sound booms. Matt kept quiet, hoping his words had been enough to persuade them. Dame Bridget looked crumpled and close to tears.

Feltz looked over his shoulder to see if anyone in the audience would speak up. But nobody did. Never one to miss an opportunity, he seized the moment with a rabble-rousing cry: 'Gaga? I'll say we are!'

Stirred into action, the audience found its voice. 'Yeah – Gaga! Gaga!' People were shouting and looking round, rallying each other to pillory and condemn the scapegoats.

Feltz wasted no time. He leapt to his feet and shouted: 'Now's our chance! Let's go for it! Get real!'

It was clear to Torment that he was losing control. Then to his amazement, Matt pushed back his chair and stood up, revealing the logo on his T-shirt.

'See these letters?' he shouted. 'D'you know what they stand for? Let me tell you! 'Reality In Our Time!'

211

That's what we must fight for, 'cos right now, we're all living in a madhouse!'

'Attaboy!' shouted Feltz.

Holly nudged Feltz and pointed at the big monitor. The camera was nosing in for a close-up on Matt; the slogan on his T-shirt filled the nation's screens for a full five seconds. Holly began shouting too, cheerleading the mob by jumping up and down. 'Get real! Get real!' she chanted.

People were rising to their feet. Anything was worth a go which might change things for the better, away from the dreary desperation of the status quo. 'Get Real! Get Real!' they chanted, shaking their fists in the air.

Commissioner Buller and Dame Bradstock looked at each other in silence like two bookends without a job. Then all of a sudden Dame Bradstock buried her head in her hands. This was it, the end! The horrible slogan ringing in her ears, she cried: 'Ungrateful pigs! And to think I've devooted me *life* to them!' Her face was red with rage, but the audience was without mercy. Their chants advanced in a phalanx on her senses: 'Get real! Get real! Get real!'

Witnessing Dame Bridget's destruction had been pure enjoyment for Torment. But wait! Was there more to come? Might she throw a tantrum? It would make excellent television.

The Dame looked to the Commissioner. 'I'll not put up with this!' she spluttered, now in tears.

Buller rose to his feet. 'Dear lady, let me escort you away from here! There's nothing more to be said, I fear.'

'There most certainly isn't!' said the Dame. Standing up to leave, she stared angrily at Matt.

'Don't go!' pleaded Torment. But the crowd was getting out of control. 'The lady is clearly overwrought,' said Buller. Solemnly he offered her his handkerchief. 'You'll feel all the better for a really good blow.'

'Oh my, Commissioner, but you're *soo* very kind.' A pungent smack of lavender cleared her head. 'This has all been a terrible shock.'

'Yes it must have been, dear lady.'

She took his arm and he led her slowly to the sanity of the hospitality suite. How was he to console her? 'It is so true what they say,' he said wisely, 'About the hand that feeds.'

'Isn't it joost,' the Dame whimpered. Wallowing in the aftermath of persecution she looked into his face, and said: 'They know not what they do!'

FIFTEEN

As Dame Bradstock and her knight-in-blue shuffled off the stage, Torment raised his eyes to heaven for the camera. The audience at home would surely be delighted by the sorry spectacle of buffoonery in retreat; the studio audience was already jeering and shouting. A nice piece of television! But what about the rest of the show? He wasn't sorry to see the policeman leave but he felt cheated by the Dame's departure. Her bursting magma of emotion might have set off a comedy of happenings over which he would have had little control. It was the sort of thing he longed for, but what chance was there of it happening now? Only Godfrey Privett and Matt Flight remained and Privett was out of the running, motionless like an owl sitting in the beam of a torch.

Torment came to a rapid conclusion. Whatever happened next was best left to young Flight.

'Please! Please!' Torment shouted, maintaining a savvy smirk. 'Everybody calm down!' In the tumult his words had little effect. Shrugging his shoulders, he gestured to Matt that the floor was now his.

Matt rose from his seat and was greeted by boisterous acclaim from the audience. 'Dickie! Dickie!' the director screamed into Torment's earpiece. 'What the hell are you playing at? You can't let this guy run the show!' Torment turned down the volume in his earpiece and glanced peevishly up at the control room. How dare they panic! Couldn't they trust him after all these years?

Led by a shaven-headed youth of dubious salubrity, the audience was now chanting as one: 'Get real! Get real! Get real!' Torment smiled pityingly. Was the herd about to stampede? What sclerotic little lives they must lead. Regulated to death. This mayhem was obviously a glorious renaissance of long-suppressed emotions.

Jubilant but alarmed, Holly and Feltz looked at one another.

'Help!' said Holly anxiously. 'What have we started?'

'Jeez, I dunno. But it's gonna be big!'

As Feltz spoke, his right leg was rudely shoved aside by a passing knee. He looked up to see a line of angry-faced aesthetes pushing their way down through the audience. The Fangos! So they were here. He'd kept an eye out for them but hadn't noticed them before: they must have kept their berets hidden, so as not to be denied admittance. They looked somewhat absurd now, marching in line in their uniforms of beret and blue polyester polo-necks. Most of them were skinny and wimpish, except for one whose distended gut wobbled like that of an overweight reservist striding to do his bit at the front. Their hero and mentor Godfrey Privett gazed straight past them as if his control of them was God-like and needed no command or sign.

'Shit!' said Feltz to Holly. 'What's going to happen now?'

'Dunno!' said Holly nervously.

'Well we're not hanging round to find out!' Feltz grabbed Holly's arm and he pulled her in a hasty retreat to the nearest exit. They burst through the door into the arms of a startled security guard.

'Listen, mate, you've got aggro in there!' blurted Feltz.

'Where?' said the guard.

'In there! They're taking over the stage!' cried Feltz, pointing through the half-open door.

The man saw the Fangos in military formation taking up position in front of the set. 'Cheeky beggars!' he exclaimed, trotting off towards them. 'This is right out of order – no mistake!'

Holly peered round the door to see what would happen. Feltz hid behind her and gaped. 'You know what? I reckon we're in for a punch-up!' he said, excited by the prospect of chaos.

The shaven-headed youth had come down out of the audience and was shouting in the face of the principal Fango, an enraged don-like man with a marked facial tick. Others were shouting abuse from the audience, furious that the Fangos were obstructing their view. 'Piss off back where you came from!' one woman yelled. Another large woman in a boiler suit advanced menacingly towards the stage. Meanwhile four or five young men were interpreting the words 'get real' as an instruction to pull up seats and hurl them about as if possessed by some demonic force.

Caught in the middle, the security guard attempted to take charge. 'Return to your seats or else!' he shouted, thwacking his baton on the palm of his hand.

'Animals!' shouted a Fango.

'Say that again and you're dead!' replied the lady in the boiler suit.

The security guard took heart as he was joined by another, puffing onto the podium munching on a half-eaten burger. 'Ladies an' gents, enuff is enuff!' he cried. But the two men were outnumbered. For their trouble they collected kicks to the shins and more abuse: 'Fascist pigs!' and 'Unhand me, you moron!'

'I don't know about you, Mick,' said one of the security guards, 'but I've 'ad it up to 'ere with these fuckers!'

'Too right mate!' said the one named Mick.

216

Having counted up to three for the very last time, the two began grabbing dissenters in whatever way they could. One picked on a diminutive woman in a knitted beret who deliberately fell limp as he dragged her to the exit. The other struggled to effect a half-nelson on the lady in the boiler suit, but was defeated by a mighty right cross which knocked him to the floor.

The Fangos had by now surrounded their hero Godfrey Privett in a protective arc. Arms linked, in line abreast, they gazed implacably out at the mob. Enraged by their preposterous sense of importance, a feisty little lady began pummelling the largest of them, who shook like a jelly much to Feltz's amusement. 'Sort 'er out, girl!' he yelled in encouragement.

'For Crissake do something, Dickie!' screamed the director, opening the window of his control booth. 'You're out of control down there!'

Torment stood up. He shouted at everyone to return to their seats. But nobody listened. His hawkish posture, normally so compelling, was now utterly ineffectual except to encourage some of the 'law-abiding' types in the audience to come to his aid.

Within seconds the scene descended into total chaos as people ploughed in, tripping over cables and knocking into cameras in a furious push to get some action. Technicians, desperate to protect their equipment, lashed out at the invaders at will.

'Jeez!' cried Feltz. 'It's crazy out there!'

'Where's Matt?' Holly shouted.

'If he has any sense, he's already outa there!'

Then Holly saw Matt jump up from the melee of flailing arms onto the panel table. He held his arms high in an appeal for calm. But the crowd wanted none of it; forcing their way through the Fangos, they surged towards him, reaching up to touch him, their faces hot with adulation.

'Well, bugger me!' exclaimed Feltz. 'Feast your eyes on that! They love 'im! The guy's an instant celebrity!'

Matt leant down to shake the hands of his admirers and accept their blessings. He was their conquering hero. Holly looked on, concerned for his safety.

'What's happening now?' shouted Feltz, distracted by a kerfuffle at the back of the auditorium.

Holly followed his gaze. The double doors at the entrance had flown open. She stood on tiptoe for a better view. Some pretty ugly-looking men were pouring in. 'It's guys in riot gear.'

'Riot gear?' said Feltz with dread. 'Must be the IRU!'

He was right. An Instant Response Unit had been called in by Cityvision. Feltz gazed at the sinister men in black and was terrified. 'They're the real hard men!' he said, quivering.

Following a moment of rapid appraisal, the unit's five men zipped up their jackets and adjusted the chinstraps on their helmets. Then, with jaws firmly clamped, they charged down the aisle towards the set, twirling their batons with menacing zeal. On entering the fray, they began dispatching anyone who happened to be at hand with adroitly placed blows to the head. Pleas of 'Oi! I work 'ere, mate!' counted for nothing.

'Get stuck in, lads!' urged their leader. 'An' no pussy-footin' abaht!'

Holly was shocked by their brutality. 'Quick!' she cried. 'We have to get Matt out of there.'

Feltz followed her, making no attempt to hide his fear. The two made their way close to where Matt was holding court like an emperor.

'Will you look at the prick!' exclaimed Feltz, watching Matt glorying in the pawing attentions of his admirers, oblivious of the punishment being meted out all around.

'Matt! Matt!' Holly called. To her astonishment, she had to call several times before he deigned to turn round.

'Come on!' yelled Feltz, catching his eye. 'Plod's on the warpath. Can't you see?'

'Yeah, I know!' Matt shouted back. Then, with an innocence as if his life was charmed: 'But they're not after me!'

Feltz was astonished. 'You twat!' he bawled. 'D'you think they give a toss who you are?'

Torment swivelled to face Feltz. 'Relax!' he shouted. 'Matt'll be fine. He's with me!'

'This is unbelievable!' Feltz cried. He knew danger when he saw it. 'Goddamned unbelievable!'

'Matt, come on down!' Holly pleaded. 'We've got to get out of here!'

Matt turned back to the crowd, but in a matter of seconds the reality of his position struck home. Not only were bloodied heads now clearly visible, but a man in a helmet, his face concealed by a black visor, was going to extraordinary lengths to reach him. The force of his passage through the crowd was leaving wounded people in its wake, clutching arms and heads in dismay.

Glancing to his right, Matt saw that Godfrey Privett had already seized his chance to leave. In the company of two Fangos, the man was down on all fours, scuttling off the set, desperate not to be seen. 'Jesus!' muttered Matt. 'I've gotta go!' With admirers still tugging at his jeans, he lept from the panel table and ran to Holly's side, his clothing in temporary disarray. 'God,' he said. 'That was pretty close.'

'You're insane!' Holly scolded him. 'You could've have been badly hurt.'

'Yeah, beaten to a pulp!' added Feltz, relieved to have his protégé safe.

'Let's get out of here before those bastards lay into us too.' Reaching for Matt's hand, Holly pulled him away and together they ran for the exit. Feltz hurried along after them.

'Pathetic!' muttered Torment as he saw Matt disappear. He had been timing things for a grand finale; in the closing seconds of the show he was going to leap up and join Matt on the table; the credits would roll on Torment himself, his arm around Matt's shoulders: his discovery, his 'star'. Now, with a minute to go, there was only mayhem and bloody heads; sensational maybe, but hardly a moment of media history. What a letdown!

But he had not reckoned with the zeal of the I.R.U. As the only camera left working closed in, a huge and beefy I.R.U. man got him in a headlock. Torment struggled, but was powerless to stop the man's other gloved hand from mercilessly entwining itself into what was arguably the most expensive hot-curled coiffeur on TV.

From the safety of the corridor Holly and Matt paused to watch the denouement. 'Look!' Matt exclaimed. 'They've got Torment!'

Bent down in the I.R.U. man's grip, the presenter was manhandled towards the exit. Zooming in on his backside was the only camera left working, gleefully catching the scene.

'I'm Richard Torment! Let me go!' shouted the great man.

The human brute tightened his grip. 'Shut the fuck up! An' let's be 'avin' yer!'

Holly called Feltz back to witness the sight. 'Bernie, come back! This you gotta see!'

Feltz trotted back reluctantly. 'Hell, what now?' he puffed. Pushing between Holly and Matt, he joined in their astonishment as Torment was booted viciously into a back room, his humiliation complete. The door closed behind him with a bang. Another I.R.U. man appeared; the two flicked up their visors and one took a packet of cigarettes from his pocket.

'Oi, who's Torment?' he asked, offering his colleague a cigarette.

'Search me, guv,' the other man said. 'Never heard of the bugger.'

SIXTEEN

Holly was more affected by Cyril's death than Matt expected. 'I should have taken him home,' she said. She blamed herself ever since the moment she listened in horror to an appeal for information concerning an elderly man found dead on the pavement a short distance from Holland Park Villas.

'Look,' said Matt for the umpteenth time, 'no amount of recrimination will bring him back.'

Now, as they stood outside the chapel, all that remained was the question of what should be done with Cyril's ashes. The man from the funeral parlour offered several suggestions. Holly could call for them in a couple of days; or, if she preferred, he would make arrangements to see they were scattered there in the Garden of Remembrance.

Holding back tears, Holly chose the latter. 'But not on the lawn,' she stipulated. 'In a flower bed. He loved flowers, you see.'

'Quite, Madam. As you wish.' The man backed away respectfully, conscious that he had impinged on her grief. But the question had to be asked of someone – and Cyril had no traceable family.

'I can't believe we're the only people who came,' said Holly. But this was so – apart from the curate, who worked alternate Saturdays on a roster. And even the curate was keen to get away, feeling through his cassock for the whereabouts of his cycle-clips whilst conveying an air of reverential gloom.

'My deepest condolences,' he said, slowly retreating to the vestry to change.

Matt felt a lump in his throat. 'Poor Cyril,' he said, looking sadly at Holly. 'Nobody giving a shit.'

'Don't!' she said. She was shocked by the lack of any flowers apart from her own. She had sent a little bouquet carrying the message: 'To Cyril. With Love, Holly Tree.'

'I thought some official might tip up from the palace,' said Matt. 'You know, *noblesse oblige* and all that.'

Holly shook her head. 'Not these days. Besides, I don't think Cyril was important enough. Anyway it's years since he worked there.'

Matt put an arm round her shoulder. 'You more than made up for things by reading that little poem.'

'D'you think so?'

'He'd have loved that. It was one of his better ones.'

'It was an odd way to write, as if Time itself was talking,' Holly said.

'Perhaps he felt like Old Father Time himself,' said Matt. Then, reflectively: 'He was a bit of an anachronism, really.'

Holly couldn't disagree. She looked at the piece of paper in her hand, its wrinkles smoothed out for the occasion. She scanned the scrawled lines once more. 'This must have been the last thing he wrote,' she said.

'Lucky the police found it,' said Matt. 'Crumpled up in his pocket like that, it might have been thrown away.'

'I hope I read it well enough,' said Holly.

They walked down the drive past banks of rhododendrons, their leaves drooping in seeming tribute to the dead. Holly looked over her shoulder one last time. She imagined Cyril heading skywards with an angel at each elbow and mentally wished him Godspeed.

'At least it's a sunny day,' said Matt.

Back at No.17 they sat on the terrace steps thinking. It had been an extraordinary few days, the joy of success in his television debut muted by tragedy.

Matt looked up at Cyril's flat. 'We should've known something was wrong, what with his window being open all that time.'

'Three whole days,' said Holly. She noticed it was now firmly closed, entombing his possessions behind a memorial of wilting pelargoniums.

'What will you do with his book of poetry?' Matt asked her.

Holly looked at him. 'What d'you think I should do?'

'Keep it,' said Matt. 'I'm sure he'd have wanted you to. I mean, what's the alternative? If you take it back to his flat, it'll only be at the mercy of the house clearance guys.'

'You're right,' said Holly. Her sympathy for Cyril outweighed the wrongfulness of keeping something that didn't belong to her.

'Anyway, if you took it back you'd have to meet that geezer Gittins again.'

'Urgh!' said Holly. 'The stuff of nightmares.'

'Exactly,' said Matt, amused by her grimace.

Cyril's cremation was the second Holly had attended in a year. The first had been Uncle Henry's. 'It makes you think,' she said. 'When someone dies, I mean.'

'Yeah,' said Matt. He was surprised by Holly's sensitivity. It was a side he had not seen. 'It reminds you what's round the corner for us all.'

'I never want to grow old,' said Holly. Her thoughts flashed back to Uncle Henry's last days, when he had refused all medication. Demons were giving him nightmares the like of which he'd never known. They'd finished him off as he lay groaning in his own bed, determined that home was the best place to die.

'Old age is so cruel,' she went on. She half-smiled at Matt: 'I can't imagine you as an old man.'

'Perhaps I never will be,' said Matt with a maudlin look. Long ago he'd promised himself he'd never reach that grisly stage. No, better dispatch himself than face its monstrous debilitations.

'Fool! Of course you will.'

'You don't know that. I might fall under a bus!'

'How boring,' Holly teased. 'You'll have to do better than that.'

'OK,' he said, grinning. 'How about doing a Jimmy Garridge?'

'Crashing? Yeah, that's cool,' said Holly. 'Kind of heroic.'

'Right, that's it then!' said Matt, ruminating on how Jimmy's early death had magnified his significance.

Holly looked fondly into his eyes. 'You're a prat,' she said. She had a soft spot for his vanity and it made her smile. 'But don't bump yourself off yet. Not now you've got all this lolly!'

'No way!' Matt smiled. Feltz had just given him a cheque for a little under fourteen thousand pounds. It was by far the biggest he'd ever banked.

'What will you do with it?' she asked him.

Looking up at the sky, Matt admitted he hadn't given the matter much thought. For the moment, simply having money was a big enough buzz in itself.

'There's one thing you must do,' she said.

'Yeah?' said Matt, guessing what she had in mind.

'Get yourself some decent clothes.'

To her surprise, he nodded in agreement. 'Yeah, I might just do that,' he said. He was thinking back to his appearance on Torment Tonight, when Willie Fitz's creation had set him apart and imbued him with confidence and power.

Holly encouraged him further: 'After all, you're somebody now.'

'Yeah,' Matt grinned. 'I suppose I am.' He remembered standing on the panel table, receiving the tributes of the crowd. 'You know, I can't think what got into me on that show.'

Holly chuckled. 'Well, whatever it was, it went down a storm. You really spelt it out!'

But that was Matt all over, she thought to herself. He was either off the scale or stuck fast at the bottom, racked by self-doubt.

Matt smiled. 'And I got Bernie off the hook!' The Council for Moral Issues had dropped its case after the show; suddenly Matt was perceived as a positive moral force and the Council would have shot itself in the foot by pursuing him. 'He's cock-a-hoop.'

'I bet he is!' said Holly.

'Says he's going to rub the bastards' noses in it.'

'What a berk!'

'That's what I told him,' said Matt. 'Forget them, move on.'

'Exactly. He's got enough on his plate as it is, with Cityvision getting all these calls. They told me this morning they've had over twenty thousand, nearly all people wanting to know where they can buy the T-shirt.'

'That's incredible!' said Matt.

Ill-prepared for such a massive response, Feltz had been rushing about for days negotiating licensing deals. Manufacturers were anxious to get in on what was generally perceived to be the next big thing. Christened the 'RIOT phenomenon' in the press, it was taking the nation by storm. A leader in *The Times* that very morning had pronounced the educated verdict: 'Mollycoddled into insensibility by decades of liberal nannying, the public is reacting with a call to traditional values and standards. The politicians should take heed, for it is worrying for all of us when political ends are pursued outside political means.' But it was a forlorn hope to expect more than a few dozen people to pay any attention to advice of that kind, especially when power and large quantities of money were up for grabs.

* * *

The next morning Holly walked into the gallery to find Feltz at his desk, feverishly hammering away at a calculator.

'Jeez!' he said, scarcely bothering to look up. 'Matt's so hot, you need a fire-suit to go near him. The deals I'm lining up – you wouldn't believe it!'

Holly sat herself down. 'Great,' she said. 'Like what?'

Feltz leant forward to impart the good news. 'To start with, the T-shirts. I've got this wholesaler guy who wants to do a run of a million!'

'Wow!' squealed Holly. 'A million?'

'Yeah, a million!' Feltz assured her. 'I tell you, that image has put Matt on the map. He's a cult figure now. People are busting a gut to jump on the bandwagon. And all thanks to my getting him on Torment Tonight!'

Typical Bernie, Holly thought to herself; self-congratulatory as ever. But a million! The word bounced around in her mind like a jolly beach ball.

'What's an order like that worth?' she asked.

'At retail prices? Well, say twelve quid a shirt – about twelve mill.' Feltz salivated at the thought of the chunky commission he'd earn.

'Matt's going to be rich,' said Holly.

Feltz cautioned her: 'Yeah, but he doesn't get all that!'

'I know. But he gets a fair slice of the cake.' After thinking for a moment, she added: 'As will Libby, I suppose; and me too, come to think of it.'

Feltz looked up in astonishment. 'You? And Libby? What on earth makes you think that?' Cakes can be shared, he thought, but this is going a couple of slices too far.

'In case you've forgotten, Libby painted the face,' Holly reminded him. 'And it's my photograph, isn't it?'

Feltz had the uncomfortable feeling he was on sticky ground. 'But you said you wouldn't charge me!' he said, as if deeply hurt. 'And as for Libby, I thought she made Matt's face up for fun, like.'

Holly re-appraised him. 'Sure we did it for free,' she said. 'But it's still our copyright, isn't it? Fun or no fun.'

Feltz was boxed in and he knew it. 'Yeah, yeah! Get to the point,' he said huffily.

'Don't be like that! All I'm saying is that three of us worked on the idea, so three of us should benefit.'

Feltz scowled. Unable to think of a way out, he realized he'd have to cut the girls in. 'OK, OK, I get the message. I'll see you both right.' Then, as a sop to himself for having come to this painful decision: 'I mean, there'll be plenty to go round.'

'Yes. It's a big enough cake, after all,' Holly said, smiling at how Feltz must be seething inside.

'Bloody copyright!' he cursed under his breath as she left the room. 'Who'd have thought she knew anything about that?'

SEVENTEEN

Two months after appearing on 'Torment Tonight', Matt was back in his studio. He was intending to get back to work, but looking around he found little to inspire him. The place felt ransacked – dishevelled, unloved, untidy and all his work gone.

The exhibition had been a sell-out and for the first time in his life he had money in the bank. Lots of it. Yet he felt strangely flat. Was it just the solitude, after spending weeks in the public eye?

It had been a whirlwind of a time. Every day Feltz bombarded him with instructions: be here, be there, be everywhere. He was always facing questions: interviewers squeezed as much as they could from him about his life, his *raison d'être* and his hopes for the future. Journalists, curators, businessmen, even politicians – each had an angle to pursue. It seemed there was no one on earth who didn't want to talk to him.

Thank God for Holly, he thought, sitting in the gallery and filtering their calls. Otherwise he'd have gone mad. There were cranks too, who made abusive remarks then hung up. On top of that there were stalkers, celebrity junkies of both sexes wanting to 'get it on' with him. 'Anytime, anywhere, you name it and I'll be there!' one had said, having fooled Holly into passing him the phone.

'Jesus, what's with these people?' Matt had ranted.

'What it is to be wanted!' Holly had said. 'Come on! You have to see the funny side of it.'

Perhaps she was right, but even so!

He couldn't do without her now, he admitted to himself. That wasn't so with Feltz, who really pissed him off. To Feltz he was no more than a cash cow, to be milked for all he was worth.

They'd already had a row about it. Feltz was insistent that under the terms of his contract Matt had to make available his name – and his time 'as requested, within reason' – for promotional purposes. This was a broad commitment and it lay him open to an uncomfortable degree of exploitation.

Endorsing a new range of face paints was one of many propositions he'd had to consider.

'Stuff that!' Matt had shouted, storming grandly from the gallery. Later in the day he had second thoughts: he called up Holly to ask if she thought he'd been a fool.

'Well, put it this way,' she'd said. 'I had a peek at the offer. There's fifty thousand smackers on the table.'

'Jesus! Is that what it's worth? I had no idea.'

'No, because you flew off in a rage before Bernie could tell you.'

His change of heart had followed quickly. After all, turning down such a sum would be wholly unreasonable. Moreover, it would be snobbish and ungrateful to a company whose products had helped put him in the public eye.

He pinned a fresh piece of paper to his drawing board. There was something wonderfully clean about its surface. He ran his hand over it, pure and smooth and white. But his pleasure at working once again with familiar materials was tinged with horror at how much work he'd need to do before even a single completed picture would see the light of day. His old familiar working practice was to sketch out ideas, then pace up and down thinking how to turn them into finished work. Such subtleties of craft and contemplation could take him weeks, even months.

There was an irony here, he thought. When he had no money, time seemed less relevant. He could devote weeks to a single piece of work. The meagre amounts of money he had to find for rent and cheap food could be scraped together somehow. Now he was rich, those weeks of work seemed like an annoying obstacle between him and the admiration the work would bring him.

He put down his charcoal. How life had changed since his appearance on 'Torment Tonight'. Creativity was suddenly a different thing altogether – oddly demanding. He was an important artist and expectations were high. Yes, the pressure was on. What he did next had to be significant: nothing less than a triumph!

His thoughts turned to poor Cyril Pout, so out of step with the world. Diffidence had confined him to a world of his own. Matt recalled the evening spent listening to the old man's poetry. Cyril had surprised them: he'd expressed sentiments each of them could identify with. Then things had gone downhill and his navel-gazing had bored them all to tears.

And the very next day, Cyril was dead.

Matt thought of the crumpled piece of paper Holly had read from, the poem on Time: it was quite an original idea, being talked to like that by Time.

I could do something with Time, Matt thought. Something new, something conceptual. Art had changed – he should change with it. Sylvester had assured him he possessed 'that rarity, a liberated mind.' With an adoring public hanging on every word it was right for him to indulge himself and to let people experience for themselves what his 'liberated mind' came up with.

Time. How it enslaves us, he mused. Silly, really, when it's entirely neutral, even benign – unless we let it rule our lives.

Looking up at the old station clock hanging on the studio wall, he thought: if only we could forget all about it – cauterise the brain against its tyranny.

Taking a stepladder, he climbed up and examined the clock face. What if I were to remove the hands and blank out the numerals? he wondered. Eradicate all references to time: make time faceless.

Then, expanding on the thought, he decided it would be better still to blank out the entire wooden case, portico, pillars and all, by stippling it with a heavy white paint, so that all that remained would be the form of the clock – a clock but not a clock.

Yes, it would be symbolic of what time actually is, he thought. Something that in itself has nothing to say.

Stepping down to the floor, he called Holly up on his mobile to tell her his idea.

'You're a screwball!' she laughed.

'Oh!' said Matt, surprised. 'But think of the problems we face when we let time into our lives – cutting it up into hours and minutes, then into seconds and even right down to nanoseconds. That's when the trouble begins.'

Holly was confused. 'What trouble?' she asked.

'We constantly have to know what the time is,' he explained. 'It's an addiction.'

'You and your addictions!' Holly mocked him.

'But it's true!' Matt insisted. 'Time rules our lives by having us run around like blue-arsed flies.'

'But who's going to buy work like that?' Holly asked him. 'I mean, it's a joke, isn't it?'

'A joke?' said Matt, indignant.

'Well, it has to be, doesn't it?' said Holly. 'You're talking about a clock that doesn't tell the time.'

'Huh!' said Matt. 'But that's the whole point of it.'

Holly didn't argue, but she thought it was a pity he wanted to pursue a thought that would benefit no one.

'So what will you call it?' she asked him.

'*Now,*' he said.

'*Now*?'

'Yes, because when you think about it, that's what the time always is. Not an instant, like a quarter to this or a quarter past that, but, *now* – a continuum where the future becomes the past even as we speak. Try to catch it and you can't.'

'Oh,' said Holly, imagining people scratching their heads trying to puzzle out this esoteric nonsense. 'So what's Bernie going to say about an idea like that?'

'Bugger Bernie!' said Matt. 'If he wants more work, this is the kind of thing he's going to get! Sylvester says it's the future.'

'But Bernie's crying out for more paintings.'

'Well, he ain't going to get 'em!' Matt said, aggressively. 'The studio's cleared out.'

'Are you sure?'

'Yeah. He's had the lot. Even the junk!'

'I thought you had several stacked behind the bed.'

'No,' said Matt. 'That was the stuff I was going to re-work, remember? But Bernie insisted I bring it in. To show potential buyers, because he'd run out of stock.'

'Oh, shit!' said Holly, recollecting. 'Those must be the two he sold yesterday.'

'Oh, no,' groaned Matt.

'Sorry, I meant to tell you. But with so much going on, I forgot.'

'Bernie's a sod,' said Matt. 'No conscience whatsoever.'

'I know,' said Holly. She refrained from telling him how over-the-moon Bernie's customers had been being 'given the chance to acquire such a unique artist's work'; and how grateful they were to Feltz for 'persuading the artist to part with them.'

'Honestly,' Matt said. 'He doesn't give a monkey's, does he?'

'No!' admitted Holly.

'He'd sell any old shit!'

'Well, your shit is hot!' Holly joked.

'Ha, ha,' said Matt. It seemed that control of his career was slipping from his grip. 'Things are getting out of hand.'

Holly could hardly disagree. Working at her desk in the gallery, she'd listened to Feltz talking up Matt's name on the phone as if he were the saviour of civilization – nothing less than a Messiah.

'He's furthering your career,' she said. 'At least, that's what he says.'

'Lining his wallet, more like!'

'Yours too!' Holly reminded him, lest a bout of self-righteousness carry him away. 'The T-shirt deal alone will bring you eighty grand – and that's after Bernie's cut.'

Matt felt ashamed. Holly was right. 'Well, you and Libby will get something out of it, too,' he said, defensively.

'Yeah, but only thanks to me! Otherwise we'd have got sweet F.A.'

'Let's not talk about money,' said Matt, feeling the tentacles of avarice seeking to entwine them. 'It screws up everything.'

'I agree,' Holly said. 'So when are you going to spring this clock thing on Bernie?'

'*Thing*?' he said, insulted. 'It'll be a sculpture!'

'OK, sculpture!'

Matt thought for a moment. 'I don't know whether I'll tell him about it.'

'What d'you mean?'

'I might offer it to Sylvester,' said Matt. He was half-watching a spider as it sucked out the insides of a fly. 'It's right up The Rich's street.'

'Bernie'll kill you,' Holly said.

'No, he won't. He'll still get his cut, it's in my contract.'

'So why not let him handle the sale?'

''Cos he got so bloody bolshy when I told him I was pissed off with painting and wanted to work on something new.'

'Yeah,' said Holly. 'Only yesterday he was bellyaching to me about that.'

'I bet he was!' said Matt with feeling.

'He says you don't understand the importance of continuity.'

'I know, I know,' said Matt impatiently, 'I've heard it all before – 'it's what the market likes to see' and all that. Well, sod the bloody market! I'm not a performing seal.'

'OK, OK,' said Holly, to calm him.

'Anyway, I figure if Sylvester buys the work it'll shut Bernie up. I won't have the hassle any more of trying to justify my change of direction.'

At least there was logic in that, Holly thought, even if his change of direction was a bad thing – though she'd keep her feelings to herself on that. Matt was hell-bent on pursuing it, so she'd bide her time and see what transpired.

But she saw an ill omen in Matt turning towards Sylvester. Sylvester's flattery was making him over-confident. Any idea for new work he came up with was now the sacrosanct pronouncement of genius. She'd already tried to warn him: 'Sylvester's a cold fish, can't you see he's using you?' But her words had fallen on deaf ears.

'Hey listen,' said Matt, noticing the sun's mid-morning trapezium emblazoned on the studio wall. 'I'd better get down to some work!'

'Yeah, I must go too,' said Holly. 'Bernie'll be back soon.'

'Where's he been this time?' Matt asked.

'He was meeting some publisher for breakfast, then he was off to a printer's.'

'Hell,' said Matt. 'Will he ever stop?'

'I doubt it,' said Holly. 'He's really fired up.'

'It's a wonder he doesn't overheat and blow up!'

Holly chuckled. 'Look, I'll see you later,' she said.

'Sure,' said Matt. He noticed the spider again: it had now completely eviscerated its prey. The fly was a husk.

'Love you,' said Holly.

'Yeah, you too,' said Matt. Hanging up the phone, he pondered how his early doubts had vanished and his love for her had grown. As for Holly – even at parties she always returned to his side. That was a sure sign, he reckoned, of an altogether deeper relationship, free of uncertainty and the confusing aberrations of wayward promiscuity.

EIGHTEEN

It was late October, six months into the 'game' as Feltz liked to call it. Matt was sitting at a junction in his gleaming Porsche Cabrio. He grinned at a fan approaching for an autograph. Before he could oblige, the lights went green, forcing the man to jump back on the pavement and curse his bad luck.

'Another time!' Matt called to him, as he slammed into first and roared off.

And there would be other times, too – if not for that fan, then for others. Autograph hunters seemed to pop up out of nowhere, wherever he went.

He peered through his wrap-around shades in search of admiring glances. Posing? The thought never entered his head.

Turning off Holland Park Avenue into a side street, Matt came to a halt in a cul-de-sac of lock-ups. He blipped the accelerator one more time and thrilled at the engine's roar. Then he pressed his remote to raise the garage door and tucked the beast away for the night.

Smiling to himself, he pocketed his keys and walked the short distance to 17 Holland Park Villas. The odd nights he stayed there had now turned into weeks and Holly had decided life would be simpler if he moved in.

She met him as he entered the hall.

'Libby's gone!' she cried, tearfully.

Matt collected her in his arms. 'Gone? What d'you mean?'

'She left this letter.'

He looked down at the tear-stained notepaper in her hand. Oh, that sort of gone, he thought to himself. A genuine 'Dear John'.

Holly pulled him into the drawing room. 'When I got back, she'd left it in front of the clock.'

'What does it say?' he asked.

'Stuff about how she knew I loved you, and her being in the way...'

'Jesus,' said Matt. 'I never meant to...'

'It's not your fault.'

'I know, but...' said Matt, sitting down on the sofa.

Holly sat down beside him. 'She says she doesn't see any future with me.' Then, sobbing into his shoulder: 'But she says she'll always love me.'

'Oh, shit!' said Matt, her tears playing on his own sensitivities. 'She must really hate me.'

Holly wiped her eyes. 'It's not like that, I promise. This was bound to happen sooner or later. But I hadn't thought it would be just yet. You know?'

'Sure,' said Matt. Lately Libby had been reluctant to join them when, on the odd occasion, they ate in. 'It seemed to me recently she was a bit off sometimes, like she was in a moody. I thought it was probably to do with me.'

'No. If anything, she fancies you. At least, she used to.'

'Used to?' said Matt, his pride dented.

Preoccupied with sorrow, Holly failed to notice his offence. 'She reckons you've changed.'

'Changed?'

'Yeah. She said it's since you started earning all this money. Buying that car and things.'

'Oh, that,' said Matt, shaking his head resignedly. 'Yeah, that went down like a lead balloon.' Petrol consumption, despoiling the natural world – but those were *her* hang-ups.

Holly managed a little smile. 'She hated it. Said you'd become one of 'them'.'

'Oh yes? Anything else?' Matt asked.

'She said you'd lost your soul.'

That comment stung. 'Can I see the letter?'

'Sure,' said Holly, handing it over. 'It's not *all* about you, you know!'

He read the letter slowly and painfully. Her comments about him were all the more troubling because they were affectionate and admonishing rather than vindictive; they did not blame him for chasing her out.

'Matt's a great guy, but fame has changed him,' he read out loud. 'Once, his work really said something. Now it doesn't any more.'

Matt handed the letter back. 'What's she getting at?'

'It's something she's been banging on about for a while,' said Holly. 'She thinks you sold out.'

'Why? I'm doing the work I want!'

'Yeah, but she thinks you should be painting. Not doing all this other stuff.'

'Other stuff?' Matt said, indignantly.

'She calls it conceptual crap.'

'That's *her* opinion!' said Matt, now thoroughly miffed. 'Conceptualism's the genre of the age, for Crissake!'

'I'm only telling you what she said.'

'Well I wish you'd told me before!'

'I didn't think you'd want to know,' said Holly. Her real reason for not telling him was his sensitivity to criticism. 'I mean, everything's going so well for you now.'

That was true. There were Feltz's triumphs on the licensing front and Sylvester Rich had snapped up his two latest sculptures. *Now!* was, according to Sylvester, 'a work of pure genius! It'll stop people in their tracks'. The other piece was called *Memorial*. A gigantic pile of dead leaves shaped into a cone, it was inspired by another of Cyril Pout's poems. Its subject was the passing seasons and it 'brought tears to people's eyes', so the gallery attendants told him.

Most exciting of all, Sylvester had taken to commissioning him direct, granting him free rein to utilize an entire hall in the Rich Gallery. His only stipulation was that whatever Matt chose to do should be in the gallery tradition of being 'open to all means of expression'.

Bearing in mind the strength of Sylvester's backing, Matt felt justified in resenting Libby's disapproval. 'Yeah, well,' he said huffily, 'there's no pleasing everybody, is there?'

'True,' admitted Holly.

'I still can't see exactly what it is she's objecting to,' he said, getting up from her side.

'She says your work's become banal.'

'Sylvester doesn't think so. He paid twenty grand for my clock piece, and another twenty-five for the leaves. And look at what I'm going to get for *Woolly Aeroplane*! Fifty grand!'

'I know,' said Holly. She thought fifty thousand pounds was an inordinately large sum of money for a section of windowless fuselage with a womblike woolly interior in which people were invited to sit. The absolute silence of the interior was apparently 'totally appropriate for a cacophonous age'. Silence as art? What a frig!

'All she's saying is that when you were painting you had passion. A cause.'

'Oh, great! And now I don't, I suppose!'

'*I* don't think that!' said Holly, wanting to avoid war. 'What you're doing now is, well – just different.' She kept to herself what Libby had actually said: '*Woolly Aeroplane*! Anyone would think he'd O.D.'ed – on laughing gas.'

Matt stood at the window in a grouch of hurt pride. Presumably Libby was equally hostile to his plans for his space in the Rich Gallery. He proposed to create an *If Room*, an installation celebrating supposition and possibility, encouraging viewers to open their minds to all the things art can be.

'Did you tell her about my *If Room* idea?'

'Yes, and she said she couldn't see the point.'

'I'd have thought the point was obvious,' said Matt. "If" is the precursor to everything. A hugely significant word! I mean, everything follows on from it! If this, if that… What if? And if what?… It's not just a question, it also presupposes the demands of action.'

'But why theme an entire room around a word?'

'Impact!' said Matt. 'It'll make people think.'

'About what?' Holly asked, not wanting to sound too much like the little girl who pointed out that the Emperor was wearing no clothes.

'Well, whatever,' said Matt, opening up his arms to the galactic enormity of prospective thought.

'Yeah, whatever,' said Holly with a sigh. His interpretation was so vague it left her bemused. She didn't want to admit, even to herself, how close she was to agreeing with Libby: she thought his new work, airy-fairy in concept and huge in size, reflected a growing self-indulgence, the very thing he'd railed against only a few months ago on *Torment Tonight*. 'Get Real?' Libby had said. 'It's like he'd never even heard his own words!'

Holly worried that if Matt had to choose between vanity and love for her, vanity would win. He was in the grip of it now – puffed up and flying high. The thought brought on fresh tears.

'Libbs thinks you're becoming a pseud,' she said, the comment bursting out. Then, to temper the blow, she joked: 'And if it isn't that – well, you're off your trolley.'

'Huh, and that coming from her!' Matt stared moodily into the street. 'Let me tell you, Sylvester's really sold on the *If Room* idea.'

'I think that's her point,' said Holly.

Matt turned about sharply to face her. 'What d'you mean?'

Holly feared a row, but things had reached a point where they were better out than in.

'Libby said Sylvester exhibited human shit at the Rich and it was considered art.'

The words seemed so offensive, Holly dreaded his reaction. But to her relief, Matt wasn't offended.

'Yeah, people are always bringing that up,' he said. 'It's just spite. They don't understand the significance of context.' This sort of criticism was nothing new and as Sylvester's protégé it was his duty to ignore it. Libby was probably jealous; but Holly had no reason to be. 'So what do *you* think?' Matt asked her. He looked at her directly, suddenly assailed by doubt. Could it be true – had he made it to the top only to succumb to the temptations of money and Sylvester's praise? Had he been a fool?

Holly was evasive. Matt was now a success. Who was she to judge his work? The pressures on him were huge. Besides, there was something sexy about his success – and about his vulnerability. Above all, she wanted to keep him. 'Come and sit down here,' she said, patting the cushion at her side. 'I can't talk while you're over there.'

Matt did as he was bidden. 'Hey, what's this?' he protested, as she slipped her hand inside his shirt.

'I'll tell you what I think,' she said, working at his flesh with her fingers. 'Someone is taking himself a teeny bit too seriously.'

'Yeah, well,' said Matt, struggling to keep a straight face. But it was useless. Within a minute, lust had barged up on deck and was demanding a turn at the helm.

'Ooh!' said Holly, breaking into a giggle.

'Oh sod it!' thought Matt, his mood overridden by a fundamental urge. They would have plenty of time to make love; Rollo Leaf wasn't due for at least a couple of hours.

Later that night Matt lay awake, unable to sleep. He had taken to waking up in the small hours and thinking over his life. By nature he was inclined to sink into introspection, but during waking hours he was rarely allowed to. Apart from Holly's insatiable libido there were endless parties, either at Holly's house or with friends whose take on life was equally sybaritic.

Sex, Drugs and Rock 'n Roll were now a long-established part of the Bohemian tradition. But the impulse behind them had changed. In the early days, they were part of the quest for hope and freedom. Now the future was full of fear, and the quest was not so much for enlightenment as for blotting out past, present and future together in a buzzing confusion of sensation. The rhythm and harmony of rock 'n' roll had morphed too, into a perpetual drug-confused cutting-edge lament.

That night Matt lay awake wondering why he joined in the orgy of self-obliteration. It wasn't as if he needed to. Doors were open for him everywhere – invitations falling like confetti, their path a fast track to opportunity.

Holly was the reason. He didn't want to lose her. They were a pair; she was carefree and jolly and he was moody, a reactionary and a dreamer rolled uncomfortably into one.

But he was troubled by their conversation earlier that evening and by Libby's dismissal of him. Was he himself anymore, or was he just playing a part? Was he an actor high on self-regard, so at the epicentre of his own conceit that he does not even notice it? Blinking in the darkness, with Holly fast asleep at his side, his thoughts drifted back to his childhood. It gave him comfort. It was solid ground, known facts, a familiar story.

His had been a simple upbringing. The family house was a tiny hive of industry living on hope and occasional bequests from his mother's extended family – bachelor uncles, forgotten cousins and old aunts they had hadn't seen for years. Whatever creative skills he had he owed to his parents. His mother's passion for flower studies had given him an eye for detail and his father's preference for sculpture, an understanding of form.

Their art had earned them little and it was a source of great satisfaction for Matt that he could now send them money. They rather disapproved of his gifts: they felt there was a certain virtue in poverty and he was careful not to overdo his generosity. But he had noticed as a child that, though they considered money vulgar, they were always grateful for its blessings. Each little dollop from the dead would be greeted as 'the relief of Mafeking'.

With Matt still a teenager, they had retreated to an island off the coast of Scotland to escape the modern world. Nowadays his mother was too ill to travel so they'd been unable to partake directly in his success and he was spared their reactions. What they would think of his new work? He did not want to know.

Perverse to the end, they were among the last of their kind, he thought – the art for art's sake generation. How lucky they were; they had to struggle, sure, but their conscience was always happy and clear.

He recalled the mish-mash of schools he'd attended. At first they'd been private; small-minded and oppressive maybe, but protective. When the family funds dried up he'd been surrendered to the State. The last place he attended was the pits, he remembered – a hellhole devoid of all decency, where betterment was frowned upon in order that the crude and the crass could feel at ease.

Matt's generation was the first in the family for a century or more not to be born with the promise of a worthwhile inheritance. This gave Matt the feeling of having been cast adrift in a coracle, its worrying fragility imbuing him with a sense of unease. There was no one *he* could look to for dollops of money or even for emotional support – his cousins, aunts and uncles were all far too busy scrabbling for their own survival. His years in London before meeting Holly had been dogged by fear and loneliness.

Dormant for the most part, his insecurity would suddenly emerge, rampaging through his psyche like a whirlwind.

Is Libby right? he asked himself. Have I become another opportunist cashing in on celebrity? That he could even ask the question was cause enough for concern.

Suddenly Holly's voice sounded clear as a bell in the darkness. 'You're awake, aren't you?'

'Yeah.'

'So am I.'

'You don't say!' Matt chuckled.

'I keep waking up,' she said, feeling for his hand. 'It must be all that black coffee.'

'I reckon so,' said Matt. They'd knocked back a lot, keeping themselves awake for hours of 'meaningful dialogue' after the publisher Rollo Leaf left. Rollo had dropped by for a discussion with Matt about his forthcoming autobiography. He'd found the business of the evening extended when Holly persuaded him to have a look at her portfolio.

It had certainly been worth it. Leaf became more impressed at each turn of the page.

'You're not just a one-off wonder, are you?' he'd said to Holly, alluding to her portrait of Matt. 'In fact, most of your faces are quite brilliant!'

One thing had led to another. He suggested a collaboration with her on a book of portraits – a hundred, maybe, in glossy coffee-table format.

'How exciting!' she'd squealed. 'We could get it out for Christmas!' But Leaf saw a problem with that; apart from Matt, all the other faces were unknowns. 'Not a good thing if you're after high-volume sales. We need names: household names, whose celebrity will guarantee a market.'

Forced to confess she knew nothing like a hundred celebs, Holly had found herself pulling a long face. The effect on Leaf was electrifying.

'That's it!' he cried. 'You little beauty!' Leaping to his feet, he rushed to kiss her. She recoiled in amazement.

'What are you on about?' Matt asked.

'Gurning!' Leaf explained. 'You know – pulling faces.'

'Yes? But who?' Holly had asked.

'Celebrities, of course!' Leaf had exclaimed. 'It's one hell of a gimmick! A book of a hundred celebrities, all pulling faces!'

'But they wouldn't like that, would they?'

'Of course they would! They do it all the time, crossing their eyes and tonguing the air like loons on the loose. You know – 'I'm so beautiful I can afford to pull a face like this.''

'But I don't know a hundred celebs!'

'That doesn't matter a bit,' Rollo had said. 'Once I put the word out, they'll be falling over themselves to get in on the act. You know how they love to show off!'

Holly sat up in bed and switched on the light. 'Rollo's idea's great, don't you think?'

'Yeah,' said Matt. He was happy for her, but thought the project pretty tawdry.

'You know, I was thinking we could fix an exhibition to coincide with the launch of the book,' said Holly. 'I mean, this *is* art, isn't it?'

For Holly, here was the chance to confirm her reputation within the mainstream of contemporary photography. Even more importantly, it would counter her suspicion that people looked on her as little more than a groupie, the girl who'd got lucky on Matt Flight's back.

She rolled back towards him. 'I can't stop thinking about it,' she said. 'It'll be humungous fun!'

'Yeah,' said Matt, gazing at the ceiling. It would be fun. But was it art, as she would have it? Well, why not? She was only reflecting the culture of the times.

But what sort of culture places a value on such trivia? he asked himself. In an edifying moment, the truth struck. 'Crap culture! Crap art!' Four little words that were an indictment of the age, and one from which he could hardly expect to escape. He was a part of his age, at risk in the same way as every other artist alive of just adding more to the largest collection of contemporary junk the world had ever seen.

'What are you thinking now?' Holly asked him. His fidgeting silence told her something was still on his mind.

'I've got this feeling that Libby might be right.'

'Oh no,' said Holly. 'We're not back on that again, are we?'

'Well, she could have a point.'

Holly had a project of her own now and she was less inclined to be critical. She turned away from him and smiled.

'OK, OK,' she said, reaching to switch off the light. 'From now on just do what's right for *you*. Don't let Sylvester lead you by the nose. I mean, you've no need to. With this RIOT thing spreading like it is, you've got the world at your feet.'

'Yeah,' sighed Matt, Holly's words and his bitter indictment of the age churning in his mind.

NINETEEN

T here it is!' said Feltz from the depths of the stretch
limousine cruising a darkening freeway. 'New
York!'

To Matt, the grey geometric outline of the city looked
as if it was made of digital cells – a trillion tiny squares
and oblique lines. The only visible reminder of anything
beyond the works of Man was the sunset covering the
western horizon. But to Feltz it resembled a bar chart – a
measure of America's indefatigable spirit of 'Can do!'

'The Big Apple,' Holly said sadly. She felt as if she
was approaching a temple desecrated by vandals.

But Feltz was full of joy. 'It's still where it's at!' he
said brightly. Then with a mid Atlantic twang, 'So take a
big bite, baby!'

Matt sipped his bourbon and looked through the window, reflecting on the events of recent years that had laid
America low. Feltz was unconcerned, of course. That's
him all over, thought Matt. No sense of compassion, just
an eye for the main chance.

'It's great, isn't it?' said Feltz, watching Matt's face as
he took in the sights.

'It's just as I'd imagined,' said Matt. The huge struc-
ture replacing the Twin Towers was now almost complete. Its outline dominated a whole section of the skyline
and the giant cranes were still busy lifting.

Feltz, Holly and Matt were en route for Manhattan as guests of the multi-media conglomerate Globalcorp. The US government was funding Globalcorp's attempt to repeat the success of the RIOT campaign in America. A 'peacenik lobby of bleeding hearts' was undermining its activities as the world's policeman, blurring America's 'manifest destiny' with liberal scruples. America's enemies abroad were taking advantage and collaborating with domestic malcontents to subvert the country from within. Never was there a time when a slogan was more needed than now – 'Get Real!' – 'Get Real!' – 'Get Real!'

Feltz sat back enraptured, fingering his drink and dreaming about Hiram Grouper, President of Globalcorp. They would be meeting him next day to discuss licensing arrangements for the use of Matt's image and merchandise in every state in the Union.

Matt's campaign was to be part of a joint corporate and government attempt at uniting the country. The ramifications for Matt would be considerable. If things took off in the States, the movement would spread throughout the world. He had already been offered roles in blockbuster movies, saving planet Earth from rogue asteroids and the like. But Holly and Feltz had both told him to take things one at a time.

Holly gazed into his eyes. 'Kiss me,' she said, caught up in the romance of entering a place that was to each of them still the greatest city on earth. The perpendicular magnificence on the horizon was surely a gateway to experiences none of them would ever forget.

Matt put an arm around Holly's shoulders and kissed her. Relaxed by the Lincoln's soft and creamy-smooth ride, Holly's thoughts drifted back to when they'd first imagined covering the side of a building with Matt's image. How could anyone have believed then that their fantasy would become reality – and inside eighteen months!

'I can't wait till tomorrow,' she said. 'Imagine, your image a hundred and twenty foot high!'

'I'm not sure I want to,' said Matt. He was nervous at the prospect of confronting an alter ego on this scale – one that had all but taken over his life.

Holly squeezed his hand. 'It'll be awesome!'

Flushed with the success of her book *Funny Faces*, Holly was treating coming to New York as a bit of a holiday, a chance to wind down. She'd had her own share of media pressure since the launch of the book and the accompanying exhibition of photographs.

As expected, Godfrey Privett had panned it: 'An imbecilic exhibition of imbecilic people. Only Lagoon Art could have staged it.' Not that it mattered: limited editions of the photographs had sold well. As for orders for the book, well, Rollo Leaf had been ecstatic: 'If this isn't bound for the best seller lists, I'm a gnu!'

Yes, this was good time to be away, she felt – let things take their course.

Feltz was keen to get to their hotel, the infamous Godolphin on West 44th. If they were lucky with the traffic, there'd be time to freshen up, down a few Martinis, and enjoy dinner. Then after dinner there'd be a racy cabaret, which he certainly didn't want to miss. The star turn would be Trixie Katz, the cutest little songbird in town, whose risqué performances were currently the toast of Manhattan.

Holly had other ideas. She wanted to go via Times Square, just to get a feel for the place before the launch of Globalcorp's campaign on the morrow.

But Feltz was adamant. 'No point,' he said. 'The traffic's diabolical at this time of day.'

'Oh,' said Holly, disappointed.

'So what time's the meet with Grouper?' Matt asked.

'It's scheduled for breakfast tomorrow,' said Feltz. He pronounced 'scheduled' with a 'k' – one of many Americanisms he'd adopted since meeting Grouper. Other expressions he liked from 'across the pond' were 'it sucks', 'motherfucker' and 'bum steer'. For Feltz this was straight-talking – the mark of men who cut to the heart of the matter.

Feltz began boring them again with everything that impressed him about Grouper. 'Hiram's got this penthouse. The view's a knockout. And hey, the guy's got this *fabulous* art collection. Everything from the most up-to-date modern stuff right back to a sketch by Leonardo – I mean, phworr! Think of the lolly in that.'

Matt didn't doubt he was right. But they weren't here to take in the view or admire a collection of art, however highly valued. Rather, it was to finalize a deal about which Matt had growing reservations. In particular, he worried that Feltz, overawed in the presence of such opulence and power, had already been taken for a ride.

'The guy has a reputation for gobbling up minnows, you know,' Matt said. It was the third time he had expressed his concern in so many hours.

'Well, I ain't no bloody minnow, so relax! Like I told you on the plane, I can handle the guy.'

Matt watched unconvinced as Feltz puffed complacently at a cigar – always a sign there was some covert scheme afoot.

'Give me a break!' Feltz continued. 'Hiram's no problem. He's a regular guy. Always smiling.'

'I bet he is!' said Matt. He was deeply mistrustful of smiles, especially those following in the wake of an agreement. 'Well, let me tell you now,' he said. 'I'm not putting my name to anything until we've been through the contract with a fine toothcomb.'

Feltz became irritated. 'Come on, be reasonable!' he said. 'You have to give the guy his fair whack. I mean, he's organized the whole caboodle over here. The launch in Times Square, media coverage, the merchandise, you name it.'

'I accept that. But I don't want a repeat of when we had to serve an injunction on that PR agency. Against Globalcorp, that might not be so easy.'

'Yeah, well,' said Feltz, needled to be reminded of past failures.

'I mean, that was some loophole!' Matt pressed on.

'Alright, alright,' Feltz grumbled. 'This is old ground.'

Holly giggled, remembering how angry Matt had been. Feltz had given a company the right to print his image on packets of contraceptives, along with his slogan 'Get Real!'. The message was that with so many sexually transmitted diseases around, protection was a must. It wasn't the kind of thing Matt wished to be linked with.

Matt grinned. 'What a fuck-up that was, eh?'

Feltz emitted a noise indicating he was sinking into a major sulk. 'Better check the e-mails,' said Holly, reaching for her laptop as a timely diversion.

Most e-mails were greetings from fans, but there were also requests for him to speak at seminars and appear on chat shows and promotional events. Then there were appeals for money – some blatant, as if he had a moral duty to respond, and others more devious, like those couched as proposals to take part in joint ventures, each one portrayed as 'mutually beneficial, guaranteed'.

There were scary messages too, warnings from shady organizations and crazy individuals. He should back off; he was a threat to universal human rights and would be killed; he was a threat to progress; he was a murderer of the weak.

'Anything interesting?' he asked.

'No. Just the usual, really,' said Holly. It was her habit to dismiss anything unpalatable as just an inevitable consequence of celebrity.

Matt's trust in her judgement was absolute. After all, she'd seen through Sylvester way before he had and she'd torn him out of his clutches. Not that Sylvester cared. Artists were like the unemployed to him: there were queues of them, winding round the block. Lose one and another was right there, desperate for a break.

The limousine swept up to the Godolphin Hotel and it was surrounded immediately by reporters, photographers and cameramen all jockeying for position.

Feltz briefed Matt before he stepped out: 'Be civil, for Crissake. These hounds can make or break you.'

'Matt! Matt!' one shouted. 'Welcome to the US of A!'

They crowded in on him, all talking at once.

'Yo! Can you give us a few words?'

'Hey, who's the broad?' someone said as Holly stretched an elegant leg out of the limo.

'Nice one, Matt! Very foxy!'

'A real class act!'

'Lady, can you tell us your name?'

'Yeah, won't you give us a break?'

Holly took Matt's arm. Smiling behind her dark glasses she looked suitably gorgeous and mysterious for the flashing cameras. Feltz meanwhile had scrabbled round the car from the other side and he pushed in front of Holly: 'Leave the lady alone, will you!' he cried, peeved that the press were showing more interest in her than in him.

'Move over, fat boy! I wanna picture!' a photographer barked.

'Yeah, yuh dumb schmuck. Get yuh ass outa here!' added another.

Feltz backed to one side. 'Shit, I'm the guy's agent, for Crissake!' he cried. But his words were lost in the hullabaloo. A dozen microphones materialized in front of Matt's face.

'OK, OK, fellas, cool it!' Matt cried, hushing the throng with his hands. And when the hubbub had died down: 'First, let me say how great it is to be here. We look forward to working with you all.'

Murmurs of appreciation merged with a frenzy of flashes and whirring cameras which seemed to be bursting with excitement themselves.

'Matt! Matt! For Newsday!' A reporter piped up. 'What's the big picture here – is it true you're takin' over Times Square?'

Matt smiled. 'Be there tomorrow night and you'll find out!'

'Gee, that's one kind of stunt, Matt?' said a journo from CNN 'Are yuh gonna pull it off?'

'You bet!' said Matt. 'It's the launch of the RIOT campaign!'

'The 'Get Real!' thing?'

'Right!'

'Hey, Matt! For Time Magazine. Is this thing gonna go global?'

'With Globalcorp behind it!' said Matt. 'What do you think?'

'Global!' exclaimed the man. 'No question!'

'And now, fellas, please, we need to get to our room.'

Guffaws followed. 'Hey, what a guy!' one cried, nudging and winking at his neighbour. 'Yeah, he's really gonna tell it like it is!'

Feltz had already checked them in; Holly spied him sulking in the lobby. Throwing them a surly glance, he announced grumpily, 'I've sent the luggage up already.'

'Bernie, what happened?' Holly asked him, amused. 'You just vanished!'

'Some fucker shoved me aside!' He straightened his collar.

'You can't blame the guys for wanting Holly's picture,' Matt said.

'But I'm your agent, for Crissake!'

Matt put a hand on his shoulder, 'Maybe. But you're not half as pretty.'

'Ha, bloody ha!' said Feltz.

Feltz looked at his watch. It was ten o'clock. The last sitting for dinner had passed and the cabaret was about to begin. Taking advantage of their table's position – discreet and a little way back from the stage – he adjusted his chair to be first in line should the delectable Miss Katz decide to wiggle and jiggle her 'cute little booty' his way.

Hastily wiping the vestiges of a syllabub from his lips, he gave the small stage his full attention. The concierge had described Miss Katz as 'a broad with mazoomas like you've never seen, pal.' He couldn't wait!

'This is the moment!' he thought: but frustratingly, it was the hotel manager who appeared. Having extended a welcome to all in the room, he turned to face Matt. 'Ladies and gentlemen, I can't let this moment pass without extending a special welcome to Mr. Matt Flight.'

Tired from the journey, this was the last thing Matt wanted.

'Stand up!' whispered Feltz. 'They want to get a look at you.'

Reluctantly, Matt rose from his chair.

The manager respectfully bowed his head and continued: 'Over from the UK to promote his campaign, he is with us here t'night.' Then, looking around to rally the diners: 'Sir, on behalf of everybody here, may I wish you all the luck in the world. We in New York are especially mindful of how important your message is for the civilized world.'

Matt nodded and smiled, to general applause from the room.

'And now, ladies and gentlemen,' he went on. 'Will you give a big hand for that ol' favourite of yours and mine, Mickey Love, who's gonna kick off the entertainment t'night.'

Feltz was visibly annoyed. Having to sit through the routine of a stand-up comic was something he hadn't bargained for. Looking glum, he sat tapping at the tablecloth during the performance – an assortment of *double entendres* ending with a personalized rendition of *I Did It My Way* that tailed away on an extended and quavering bum note.

'God bless yuh all!' the man cried, skipping from the stage to a round of applause.

The manager re-appeared. 'And now, ladies and gentlemen, the lady you've all been waiting for! It is my pleasure to welcome a singer who, in a short space of time, has captured the hearts of Americans – and not just the heart!' Then after a deliberate pause: 'As any red-blooded male will testify!'

Raucous laughter followed from all and sundry.

'Get on with it!' muttered Feltz. Holly nudged Matt to take a look at Feltz, who was somewhat resembling a pug with its tongue hanging out.

'The lady in question,' said the manager, striving to be heard, 'is, o'course, is o'course, that regular tonic for the blues... MISSS – TRIX – EEEE – KATZZZZZ!'

The spotlight swung across the stage to discover the singer posed with hands on hips, peering under a fringe of blond hair hanging seductively over one eye.

'Phworr! Get a load of that!' Feltz said. What a vision of loveliness! Gold clothes, blonde hair and ivory skin, offsetting a Cupid kiss of glossy red – the sexiest little pout he'd ever seen.

Flicking her hips to an opening refrain, Trixie unhitched the mike from its stand. 'Hi!' she said, with calculated economy. Her sexy southern drawl was the envy of every woman in the room and the men applauded with gusto.

'Now,' she said, stretching her arms up high to reveal the beauty of her assets. 'What you all doin' starin' at lit'le ol' me?'

There was a roar of male appreciation. 'Naughty, naughty,' she went on. 'I know what yuh want, and it ain't just a priddy song now is it?'

'Shit! She's hot for it!' muttered Feltz. His heart was throbbing.

Holly looked at Matt, then back at Feltz. 'Men!' she thought. Pathetic and disgusting. They were both ogling. Trixie Katz, indeed – nothing but a tart up from Vegas!

Trixie walked over to the pianist and the spotlight followed in her wake. 'But, hey, *you* seen it all before, ain't yuh babe?' She brushed the pianist's cheek with the back of her hand. He cocked his head and smiled.

'Phworr!' Feltz muttered again, as she leant to kiss the man's forehead. Lucky sod, he thought – treated to a proverbial eyeful.

'You know, folks,' said Trixie, 'he's just the sexiest li'l piano man I know.'

The audience hollered.

'She's had a boob job,' Holly said. 'No real tits stick out like that!'

'No, they're for real!' Feltz said.

'They're implants!'

'Shush!' whispered Matt, conscious that their table was attracting attention.

Trixie sidled up to the bass player and stood behind him, fondling his thighs as he played. 'So how about you, Mr. Bass Man? Are you up for it?'

The bass player plucked his strings wildly in a frenzied simulation of lust. It was a trick the audience never failed to enjoy. Trixie laughed along while they whooped and whistled.

'Seriously folks,' she said, ambling back centre stage, 'won't you big it up for these guys? Ivan, my piano man, yeah? And, Leroy on bass, if yuh will – two bad, bad boys, I godda tell yuh!'

Laughter and applause filled the room as Trixie sashayed round the stage, warming up for her first

number. Men craned their necks, watching how her miracle of a dress revealed more of her buttocks than naked-
ness ever could, peachy pink and flashing up at every
twirl.

Holly read Feltz's mind: 'Dream on, Bernie,' she said.
'Dream on!'

The tempo picked up. Trixie kicked off the evening
with her own raunchy version of a bouncy little number
called *Sugar Town*. Soon she was down from the stage
and singing her way between tables, stopping to glad-eye
the men and run her hand under their chins.

Feltz gripped his knees and drooled. Would she come
his way? That's what he was here for! For a while it
seemed she never would – moving closer for a moment
and then away, driving him mad.

'God, Bernie, you're pathetic,' muttered Holly. But
she could not help admiring the singer: her slinky
manoeuvring and teasing of men was quite a turn-on.

At last, Trixie came to a halt. Looking over her shoulder as she sang, she caught Feltz's eye: beady, intense,
desperate. The chorus was approaching and little by little
she shimmied towards him, alternating her gaze between
his hopeful expression and his lap, to which in a final
abandonment of decorum he had shamelessly decided to
point.

'You silly old git!' Holly scolded him. 'You ought to
know better.'

Feltz smirked at her, confident in his ability to cope.
But, to his surprise, he suddenly began to shake.

Holly noticed and whispered to Matt: 'Shit! I think
he's having palpitations.'

Matt poured a glass of water. 'Here, drink this,' he said
to Feltz. But Feltz paid no heed. He was consumed in the
coming moment when he would be able to peek into the
contents of Trixie's loosely buttoned top.

Holly was worried. 'Little bitch – I'll give her *Sugar Town*!' she hissed, doing her utmost to ward off the singer with an icy stare.

Feltz prayed this would be his night. He was a visiting dignitary, after all; maybe Trixie would make up for the years when to 'pay for it' had been his only option.

The spotlight was now on Feltz and Trixie both. Placing a hand on his shoulder, she gently rubbed her knee against his thigh.

'My, but you's awful hot,' she said. Sitting on his lap, she picked up his napkin and dabbed at the sweat on his brow.

'I could get hotter,' Feltz stammered, his eyes wide. Trixie's concealed mike picked up his voice and amplified it for all to hear.

'Whoa there, tiger!' said Trixie, much to the audience's delight.

Despite his inability to stop shaking, Feltz was in heaven. Grinning wickedly, he placed an arm round Trixie's waist and drew her close. She responded with a peck to his cheek.

'So, what's your name, big boy?' she asked him.

'Bernie,' said Feltz, ecstatic that for once in his life he was the envy of every man there. What a winner, sitting in the spotlight and cuddling a beautiful star! Eat your hearts out, guys! His mind raced ahead to after the show. Would he be able to get together with Trixie? Oh please God, let it happen!

She stroked the end of his nose. 'Say, honey, how about joinin' me in the chorus of this li'l old song?'

Grinning inanely, Feltz nodded his consent. But as the music picked up he felt more and more breathless. Unaware that anything was wrong, Trixie gestured to the audience to sing along with them. Her little radio mike was hidden in one cup of her brassiere; she moved it close to Bernie's mouth so it would pick up his effort at singing. 'Here we go now!' she said, snapping her fingers to the beat: 'Shoo, shoo, shoo – Shoo, shoo, shoo – Shoo-shoo-shoo-shoo-shoo-shoo… Sugar Town.'

Bernie felt the world turn upside down. Only a gurgle issued from his mouth, as if the diva was accompanied temporarily by the flush of a lavatory.

'C'mon now, baby,' said Trixie. 'You can do better'n that.'

But Feltz heard nothing. Rolling his eyes, he passed out.

'Jesus Christ!' Trixie screamed, grabbing at the table-cloth as Feltz's body slid sideways off the chair. The two of them crashed to the floor amidst a cascade of bottles and half-empty glasses.

Matt leapt from his chair. 'Shit! He's having a heart attack!'

Holly looked down at Feltz's eyes, blank and redundant in their sockets. 'Bernie! Bernie!' she called.

Shocked but unhurt, Trixie rolled herself clear. 'Oh my God! Is he dead?'

'I dunno,' said Matt now kneeling at Feltz's side. Others gathered round in consternation.

'Oh shit! Have I killed 'im?' squealed Trixie. 'Oh my God! My God!'

Holly fumbled for Feltz's pulse, but couldn't find it. 'Quick!' she shouted. 'Get a doctor!'

'A doctor!' someone standing by cried out. 'Is there a doc in the house?'

The hotel manager arrived. 'Please, everybody! Stand back and give the gentleman some air!' He fumbled frantically for his mobile to call an ambulance.

'He needs a cardiac unit!' Holly shouted.

'Sure, sure, I'm doing all I can!' puffed the manager, anxiously waiting to be connected.

Feltz's face was turning from an overheated red to a deathly white. Holly glanced around for a doctor, but if there was one in the house he or she was keeping a low profile.

Matt pulled off Feltz's dicky bow and opened up his collar. 'We'll have to do something ourselves. Otherwise he's a goner!'

'Sweet Jesus!' cried Trixie. 'We can't just let him die!' She knelt down astride Bernie and took his head in her hands.

The Maitre-D arrived and whispered something to the manager, who announced triumphantly 'A cardiac unit's on its way!' On sighting Trixie straddled across Feltz, the Maitre-D was visibly alarmed. 'Trixie babe, you sure you know what you're doing?'

'Sure, I do!' She drew a deep breath, put her lips to Feltz's open mouth and blew for all she was worth. Then she lay him back and pummelled him violently on the chest.

The onlookers crowded closer, amazed. 'Gee, where did a broad like *that* learn to do *this*?' a man whispered to his companion.

Trixie put an ear to Feltz's chest.

'Any sign of life?' asked Matt.

'Could be!' she squeaked, detecting the faintest of heartbeats. Then she got back to work on Feltz's mouth, this time holding his nostrils shut with finger and thumb.

Concern for Feltz had, for most onlookers, turned to fascination with Trixie. Several men were jockeying for the best view of her rear end while she worked to resuscitate Feltz. One was grabbed abruptly from behind by his wife.

Holly detected the wail of a siren from the street. 'Thank God!' she cried, clasping Feltz's hand. 'That must be the ambulance.'

'Just in time, with luck,' said Matt, getting to his feet.

'OK, folks! Make way, now! Make way!' the manager shouted.

Their route clear, a team of paramedics rushed to Feltz's side. They worked with alacrity to save him.

Trixie leant over them. 'Gee! D'you think he'll be OK?'

'Maybe, lady,' said one, turning to see who owned the husky voice. He blinked, as if momentarily stunned by a blow to the head: instead of a face he was confronted by the most astonishing pair of breasts he had ever seen, threatening to fall out of a gold brassiere. 'Jesus, lady! Would you mind standin' back?' he said. 'We gotta a job to do!'

'Oh, I'm sorry!' said Trixie, upset. 'I sure meant no harm.'

Matt helped Trixie to her feet. 'Hey, you were great!'

'Why, thank you,' said Trixie. 'Say, ain't you the 'Get Real' guy?'

'That's right!' said Matt. Being recognized by pretty women was one of the more welcome dividends of celebrity.

'Well, have I been wantin' to meet *you*!'

Holly bristled. 'Like half the world,' she cut in, brusquely.

'Sorry,' said Matt. 'This is Holly Tree.'

'Nice to meet yuh!' said Trixie cheerily.

'Hi', said Holly, less than enamoured.

Trixie took the hint. 'Yeah, well, guys, I guess I'd better be movin' along.'

'Sure,' said Matt. 'But hey, that mouth-to-mouth stuff – where did you learn it?'

Trixie smiled wryly. 'It's easy, ain't it? Just like kissing – only instead of sucking, yuh blow!' She pursed her lips and blew him a kiss.

'Oh!' said Matt, stunned.

'You've obviously done it before!' said Holly, with discernible disapproval.

'I have,' Trixie admitted with a saucy grin. 'Only, I ain't tellin' *you* 'bout that!' Nor anyone else, she thought to herself: she'd picked up the skill while working as a hooker. An overweight executive had hired her together with another girl and her friend had had to revive the man when, too low on puff to stay the course, he'd threatened to die on them.

Trixie's about right, thought Holly, hazarding wild guesses of her own.

'Hey!' Trixie called back. 'Remember me to the li'l guy when he comes round!'

'You mean, if he comes round,' Holly said quietly, watching the paramedics lift Feltz's limp body onto a stretcher and carry him from the building.

TWENTY

Matt and Holly walked arm in arm from the clinic into the cold of the early morning. Matt looked up. The sky was red and the tops of the buildings were suffused in an ominous pink glow. There were few other people about, just some early birds scurrying about their business with heads bowed. Plumes of steam escaping through manhole covers seemed like vents for the simmering cauldron of uncertainty the city had become.

An armoured vehicle was parked half on the kerb. It was a Humvee, in the midnight blue livery of the Urban Security Service. It had been there when they arrived; it must have been there all night. The curfew hours were just over, but Matt sensed the crew watching them anyway. Trained anti-terrorist units were stationed at junctions all over the city. An attack could happen anytime, anywhere; such normality of life as once had graced the city was now on hold 'twenty-four-seven'.

'Bernie looks bad,' said Matt. He peeked surreptitiously at the Humvee's caged windows, but through the blackened glass nobody was visible.

'I'm glad the doctors let us see him,' Holly said. She was so absorbed in thought she barely noticed the vehicle. 'At least he's not dead.'

'Next best thing, though,' said Matt. 'I mean, he can't speak. And did you notice that stare?'

'Like he sees no one.'

'Do you think he'll recover?' Matt asked grimly. 'I mean will he be… a bit of a veggie?'

'Poor Bernie,' Holly said. 'That would be just so horrible.'

Back in their chauffeured limousine, Matt picked up a copy of Newsday.

'Anything about us?' Holly asked.

'Yeah,' sighed Matt, pointing to a photograph taken on their arrival at JFK. 'Says underneath I'm 'a rioting messiah'.'

'You've Bernie's press release to thank for that,' said Holly.

Passing the paper to Holly, Matt spoke to the chauffeur: 'How far are Globalcorp's offices from here?'

'About fifteen minutes, I guess.'

Holly sensed Matt's concern. 'Don't worry,' she said, as if nothing untoward had occurred.

'You say that, but Bernie keeling over like this hasn't half dropped us in it.' Matt fished for his wallet. 'Have you got Grouper's private number? I'd better ring to say it's just two of us coming now.'

'Relax, will you? We can handle everything.'

Matt was keying the number into his mobile's memory. 'You've heard the guy's reputation,' he said, believing every word of what he had learnt about the man: that, far from being a man of sophistication and charm, Hiram Grouper III was an inelegant throwback to meat-packing forbears on whose long since laundered exploits, the Grouper fortune was founded.

'They say he's a pig to do business with!' Matt emphasized.

'So,' said Holly, 'you know what I think would be best?'

'What?'

Holly gripped his forearm and looked him in the eye. 'Let me deal with him. You just hold back – *Play the artist,* you know?'

Matt was relieved. He handed her the phone. 'You've been dying for a chance to do this, haven't you?' he said.

'What if I have?' said Holly, with an impish smile. She pressed 'dial'.

'Ever since that condom business,' added Matt.

'Yeah, well. I probably shouldn't say it, but Bernie's made a few boo-boos lately, you have to admit.'

'He has,' Matt conceded. 'And always on the larger deals.'

It was uncanny. Talking big numbers seemed to blind Feltz's otherwise razor-sharp instincts.

'He's too busy thinking of his commission,' said Holly.

'Ain't that the truth!' said Matt in a fake accent.

'Shush!' said Holly. 'Someone's answered.'

'The Grouper residence,' said a very dignified voice.

'Oh, good morning!' said Holly brightly. 'Is Mr. Grouper available?'

'Who is calling, madam?'

'Miss Tree, on behalf of Matt Flight.'

'Flight, you say? Ah yes, hold the line please.'

Holly turned to Matt, her hand over the mouthpiece. 'This is all frightfully formal,' she giggled. 'I'm talking to some plummy English guy. He must be the butler.'

Matt leaned towards her so he could listen in. Together, they heard Grouper's voice in the background. By the sound of it, he'd just got out of bed and wasn't taking much in.

'Limey broad, yuh say?' he said, walking to pick up the phone.

'I'll give him limey broad!' whispered Holly.

'Hullo, Grouper speakin'.'

'Oh, good morning,' said Holly, her voice forceful and clear. 'This is Holly Tree.'

'Do I know you?'

'No you don't. I'm travelling with Matt Flight.'

'Ah, Matt Flight,' said Grouper, sounding like he had a blocked nose. 'Yeah, that's right. I'm expectin' the guy.'

'Right,' said Holly. 'But I'm afraid I've some bad news.'

'Yuh, what? Has he had an accident?'

'No,' explained Holly, 'it's his agent.'

'You mean Feltz?'

'Right,' said Holly. 'I'm afraid he won't be with us.'

'Why, for Crissakes?' shouted Grouper, getting edgy.

Holly held the phone from her ear. 'He's had a heart attack.'

'What!'

'It happened last night,' explained Holly. 'We were watching the cabaret at the Godolphin Hotel, and…'

'Trixie Katz?'

'Right,' said Holly. 'She sat on his lap and, well – he just pooped.'

'Pooped?'

'Yeah, collapsed.'

'She's a hot number, that one,' said Grouper. 'But is the li'l guy gonna live? Only, we got negotiations!'

'They think he'll live, but beyond that nothing's clear.'

Grouper sighed. 'You mean he could end up cuckoo?'

'I'm afraid so. All he can do at the moment is stare.'

Matt was still listening in. Little guy? he thought. He'd never heard Bernie described like that before. Little shit, maybe! But thinking of him lying in a coma, he felt ungrateful; if it hadn't been for Bernie, his career would have got nowhere. And besides, he'd grown fond of the man: his roguishness was in many ways endearing.

'So where does this leave us?' asked Grouper. 'Only we got the promo kickin' off t'night an' a raft of things to talk about…'

'I'm taking over,' said Holly robustly.

'Hey, lady! What do *you* know?'

'What do you mean?' Holly cut in aggressively.

'Well, I was only gonna say...'

'What?' demanded Holly.

There was silence on the other end.

'Listen,' said Holly, abruptly. 'We'll be with you by eight as arranged.'

'OK OK! I hear yuh,' said Grouper, bemused. But the line was already dead.

'That was a bit sharp, wasn't it?' said Matt as they swung into Fifth Avenue.

Holly smiled smugly and settled back to enjoy the window displays: Saks's, Tiffany's and Macy's were among the ones she was determined not to miss.

Matt shifted in his seat, unable to relax. 'Bernie told me that when RIOT gets underway in the States, resistance to it won't be tolerated,' he said.

Holly didn't like the sound of that. 'You mean they intend to use force?'

'Oh, yeah!' said Matt emphatically. 'The FBI's been ordered to flush out the wreckers. They're really going to put the boot in. Sort out the 'rat-fink wise-asses' or whatever they like to call them. I guess you can't blame them though, when you think of the shit that's come down on them.'

'Maybe. But using that kind of force isn't going to help us.'

'I had the same thought,' said Matt.

'I mean, supposing there's a backlash. It could be you they come after!'

'It's a risk.'

'What if something happens to you?' Holly thought of Bernie lying insensible in hospital. She shuddered.

Matt shrugged his shoulders. 'It won't,' he said.

Holly was unconvinced. 'I think after tonight's launch we should go home, and not do this whistle-stop tour Grouper's got planned.'

'I can't. That's all been agreed.'

'If I'd had a say, I'd never have let you sign up for it.'

'Don't worry. We're riding high in the popularity stakes, we'll be fine. And besides, according to Bernie, the State Department has promised massive security.'

'I hope you're right,' said Holly. Then, smiling, 'Only it's not just us to think about now!'

Matt smiled. 'I know.' He glanced at her tummy. He smiled then gazed out of the window, enjoying his thoughts in the comfort and peace of being driven.

The discovery that Holly was pregnant had come as a shock, more so to him than to Holly. But then he'd adjusted to it, joining with her in laughingly trying to guess when and where it had been conceived.

Was it that time after a party, when they'd made love in the gazebo at three in the morning? Or was it the afternoon he'd taken her by surprise in the kitchen? Or that night a few days later, in a tiny hotel in St. Germain, when they'd both been turned on by an erotic house movie?

It was impossible to say. The pregnancy was an accident, but a happy one. Like the chance stroke of a brush that is the making of a picture, it engendered a sense of completeness between them.

Matt had even thought about marriage. He'd held back from proposing on the grounds that they were happy enough as they were. But what would become of Holly and the child should he die young? He had often spoke of this to Holly.

'Honestly, you've got a thing about it!' Holly had once chided him. 'Anyone would think you had a death wish!'

'But these days, the higher a person's profile, the greater the risk of falling victim to some crank,' Matt had responded.

Eventually, he'd made a will in secret and only told her about it afterwards. The thought first occurred to him when he learned that Holly's Uncle Henry had made one in spite of his bohemian ways and total disregard for convention.

Matt had called on Sylvester's lawyer, Royston Rigg, who knew all about the fortune he was amassing. 'You're a man of substance,' Rigg had observed. 'And in the dangerous world in which we live, the action you wish to take is a measure of your foresight.'

'That's what I thought,' Matt had said, flattered. 'I mean, imagine what would happen if I died tomorrow!'

'God forbid!' Rigg had said, putting up his hands in horror. 'But, rest assured that should the unthinkable occur, it'll be my pleasure to personally attend to your affairs.'

With those comforting words their meeting had ended, Rigg smiling benevolently at Matt the wealthy innocent.

Holly had been astonished when Matt said she and the baby were to be his only beneficiaries. 'Why me?' she'd said.

'I've no one else – except my parents,' Matt had told her disarmingly. 'And I'll trust you to take care of them.'

Holly had been overcome, accepting it as proof of his love for her. 'I know it sounds silly, but until now I wasn't really certain,' she'd said between sobs.

Matt had then broached another of his preoccupations: 'And someone has to know what I'd like done with my body.'

'Oh!' she'd said, surprised. 'And what *do* you want done with it?'

'I don't know!' he'd said with intensity. Then, dismissively: 'What happens to it isn't important. For all I care, they can chop it up for spare parts.'

'Fine,' Holly had said. But even to Matt, it was obvious that his grim solution wasn't sincere.

'D'you know what I fear most?' he'd asked.

'What?'

'Being forgotten! I mean, think of old Cyril – if it hadn't been for us, nobody would have given a shit.'

'But you're not Cyril, for God's sake!' she'd said impatiently. 'And you won't be forgotten.'

'You don't know that!'

'Of course I do,' she'd said, 'and so do you!'

'Just because I'm known now, it doesn't mean to say I'll be remembered.'

'Why is it such a worry?' Holly had said. 'Unless you believe in an afterlife, you won't be around to care!'

'I don't know. It just is.'

'If it makes you happy, I'll create a foundation in your memory,' she'd said, tongue-in-cheek. 'Or build you a memorial!'

Impatient to end the conversation, she had assured him yet again that he wouldn't die young. 'You'll live till you're a hundred!' she had said, tossing in a platitude for good measure.

* * *

Globalcorp's headquarters tapered from an arched base to the sky, its profile like a giant shard of blackened glass. A hundred and ten floors of offices fed the company's might and crowning them all was Hiram Grouper's penthouse apartment. Sumptuous in every way, it housed the tycoon's obligatory art collection – one to rival any in the hands of the city's major players.

The chauffeur drove onto the forecourt and came to a halt by a bronze bust of the company's founder, the illustrious Hiram B. Grouper the First. It seemed the old man's penetrating gaze, standing high on his pedestal, was no defence against graffiti, for newly-sprayed on the base in red and visceral hues for all to see were the words 'GLOBALCORP SUCKS!'

Matt leaned towards the chauffeur. 'We may be some time,' he said. Stepping from the limousine, he looked up. The building was moving against the clouds like a surreal heaven-slicing knife.

Holly sensed his thoughts. 'Those glass edges! They look razor sharp.'

Matt lowered his eyes. 'Yeah. Just like Grouper, I reckon.'

'Don't you worry,' said Holly with a grin. 'This Mr. Big is not going to get things all his own way.'

Through the revolving doors they were met by two burly armed guards who surveyed the new arrivals with suspicion.

'We've an appointment with Mr. Grouper,' Matt explained.

'Your names, please?'

'Matt Flight and Holly Tree.'

'ID?'

Matt hadn't expected this request. 'No.'

'You're kidding!' He looked at his companion as if to say, 'Who are these bozos?'

'In England,' said Matt, with a shrug of his shoulders, 'I'm never...'

'The lady?' the man interrupted him.

'I have none either,' said Holly.

'OK, if you folks'll step this way, please.' He ushered them to the side of the foyer.

'Is this necessary?' asked Matt.

'Security check, sir,' drawled the guard, running a detector over Matt's clothing.

'This is Matt Flight!' protested Holly. 'Surely you...'

'Beg pardon, ma'm,' the second guard cut in. 'Evr'body gets checked out just the same. Now if yuh wouldn't mind spreadin' 'em, please.'

'This is ridiculous!' said Holly. The man was scanning her legs in a manner far too close for her liking. 'You guys are paranoid!'

'It's company policy, ma'm.'

'So what's the worst thing you've ever found?' Matt asked, trying to make light of the situation.

'A Fed-Ex delivery, surrh,' said the guard, scanning Matt's legs.

'Really?' Matt said.

'Yup. A turkey.' The man strung his story out in a slow drawl while going through their pockets and belongings. 'Corn-fed, just how Mr Grouper likes 'em. Nice thoughtful gift, in a big fancy box with a bow on it. From a well-wisher. Only thing was, it was stuffed with plastic explosives!'

'Wow!'

'Lot o' people gotta grudge against the comp'ny, surrh,' the other guard added.

Hardly surprising, Matt thought, given Globalcorp's almost universal power.

'OK folks, you're clear to go,' his colleague said. 'Hundred and twelfth, have a nice day.'

Holly was the first to walk into the lift. 'So much for the land of the free. The security is a nightmare!'

'Yeah, they're manic about it, but what can you expect?'

'Things are much worse here than at home!'

'Well, they're in no position to trust anybody,' said Matt. It had been much the same in England, he reminded her, before the RIOT campaign took hold: sporadic gunfire and bombs going off day and night.

The lift doors closed and the electric motor hummed into life, moving through various gears. Would things change for the better here as they had done in England, Matt wondered? Even now, he found it hard to believe that an everyday expression like 'Get real!' had become a slogan of such power. But, it was true! In England, Unity had risen again, marshalling her forces into a campaign for change that had sent dissidents scurrying for cover. The crazed logic he'd fought against was dying in the face of a new-found passion and conviction. Now, commandeered by politicians keen to be *on message* with the new mood, the movement he'd founded had been largely taken out of his hands.

Not that it had all been plain sailing. Active supporters of RIOT had suffered reprisals. People displaying the poster had been victimized, their houses damaged and splashed with red paint. Matt, too, had had to contend with ugly incidents, not least when a grenade was hurled through the window of No. 17. It failed to explode, but the experience was nonetheless terrifying, as was the destruction of his car that same night. He'd witnessed the whole thing, powerless to intervene; five men in balaclavas had smashed it to pieces with baseball bats before setting it alight and running away. Rumour had it this was the work of an organised gang of benefit frauds. They'd been working the system for decades and wanted revenge for the loss of a cushy livelihood.

The lift was propelling them vertically at a speed they could only guess at. A slowing in the motor's hum signified they were nearing the building's summit. Holly's fingers tightened on his hand.

TWENTY-ONE

The lift doors opened onto the lobby of Hiram Grouper's penthouse. Holly stepped out first.

'Look at that,' she said, pointing at the huge curlicues of a monogram set in the centre of a white marble floor.

'There's no doubting who lives here!' said Matt, deciphering Grouper's initials.

'God, how naff!' Holly said derisively.

'The guy's gotta be an egomaniac,' Matt said softly, trusting to luck that no one could hear him.

The lift closed gently behind them. The only other exit from the lobby was a tall pair of double doors of mock-baronial solidity. Holly noticed there was neither a knocker nor a door-bell. 'How d'you suppose we make ourselves known?' she said.

'I haven't a clue.' Glancing up at the ceiling, Matt spotted a monitor. 'But I think you'll find someone knows we're here.'

'Oops! Do you think they heard us?'

'I hope not!' said Matt.

They stood in a quandary waiting for something to happen. Eventually a latch clicked and the double doors opened slowly, revealing a circular hall. What seemed like daylight filtered down from a cupola onto another marble floor, this time laid in the design of a compass.

Dozens of gold discs were set irregularly into its circumference. Matt presumed they signified Globalcorp's various interests around the world.

They entered gingerly, expecting to be met. Several corridors radiated from the room but no one was about.

'So what happens now?' asked Holly.

'We wait.' Matt was admiring the carver chairs around the edge of the room.

Holly spotted them, too. 'Louis XIV, I reckon,' she said. Then, suddenly quizzical: 'Hey, is there a Mrs. Grouper?'

'I've no idea. Why?'

'I just get the feeling there isn't,' she said. From the decor she guessed Grouper was a bachelor; and from his reaction on the phone, a grumpy old misogynist too.

'Hey, look at this!'' Matt said, venturing towards one of the corridors. 'A Lichtenstein!'

'Ooh!' said Holly. 'I love Lichtenstein!'

They wandered together into a small room at the end of the corridor and gazed at painstakingly painted little dots making up the face of a beautiful blonde. With a tear in her eye, she was declaring her undying love for a guy called Chuck, whom the eye was not permitted to see.

Holly pulled at Matt's arm. 'Hey, look over there! Isn't that one of Monet's haystacks?'

But Matt was absorbed with a discovery of his own: 'Lucky devil's got a Magritte. In fact, a whole wall of them!' Walking on, he peered into two further rooms. 'Look down here! Pollocks and Rothkos, a mass of them!'

'Ahem!' said a voice behind them. They had failed to notice the arrival of the butler. As Holly had suspected, he was an Englishman. Middle-aged and conventionally attired, he had a dejected look. His jacket and trousers were ill-fitting. Holly wondered if he was an out-of-work actor.

'Good morning,' the man said. 'Mr. Flight and Miss Tree, I presume.'

'Yes,' said Matt. 'Mr. Grouper is expecting us.'

'Of course. Follow me, if you will.'

'You're English!' said Holly.

'Thank you ma'm,' said the butler, as if her observation was the height of compliments. 'Indeed I am.'

Behind the man's formality Holly detected a hint of oppression. Count Dracula's servant Igor sprung to mind.

'Have you worked in America long?' she asked.

'Rather more than long enough, I fear.'

'Oh,' said Holly, intrigued.

'It's a case of needs must.'

'Why, whatever happened?' Holly hoped the interminably long corridor wouldn't come to an end before he answered.

'Ah, it's a delicate matter, ma'm,' the butler sighed.

'Oh, dear,' Holly said sympathetically.

'This is quite some collection,' Matt said, to change the subject.

'Indeed! It spans from the sixteenth century to the present day. From the Dutch school through to the Impressionists and beyond.'

'You must enjoy working here.'

The butler threw a sepulchral look over his shoulder. 'If you mean the art, sir, yes. Once one has had the good fortune to care for a collection of some distinction, a love of fine work never deserts one.'

'Oh!' said Matt, his curiosity aroused. 'Were you a curator once?'

'In a manner of speaking, sir...' the man tailed off dolefully.

'Well, this is certainly a collection of distinction!' Matt said, regretting his words somewhat as he caught sight of a piece by Damien Hirst, a sentimentalised carcase suspended in formalin. It sat in gory isolation in a passing room.

'That is primarily due to the *previous* Mr. Grouper, sir,' said the butler. Then, with quiet but withering disdain: 'The present Mr. Grouper – who is the third – has a preference for more *modern* work!'

'I see!' said Matt, smiling at how Hiram's meat-packing forbears would have approved.

Reaching the end of another corridor, they encountered two Hispanic servants with eyes downcast. Carrying salvers of hot food, they stood deferentially to one side so the butler and his party could pass.

All men! Holly thought to herself.

Ahead was a room with an open door. They could clearly hear the tycoon talking on the phone. His tone was far from amicable.

'One moment, please,' the butler requested, detaining them lest they distract the man of power. But Grouper had noticed his guests; waving them in, he gestured them to some chairs while he continued with his conversation.

'You tell that cocksucker this!' he ranted, pacing up and down. 'If he ain't agreed by tonight, I'll bust his ass!'

Whoever was incurring such wrath had better be a big man, thought Matt. Standing up to Hiram B. Grouper the Third, striding about tank-like in a quilted silk dressing gown, was not for the faint-hearted.

'I don't wanna hear it! I don't wanna hear it!' Grouper was evidently crushing some attempt at resistance. Obese, balding and enormous in every way, he had the aggressive presence of an antagonized bull walrus.

For Holly, Grouper was just as she'd imagined – a loudmouthed bully who'd stop at nothing to get his own way. As the butler withdrew, she sensed he was relieved to escape his master's coarse invective.

Matt's sense of unease increased when he felt something probe his nether regions. He turned round to find a grossly overweight hound had slunk noiselessly into the room, bent on making an assessment of its own. He stroked the animal's head, hoping to divert its attentions from his most vulnerable parts.

Grouper put down the phone. His rage was forgotten in an instant. 'Matt, baby!' he gushed as he lumbered across the floor, his long arms reaching out in readiness to greet him. 'Well whaddya know? We meet at last!'

Matt extended his hand, only to have it firmly enveloped and crushed. 'Hiram,' he said, doing his best to ignore a twinge of pain. 'Good to meet you!'

'Call me 'H', please!' said Grouper, giving him a hearty slap on the back.

Turning to Holly, he greeted her too: 'Hey, hey, Miss Tree – one fiery lady!' he said, his eyes narrowing guardedly.

Holly forced a grin. 'Please! Call me Holly.'

'Sure! Holly it is,' said Grouper, surprised at her youth.

'Have we come at a bad time?' said Matt.

'Have yuh what?' Grouper blinked, momentarily flummoxed. He'd forgotten that only seconds earlier he'd been laying down the law in an extreme manner. 'Aw, shucks!' he said, his outburst remembered. 'I do apologize. Believe me, I'm a big pussy at heart. But, hey! Sometimes you gotta kick ass.'

'I understand,' said Matt, struggling to accommodate Hiram's curious intonation.

Big pussy, indeed! Holly thought to herself. That's a laugh!

'No, things are gonna be fine,' Grouper assured them, confident as always that threats of assault on a person's backside would be enough to carry the day.

'When do we go live?' Holly asked.

'Nine t'night. That's two hours before curfew kicks in.' Then, his eyes round with excitement, he told them: 'There's gonna be some party, I tell yuh!'

'A party?' Matt queried.

278

'You bet!' said Grouper. 'We got a dispensation – Times Square's gonna be hummin' like it ain't done in years!'

'Great!' said Holly anxiously. Matt's safety was increasingly worrying her.

'No fireworks, mind!' Grouper went on. 'Too much shit goin' down in this city for that. But hey, we got jugglers, guys on stilts, a big band, all kinds of stuff to liven up the night.'

'Really?' said Holly. She was pondering his flattened nose. Probably the result of his bar-brawling youth, she thought; he'd bragged about it to Feltz, who was duly impressed.

'Yeah, we're gonna have ourselves a ball. But, Gee, I'm sorry Bernie's gonna miss it!' And with dubious solicitude he added: 'Say, I guess you guys are as cut up 'bout that as I am.'

'Yeah, it's bad news,' Matt agreed. 'He's been my agent since the beginning.'

Grouper shook his head sorrowfully. 'You had a good 'un there.' Turning his back, he made for the sideboard, where he selected a hash brown from under a silver salver. 'Sheez, that's hot!' he said, tossing it to the dog with total disregard for it landing plumb in the middle of an ancient Persian carpet.

'You know, me and Bernie was gettin' on famously,' he went on. 'And hey – the guy was awful cute when it came to protectin' your interests!'

'Yeah?' said Matt disbelievingly.

Holly watched the dog's tongue flicker in and out as it padded round the titbit waiting for it to cool. 'That's some dog you've got there,' she said. 'What breed is it?'

'Rattler? Why, he's a bloodhound, ain't yuh, son?' Grouper gazed fondly at the fat-laden animal.

'Weren't they once used to track slaves on the run?' Holly asked.

'Darned right!' said Grouper, patting the animal proudly.

Holly thought it unlikely that this snuffly descendant from an age of barbarity, could hunt a man down anywhere, let alone through a swamp in which it would surely sink.

After a further geniality about Feltz being one of the most likeable men he'd ever done business with, Grouper got to the matter in hand. 'As luck would have it,' he said, 'Me and Bernie have gotten most of this agreed!'

Matt feared the worst. Had Feltz acceded to his every demand, the bigger rogue twisting the 'li'l guy' round his finger?

Grouper summoned the butler. Then, turning back to his guests, he spread his arms expansively: 'Please, won't yuh join me for some breakfast?'

Hiram parked himself at the head of a table and directed Holly and Matt to chairs on either side. Holly's was opposite the panoramic window and the view was all that Feltz had cracked it up to be. She could see right across Central Park to the Hudson River and beyond.

Grouper beamed at his butler – much to the man's resentment, it seemed to Holly. 'Harvey, make with some coffee for my English friends!' Then he ostentatiously divulged from behind his hand: 'Hey, Harvey's an aristocrat! Ain't yuh, Harvey?'

'Yes, sir,' came the reluctant reply.

Holly was stunned. 'Really?'

'Yeah, meet Sir Harvey Haugh,' said Grouper. 'The guy's a real live baronet, right?'

'Oh,' said Matt, embarrassed for the man, who studiously avoided eye contact with everybody in the room.

Grouper sat back proudly. 'Yeah,' he went on, 'Harvey owes a lot to me. Ain't that right, Harvey?'

Harvey nodded meekly. 'Will, that be all, sir?' he asked, seeking to exit.

'Yeah, yeah. That'll be all.'

Once Harvey had left the room, Grouper treated them to an explanation.

'It was back at Thanksgiving. Me and four buddies had taken a trip down to Reno to play us some poker. And whaddya know? This guy tips up at our table – a real dandy lookin' dude. Yeah, it's Harvey, half cut and wavin' a wad of cash as thick as my arm! Tells us he's on a roll. 'Will you gentlemen permit me to join you?' he says in that fancy way of his – so we duly oblige. But – surprise, surprise – the guy ain't so savvy. In a couple of hours he's down to his last buck.'

'Poor Harvey!'

'Wait – here's the crazy thing! He keeps writing out IOUs to stay in the game — all showy like, as if he does it all the time. Me and my buddies, we don't want to be discourteous – I mean, the guy is Sir Harvey Haugh, an English aristocrat for Crissakes!'

'Oh, no!' said Holly, having a strong idea where the story was going.

Grouper grinned. 'Yeah, you got there before me. Some hands later, the guy's in a muck sweat. Says he's wiped out. Then he comes clean – tells us what he sat down with was all he had left in the world!'

'No!' said Holly.

'Oh, yeah!' said Grouper, reliving the horror. 'So, I says, 'Come on, Harvey, ain't you got a stately pile or somethin' back in the UK?' 'Not any more!' he says, like the four us would be sympathetic! So, I says, ain't yuh got nothin' – pictures, silver, jewellery, for Crissakes? And he says, 'I did have!' And he tells us how his bankers just took the lot.'

Holly shook her head in amazement.

'So what happened then?' asked Matt.

'I asks him, what the fuck was he playing at issuing IOUs?' Suddenly conscious of his language, Grouper leaned towards Holly and said. 'I do apologise – I was forgettin', we have a lady present.'

Holly waved his transgression aside.

Grouper went on: 'You know what Harvey says? 'Gentlemen, it was an act of desperation.' Like we should all understand and forgive him. I mean, I ask yuh! Anyways, he has this story about how he's lookin' for a rich widow to marry and would we all wait till he found one.'

Holly and Matt found it hard not to laugh. Grouper sensed this and with a hint of annoyance, said: 'Hey, fellas, I'm bein' serious here! Anyways, the guys say to Harvey: 'Are you crazy? We ain't waitin' on that. We want our money!' And you know what? Harvey just shrugs his shoulders!'

'Mad!' said Holly.

'Yeah it was! 'Cos the guy next to me stands up to whack him. A big guy, too – cattle baron buddy up from Texas. Anyhow, I tells him to cool it. Then I gets this idea, how it's Thanksgivin' an' all, and I could be of some assistance to Harvey. So, I says to my buddies, 'I'll make good Harvey's debt' and of course they looks at me like I'm goin' loco.'

'You mean you bailed him out?' Matt asked.

'Sure!' said Grouper. 'I figured Harvey could be useful. You see, aristocrats have rarity value.'

Matt looked at Holly, wondering if Grouper's appetite for collection was about to reveal a certain perversity. Was there a room somewhere with aristocrats hung on hooks?

'Harvey thought it was Christmas!' Grouper chuckled. 'He's so goddam grateful! Is there anything he can do, etcetera etcetera blah blah blah, so I says, 'Sure, Harvey, there's something you can do. You can come back with me to New York and be my butler!''

At this, Hiram burst into cacophonous laughter like gunfire. Poor Harvey, Holly thought to herself. What a nemesis!

'Yuh shooda seen the guy's face!' exclaimed Grouper before continuing with his clattering laughter.

Matt looked down at the table. 'I can imagine.'

'I couldn't do fairer'n that, now could I?' Grouper pleaded. 'Getting the guy off the hook cost me a fortune – a hundred grand, for Crissakes!'

Now Holly understood Harvey's misery. How could he have envisaged life would take this course for him? His only consolation was that he'd narrowly escaped a bruising from a cowpoke in a ten-gallon hat.

'Hey, but I figure Harvey was worth it,' Grouper went on. 'You see, the fellas come and play *here* now. They love him, he makes 'em feel like lords!'

'I'll bet,' said Matt, imagining Harvey mixing drinks for barbarian chiefs and lighting their cigars.

Harvey returned with the coffee.

'Say, Harvey! Am I a reasonable man?' Grouper asked him with a sugary smile.

'Yes, sir,' said Harvey, having learnt long ago it was folly to disagree with his master. He'd once suggested there might be a let-up in his subservient formality – rather less of a master–servant caricature in their relationship. At this, Grouper had flown into a rage: 'But that's what you're here for!' he'd roared. 'To give the place some class, for Crissakes!' Then while berating the man for ingratitude, Grouper had grabbed him by the shoulders and shaken him – a humiliation made all the worse for being witnessed by the house staff, themselves frequent victims of his abuse.

Holly studied Harvey's doleful expression and wondered how long his imprisonment would last. Likely an age, she thought, given the money he would have to pay back. Perhaps Harvey would never be free, and he would die out of despair. Would Grouper then have him stuffed – his parting with such a treasure too much to bear? She could imagine him lamenting his passing to pals: 'The guy even laid out my underpants!'

Matt was puzzled as to why Harvey just didn't walk out. Perhaps he was so ineffectual, life on the outside was too much to cope with.

'How long yuh been with me now, Harvey?' Grouper asked him.

Harvey placed the percolator on the table. 'I couldn't exactly say, sir,' he said, not wishing to recall a single instant of his cruel incarceration.

'There yuh go,' said Grouper, satisfied. 'It's like they say – time flies when you're happy!'

Hiram and Harvey. What a pair, thought Holly. The tyrant and his titled serf.

Grouper eyed the salvers on the sideboard. 'Hey, we got anythin' you want! Juices, waffles, cereals – and eggs, sunny-side-up or over-easy. Then there's bacon, sausages, cold meats, kidneys and kippers. So, folks, enjoy!'

Holly felt suspicious. Was this generosity his way of softening them up? She chose to eat modestly, just fruit juice and cereal. But Matt saw no reason for wariness. If Grouper was concealing some con, Holly would spot it. 'What a feast!' he said, helping himself as Harvey passed by, proffering salver after salver of food.

Grouper saw Matt tucking in. 'Hey, I can see you're a guy after my own heart!'

'Well you've gone to some trouble here,' said Matt.

Flattered, Grouper turned to Holly. 'And how about you, my dear? Can we tempt you to something other than fruit juice? Or are you concerned for that delightful little figure of yours?'

Holly forced a smile. 'I'm fine, thank you.'

Grouper piled waffles onto his plate until they were inches high then smothered them with cream and maple syrup. Holly felt vaguely sick.

Grouper noticed her expression and leered at her, delighting in her obvious distaste. As the rubbery protuberance of his lips closed on a calorie-saturated mouthful he looked for all the world like a huge frog. To Holly it seemed he might swallow the world and not notice.

'Now fellas, let me bring you up to speed,' he went on, wiping maple syrup off his chin. 'As you know, Congress has granted a budget for this campaign.'

Holly pricked up her ears.

'Ten million bucks!' Grouper was pleased to inform them.

'Bernie told us you've produced a whole range of promotional gear,' Holly said, giving the impression she knew rather more about the deal than she did.

'Yeah, we went overboard for you guys. We got the lot! T-shirts like the ones you have in the UK, flags, badges, stickers and a lot else besides. Hell, you know how a promotion goes.'

'So it's all systems go,' said Holly.

'Sure,' said Grouper. 'Come t'night, there'll be vendors staked out all over.'

Holly looked at Matt. 'Sounds great, yeah?'

'Yeah, great,' said Matt, enjoying his first taste of bacon with maple syrup.

Grouper shovelled in another mouthful. 'Hey, did Bernie tell you I fixed us up a motorcade?' he asked.

'A motorcade?' queried Matt.

'Yeah,' said Grouper. 'What did you think you'd be doin'? Trottin' into Times Square on a donkey?' He burst into another grating roar of laughter.

Holly covered for Matt's ignorance. 'You remember,' she said to him. 'Bernie told us about it on the flight.'

'Oh, yeah, of course,' said Matt, pretending that the fact had slipped his memory, 'Bernie did say something about it.'

'We even got cheer leaders headin' it up,' Grouper added.

'Great!' Holly enthused.

'Great? It' gonna be the greatest!' exclaimed Grouper. 'Yuh gonna love it!'

'Sounds like a circus is rolling into town,' Matt said.

Grouper beamed. 'Yeah, I guess that's about right!' He'd whipped up a frenzy of hype to make sure the media would turn up in force.

Continuing in an excitable vein, he explained that when the campaign was launched and Matt's image finally flashed up, balloons would be simultaneously released in every state right across the Union.

'Yeah, thousands!' he gleefully assured them. 'Some of 'em real whoppers, that'll pick up the jet stream. Jesus! They could come down anywhere.'

Matt imagined tribesmen in remote corners of the world scratching their heads in bewilderment as shrinking balloons bearing his image sunk slowly in their midst, their epic journey at an end.

But Holly was concerned with more practical things. 'So when can Matt expect his signing-up fee?' she asked, nonchalantly stirring her coffee.

'Signing fee? This is news to me, lady!' said Grouper with a note of alarm.

Holly's suspicions were confirmed. Feltz must have been dissuaded from seeking a down-payment for Matt, doubtless on the grounds that any such sum would be a trifle compared to the enormous royalties he was in line to receive. This would be far from ideal: if something went wrong and the campaign was halted, Matt would emerge penniless. No, a sum up front was essential. She decided it was time for a little bluff.

'Matt's services never come without a golden hello,' she said. 'Surely Bernie said?'

Grouper put his hand on his heart. 'Lady, I'm telling yuh I know nothing about no golden hello!' Then he turned back to spike another forkful of hotcakes.

Holly shrugged her shoulders. 'Bernie told us the agreed figure was half a million dollars,' she said. 'Isn't that right, Matt?'

'Yeah, right,' said Matt, knowing this to be a lie.

Grouper downed his fork, his appetite gone. 'Five hundred grand!' he roared. 'No way!'

"H," Holly said, taking advantage of the shortening of his name in a calm and very English way. 'That was the figure Bernie gave us.'

For a moment Grouper said nothing. It was true Feltz had broached the subject of a signing fee, but he was confident the matter had been buried under layers of guile. What had Feltz been playing at, agreeing one thing then promptly telling Matt and Holly Tree something else?

'Now, listen up!' he said, downing his napkin on the table. 'Matt's deal's based on royalties. Ain't no other fee comes into it!'

'Come on, H! You know as well as I do, until the goods are sold, royalties are pie in the sky,' said Holly.

Tired of her calling him 'H' in a manner that lacked respect, Grouper pushed back his chair and stood up, leaning over Holly with his fists on the table. 'Yuh'd better wise up, lady!' he barked. 'Coz I'm tellin' you now, Globalcorp ain't paying no 'golden hellos' to no one!'

Holly glowered at him. 'No?' she said. She clenched her own fists on the table. Matt couldn't help noticing how tiny they were next to Grouper's – like cocktail sausages taking on four-pound saveloys.

'Well, if that's the way you feel, we're out of here,' Holly said calmly. 'It's that simple!'

Grouper stabbed a finger at her. 'Yuh think you're pretty cute, don't yuh?' he said. Then he looked at Matt, trying to judge where he stood on the matter. But as previously agreed, Matt played dumb. Looking down at his plate, he carried on eating as if commercial concerns were either above his head or beneath his contempt.

'Come on, Matt, we're going home,' Holly said, upping the ante. Standing up from the table, she made for the door.

Grouper's face turned from red to puce. Was the deal about to *crater?* Striding to the window, he glared at the sky. One thing was clear to him. He was in a no-win situation. His eyes wandered to the treetops in the distance of Central Park. How he'd rather be there, exercising with Rattler as his doctor ordered; anything, rather than face a humiliating climb-down with this two-bit limey bimbo!

'Well?' said Holly, turning back for a last word. Matt had stood up and was wiping his face.

'Jeez! I have no idea how Bernie arrived at that figure,' said Grouper. He turned round to face them, for once in his life bamboozled.

'That's simple,' said Holly. 'It was based on the budget – ten million dollars.'

Matt marvelled at her nerve.

'Five percent of that is half a million,' Holly went on. 'Bernie reckoned that was fair.'

Grouper was mystified. 'All right, all right!' he said, stomping back to the table. 'I ain't an unreasonable man.'

'So it's agreed?' said Holly.

'Yeah. You gotta deal,' Grouper nodded reluctantly. The meal resumed in an atmosphere of thin cordiality. Holly did her best to cheer things up by telling Grouper how she envied him the view from his apartment.

'We were admiring your pictures, too,' said Matt. 'Bernie told us you had a wonderful collection.'

'That's right,' said Grouper, sufficiently recovered to enjoy a plate of devilled kidneys. 'It was started by the old man – back in the last century, you know?'

'He must have been a man of vision.'

Grouper warmed to Matt's flattery. 'Yeah, the ol' man had what it takes. Always knew a good thing when he saw it.'

'I see you like to buy art yourself,' said Matt.

'Oh, sure,' said Grouper, pausing to wipe his lips. 'I got dealers popping in and out the whole time, yuh understand. They keep me briefed on what's hot.'

His humour improved, Grouper remembered he had a little surprise up his sleeve, something he thought would please Matt.

'Hey,' he chuckled, 'when we're through eatin' here, remind me I got something to show yuh.'

'Really?' said Matt, curious.

'Yeah, you're gonna love it!'

Thrilled at having pulled a fast one on Grouper – nothing more than he deserved – Holly sat quietly detached from the conversation. But when breakfast was over, she wished to banish any lingering resentment.

'I'm sorry for the misunderstanding,' she said to Grouper.

'Hey, lady!' he said, with convincing nonchalance. 'That's nothing! Some you win, some you lose!' Grouper was fond of little sayings, and he was comforting himself with one he'd coined since the accession of President Bush III: There's nothing like a dame presiding over things, for allowin' gentlemen to do their worst!

Holly gave Grouper a wry smile. Cheeky sod, she thought; he's not so much a grouper fish as a shark.

'Now,' said Grouper, his face breaking into a grin. 'About this thing I wanna show yuh!'

TWENTY-TWO

Matt was desolate.

'Some bloody surprise!' he exclaimed, as they descended in the lift. The very act of going downwards was compounding his misery.

'I know. I couldn't believe it,' Holly said in sympathy. 'It was the last thing I expected.'

'Sylvester's a bastard!' Matt ranted. 'I mean, how could he do such a thing?'

'But that's Sylvester all over.'

'To sell it to Grouper, of all people!'

Matt was agonised. *The Orchard* had been sold to a greedy old vulgarian who would just sit in front of it and gloat, his only satisfaction that he'd acquired another 'masterpiece' accredited by others. As for Grouper understanding the picture – well, forget it!

'But you can hardly blame Grouper,' said Holly. 'He just sees it as a coup for his collection.

'But *The Orchard*!' Matt wailed, feeling deep inside that it was the only true and good thing he'd ever done.

Holly commiserated. 'I know, I know…'

Matt couldn't have been more upset. Yes, the painting belonged to the Rich Gallery; but he had thought Sylvester prized it so much, he would never sell it on. He'd imagined his *tour de force* hanging there in perpetuity for coming generations to admire. Just as Libby had said, the picture was art: it embodied deeply-held convictions, it came from the heart, it was untainted by mercenary considerations.

'I feel gutted,' he said. It was as if every ounce of his integrity was laid waste.

'I know,' said Holly. 'But to Sylvester, the sale was just another deal.'

'That's what really gets me!' Matt said bitterly. It was a breach of trust, trust he'd taken for granted.

Back at the hotel he lay on the bed, hands behind his head. Holly sat beside him, idly leafing through a glossy magazine.

'God, I'm whacked,' she sighed. Lying back, she let the magazine slip from the bedspread to the floor.

'Did you see the way Hiram was eating?' she said. 'I thought he was going to eat the table-cloth!'

'Given half a chance he'd have eaten us!' Matt said, remembering the hugeness of the man. 'You did well.'

Matt looked at his watch. It was half-past three; the afternoon was dragging. He suggested she try and get some sleep. He needed sleep too; but, mortified by the sale of *The Orchard* and apprehensive of the evening ahead, he sensed he was unlikely to get it. Adrenalin kept surging through his body in waves.

Holly reached back to puff up her pillow. 'What time did Mr. Big say we should be ready?' she asked. She was still gloating over her victory.

'He's picking us up at eight.'

'Oh, yeah.' Thinking pleasurably of the empty hours ahead, she curled up and went to sleep.

Holly was amazing, thought Matt. She could drop off to sleep in an instant, while he was fidgety and restless even when tired.

Pressing the remote, he switched on the television. It crackled into life and he lowered the volume a little. Holly could sleep through chatter and music; it seemed to soothe her even. Yet, switch it off and she'd probably wake up.

He channel-hopped from station to station, searching for something of interest, anything to avert his mind from its mounting apprehension. A channel devoted to religion caught his attention. Its evangelical maestro was in full cry:

'Friends, I stand before you as an emissary of the Lord!'

'Hallelujah! Hallelujah!' the congregation cried, raising and lowering their hands in the grip of devotion.

The man reached out and 'laid hands' on a woman sitting hunched in a wheel chair.

'Sister Mabel! With the power of HIS Love which is vested in ME, I say to you: 'Rise!''

'Hallelujah! Blessed is His Love!' the congregation chanted.

The woman called Mabel sat transfixed, staring into the gloom of her lap. A nurse at her side leant and whispered in her ear.

Mabel looked up. Finding sudden strength, she heaved herself out of her wheel chair and stood on her feet. The congregation burst into astonished and uninhibited emotion.

Was it a set-up? Matt wondered. Or had she undergone some kind of hypnosis that enabled her to transcend the pain of her disability?

A break for commercials interrupted. More hypnosis, thought Matt; always selling, selling, selling. Even the evangelists were selling; their hold over people earned them millions.

Were they a force for good? The relief they brought was short-lived, so he'd read. Did that matter? Surely a moment's relief was better than no relief at all?

The show came back on, 'brought to you by courtesy of Divinity Digital.' The evangelist signalled to his sidesmen that it was now time to start hauling in the cash.

Hard currency in return for miracles. Hardly the Jesus tradition, thought Matt: he'd thrown the money-men out.

Then it occurred to Matt: wasn't he himself a salesman too, making a fortune out of misery? Would his remedy for social ills last any longer than the disabled woman's cure? Of course not; it was in the nature of life that struggle was continual; there was no permanent victory. He was simply a pawn that Fate had seen fit to bring into play, to counter the sophistry of a generation who'd lost its way.

Would his work make any lasting difference? No, time submerges all things. He would amount to no more than a footnote in history. Human memory is short and changes soon meld into the torpor of casual acceptance. So what is the purpose of any action at all, when fate makes such a mockery of all we do? We're sunk before we even begin!

The evangelist was back. With his perma-tanned looks, bootlace tie and frock coat he looked more a Doctor Feelgood from the days of the wagon trains than a twenty-first century emissary of God. The snake-oil on offer was hope. Perhaps that's all hope is, thought Matt – an illusion: the illusion that there's more to life than daily immersion in the horrifying cesspit of reality.

Looking at things like that, he said to himself, the struggle I've had to paint the truth has been pointless. The sense of purpose I've felt is self-delusion.

Turning his head to one side he closed his eyes. The blankness became a canvas for drowsy imaginings which slowly coalesced into the fullness of a dream.

Like a bird he was flying high over the streets of New York. People below him were rushing hither and thither and calling for him to come down. He fought hard against doing so, but their adoration was impossible to resist.

He swooped downwards, the wind screaming in his ears. He stopped and hovered above the crowd. But he still wasn't low enough for their liking.

'Lower! Lower!' they shouted, reaching up and beguiling him with smiles.

He dropped through the air inch by inch until he was tantalizingly close but still safe from their grasping hands: or so he thought, for suddenly a man jumped up on his blind side and grabbed him by the ankle, pulling him kicking and struggling to the ground.

Matt woke up to find Holly at the end of the bed, shaking him by the foot.

'Come on!' she said. 'It's after seven! Time we got changed.'

Sitting up sharply, Matt swung his legs over the edge of the bed. 'I had this weird dream,' he said, rubbing his eyes.

Holly was brushing her hair. 'No change there, then.'

'I was flying high…'

'What, like you'd had a joint?'

'No, it was an incredible sensation, like I was free.' Then he told her the dream, ending with his struggle on the ground with the man who'd caught him. 'By the look on his face, he was going to kill me!'

'Sounds like a good omen!' said Holly.

'What?' said Matt, confused.

'Think how often you dream something bad's going to happen, and it never does. It's like an anxiety… then you dream about it, and as soon as you do, you know it won't happen.'

'Huh! I hope you're right,' said Matt, impressed by her creative management of the dream-world. He stood up to answer a knock at the door. Room Service was returning his scarlet jacket, newly pressed. He gave the boy a ten-dollar bill.

'It's funny,' he said, laying the garment on the bed. 'Of all the clothes I've got, Willie's jacket is the one thing I wear most – and it was made for someone else.'

'Well, it's become iconic, hasn't it?' said Holly.

'I suppose so,' said Matt, inspecting it. 'But iconic of what?'

'Don't start on that now!' said Holly. His self-doubts and ruminations were becoming a positive nuisance. And when everything was going so well, beyond their wildest dreams!

'This conceit that we matter is laughable,' Matt moaned.

Holly looked at his glum face. Probably, he should get into Buddhism like Libby had recently. At any rate, nothing *she* could say on the matter would make any difference.

'I think life is a con,' he went on. 'I mean, what I'm doing is a complete waste of time.'

'What crap you talk,' she said. 'You *have* made a difference. And that *does* matter!'

'Why? I mean ultimately, nothing changes the way we are as human beings.'

Holly turned and stared at him, eye-liner in one hand and only one eye made-up. 'Who the bloody hell do you think you are? God or something?'

She looked so funny and she spoke with such a mixture of reverence and profanity that Matt laughed.

'You're right of course,' he said. 'Things are completely beyond our control.'

Jolted out of his pessimism he pulled on his hallmark white T-shirt. He even began humming a little tune. Holly smiled in exasperation. What a case! she thought.

Matt reached for his red jacket. 'Someone up there,' he said, raising his eyes, 'is having one hell of a laugh!'

TWENTY-THREE

att was watching television in the rear lobby of the hotel. He and Holly were waiting to be collected for the short limousine ride to Times Square and Holly was making a last-minute visit to the ladies.

'This is Ed Ramble for NBC, coming to you live from Times Square. Within a few minutes we're expecting the arrival of Matt Flight, the British-born founder of RIOT. He's here to attend the launch of his stateside campaign and I spoke to him on his arrival in the city yesterday.'

There was a close-up of Matt arriving outside the hotel then a shot of Holly getting out of the car with her film-star looks. Ed Ramble's voice continued over: 'While he wasn't givin' much away, I can reveal that the famed image of his face – some hundred-and-twenty foot high, so we're told – is shortly to come up on a billboard directly across the street.'

The huge blank billboard was pulled into close-up. Then the camera cut back to Ed.

'What effect Flight is gonna have on the crowds here tonight, we can't be sure. But the very fact that people have turned out in such numbers shows us one thing for certain. There is a big weight of expectation on the young man from Britain.'

The camera panned to a new face on Ramble's right. 'By my side I have NYPD Chief Mitch McClusky, responsible for security in Times Square tonight.'

McClusky nodded.

'Whaddya say, Mitch? Are we ready for this guy Flight and what he has to say? Do you agree we've gone too far enough in our tolerance of out-of-left-field behaviour?'

Mitch looked reluctant to answer. Mixed messages from his political masters, and his own dignity as a law enforcement officer, meant there was only one practical response – to stay strictly within his professional remit.

'Well Ed, I don't know exactly what you're wanting me to say here, but we got five hundred officers out there and we're lookin' to contain any trouble.'

'That's great to hear, Mitch! Now let's move on and hear from some of the other good folks gathered here tonight.'

A woman waving a flag emblazoned with 'Get Real!' was first to be asked for a comment. 'Well I guess we're lookin' for a new approach,' she said. 'A moral majority kick-back.'

Ed approached a black man with a Rastafarian head of hair.

'What do you think, sir?' he asked.

'No change!' the fellow said briskly. 'Just 'the man' findin' new ways to screw things up.'

'Politicians – they're all on the take!' said the woman with the flag. Then, glancing about wildly: 'Who *can* you trust? That's my question.'

'Friggin' do-gooders is the problem!' shouted someone else, uninvited.

'Yeah!' cried a middle-aged woman pushing through from behind. 'We little people gotta wise up. We been pushed around too long. People think they know what's best for us, but they don't!'

'Wise up to what?' said a doubting voice from nearby.

'Reality, stoopid!' snapped a man at his side.

'Hey, jerk-face, don't call me stoopid!'

'Whoa! Cool it, folks, will yuh?' pleaded Ramble. 'We're going out live here!'

A drunk man with tattoos elbowed his way towards the camera. 'Hey Ed! Let me tell yuh what's goin' down here!' he shouted. 'We're gonna start sortin' out the schmuckos who are lousin' up our lives!'

'Yeah, no more friggin' around!' called another.

'We gonna kick some ass!' yelled a man at the back.

'You bet, pal!'

'Oh yeah, who's ass ya gonna kick?'

The sound man pulled away from the crowd as the objector and the tattooed man began to exchange purple insults. Ramble and the camera also moved discreetly away. 'And there you have it,' Ramble was saying. 'Along with the excitement there's also anger. You may think it ugly, you may think it justified, but it is surely a natural result of all the frustration the good people of this country have come to feel.'

Matt could see the crowd behind Ed surging in response to some off-camera fracas. Police with batons drawn lumbered past, as Ed carried on with his patter: 'Will this campaign bring about change? A radical re-appraisal of attitudes? Who can say? But what I do know is, this fine country of ours will always rally in the face of adversity. And what better time for that to happen than today, with a new President in place committed to defending our nation against enemies from within and without.'

Matt wrenched his concentration away from the television screen; Grouper had arrived, puffing on a cigar.

'Where is the delectable Miss Tree?' he asked anxiously. 'Only, we gotta be makin' tracks.'

'She's gone to the john,' said Matt, hoping he'd picked the right euphemism.

Grouper grimaced. 'That's broads for yuh,' he sneered. 'Always playin' with their faces.'

Matt forced a chuckle.

'Hey, I meant to tell yuh,' Grouper went on. 'We're waitin' on Senator Dick Connor and City Mayor Baumberger too.'

'Yeah?' said Matt, looking surprised.

'They'll be travellin' with us.'

'They're real political heavyweights, aren't they?' said Matt. 'How did you get them along?'

Grouper grinned. 'They got vested interests.'

'What?' said Matt.

'Sure!' said Grouper. 'It's thanks to those guys Globalcorp got the contract.'

'How did that happen?' Matt said

'Hey, what is this?' asked Grouper jocularly. 'The Spanish Inquisition? That's the way it's done here; influence!'

'You mean they're in on the deal?' said Matt.

'I have a little saying for you,' said Grouper, in a tone Matt had not heard him use before. 'Politics is the continuation of business by other means'. One of your European guys said something similar.' Grouper's eyes were narrow and Matt fancied his obstreperous bonhomie was a facade for all the intelligent evil the world could muster. 'Let's just say, I smooth the way for them, they smooth the way for us,' said Grouper, gesturing calmly with his hand.

Matt looked down at the seal on Grouper's gold ring. No honour there, he thought. He wondered if Hiram even knew the meaning of the word 'corruption'.

'C'mon, you know 'bout these things,' Hiram said, looking at his watch.

'All too well!' said Matt with resignation. Then, just as he was wondering how much the mayor and the senator stood to make, Holly came up and joined them.

'Ain't no room for Holy Joes in this game – is there, Miss Tree?' Hiram said to round things off. 'End of story!'

Holly smiled breezily. 'No!' she heartily agreed.

Seeing Connor and Baumberger arrive, Grouper made the introductions and they went outside to the waiting cavalcade. Matt found himself seated in the back between Connor and Baumberger, two groomed men of politics. Grouper and Holly were on seats opposite.

Connor turned and leaned towards Matt, gazing into his eyes. 'You know son, since the assassination of President Schwarzenegger, the idea of a saviour from outside has become a significant political possibility. Do you get my drift?'

Matt looked at the man with no idea of what he was talking about.

Connor placed a hand on Matt's knee. 'You know the Constitution was amended to allow Arnie to run?' he confided.

'Maybe we should talk about this some other time, Dick,' said Baumberger to Connor.

Matt looked from one to the other, his mind numb. What were they suggesting?

'Just wanted to plant an idea in the young man's head, that's all,' said Connor to Baumberger.

They had set off through the streets. Matt looked at Holly; she was staring at him as if frozen.

Their car, escorted by a phalanx of police on Harleys, was followed by two further vehicles. Both were black saloons: one carried a team from the FBI's anti-kidnap unit and the other an assortment of Globalcorp executives.

Safe behind bullet-proof glass, Matt waved to people leaning toward the car from behind barricades. They all seemed to be cheering him on with unbounded enthusiasm.

'Hey, what did I tell you?' Grouper said. 'The folks out there are crazy for you!'

With Senator Connor's words still on his mind, Matt's gratitude was muted. Overhead, the beating blades of a helicopter were sending shock waves through roof of the armoured limousine, filling the air with subsonic vibrations. On the ground, heavily-armed police punctuated the front line of the crowd and neon advertising signs flashed and flickered from every direction. What chance for *reality* in the face of all this? he wondered.

He looked at Hiram and at the grey power-brokers on either side of him. They have no more interest in my message than a triumvirate of mafia hoods! he thought. This whole thing is more like a masquerade: a battle for power under the banner of enlightenment.

Staring out of the window, he had the uneasy feeling he was being used. But what of the people? Were they using him too?

The car drew to a halt. A massive policewoman was standing near, chewing gum. She must be six feet tall with a circumference to match, thought Matt. Festooned about her metal jacket was an armoury. Matt counted a baton, a holstered handgun, an antipersonnel aerosol, and a belt of stun and teargas grenades. At the ready in her hands was a pump-action shotgun. The driver lowered his window.

Senator Connor leant forward. 'Is there any kind of problem?' he asked.

'I don't believe so, surrh,' the policewoman said, glancing left and right before peering into the back of the vehicle. 'But I'd sure be obliged if yuh'd pass on my goodwill to the young man in the back, surrh.'

'Sure thing, Sergeant,' the Senator agreed. 'There's a lot for all of us resting on his initiative.'

Despite her overall impression, there was gentleness in the contours of the woman's face. Matt's disillusionment deepened. It was as if she no longer felt any allegiance to her sex and had turned into something else: her body like a porcupine's, bristling offensively and devoid of allure.

Progressing now at a snail's pace, the entourage neared its destination – a roped-off stand erected on the pavement some hundred yards ahead. Numbers of pressmen and photographers were there waiting. Along with the crowd they had been enjoying the antics of stilt-men, fire-eaters and jugglers.

Such was Globalcorp's grip on the media, Matt was already a hero to the waiting crowds. Over the past month, reports had stirred up a frenzy of expectation.

'Come, hurry!' the press now exhorted. 'Let the good folk of this city make their way to Times Square!'

Matt stepped out of the limousine to face a barrage of questions from hordes of journalists caged behind barriers that were straining to keep them at bay.

Just twenty feet away, he noticed Ed Ramble, now suspended in the pulpit of a hydraulic lift. His commentary never reached Matt; it was drowned in a roar, a Mexican wave of approval that swept through the crowd.

'Unbelievable!' said Matt. Everywhere people were shouting and smiling and waving flags. His fears that he was being used evaporated in a swell of euphoria. The mass of people were his.

'Wow!' Holly exclaimed. 'I've never seen so many people.'

'Make sure you stick by me, once we're up on that stand!' Matt said.

'Don't worry, I'll be there,' she said, clasping his hand.

Dazzled by spotlights whose punishing glare seemed to search every pore of his skin, Matt momentarily lost sight of everyone.

Grouper cupped his ear to the crowd. 'Will yuh listen to that?' he said. 'Music to my ears!'

Holly pointed to a video screen fixed above the heads of the crowd. 'Look!' she said, nudging Matt. The two of them were on-screen, in close-up. 'Isn't that... amazing?' she said, struggling for a word to describe how she felt.

Blinking, Matt took in the scene. Holly leant to kiss him. Touched by the humanity of the moment, the crowd erupted into whoops of frenzied glee.

Grouper was ecstatic too: this unscheduled touch had worked wonders. 'Matt baby, this is gonna be the night of your life!' he cried, walking up the steps to the stand.

Matt gulped. Never before, even at the height of his campaign in England, had he faced such tumultuous acclaim.

'Some turnout, eh?' said Grouper. Sales figures ratcheted upwards in his head beyond his executives' wildest projections.

Matt made no comment. Standing on the bottom step of the stand he was seized by fear. In seconds he would be a celebrity in full view of countless thousands: a celebrity, replendent in red. So many before him had been killed – pop-up targets of a barbaric age, murdered for no reason other than some psycho had a motive.

Don't be irrational! he told himself, trying to shake off the feeling that this might be the moment Fate decided to write him out of its farce.

He reached the last step and waited for Holly to join him. Then, to the triumphal oompahs of the band, he took her hand and together they walked onto the stand. His fear was swept away by sheer razzamatazz.

As the crowd roared on and on, illuminated in the brightness of neon, it was as if it had erupted into a hot and heaving larva of liberated humanity. Matt breathed in the adulation. Surely, he thought, this is the people's ultimate acceptance of my message that, however we may wish things to be, we are bound by realities we cannot escape from: the struggle, the doubts, the ruthless Darwinian contest of natural selection.

Close at hand, Ed Ramble was commenting to the nation from his hydraulic lift. The spectacle so far had been a commentator's dream; the crowds, the band, the cheerleaders with their pretty costumes and high stepping routines; then at last Matt Flight and his cavalcade of limousines.

'Well, darn me!' Ramble announced to the nation, his breath taken away. 'Ain't this a sight for a billion sore eyes!'

Ed noticed the mayor standing somewhat discreetly behind the bulk of Hiram Grouper III. Ed reckoned he was staying out of harm's way, though he did not say so to the nation. There had been an attempt on the mayor's life earlier in the year and illuminated as the party was, ten feet above the ground for all to see, he might well fear another.

'Well, whaddya know?' Ed announced, checking the time. 'Zero hour's coming up! Things look to be on schedule, so any second now Flight will be invited to throw the switch. That will flash up what everybody here's waitin' to see.'

Matt looked up at the huge billboard where he would shortly appear magnified many times. High above the square, two choppers threshed through the night sky, their thermal imaging cameras probing the surrounding rooftops for signs of malevolent intent.

Matt acknowledged the crowd one more time. Standing back and looking at his watch, Grouper counted down from ten, then with a flurry of his hand he gave the signal to proceed.

His heart in his mouth, Matt threw the switch. Across the street, the vast image of a face slowly emerged from the darkness, its admonishing three-eyed gaze subjecting the multitude to scrutiny. The crowd's response was one of awe, a singular gasp that hung in the air. The scale of the spectacle was astounding to one and all.

Even Grouper was humbled. 'Wowee! Will you look at that Cyclops eye? It kinda looks straight through yuh!'

Underneath the image, Matt's slogan began flashing in pulsating brilliance. The effect was extraordinary. The crowd was galvanized; a resilience, a sense of empowerment seemed to well up inside every one of them. Then it brimmed over into words, uttered quietly at first, but then louder, and then louder still: 'Get Real!' 'Get Real!!' 'Get Real!!!'

Matt felt jubilant. The crowd's response was magnificent. Their heartfelt identification with his message was all he could wish for. His life hadn't been a waste of time and Holly was right: to make a difference, if only for a while, is what matters. What happens after we've gone is not our concern. Our wish to leave a lasting legacy is a vainglorious aspiration. He turned to share his joy with the others on the stand.

Grouper beamed with satisfaction. Whipping out his mobile, he fired off instructions to his staff: 'Get them balloons in the air!' he shrieked. 'And tell those vendors to go for it! *Everybody's* hot for this guy!'

'God bless America,' said Ramble from his pulpit. His voice faltered with pride as, along with the crowd, he witnessed thousands of balloons take to the air, each carrying its message onwards and upwards, deep into the night.

Elated, Matt went to take Holly in his arms. But as he drew near her, he lurched forward, the joy draining from his face.

'Oh, no! Oh, God, no!' she cried. Something warm was on the right side of her neck, moving down towards her breast. She held him for a second before collapsing with him onto the metal grid floor.

For a moment, nobody was sure what had happened. But Holly knew. Her bird of paradise had flown.

TWENTY-FOUR

Matt had been dead for nine years before Holly decided the time was right for Luc to 'meet' his father. Matt was now a hero from History, his every detail plastinated by impregnation with reactive polymers. Preserved in this way for all time, he was on display in the new and popular Hall of Fame at the British Museum.

Matt Flight's body was just one of many fine examples of a remarkable technique that helped to keep the past alive. Parties of schoolchildren studied these exhibits on their history trips. Here was the closest thing to history brought to 'life' – the actual bodies of the dead, sitting or standing just as they had done while alive.

Matt's permanized posture had been decided upon by democratic public competition. As befitted a man whose guiding light was a simple philosophy, popular consensus was in favour of a seated posture deep in thought – like Rodin's *The Thinker*.

Holly visited the museum often, but until now she had been reluctant to take her son. The realism of Matt's figure in his dazzling scarlet jacket was a sight too disturbing, she felt, for a boy younger than nine years old.

'Which one's my father?' Luc asked as they walked along slowly side by side, gazing with others at the heroes of yesteryear. All were cultural figures whose next-of-kin had acceded to public demand that they should be neither buried nor cremated but preserved for all time, clothed in the fashions for which the public best remembered them. Occasionally, there was a public outcry when a figure, judged to be no longer 'historical', was removed for burial or storage. A humiliation indeed! But Matt was still valued for what he'd achieved and such a fate was unlikely to befall him – yet!

There had been something of a conflict between Matt's ageing parents and Holly over his plastination. Eventually the matter was resolved by a phone-call to Mr. and Mrs. Flight from the Minister for Public Heritage and the Arts. It was in the public interest, the lady had said, that Matt be the inaugural inhabitant of the new Hall of Fame. Holly had been agreeable to the idea from the start; it would keep her promise to Matt that he wouldn't be forgotten. She thought it a benign irony that Matt, an artist, would become an exhibit himself, a permanent celebration of everything he believed in.

Drawing near to Matt's podium, Holly took Luc's hand. 'He's over there,' she said, suddenly overwhelmed. 'See him? He's the man in the red jacket up on that stand.'

Holly dabbed her eyes with her handkerchief. Luc let go of his mother's hand and walked up to the figure, his mouth agape in wonder. Holly allowed the boy time to adjust.

'He looks really real!' exclaimed Luc, moving as close as he could.

'Well, he is,' said Holly, smiling through her tears. 'It's just that the life has gone from him.'

'Can I touch him?' Luc asked.

'Of course!' said Holly, thinking it right to encourage him. After all, touching and looking were all that was left to the poor boy.

Luc rested a hand on his father's shoe.

'Oi! Fingers off, sonny!' said an attendant. 'Can't you read?'

'Sorry!' said Luc, stepping back.

Holly glowered at the man. 'Don't be so officious!' she told him. 'Matt Flight was the boy's father.'

'Oh,' said the man. Then, begrudgingly: 'Well, 'ow was I to know?'

'Please leave us,' said Holly, taking hold of Luc's hand once again.

The attendant sloped off back to his chair, grumbling under his breath: 'Rules is rules! I got a job to do, ain't I?'

Once he'd gone, the two of them stood there for ages. Luc listened hard as his mother talked gently of golden days she'd been lucky to share with his father before he was cruelly struck down.

No one ever found out who killed Matt. His death was portrayed around the world as a straightforward celebrity shooting but Holly, distressed and overwrought, had refused to accept this version. She believed Matt was martyred and that the CIA was behind it. It was a ploy, she believed, to discredit the enemies of American power; to encourage an authoritarian backlash; and to make sure that Matt, an outsider, would have no influence over public minds. Matt was, after all, unpredictable: a bit of a loose cannon. Such double-dealing seemed to Holly entirely plausible – well in line with the shadowy practices of the CIA.

The immediate aftermath of Matt's death was the unhappiest period in Holly's life. She was saddened still further by the news that Bernie Feltz would never recover from his vegetative state. He would be confined for the rest of his life in a north London clinic for the living dead. She found herself weeping for him too: the sight of him hunched in a wheelchair was too much to bear.

Alone, pregnant and in need of someone to turn to, Holly had sought solace in the company of Rollo Leaf. Attracted to her from the first, he was only too pleased to oblige. He was kind and practical by nature and he proved a tower of strength. It wasn't long before their relationship developed to the point that he was rather more to her than her publisher.

In time, when her grieving for Matt was over, she fell in love with Rollo. Though it was not quite the same the second time around, Rollo's devotion to her and to Luc more than made up for any shortfall in her expectations. More for the sake of her peace of mind than out of conviction, Rollo had brought her round to another view of how Matt died.

It was more likely, Rollo said, that Matt had been the victim of a fatwah. Fundamentalist fanatics were targeting western public figures at the time and they had decreed that his campaign was yet another assault on Islam. They had a particular internal reason for doing so: Matt's godless logic was drawing young Muslims away from the Faith. His message was being taken as a moral justification for violence – like socialism in its time – that required no religious content or limitation. His helmeted face was appearing, spray-painted on walls, in shanty-towns where fundamentalists were accustomed to a recruitment monopoly. Matt's message, said the mullahs, was yet another symbol of western society's decadent morality.

Of course, Matt had also attacked decadence, and it seemed ironic to Holly that he should have been killed for promoting it. That was something she would never quite get over. But at least from then on she could look back with pride and with her bitterness forgotten. Yes, Matt had died a hero in pursuit of a cause, and he had made a difference.

She was trying to explain some of this now to young Luc, but the machinations of his father's enemies were hard for Luc to understand. He asked her questions and she held him close, answering as best she could through the pain of recollection.

'Do you think he minds being dead?' Luc asked, looking deeply into her eyes.

'No,' she said, touched. 'In a funny way I don't think he does.'

'Why?'

Remembering Matt's vanity, Holly smiled. 'Well, lots of people come to admire him.'

'Lots of people?' said Luc, seeking reassurance that his father didn't feel alone.

'Yes, lots,' said Holly, confident.

'And every day?' Luc asked her.

'Yes every day, I'm sure.'

'Because otherwise, I think *we* should come every day!'

'Shall we come next Sunday?' she said.

'Yes. I think we should,' Luc said solemnly. 'Shall we go now?'

'Yes.' They stood quietly for a few seconds, contemplating Matt's strange lifeless stillness, before turning away.

Walking by with his two teenage sons, a bluff-looking man caught Holly's eye. 'Blow me down,' the man said, pointing up at Matt, 'if I didn't 'ave that geezer in the back of me cab once. Honest to God!'